A Shift of Time

The Finest in DAW Science Fiction and Fantasy
by JULIE E. CZERNEDA:

THE CLAN CHRONICLES

Stratification
REAP THE WILD WIND (#1)
RIDERS OF THE STORM (#2)
RIFT IN THE SKY (#3)

The Trade Pact
A THOUSAND WORDS FOR STRANGER (#1)
TIES OF POWER (#2)
TO TRADE THE STARS (#3)

Reunification
THIS GULF OF TIME AND STARS (#1)
THE GATE TO FUTURES PAST (#2)
TO GUARD AGAINST THE DARK (#3)
TALES FROM PLEXIS

***

NIGHT'S EDGE
A TURN OF LIGHT (#1)
A PLAY OF SHADOW (#2)
A CHANGE OF PLACE (#3)
A SHIFT OF TIME (#4)
A TWIST OF MAGIC (#5)*

***

SPECIES IMPERATIVE
Omnibus Edition
SURVIVAL | MIGRATION | REGENERATION

***

ESEN

Web Shifters
BEHOLDER'S EYE (#1)
CHANGING VISION (#2)
HIDDEN IN SIGHT (#3)

Web Shifter's Library
SEARCH IMAGE (#1)
MIRAGE (#2)
SPECTRUM (#3)

***

IN THE COMPANY OF OTHERS

THE GOSSAMER MAGE

TO EACH THIS WORLD

*Coming soon from DAW Books

A SHIFT OF TIME

Ansnor

JULIE E. CZERNEDA

Copyright © 2025 by Julie E. Czerneda

All rights reserved. Copying or digitizing this book for storage, display, or distribution in any other medium is strictly prohibited. For information about permission to reproduce selections from this book, please contact permissions@astrapublishinghouse.com.

This is a work of fiction. Names, characters, places, and incidents are products of the author's imagination or are used fictitiously. Any resemblance to actual events, locales, or persons, living or dead, is entirely coincidental.

Cover illustration by Matt Stawicki

Cover design by Katie Anderson

Maps by Julie E. Czerneda

Photos by Roger Czerneda Photography

Edited by Madeline Goldberg

DAW Book Collectors No. 1985

DAW Books
An imprint of Astra Publishing House
dawbooks.com
DAW Books and its logo are registered trademarks of
Astra Publishing House

Printed in the United States of America

Library of Congress Cataloging-in-Publication Data

Names: Czerneda, Julie, 1955– author
Title: A shift of time : Ansnor / Julie E. Czerneda.
Description: First edition. | New York : DAW Books, 2025. | Series: Night's edge ; #4 | Summary: "The 4th book in the Aurora Award-winning Night's Edge series returns readers to a rich and atmospheric fantasy world.Perfect for readers of Charles de Lint, Naomi Novik, and Katherine Arden, A Shift of Time is a charming, heartwarming, hopeful fable"--Provided by publisher.
Identifiers: LCCN 2025010274 (print) | LCCN 2025010275 (ebook) | ISBN 9780756410711 hardcover | ISBN 9780698193550 ebook
Subjects: LCGFT: Fantasy fiction | Novels
Classification: LCC PR9199.3.C92 S55 2025 (print) | LCC PR9199.3.C92 (ebook) | DDC 812/.54--dc23/eng/20250310
LC record available at https://lccn.loc.gov/2025010274
LC ebook record available at https://lccn.loc.gov/2025010275

First edition: July 2025

10 9 8 7 6 5 4 3 2 1

The Brothers Three

I dedicate this book to my Czerneda brothers:
Anthony (Tony) Charles Czerneda, always
thoughtful, Philip Peter Czerneda, ever exploring,
and Roger Henry Czerneda, perpetually youngest
(and thus forever appointed carrier of the canoe).

Thank you for the gift each of you are to my life
and for letting me share in your remarkable bond.
The sum of you is delightful, powerful,
and utterly irreplaceable.

I couldn't love you more.

To the brothers three!

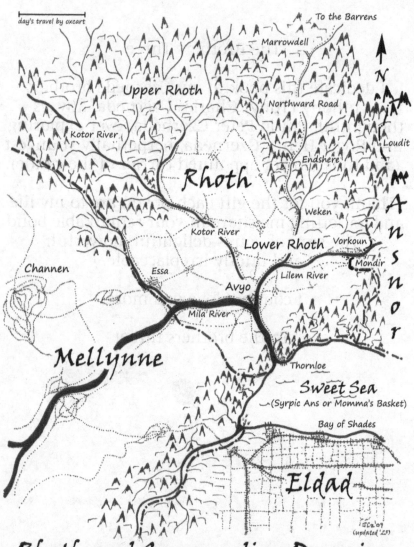

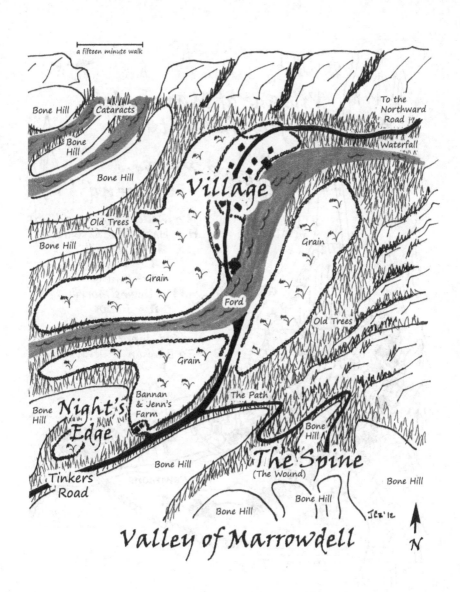

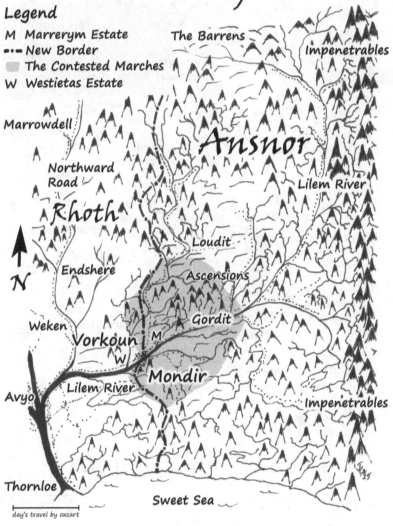

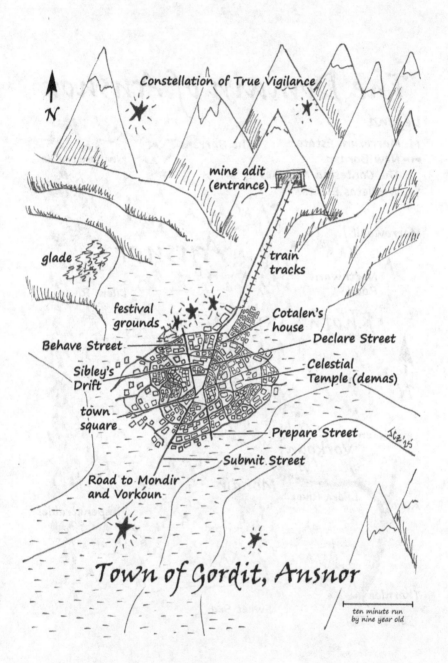

Prologue

TWENTY-THREE YEARS AGO, Within the World of Books and Students...

Kydd Uhthoff paused his furious packing, a book in each hand, books he wasn't to have and certainly wasn't to take with him, abruptly aware he was no longer alone.

Lowering his chin, he turned his head just enough to see through the fall of his hair. Enough to glimpse the shadowy figure in the open doorway, the door he'd meant to lock, he was sure of it, but he'd no more right to privacy now than he did this room or books.

Prince Ordo had seen to that.

"Go away," he growled, giving his attention to his task.

Most of it.

He heard footsteps as the figure entered and the soft closing of the door. Caught the fragrance of lavender and Kydd knew then who'd dared interrupt him was his brother's wife, Larell. He swallowed what else he might have said.

She deserved none of his anger.

In silence, she moved around his small room, a match for any student's at the university with its wax-splattered desk and once-cluttered shelves, its narrow bed with drawers beneath, now pulled open and empty. He felt more than saw her stop by his easel. Heard her fingers stir the brushes waiting for paint and about to be abandoned.

His heart lurched with despair. He shoved in another book, heedless of damage.

"Dear Heart." Her hand found his shoulder. He froze, bent over the bulging case, hair in his eyes. "How are you?"

How? It hurt to breathe, stung to think. Ancestors Bloody and Broken, he couldn't imagine leaving, let alone the scene tomorrow morning when they'd pile into the wagons allotted them by the Settlers' Bind and go—where?

The word fell from his lips. "Where?"

"North," she answered, which everyone knew, that those of Naalish blood, exiled and stripped of wealth by decree, were granted lands in the desolate Barrens where none lived now and likely, he thought bitterly, none could. Then Larell surprised him. "We'll make first for a place called Endshere. Arrmand Comber, a distant cousin of your grandfather's, made a home there, on the Northward Road. The pair exchanged letters over the years—an exchange I gladly continued with Arrmand's daughter, Cammi." A soft chuckle. "She's started work in the post office. Your brother's pleased to have an impeccable forwarding address for his academic correspondence."

How dare she make it all sound normal, even sane? As if they'd simply continue life as they had, instead of die horrible deaths in the wilderness. "Dusom's a—" Kydd shut his mouth. His brilliant brother was hardly a fool, but still—

"—an optimist?" Larell finished charitably. She tucked a lock of his hair behind his ear, straightened his collar, then gave his shoulders a motherly squeeze, despite being his elder by a mere nine years. "He puts on a brave face, Dear Heart. As do we all."

"Except Wainn." His nephew hadn't stopped talking about the trip, considering it the biggest adventure in his short life.

"He hopes to see bears. I hope the baby sleeps most of the trip." Larell perched on the edge of Kydd's bed, giving the contents of his bag an unhappy look. "Can you not leave them behind? Be done with it?"

With magic, she meant. With the study he'd devoted years to and ideas he'd come to believe were more important—and dangerous—than the decrees of any prince, no matter that they were scoffed at by most and skirted the law.

Skirted? The possession of such books, along with his Naalish heritage, was a sure path to prison.

The effort to obtain them, the time to assemble such a collection, mattered naught to him. The knowledge they contained did, for it might prove the only way he could protect his family once they left civilization behind. Sick with dread, Kydd pushed in the last volume and began tucking clothes on top, as he had when filling his trunks. "They can't stay here."

"As you wish," Larell conceded, though her frown remained. Deepened as she noticed what he'd piled in the crate to be burned before they left. Torn paintings, abandoned sketches. Nine journals, their clasps polished and leather worn smooth with use. Her sigh held a wordless protest.

Kydd shook his head once, hard, to forestall more. His scribbles were useless, his scholarship perilous, and neither did he dare set close to his family.

Larell stood, accepting. "I'll send Dusom to help carry down your things. Kydd. Dear Heart." He looked up. "We'll be together," she added gently, her deep brown eyes full of warmth and compassion. "Everything will be all right. You'll see."

He nodded, having nothing to say.

On her way out, she collected his brushes, tucking them decisively under an arm.

As if he'd ever want to paint again.

Four Hundred and Seventy Years Ago, Within the World of Toads and Dragons...

There was magic, enough. Beings who used it, or were it, or both. There was sky and earth and seasons, of a sort, though it didn't snow.

How could it? Water stayed where it was summoned, in fountains and wells, and what rained from sky to earth in its seasons was mimrol. Silver and warm, mimrol carved rivers and filled lakes, spreading magic as it flowed.

Dragons hunted the air, kruar the ground, and toads, though cousins, stayed out of sight. Terst farmed and built, bringing peace where it could flourish, and avoided dragons and kruar too. All had their place, whatever they thought of it, or if they even did.

But there were those, the sei, who thought a great deal. Sei pondered what was beyond the ken of others, being as curious as they were powerful, and one fateful day the sei wondered . . . was there more?

And one day wondered . . . could they touch it?

And all would have remained as it was, with magic enough and peace, but on a day when the light of an unseen sun dimmed, on a day when anything seemed possible, one sei reached from the world of dragons and toads, into that of books and students . . .

Tearing both worlds open.

Making both worlds bleed.

Spilling magic.

The sei mended that tear, as best it could. Used itself like thread. Held on, accepting that penance.

While dragons and toads, as well as kruar and terst, explored what the sei had wrought.

Today . . .

There's a world of books and students.

There's a world of dragons and toads.

Writhing through both is the edge where they meet, for the sei holds, still.

Magic, wild and potent, lives there.

And so does Jenn Nalynn.

ONE

A WIDE PATH WOVE through Marrowdell's village, linking porch to porch, wrapping around homes to reach barns and outbuildings, connecting all to the fountain at its heart before scurrying off to the commons pasture and the river. Once across, it became the Tinker's Road and coursed the length of the valley, first to the farm of Bannan Larmensu and Jenn Nalynn, slipping past the meadow known as Night's Edge and the hidden one home to a dragon, to its seeming end at the base of the Bone Hills where no one went. Seeming, for the road's end marked the crossing to and from the magical Verge used by the seven terst turn-born, who came to Marrowdell on occasion and their own business, being tinkers and traders. And friends, as best they could be, having only the memory of hearts.

Leaving the village in the other direction, the path passed through the ever-open gate—the hinges had rusted so it couldn't be closed, not that any thought it should—and grew wider and straightened, having more serious purpose. For this was the way out of Marrowdell to the Northward Road and hence to the wider world, leaving the edge and magic behind.

And bringing all other visitors. There'd been, since last fall, a multitude of unexpected arrivals. Dema Qirmirpik of Ansnor with the Eld, Urcet a Hac Sa Od y Dom—in a fine caravan complete with servants. Allin bringing his new wife, Palma Anan, to meet his family and friends. Less happily, Tir Half-face with Bannan Larmensu's nephews, fleeing a deadly midwinter's pursuit, and they'd have died in the snow if not for Wisp. Bannan's formidable sister, the Baroness Lila Westietas, come to save her youngest from a dream then take her family home to Vorkoun.

Marrowdell no longer felt as isolated as it had before. With a tingle of anticipation, Jenn Nalynn shaded her eyes, the better to see if anyone came today.

Not, she thought, being reasonable, that it was at all likely anyone would. This spring's cavalcade from Endshere were long gone, off to see to their own homes after the flood, having come to help in Marrowdell and been most welcome.

Marrowdell's paths were smooth again, Battle and Brawl having dragged the rake over them this spring to smooth away the ruts. Twice from the Northward Road to the river, and from the river to as close to the end of the Tinker's Road and Bone Hills as they were comfortable to do and they'd have made a third pass, if Davi Treff had listened to his mother Lorra's continued complaint about an uneven spot in front of their house, but the draft horses had been needed to till the gardens and planting not something that could wait.

Now, with the days long and the sun summer-warm, Jenn smiled to herself, everything was in a hurry. Bees skimmed through the soft warm air, newly arrived in their hives and eager to fill them with honey. Six of the seven carried off by the flood had been recovered, scraped clean of the paper lining made from Kydd Uhthoff's forbidden books of magic before he'd invited new bees to take up residence. Little birds sang and chattered in the hedges, their nests full of hungry hatchlings, while the riverbanks came alive each night with the chorus of frogs.

Which weren't like house toads, those being little cousins and magic, but did make her curious. Did house toads sing? Have babies? They'd proved to be more than anyone thought and—

"Heart's Blood! Can you not brew it outside for once?"

"Now, Dear Heart—"

Jenn's lips twitched at the commotion in the house behind her. If Peggs protested, the beverage in dispute would be bog tea, introduced to Marrowdell—and their aunt—by Tir Half-face, Bannan's long-time friend. The former soldier had learned to make it while on patrol in the marches and drank it daily. Unfortunately, when brewed bog tea produced an aroma most kindly described as pungent, an odor the still-pregnant Peggs couldn't stand for an instant.

Tir must have slipped into her kitchen to make some for their aunt, the Lady Mahavar, who'd acquired a taste for what she called a fine and bracing tonic, regardless the commonness of its ingredients.

Poor Peggs.

Now sworn to the lady's service, Tir would stay in Marrowdell so long as she did, brewing his tea as long as the supply lasted—and he was certain he'd spotted the key ingredients in the valley.

And of course Aunt Sybb wouldn't—and mustn't—budge from Marrowdell any sooner than the harvest.

Meaning a long summer of bog tea in Peggs' kitchen. Maybe her sister would get used to it—

The kitchen door closed emphatically. Roses shuddered.

—eventually.

She might, Jenn mused, have to resort to what Old Master Jupp called "shenanigans" to spare her sister. Maybe Wisp could hide Tir's odorous tea until Peggs had her baby—or she herself send it away with someone else entirely, a thought arriving with the two women striding briskly past the Nalynn porch toward the commons.

The pair were sisters, Emo and Elsinore Anan, arrived with the rest from Endshere but who'd lingered, agreeing to take Marrowdell's livestock to summer pastures beyond the Northward Road. The task had been Tadd and Allin Emms' since they were old enough to ride with Uncle Horst, but Tadd was lately become the miller's apprentice—and father of twins—while Allin had moved to Endshere to become an innkeeper with Palma, who was the sisters' cousin.

Even if Jenn waved, she doubted she'd catch their attention.

Massed curls met as the sisters chatted earnestly: the elder's, Emo's, hair was black and expanded like down in the warmth. Elsinore, the younger, had hair the orange-red of sunrise, though just as fluffed.

Their hair appeared their only softness, for the pair dressed in sturdy leather and canvas, with well-oiled boots rising over their knees as suited drovers. Bows and quivers hung over their wide shoulders, shoulders draped with worked deerskin, and they'd each two knives secured to their belts.

According to Bannan, Tir was entirely smitten. A shame the sisters had their sights on Devins Morrill.

While Devins' role, Hettie reminded her stepbrother at every chance and with a mischievous grin, was to pick one and make ready to outrun the other.

Poor Devins. Or lucky Devins, Jenn supposed, depending—the point being Emo and Elsinore would leave tomorrow morning with most of the horses and yearling cattle, not to return till the harvest reopened Marrowdell's fields to grazing. She felt sorry for Devins, who'd already started to pine—not that he'd admit for whom—but, as Aunt Sybb would and did say, regularly, absence was the surest test of affection.

Which had to do with leaving her beloved husband, Uncle Hane, in Avyo every spring and summer, but also, Jenn decided, explained her own current restlessness. Bannan Larmensu, who held her heart, had left the valley yesterday and not yet returned, an absence unremarked by anyone else, for he'd not used the road at all.

After the flood, she'd made a wish to open a special crossing in her meadow—a door—just for him. She cast a longing look toward it. A look only, Jenn careful not to wish or want or worry in case her turn-born magic pulled the truthseer home before he was ready.

Or cause a storm. Or summon crows. Frustrating, never to know how Marrowdell would answer. Perilous, as well. There were always consequences.

And, Jenn sighed, she'd made the door in the first place to let Bannan visit his family in Vorkoun—a secret they both kept, though she'd told her sister Peggs, having promised to be truthful, and Peggs told Kydd, her husband, having done the same.

Wainn, who listened to Marrowdell, doubtless knew but wouldn't tell.

She hoped.

Wisp, her dragon, knew of the door and remained uneasy about it, though the terst turn-born had given their consent and the sei, who'd created every crossing from Verge to edge to control passage between, permitted her small act of trespass. Or hadn't yet noticed or didn't care. Difficult, Jenn reminded herself, to tell with sei, even being, in part, one herself.

Spirit and Dauntless, the kruar who'd attached themselves to Bannan's nephew Werfol, used the door to relay messages from his sister Lila, for such creatures had the power of speech within the edge, and the edge included, they'd discovered, not only Marrowdell but the slope and part of the forest behind the Westietas home.

The latest had sent Bannan off in a hurry. A new concern over Werfol and his gifts, for the brave young boy was a truthseer like his uncle and a truedreamer like his mother, Lila, and struggled for control more often than not.

Making it, Jenn sighed again, softly, much too soon to expect Bannan back.

Eyes of molten gold glared from a mud-smeared face. "You're a dirty stupid liar!" Werfol Westietas' hands curled in fists as he struggled to get free. Dutton Omemee kept hold of the boy's coat, the big guard throwing Bannan a pleading look.

"I am not!" The other half of the current dispute stood his ground, defiance in every line and boots deep in a puddle. Semyn Westietas, heir and elder brother, appeared no less muddy and equally furious. "You're wrong, Weed. Your gift isn't perfect. Admit it!"

"WILL NOT!! LI—"

Gently but firmly taking hold of Semyn's right ear and Werfol's left, Bannan waited in stony silence until his nephews stopped squirming to stare up at him like little owls, tears now streaking the mud. "Enough," he ordered quietly.

An abashed mumble, "Yes, Uncle," from Semyn.

With a fierce scowl, Werfol pressed his lips together. Unrepentant, that was.

The lad didn't make it easy. The truthseer schooled his expression to neutral, aware Dutton chewed his lower lip to keep from a grin, even more aware they stood in the midst of the training yard in plain view of the windows—and so Lila, their mother.

Who'd sent the message to bring him here, as quickly as possible, before, to quote Lila, she locked her youngest in a closet for a year to gain some peace.

Poor timing, their tutor's trip to Avyo's Sersise University. Namron Setac had proved good for the boys; it hadn't hurt the man knew enough of gifts—magic—to keep Werfol's attention. Doubtless some mission, either for his secretive group or Lila. Or both.

Leaving the boys to him. Bannan released their ears, taking hold of their shoulders. "Over there." He guided his nephews ahead, sloshing through the muck where they'd had their latest fight, until they reached drier ground and the bench under the spreading elm tree. "Sit." He settled himself between the two. "We'll be inside in a moment," he told Dutton, who gave a relieved huff and headed for the kitchen to clean himself up.

Not for the faint of heart, looking after the heir and his doubly gifted younger brother.

Bannan felt daunted himself, but he'd promised Lila—and left Marrowdell and Jenn—to do his best. "What started it this time?"

"He LIED!" "I didn't!!" "He—"

Letting them bicker, the truthseer looked deeper into their faces, drawing on his own honed and trained gift. Both told the truth.

Heart's Blood, if only it were that simple. "Perception," he said, setting the word between them.

Werfol tensed as if suspecting a trap.

Semyn, clever as their father, Baron Emon Westietas, frowned in concentration, then made an "aha" face that shifted instantly to dismay. "It *was* my fault. I was only guessing about Poppa's new project but I said it as if I knew for sure." He leaned forward to look past Bannan at his brother. "I'm sorry, Weed. I didn't think of it as a lie. I didn't mean to hurt you."

To see falsehood, especially in a familiar face, caused pain nigh onto physical; Bannan had yet to find the courage to tell the young truthseer it always would. "Werfol?"

The scowl intensified.

Ah. More to the anger than Semyn's slip of the tongue, something Werfol—who'd taken eagerly and well to his lessons—should have been able to grasp. Bannan stretched out his legs, crossing one boot over the other, and laid his arms across the back of the bench behind his nephews, prepared to catch either by the collar if they went to bolt, resigned to be out in the rain as long as it took. "What's behind this? Tell me the whole of it."

Curious himself about Emon's "new project."

"Here you are, Dear Heart." Aunt Sybb stepped out on the porch. She took her accustomed seat, settling into her cushions after a wary glance beneath to ensure the Nalynn house toad wasn't joining them. Tir came behind with a loaded tray he set on the barrel that served for a summer table. "Will you join us?" Aunt Sybb asked. "Tirsan's brought an extra cup." She was the only one to use Tir's full name.

"I've had my tea, thank you," Jenn said, pointedly ignoring Tir's wink. "Where's Peggs?"

"Airing out the kitchen. She's more pies to bake in that giant stove of hers and continues to assert this delicious tea upsets her." Creases framed Aunt Sybb's eyes, Peggs not the only one upset. "Ancestors Pent and Plentiful," she sighed. "Here's hoping the baby arrives soon."

A hope having nothing to do with tea and everything to do with a date past and anxiously pending. Jenn reached over to touch her aunt's wrist. "Peggs will be fine," she said gently, careful to keep it a hope of her own and not a wish or magic.

A small, elegant hand covered hers. In a rare concession to the weather, the elder Nalynn had done without her customary waistcoat and skirt, choosing instead a simple summer frock with three-quarter sleeves. She'd draped a pale yellow shawl over her shoulders, its ends fastened above her heart with an unfamiliar pin.

Jenn eyed it curiously. The pin looked like a sprig of flowers, three in total, their long stems tied together by a metal ribbon—no, she decided, it was meant to represent a thin curled leaf, suggesting the artist worked from a living plant, if one she'd never seen before. Each flower consisted of three topaz petals above a tiny emerald, the whole a more delicate and restrained piece than the Lady Mahavar usually favored. "What a lovely pin," she complimented sincerely, such notice surely expected and deserved, as well as an easy change of subject. "A gift from Uncle Hane?"

"One from me, Dear Heart, to you." Aunt Sybb unfastened the pin, placing it on Jenn's palm, then took her cup from Tir.

Whose eyes locked on the pin, brows colliding in a frown above the fine leather mask that covered the lower half of his face, and Jenn had the strangest impression he was about to snatch the pin from her.

She wasn't the only one. "I made my decision," Aunt Sybb said gently, giving him a meaningful look. With a reluctant nod, Tir smoothed his expression and took a seat, but his eyes never left the pin.

Making it other than an ordinary gift. Of course, it wasn't her birthday until harvest, but their beloved aunt loved to shower them with little surprises from the moment she arrived. This very morning, hadn't she given Peggs a sachet of fine talc?

A gift kind and practical, her sister experiencing chafing in areas she preferred not to discuss and the talc their aunt's sovereign remedy.

Whatever Tir's problem with the pin, Jenn had her own, a bejeweled pin being more than slightly problematic in nature, her much younger self having dropped Aunt Sybb's then-favorite such item in the privy. Remembering, she gave a little embarrassed cough. "Are you sure . . ."

A glint in those wise eyes. "I'm sure you'll take excellent care of it, Dear Heart. Now accept it. You'll make me glad."

There being nothing she'd like better, Jenn smiled from her heart. "Thank you, Aunt Sybb. I shall treasure it." Without noticing the small white moth in a rafter above busy scribbling notes, she lifted the pin to her eyes, turning it to catch the sunlight.

Having expected colored glints from the gems, Jenn was taken aback to see silver letters take fire along the inner length of the metal leaf, the pin itself gaining weight—which was clearly impossible. She shot her aunt a startled look.

Receiving a remarkably smug one over the rim of Aunt Sybb's cup in answer, and didn't Tir prove himself part of what was clearly a conspiracy by passing Jenn a hand lens, though his frown returned?

Now with her own misgivings, Jenn focused the lens over the letters.

"A wish for joy to our Melly."

The air thickened as Jenn's hands dropped limply into her lap, pin and lens still in their grip. Roses leaned around the side of the porch, their dark red petals almost hidden in shadow, leaves rustling with dismay. Tir glanced at them, brows rising; Aunt Sybb, long accustomed to the oddness of Melusine's roses, did not.

Jenn stared at the pin—this *wishing*, though she sensed no power in it, other than the use of what had to be mimrol, liquid magic from the Verge, for the inscription. Feelings roiled queasily inside her. None were joy.

This—this had belonged to her mother and Peggs'. Gifted, she'd no doubt at all, by the parents who'd forbidden Melusine her happiness with Radd Nalynn, a Naalish, and locked their own daughter in her rooms, forcing her to flee by night with baby Peggs to join her husband in exile.

Parents who'd sent a soldier to Marrowdell to bring their daughter and her child back to them, causing Melusine's death—and Jenn's birth at the turn.

How could Aunt Sybb give her this? Jenn wanted to throw the horrid thing, all it represented, away.

"This is from a better time," her aunt said then, reading her face. "Melly, Ancestors Dear and Departed, left it with me in trust, to bring to her daughter once she was grown and—" Instead of faltering, the lady straightened, nostrils flared, chin high. "—grown and safe from them."

Tir growled.

Aunt Sybb ignored him. "You and Peggs deserve proof your mother was happy, once, within a family who did love her. I say this with surety, for Melusine was my protégé and dear friend long before she met my brother and fell in love."

Jenn stiffened. "You never said—" The questions she and Peggs would have asked. The stories they longed for and missed. "Why?" The word came out a whisper.

Her aunt's eyes glistened. "When Melly and Radd entered this beautiful valley they swore to leave their past behind them on the Northward Road. It was not my place to go against their wish nor—" with a hitched and unhappy sigh "—did I think they were wrong. We were all angry, Dear Heart. Afraid. Here, at last, was sanctuary. A fresh start, free from pain." She paused, letting silence wrap around them, as if to allow Jenn's heart to stop pounding—not that it did—before saying more cheerfully, "Ancestors Witness, from now on, I'll be delighted to tell you and your sister everything I recall, starting with this." She gestured to the pin in Jenn's hand.

Tir shifted on his barrel. "It'd be no simple gaud," he accused darkly. "That cursed mirror made its way back here. What says this didn't?"

"I do, Tirsan. I decided," Aunt Sybb said again, this time with rare force. "Not Melly's pin."

Not, clearly, the first time they'd argued about it. Jenn was on Tir's side. Her beloved aunt's determined blindness over Marrowdell's magic was amusing when it came to house toads and roses. This was perilous and Tir was right. Magical objects like Crumlin's mirror had a way of influencing those around them, of finding their way through the edge.

Of causing trouble.

None of it Aunt Sybb's fault. Jenn closed her fingers over her mother's pretty pin, an object still ominously heavier than it should be, summoning a warm smile. "Thank you again, dear aunt. I can't wait to show Bannan." With what she hoped sounded like pleased anticipation and not an urgent desire for his true sight.

By the glint of satisfaction in Tir's eyes, he knew better.

What no one could see? On the pretty pin held in Jenn's hand, the wishing pin given by the House of Semanaryas to their only daughter, left behind in Avyo with her sole friend those many years, brought here this very first summer of Jenn Nalynn being turn-born and magic, the words written in mimrol briefly changed themselves to read . . .

"*A second and special granddaughter. How perfect.*"

"Next you'll say we must tell Weed what we plan for his birthday months ahead." Emon looked distressed.

Lila looked *interested*.

Not the typical reaction of a mother learning the root cause of trouble in their home, but then, Bannan thought with a mixture of pride and resignation, his sister was hardly typical. "Werfol doesn't need to know everything beforehand. But—until he has better control over his gift—it would help prevent future troubles if you told him when there's a secret being kept."

Lila's lips quirked to the side. "And you, brother-mine."

As well try to hide bacon from Scourge. Bannan conceded the point with a half shrug.

Without a word, Emon spun the paper on the table in front of him and pushed it to Bannan.

It was an architectural drawing. Not of a clever mechanism or engine, the baron's usual subjects, but of a simple cottage, styled like their home in Marrowdell, with a single large room below and loft above. Bannan found himself reaching for it involuntarily, a finger tracing where their kitchen would be, then his hand flattened on the paper and he glared at the two of them. "Ancestors Impulsive and Impossible. What's this?" He whispered the words, even though they were alone in Emon and Lila's private library, the boys downstairs with Dutton and Cook having lunch.

Even though he'd no doubt at all the answer.

"The forester's hut is fit for nothing but mice," Lila confirmed lightly, as if discussing the weather. "Past time it was replaced with something useful."

Heart's Blood. In the edge. The hut was in the edge, and what she—and Emon—were proposing would draw the worst sort of attention. If it hadn't already. "Does Roche know?" Bannan demanded grimly.

Devins' older brother lived with the Westietas, fitting in well, preparing—with the best instructors in Rhothan politics—for the day he'd claim his father's seat in Avyo and become Baron Morrill. But one of Jenn's first wishes had changed Roche for life. Furious at his habitual lies, she'd ordered him to stop, unaware, then, of her power or its consequence. From that moment on, Roche told the truth. He couldn't help himself, blurting out his own dark secrets. He'd had to leave Marrowdell—to start a new life where he'd no secrets to spill.

This cottage—what it represented—was the sort he mustn't learn.

Emon took back the drawing, tugging a little to free it from the truthseer's hand. "Roche knows that it's to be a safe playhouse for Semyn and Werfol—a place of their own, away from adults. To be children"—he glanced at his wife—"while they can."

Lila, for her part, returned an innocent green-eyed gaze neither man believed for an instant. "And if it serves as a convenience for out-of-town guests who wish extra privacy—" Her hand sketched an airy line.

Meaning Jenn Nalynn.

That's what this was about, Bannan was certain of it. A way to satisfy his sister's intense curiosity about the turn-born and her power. The boys' use of the little cottage was a screen. Out-of-town guests? Another lie. "And you wonder why Werfol's riled beyond common sense?" he accused, jaw clenched.

After a quick study of his face, the baron rolled up the troublesome paper. "It was never our intention to cause Werfol—or you—distress, Bannan. I apologize. We should have consulted with you and the boys before going this far." Lila stirred and he sent her a quelling look. "We should have and will, from now on."

"Are you so against having a place here?" Lila asked quietly, then went straight to the heart of it. "A place where Jenn can be comfortable if—when—she chooses to come with you? A place we can sit and share a meal like family instead of balancing on grumpy song stones in the rain?"

The stones in question being the scree who made up the talus on the slope—beings who weren't, as a rule, ill-tempered—but she wasn't wrong. Jenn couldn't leave the edge. Would never walk into this house.

Maybe he saw ulterior motives instead of kindness.

Lila, only kind? Bannan resisted the impulse to use his deeper sight and see if his sister lied to him. Ancestors Duplicitous and Deceiving, of course she did, by omission if nothing else, and seeing it—proving it—would only cause him the pain Werfol'd felt. It wouldn't change a thing.

And he did miss Jenn. He wanted her to know his precious family—however conniving and sly they could be at times—and, oh, how he hated being apart from his love even this long. "If—if—I agree to this," he muttered at last, "there'll need to be rules."

With a grin, Emon whipped out the drawing, spreading it flat once more. He planted a fingertip on a tall pole Bannan had noticed but not understood, drawn as if attached to the roof. "This sends and receives coded messages along a series of wires. It's the Eld system, one in use between their train stations and coming here, once we've built ours. Deceptively simple—quite, quite brilliant. The concept builds on earlier work by—"

Lila raised an eyebrow.

To Bannan's relief, her husband the engineer stopped and chuckled. "With it, Bannan, you'll be able to signal us that you've arrived at the cottage. And when you're ready for company—or not. All without leaving the edge."

A marvel indeed. Jenn would love it.

He met Lila's now-somber regard, giving a tiny nod to acknowledge what Emon didn't need to add.

A system like that went two ways.

They'd be warned if strangers approached the edge, especially the sort of strangers who mustn't learn of his door to Marrowdell.

Or of the existence of Jenn Nalynn.

Emon, perhaps seeing he was relenting, gave a boyish grin. "Would you like to see it?"

"A model?" Bannan hazarded, that being something else the baron did.

Lila stretched like a cat, anticipation glinting in her green eyes. "Oh, we've done better than that, little brother. It's done."

He stared in disbelief at the drawing, shifting that look to meet distinctly smug ones from his tablemates. "I walked by the hut a dozen times or more." And seen nothing but a decrepit building, being reclaimed by the forest.

But that would be the point, wouldn't it? No one would give the broken-down hut a second look. "You built all of this inside," Bannan said wonderingly.

Emon leaned back with a contented smile. "That we did."

Kydd Uhthoff hesitated before stepping up on the porch of what had been, till his marriage to Peggs Nalynn last fall, his home every bit as much as it was his brother Dusom's and nephew Wainn's. Once on the sun-warmed wood, the door two steps away, he hesitated again, noticing small things. How, this late on a summer's day, sunbeams reached to the far right of the porch, catching the colors of the braided rug and gilding the pair of treasured wooden armchairs, brought from Avyo and made welcoming with cushions tapestried by Riss Nahamm. Barrels made handy side tables, not that any had room for a cup, being stacked with books. Dusom's habit, to be reading a dozen or more at any given time.

But these books had cobwebs on them and dust, a telling neglect. Ancestors Puzzled and Perplexed, something wasn't right here.

Kydd let out a slow breath. Or, as Peggs would say, he made much of nothing at all. Wasn't his elder brother preoccupied with new duties and distractions, Wainn having presented him Delfinn, his first grandchild? Wasn't the weather too fine for study? Wasn't—?

Yet the curtains were drawn on this fine day. They'd been drawn since shortly after the flood and Dusom's excuse of letting them dry out had passed beyond credibility to ridiculous. Every other building in Marrowdell stood open to the glorious summer air, windows cracked and doors open. Shut tight, this house, as if against winter.

Or to hide a secret—and where had that wild thought come from?

From something inside. Something reaching out, calling to him after all these years of silence and peace, something—

—*not here*. That had never been here.

Shaking off the memory, Kydd pressed his lips together and strode to the door. He raised his hand to knock—and wasn't that another change for the worst, that Dusom required it of his own—

The door opened before he touched it, his brother surging out to close it behind him, and there was no mistaking the forbidding in that.

For an impossible, heart-wrenching instant, it felt like meeting a stranger.

Kydd fought off the feeling. Like twins, the Uhthoff brothers, possessed of the same build, tall and slender, long-fingered and well-featured, and though Dusom's long years of scholarship had begun to curve his shoulders and the thick black hair over his ears was streaked with white, Kydd wasn't, in truth, far behind him.

Ancestors Blessed, they'd always been close—

Thinking that, Kydd lowered his hand, made himself smile. He bowed his head briefly. "Greetings, Brother—"

"This grows old," Dusom said heavily, his voice strained and hoarse. "I've said I want no company in the house."

As if the house had become his fortress—a defense against what? "Surely I am not 'company,' Dear Heart—" Kydd said, forcing cheer into the words. He made to move around his brother. "We'll have tea—"

"NO!" Dusom shoved Kydd back, hard enough to send him staggering down the step to the ground, and his brother had never in their lives raised a hand to him before this, and he couldn't fathom it—

Unless he'd been right, all along. Right since coming to Marrowdell, with its strange and powerful magic, and certainty crystallized Kydd's thoughts, firmed his voice. "You're under a spell, Dusom. It's this place." Seeing a flicker in the older man's eyes, he dared put a foot on the step. Pleaded, "Hearts of our Ancestors, I beg you let me help you."

But Dusom shook his head and disappeared into his house, the house that had been their home, and closed the door.

Kydd spun on his heel and ran for help, blinded by a terrible fear, the one he'd buried twenty-three years ago, the one he'd thought to erase with happiness.

Knowing he'd been wrong to forget any of it.

The kitchen smelled wonderfully of fresh-baked bread and warm berry jam—loaves lined up to cool and a pot bubbling on the big stove—and a pair of hungry boys might be forgiven thinking first of their stomachs. Before Semyn and Werfol could enter, Cook held up a thin forbidding hand, then pointed wordlessly toward the side room with its sink and tile.

Semyn stopped at once, aghast to have almost tracked mud into her spotless workspace.

Weed, naturally, tried a smile. "But Cook—we're famished." It wasn't quite the full wheedling voice the younger Westietas could produce without warning, but close.

Cook smiled back, revealing a woeful lack of teeth. "Ye'll nah starve while gitt'n clean."

Which was true, of course, and Werfol gave a happy little shrug. "Had to try."

You hadn't, Semyn said, but to himself. Bowing an apology to Cook, he led the way to the sink room, trying various oaths in his head. Ancestors Naughty and Nasty. No, Ancestors Reckless and Rude.

Yes, that one. That was Weed. Much as he loved his brother, there were times Semyn despaired of Werfol ever controlling his impulses. Or his tongue.

Setting their boots on the rack to clean last, they stripped off their muddy clothes in silence. Werfol looked smaller, in his simples, with bruises starting to bloom under the pale skin of arms and chest. Plus a good one on his jaw and Semyn might have been sorry but he'd an ample set of his own.

Filling the bucket, Semyn poured cold water over Weed's head before his brother could dodge. Muddy streaks trailed over his outraged face but before he could protest, Semyn handed him the bucket and bent over, a little, ready for his turn.

Weed refilled the bucket. Stood glaring, which he did rather well. Semyn waited, eyebrow raised in challenge.

Without warning, Weed dumped the bucket on Semyn's head, the cold making him sputter and spit. Then both were laughing and somehow found another bucket and it was just as well their clothes were on the floor because enough water flew to get those clean as well.

Cleaner.

"I'd best check on—" About to say her sister's name, Jenn froze in place.

Kydd Uhthoff, usually easy of pace and the image of courtesy, was running full tilt down the village path. He almost collided with the Anan sisters, who looked startled and a little annoyed, before charging the step to the porch, his lean handsome face so pale and grim Tir surged to his feet with a sharp, "What's to do?"

The beekeeper jerked to a stop. "Tir. Jenn." Remembering himself, he gave a short bow. "Lady Mahavar. Forgive my unseemly haste." He looked longingly at the door to the house, as if desperate to go inside.

"Peggs is fine." Aunt Sybb patted the bench beside her. "Sit. Have tea." When he hesitated, she added briskly, "It's Tir's special brew, so you needs must have it here in the open or not at all."

The former soldier poured a mug, handing it to Kydd without a word. Trapped, the beekeeper perched more than sat on the bench, one knee bouncing as if ready to leap up again. "I really must talk to Peggs, Lady—"

"Aunt Sybb," that worthy admonished kindly. "I shouldn't need to remind you, Dear Heart. We're family."

"Yes, of course. Forgive me, Aunt Sybb, and thank you." Kydd brought the mug to his lips and took a too-heedless gulp, choking. His cheeks regained their color as he recovered. "S-strong," he sputtered at last.

Aunt Sybb smiled. "And quite bracing," she agreed. "Now, what is the trouble? Surely your family can be of service?"

"Is it Delfinn?" Jenn asked, not bothering to be tactful. While Kydd wasn't yet a father, he was certainly gaining what Hettie called an "education" whenever he took his turn minding his great-niece, and, to be blunt, the man panicked at the babe's least whimper or tiniest rash.

Not that Jenn—whose child-rearing experience to date came from Hettie tossing her one or the other of her infant twins whenever she needed a free hand—thought she'd do much better.

Kydd stared at her blankly.

"Delfinn?" she prodded.

"Napping with Wainn in the orchard. I don't know why you'd—it's not—" Kydd clamped his lips together, his expression bleaker than Jenn had ever seen it.

Whatever Aunt Sybb read in his face, it drew her graciously to her feet, Tir taking her cup. "Come." She offered Kydd her arm. "Let's get you to your wife."

Setting his mug on the floor, Kydd stood and tucked her little hand into the crook of his elbow, holding it there with his other hand as if it were a lifeline.

Tir opened the door to admit the pair, closing it before Jenn, who'd jumped to her feet, could follow. When she opened her mouth to protest, he shook his head. "Whatever's amiss isn't for the likes of us."

Jenn wasn't so sure about that.

She was sure she needed Bannan home, sooner than later, even if she had to fetch him herself.

And wasn't that an interesting thought?

From the girl's meadow, where the valley floor rose to the Bone Hills that bound it, Wisp could, if he chose, lift his head and see across the expanse of field, hedge, and river to where the dwellings of the villagers crowded around their fountain and each other.

He did not, content to keep his long jaw and neck nestled in the pile of grass he'd made—grass that wasn't actually his, belonging in various rabbit nests—but what a dragon wanted, a dragon took. Such was the way of things and always would be.

He'd put back the grass before the girl came.

It being the most comfortable of moments, the sun on his body and air pleasantly dry, moving held no appeal whatsoever. Wisp had taken care to settle himself where he could, by cracking an eyelid, see the path the girl would take to the meadow from her and Bannan's farm. At the same time, he could watch the place he'd stood when she'd tried to make him into a man, her new and out-of-control turn-born power and a silly Rhothan wishing searing the meadow to ash and the flesh from his writhing bones.

She'd believed she needed a husband. The dragon growled, deep in his chest, grimly amused by the memory of how the truthseer had arrived the same day to ultimately save all three from that fate.

Having no harm in her heart, the girl had restored the meadow and, by the end, helped the sei restore Wisp's true self.

Most of him. Idly, Wisp twitched his now-intact wingtips; that his leftmost limbs remained withered and useless was old news and unimportant. When the sei deigned to notice the war between the kruar and dragons for control of the Verge, the sei ended it, giving the leaders to their own for justice. Scourge had been stripped of his armor by his fellow kruar and exiled beyond the edge to forget himself and become a legend.

Dragons had no interest in legends.

Wisp had survived his kind's attempt to destroy him not because they didn't do their utmost to rip him to shreds, but because he was too powerful—and stubborn—to die. The sei decided then on an additional punishment, or potential redemption, or continued neglect—one never knew motive, with them. They gave him to the terst turn-born enclave as a drudge, and the turn-born, unused to servants, gave Wisp the most demeaning jobs they could find except when they forgot him in the gap beneath their kitchen floor and the ground.

Not that the dragon cared.

The birth of Jenn Nalynn changed matters, the sei burdened with the promise and threat of a turn-born in the edge, where none had been before. Wisp was thrust into Marrowdell with one instruction: prevent her from leaving, by her death if necessary. Neither sei nor dragon anticipated Wisp would come to love the babe, the child, and the woman grown with every fiber of his scarred and ancient heart.

The sei gave Wisp a sanctuary within the Verge, near the crossing used by dragons, for he remained crippled and flightless and would be easy prey. Though in that they proved wrong as well, for dragonkind knew better than challenge their former lord and the kruar, who used the turn-born's crossing, soon learned better as well.

Or died.

There was, after the turmoil that almost tore the Verge and edge asunder, a third crossing created between Marrowdell and the Verge, the Wound, a gap held open by the sei trapped between and injured. None used it until Jenn Nalynn, lured by that sei, dared.

Steam left the dragon's nostrils at the thought. He—with Scourge and the truthseer Bannan—had taken that ominous crossing thinking to save the girl, who'd saved them and the sei instead.

Being power incarnate. Power unchecked, except by her own good heart, and Wisp, while proud, felt a certain wariness about that.

He cracked open his other eye, staring at the innocent-seeming spot in their meadow where Jenn Nalynn had done the unthinkable twice. First to change him into a man, then to create her own crossing.

A door, she called it. A convenience for Bannan, who apparently needed to reach his far-off family at whim, but this wasn't like any other crossing, where the first step went from a place in the edge into the Verge and to go anywhere else meant traveling through that realm to another crossing. Easy for a dragon or kruar or turn-born. Difficult for anything of softer flesh and mind. Prey they'd be, or go mad.

Impossible, for those with no magic inside.

What the girl had made crossed from here to there apart from the Verge; not even he could do more than sense that realm rushing by with unnatural speed, out of reach.

Making Bannan's door a trap, not a gift.

Each time he'd used it, Wisp felt a *wrongness*, not that he'd yet found the right words to explain what was, in the end, a dragonish instinct. Oh, he'd tried—so often, the girl had taken to throwing up her hands to dance rather than be frustrated or see him be.

He did enjoy watching her dance, especially when he added clouds of flower petals.

So be it.

The dragon closed one eye, leaving the other open to watch for the peril he knew was coming if not its shape or size. An impudent rabbit tugged away some of his grass. A trespass he permitted, the creature being hers.

As, always, was he.

TWO

DASHING FROM MARROWDELL without checking on her sister and Kydd would be, Jenn knew, the height of irresponsibility.

Unless that was leaving at all—she silenced her conscience. Peggs first, regardless.

She'd have questioned Tir about the pin, but he made it clear he wasn't in the mood to chat. Having poured himself the last of the bog tea, upending the pot to be certain, the former soldier dragged his barrel in front of the door and sat there, staring out over the village.

Every so often, he'd lift his mask, showing the ruin of cheek and chin, to drink.

As if the Nalynn household needed more guard than its house toad, who emerged from wherever it had managed to hide its round bulk once the Lady Mahavar was safely out of sight.

After a pause to glare at it, Tir resumed his intense surveillance of the peaceful valley.

Maybe if she claimed to need the privy—snuck around back—

~Elder sister?~

Rather than include Tir in their conversation, the man prone to either mock the little cousins or grumble at them, Jenn went and sat on the top step. Once the Nalynns' house toad settled next to her, its cool body against her arm, she tipped her head close and whispered, "What is it?"

~This moon cycle I laid six eggs. Last night I ate three foul nyphrit. I matter to Marrowdell.~

She nodded, summoning her patience. The little cousins did matter, in far more ways than these. Hers stayed at the farm to watch for Bannan and help his toad guard the buildings, structures a particular duty and concern of the creatures. There was nothing to be gained by rushing one.

~Elder sister, why does the man block the entrance to our home? It is~—the toad hesitated, eyes protruding, before finding the word it wanted—~unprecedented.~

A measure of the respect Tir had earned—whether he wanted it or not beside the point—that the house toad chose to assume he'd good reason and wasn't just being what he was. Difficult.

Jenn shrugged. "He wishes to ensure a private discussion between my aunt, my sister, and her husband." A wish that stung, just a little. "I should be in there."

The house toad shuddered. ~I do not think so, elder sister. The beekeeper is full of a terrible fear.~

She twisted to look down at it, no longer bothering to whisper. "What's Kydd afraid of?" She sensed Tir coming alert. "Do you know?"

One eye blinked. ~I do not. He has always been afraid, elder sister, but—~ A foot stretched. Returned to its place. ~This is a new and deeper fear.~

Always been afraid. Kydd Uhthoff had come to Marrowdell as a student of politics, but also of magic and its consequence. He'd spoken of unseen dangers here to any who'd listen, confessing to Peggs and Jenn how he'd done everything he could to urge their elders to leave the valley, only to be ostracized and misunderstood. How, at last, he learned better. He'd torn apart his books, used them to line his hives. Been content.

Or, Jenn thought suddenly, had Kydd merely learned to hide his fear, even from himself?

Kydd Uhthoff hadn't felt this alone since arriving in Marrowdell to face a peril he couldn't explain and others refused to heed, even as his own family was torn and wracked by loss. In that abyssal time, when Dusom himself shunned him, despair had been his companion and fear his only friend. Those memories kept him on his feet when the Lady Mahavar gestured him to sit, hands fisted in his pockets.

And they kept him distant from the astonishing woman he'd married, who looked at him with such warm and loving concern his heart begged to thaw—but he couldn't afford weakness. Not today. They all depended on him. "We have to leave," he repeated. "All of us."

Lady Mahavar shook her head. "The day will come when that's your choice to make. Hane and I are working hard to have the Fair Lease overturned. I assure you we aren't alone—"

Kydd gritted his teeth, forced the words out. "NOW. We have to leave now!"

"Dearest Heart, Jenn can't," Peggs reminded him, as if saying the sun rose in the east or the night was full of stars. "I won't." Her hands slipped over the bulge of their child. "We won't."

He saw memories of her own cloud the lady's face, heard them add sharpness to her voice. "What's returned you to this woeful state, Kydd Uhthoff? Tell us!"

With a gasp, Peggs came to him, her hands outstretched, ready to give comfort and strength.

Ancestors Bloody and Bruised, the hurt in her face cut his heart when he stepped back to avoid her, but there was nothing for it, not if he was to save them. "It's starting again—the way it did with the family from Weken. The madness. My own brother—" Why was there no air to breathe? "He's succumbed, I tell you. Lost. We can't know who'll be next—I warned them there'd be a price to pay for this—" He threw up his arms, encompassing this home he loved, the village surrounding it, the beautiful land beyond.

A land seething with magic and threat. Marrowdell—how had he ever thought it safe?

His eyes locked on Peggs, her rose-kissed cheeks gone pale as the finest alabaster. "What if it's you?" he demanded of his beloved, hearing his voice crack, feeling something inside poised to shatter. "How do I—how do I bear that?"

They were staring at him, shocked, disbelieving. Heart's Blood, he was no more convincing than he'd been before. Had no idea what more to say or do—

"Peggs, the summerberry wine, please." The lady's regard remained on him, held him. "We'll hear what you have to say, Kydd, I promise. First. Please. Sit and calm yourself."

Commanded as surely as if she'd cast a spell, Kydd stumbled to the nearest chair and dropped into it. He clenched the wooden arm with his left hand. His right stayed a fist, raised to press against his lips.

It was that or scream.

Peggs, moving as if her bones ached, made up a tray with the bottle and two mismatched glasses. The best they had. She poured for her aunt and for him, holding out his glass until he loosed his fist to take it, her eyes searching his face.

He couldn't smile. Didn't try. Her worried sigh was from another life. He heard Lady Mahavar thank her niece, watched her raise her glass to him in a toast before taking a delicate sip.

Civility. Courtesy. Tradition. They'd power in and of themselves. Kydd went to lift his glass and do the same. His hand shook and the precious stuff spilled over his lap and the floor.

Peggs was there before he realized what he'd done, to take the glass and lay a cloth over his lap. She cupped his face with her hand and he leaned into it, closing his eyes with a shudder. "I—I'm not myself," he admitted helplessly.

"You will be," Lady Mahavar promised. "Listen for a moment. Just be calm and hear me."

He couldn't have spoken if he tried. He nodded into Peggs' warm hand.

"I too was here, Kydd, at the beginning and since. The families who came later left by their own choice because they didn't belong in Marrowdell. The rest stayed because they did. Whatever you feared for them then—whatever you remember now? It didn't happen.

"What did were bandits. Winter. Flood. The trials of life far from help and comforts. The people of Marrowdell came together in strength and community to overcome whatever they faced. As you did and do each day." With inexpressible tenderness, "We don't forget the pain and those lost. We shouldn't and won't. But pain and loss do not define us. Nor does the past."

A kiss on his brow. A rustle of fabric as Peggs knelt by his chair, wrapping her arms around him as best she could. It was more than warmth and love. It was protection and anchor both. Seconds or an hour later, Kydd found himself able to take a deeper breath, felt the sickening panic fade back until, finally, he could make the effort to lock it away again.

His determination to save them remained. He opened his eyes. Met the steady gaze of the Lady Mahavar—*his* Aunt Sybb—drawing strength from her composure.

And when she frowned to ask most sternly, "Now, what's this nonsense about your brother?"

He managed to say the words.

Giving Tir no chance to argue, Jenn bolted around the house. Before she could open the kitchen door and leap inside to demand answers, Peggs came out, carrying, of all things, a pie.

Seeing how her sister struggled, Jenn hurried to help. The pin in one hand making that awkward—it was a most generous savory pie and their heaviest dish—without thinking she handed Peggs the pin at some point in the process, and her sister absently tucked it away in her bosom, too busy groaning with relief to be curious.

Peggs braced herself, hands against her back. "Ancestors Bloated and Ballooned, might be the last I bake," this in a dire, most un-Pegg-like mutter.

Questions could wait. Jenn kissed her sister's cheek and forgot the pin. "You'll have the baby soon," she comforted, not that she knew nor would dare wish, but surely must happen. Peggs' belly was swollen larger than Hettie's, and she'd had twins. "Just one," she stressed, aware her sister worried about exactly that despite Covie's assurances. She lifted the pie. "Isn't this tonight's supper? If you don't wish me to stay, Dear Heart," she teased, "simply say so. There's no need for such a generous and tasty bribe."

Though if Bannan made it home today, Jenn thought all at once, they'd enjoy a fine supper. Wasn't that just like Peggs? She smiled from her heart. "But thank you!"

Her sister didn't smile back. "The pie's for Dusom. Kydd's told us—his brother's in urgent need of one. And you must deliver it. He needs to see you, Dear Heart."

Not at all what she'd expected, not that she'd known what to expect, but surely with Kydd's upset and the house toad's revelation there must be more to the matter. "Master Dusom?" Jenn echoed dubiously. Their former teacher becoming Peggs' brother-in-law wasn't enough for her to lose the honorific, not that he'd mind at all, but it didn't feel right. "To see me?"

"Yes. Kydd says the matter is urgent. Please. You must go without delay."

This being a most unlikely request, especially involving Kydd and his supper, she felt it necessary to confirm, "With your pie."

Her sister gave a vigorous nod of assent. Jenn had the feeling she was about to wave her along with her apron.

Jenn didn't budge. She wasn't being contrary but something wasn't right, starting with the fragrant savory pie in her arms. While everyone loved Peggs' pies—and those she baked from the first ripe berries of spring were like the promise of summer itself while her supper pies were the most comforting of meals—for Kydd to claim his brother *needed* the Nalynns' supper seemed odd. Why not just invite him to dine?

As for being seen by him, why, yesterday afternoon, she'd waved at Master Dusom as he conducted class by the riverbank, in the shade of the oak, Cheffy and Alyssa intent on what he taught them, which might, Jenn thought in retrospect, be about the river itself, the children remembering the flood and how they'd almost lost the village beneath the roil of silt-dark water and ice, and possibly needing reassurance.

Especially as they'd almost lost the river for good when she'd made a hasty wish to get the floodwater out of her way so she could follow Bannan—taken by the toad queen—a wish that brought down a tall ridge to dam the river entirely, sending its flow over the cataract and leaving the valley dry.

Consequences. Always, there were consequences, so Jenn had been far more mindful when it was time to restore her beloved home and its river, leaning on the guidance of the terst turn-born, who'd come to help, and the aid of the little cousins.

As a result, Marrowdell's river entered the valley as a spring of sorts, bubbling to the surface at the base of the collapsed ridge, having carved its way back under the rocks, aided at the last by willing claws. It spilled into its former bed to meander the fields, babbling over rocks, shallow and sparkling at the ford, deeper and mysterious in its pools—

A sight Jenn would never again take for granted, nor would any here.

Not to forget she'd seen Master Dusom again earlier this very day, him walking to the Ropps for butter while she headed to the Nalynn house. They'd exchanged pleasant greetings, as one did, and he'd seemed perfectly fine—perhaps scruffier than his tidy habit—though she hadn't lingered nor had he, meaning she might have missed something strange in his demeanor.

Ancestors Puzzled and Prickly. "You'd tell me if there was something wrong with Master Dusom, wouldn't you?" Who was, being

Kydd's elder and a grandfather on top of it, one of the older residents of Marrowdell—not that he showed his age other than flattering touches of silver in his thick black hair—and he was important to all of them and kind, so she couldn't keep an anxious note from her voice.

"Kydd believes there is," came the alarming answer.

The forester's hut looked as ruined as before. Having come alone, by his choice, Bannan followed Emon's instructions and went to the rear of it, out of sight. He pressed the knot in the fourth log from the ground.

A door opened where no door appeared to be or been before. Bannan slipped inside before he could doubt, hearing a snick from behind as the door closed itself.

It was truly a puzzle box. The interior was lit from above, windows cunningly inset amid the seeming ruin of the roof and high along the back wall, with a curtained mirror opposite to spread the light. The furnishings had been thoughtfully chosen. Nothing new, nothing ostentatious. Simple—

Ancestors Beset and Blind, nothing about this was. A cage, as much as gift. Ploy, as much as kindness, and he'd have rushed back out again except—

What if Jenn liked it?

Bannan made himself move around the space, touching cushions, opening cupboards, trying to imagine this as a second home—a tiny estate in the mountains of Vorkoun, where he and his beloved could entertain family and share news.

From news to schemes—impossible to keep Lila, who cared about a broader canvas than little Marrowdell, from drawing them into hers for Vorkoun and Rhoth. For all he knew, the scope of her plans included Ansnor and Eldad, let alone vast Mellynne, and Ancestors save them if she'd ambitions for the edge, newly aware of its possible extent.

Yet Jenn Nalynn cared as well. He did. Was it wrong to want change?

Wrong to demand justice?

The truthseer stopped at the table. Leaned on his fists. Waited for calm. Here it was, he thought. Here was the trap Lila set, baited with his determination—and hers—to solve the mystery of their parents' murder and drag those responsible into the light of day. Those who'd used dark magic to pull a mountainside down on the Marerrym home and those inside.

This place was Lila's invitation to join the hunt. Not blatant. Never that.

It didn't need to be. His sister knew the pain that had filled him those terrible early years, a boy's grief made infinitely worse by a new and uncontrolled power assailing him with every lie and half truth from those who'd swarmed around them.

He'd survived because of Lila. Because she'd believed he wasn't mad or cursed. Hardly more than a child herself, she'd forged herself into his protector, becoming a force of will and, yes, steel others learned to fear, and how had that been right, that she'd had to set aside her grief to tend to his?

Someone had to pay. Would pay. Hadn't his years as Captain Ash, using his true sight to expose liars, been his forge? By the missing Bones of their slaughtered Beloved Ancestors, he was ready—

—to do what? Bannan hung his head. He'd left the guard and Lila. Gone north. Found peace and love in Marrowdell, a new and better purpose for his life, but at what cost? His sister needed him. This meeting place was Lila's plea for him to do for her what she'd done for him. Abandon his dreams to help her.

But what of Jenn? She'd love this place, he knew, the instant she laid eyes on it. She thought only the best of his family, blissfully innocent of the complex depths whirling around them.

The potential for darkness. If being here twisted him back into Captain Ash, however slightly? It would taint everything.

He owed his beloved better than that. To *be* better. Bannan stood up, shaking his head. He wouldn't show her the cottage. Wouldn't risk it. They'd balance on the scree-filled slope during visits and call it enough.

Emon and Lila had hidden this place.

Let it stay hidden.

The decision left a sour taste in his mouth. When he left the cottage, closing its secret door for good, Bannan threw himself toward his crossing, crashing through brush then over stones as if in flight.

Not that he fled, of course he didn't, it was simply time to be gone from here and home—

—which explained why he almost collided with the very last person he'd expect to encounter on the Westietas Estate.

Mistress Sand.

"I should have seen it." Peggs lowered herself to the sturdy bench their father had installed by the garden, gesturing to Jenn to join her, which was a relief as the pie was substantial and her arms starting to burn. Peggs lowered her voice, though there was no one nearby except a few bees; neither sister noticed the solitary white moth that, having fluttered after Jenn, landed beneath the bench. "I know Dusom. He's been acting strangely of late. For one thing," in a foreboding tone, "he's only teaching outdoors."

Peggs did know people. Ancestors Blessed, it was almost magical how she'd have a basket ready for their father before he could announce he'd work late at the mill and put a kettle on for Aunt Sybb before that worthy could ask for tea. If not bog tea.

This time, however, Jenn shook her head, on surer ground. "That's not strange, Peggs. It's his habit once the weather's this nice." And made it easier to daydream—

"And has Dusom ever, when it rains, sent a rote lesson to the Ropps and bid their children stay home?".

Well, that was unusual, Jenn had to admit, and not what those working parents would prefer, but much had changed since the flood.

Marrowdell hadn't so much been restored as adapted. Scars ringed the massive trunk of the oak tree by the river, but it was already heavy with new acorns. Melusine's roses had returned, cloaking the Nalynn home, their red blooms more splendid than ever, and all agreed the grass was a brighter, deeper green, having been enriched by the silt.

Even if some damp mornings the air had a musty taste.

The fields of kaliia grew faster than ever in memory, already bending in graceful waves before the wind, though most of the efflet tending it were new to Marrowdell, summoned here by the terst turn-born after too many of the little cousins died trying to keep back the flood.

Whose highest reach stained outer walls of buildings, ice floes recalled in nicks and notches in the wood, and the insides of every home had been thoroughly disheveled, both by the water and Wisp's quick action to pull out and dry their belongings, aided by the yling. People continued to find what belonged to someone else or, less happily, to discover something small and loved gone missing. New fences filled the gaps torn from the hedge around the commons, but Davi's forge had been tipped, its heat extinguished by the flood.

She'd helped fix that, thought Jenn with some pride. The terst turn-borns' original expectation had been straightforward, as such magic went, being a united desire for the stone beneath the forge to glow furnace-hot on command. It hadn't been so much a matter of making her own wish as of gently reminding the stone what to do.

And some good had come of the disaster. Though the neyet, the old trees of the forest, closest to the river had been uprooted from the Verge and drowned, the terst turn-born had rendered their bodies into lumber and logs, desperately needed as Marrowdell's population expanded. Uncle Horst's former home, that he'd gifted to Hettie and Tadd, now boasted a larger kitchen and nursery. Davi's cart had been rebuilt, and Devins—however slower—was making improvements to the Morrill home, while the Uhthoffs gained an attached room for Delfinn and Wainn.

Explaining matters. "Master Dusom," Jenn declared triumphantly, aware her sister waited less than patiently for her reply, "likely wants quiet in the house while Delfinn naps."

Ancestors Tried and True, if she'd learned anything from Hettie's excitable twins, it was that the person who dared disturb a peaceful, sleeping baby would be stuck rocking it. Certainly setting the disturbed babe on Crackers, Hettie's birthing day gift from Mistress Sand, to watch the artifice turning into whatever shape soothed best—charming indeed—worked, but that left the other twin wailing to be rocked or take its turn so you didn't, that was all.

Babies were a force of nature. As, it turned out—the surprise of all save her closest family—was Lorra Treff, who reliably put Delfinn into a sound sleep by telling her granddaughter long and winding stories of pottery and guilds and the wickedness of princes.

Peggs drew a lock of her hair between her lips, her habit when worried or thinking hard, though she no longer chewed on it—mostly—being a mother-to-be who wanted to set a good example. She spat the hair out decisively. "When you take him the pie you must ask him, Dear Heart."

Ask their former teacher to explain how he taught? Jenn shook her head vehemently. "Surely Kydd—or Wainn—"

"Ancestors Witness, Wainn's so besotted with his daughter he'd not notice if the moon fell from the sky."

Possibly true but also unfair. Devoted as Wainn was, he'd notice anything amiss in Marrowdell and give warning, as he had in the past.

Wouldn't he?

"Kydd, then."

Peggs' long cool fingers captured Jenn's wrist. She spoke so quietly Jenn had to lean close to hear. "Dusom pushed Kydd off his porch. Just now. Kydd's still upset."

Shocked, Jenn couldn't find a word to say. The brothers were close—the best of friends as well as blood—and for them to fight?

She'd have thought them too old for it, frankly. Not a thought to share with Peggs.

Her sister wasn't done being alarming. "Kydd told us Dusom's been acting odd since the flood. He's refused to let anyone else go upstairs. When asked why, or if there was a problem, perhaps a leak in the roof, Dusom claimed a lingering mustiness and accused Kydd of fussing." A flash of indignation on her husband's behalf, though it was true he did get worked up at times. "Yesterday Kydd tried to press the point and Dusom told him flat out the loft isn't fit for company."

"But Jenn," Peggs went on woefully, "that's where he sleeps! Or did. Aunt Sybb agrees. Something's wrong in that house. Or with Dusom."

"Maybe the poor man merely seeks privacy," Jenn said weakly. "With Delfinn—"

Peggs gave her that look.

The one meaning she'd missed something. Jenn covered the hand holding her wrist with her own, searching her sister's beautiful, troubled eyes. Caught, finally, the heartfelt depth of Peggs' worry and knew what she had to do.

"I'll see Master Dusom and ask him about everything, including his loft and treatment of his brother, Dear Heart," she promised. "It'll be easier with the pie," she added rather glumly, not looking forward to her assignment.

Rewarded by the hint of a dimple. "With pie it is."

Jenn rose and started to walk away. Remembering the pin, she stopped and turned. "My pin. Aunt Sybb gave it to me on the porch, just now. She said she'd waited for the right moment for some time. There's more I need to—" The pie being considerable and Master Dusom in distress, she moved restlessly from one foot to the other. "I—"

"You need to go. Tell me all about it later, Dear Heart," Peggs suggested, and touched her bosom. "I'll keep it safe till then."

Jenn didn't quite know how to express her concerns about the pin to a person as sensible as her sister—or if she was, when it came down to it, concerned at all, now that she didn't hold the pin in her hand.

"Later," she promised with a smile.

While the moth beneath the bench scratched notes in its tiny journal.

And the words on the pin brought from Avyo changed briefly again to read . . .

"A baby. How useful."

In this, the summer estate—before becoming their full-time home thanks to the treaty that put their Vorkoun tower into the hands of Ansnans—the Westietas lived on the second floor, where a hallway connected the guest suite, where Roche Morrill stayed when here, the bedroom Semyn shared with his brother—and a house toad—to their parents' set of rooms. Those included the library and sitting area, where the boys were welcome unless a guard stood outside the door indicating Momma was about her business and likely hosted strangers.

This summer, Semyn and Werfol found themselves invited inside more often than not, Momma newly determined they learn who their enemies were.

And friends. Chancellor Rober Milne was one. Though Vorkoun's city administrator typically brought a long list of troubles and complaints, the tone of discussion was always cheerful, for Milne believed in Poppa's vision for the coming railway and commerce with Eldad. They'd sit at the table before the great windows overlooking the fountain and entry to the house, Cook sending up a tray of Milne's favored treats and the boys'. Unless maps were involved, Werfol would be bored; Semyn could tell, though his brother no longer showed it by twitching or fiddling with his buttons.

He'd matured, Momma said, having spent time a prisoner of the worst of their enemies—not that she'd say who it had been—a situation in which Werfol had acquitted himself with honor and done the family proud.

At first, Semyn hoped he'd have done as well and was a little jealous, but Weed came away with horrid nightmares that woke them both up and could no longer bear to sleep without a light. Their house toad would sneak under his covers, perhaps thinking to help; mostly its chill softness startled Weed awake—which did, it was true, stop the nightmare, so maybe the toad did know best.

For this meeting, between their parents and uncle, the boys were expressly not invited and, in fact, Dutton had been instructed to ensure they stayed in their room, which wasn't quite punishment as they'd been allowed to bring up trays of jam-smeared bread and a small cup of cider each.

Done, Semyn went to his stack of books and—

"We should be there," Weed grumped. He threw himself on his bed, arms flailing. "To tell our side of it."

—choosing the topmost, Semyn went to the little desk now in front of the fireplace and sat, opening the book where a ribbon marked his place. "We know what he'll say," he said briskly. "Uncle Bannan will tell them I started the fight by lying at you. I didn't mean to, Weed." This with a sideways glimpse at his brother.

Who, yes, grimaced then shrugged. "I know. I didn't mean to get mad." A dramatic sigh. "I can't help it."

"I know," Semyn replied absently, already starting to read. The tome concerned the genealogy of the most recent Morrill generation including Roche and his brother in Marrowdell, as well as their mother, Covie Ropp. He'd found a fascinating sidebar concerning the connection between the Nahamm and Wagler lineages, represented by Riss and Master Jupp, with implications to—

Weed's feet hit the floor. "Wanna bet Poppa's telling Uncle Bannan about his secret project right now? We need to be there."

It was, Semyn admitted to himself, a good bet. Uncle Bannan's gift made him just as uncomfortable when those he trusted kept secrets as Werfol's, according to their tutor—the difference being their uncle had years of practice governing his expressions. But be there? "We weren't invited."

Weed began counting on his fingers. "We're clean." One finger. "We've full stomachs so won't want anything from their trays." A second. "We're not mad anymore," this with a triumphant lift of a third. "And the most important reason is that Uncle Bannan will leave soon. You know he will. He only came because I was being difficult."

"You're always difficult, Weed." And very often right, as now. Semyn closed his book, turning on the stool to face his brother—who, sensing capitulation, stopped bouncing on the edge of his bed to watch him with those golden eyes. "We could," he said slowly, "send a message with Dutton."

"Momma likes it when we're *appropriate*." Werfol grinned, looking remarkably like one of the strange new horses in the stables when offered a mouse.

Not his most trustworthy expression, but Semyn, who knew deep down he also enjoyed using adult manners and courtesies to get what he wanted, nodded. "Let's write—"

The words fell on deaf ears, Weed having launched himself at the door, opening it with a burst of "Dutton, we need you to—"

But the big guard wasn't alone. There was a strange man with him, dressed in the house livery and armed, which only someone trusted would be, but much younger.

Werfol froze and Semyn might not have guessed why except he'd overheard talk of preparations for a trip to Vorkoun. He'd told Weed and they'd assumed it would be Momma and her guard, as usual. Poppa had yet, being in exile and not allowed to be political in public, to visit his own city.

But a second guard here could only mean—

"You're leaving," Weed accused. "With Semyn. To go to Vorkoun with Poppa."

Dutton went to a knee, to meet his brother's blazing stare. Semyn started forward, stayed by the guard's gesture. "Yes. Petrill Lan will guard you, Werfol," he said reasonably. "He's the best of our new—"

"Why does Semyn get to have you!?"

"It's a temporary—"

"You swore to obey me. I won't allow it! You're mine, not Semyn's!"

Semyn winced. Dutton sighed. The poor new guard kept his eyes straight ahead, carefully expressionless, while Werfol shook with rage.

The door to their parents' rooms opened, Momma stepping out.

They were, Semyn knew, in for it now.

By one reckoning, to go from the Nalynn home to Master Dusom's—and Wainn's and Delfinn's—was a matter of mere steps, Marrowdell's village on the compact side, according to Aunt Sybb, used to the many streets and neighborhoods of Avyo.

By another, more pragmatic one, the trip depended on how many people you met who delayed those steps, a compact place tucking everyone nice and close together. Which was, Jenn and Bannan had agreed, a very good reason for two people still new to each other and discovering so much to take full advantage of the separation of the river and Tinkers Road, granting their lovely little farm—and her meadow—a rare privacy.

Because being close together was a joy as well, despite the urgency of her mission to see Master Dusom, when Jenn noticed the door of the Nalynns' nearest neighbor opening, she slowed and stopped for Gallie—for it was Gallie Emms who came out, Loee on her hip—to speak to her.

"There you are, Jenn," Gallie exclaimed with a smile, as if surprised. She'd doubtless seen Jenn walking to her sister's earlier, but residents of Marrowdell, as a rule, didn't remark on others coming and going—itself a type of privacy, Jenn suddenly realized, and most kind. "And with a pie?" Her smile widened hopefully.

"For the Uhthoffs," Jenn replied, not that Peggs didn't make pies for the Emms in exchange for Gallie's justly famed sausages—to be sold this fall in Endshere's fair, tasking Zehr with making a table that would collapse for the wagon ride there and back—but the matter of pie best settled at once.

Really, it was just as well no one suggested Peggs sell her pies at the market—there seemed barely enough for Marrowdell.

Jenn blinked, realizing she'd missed what Gallie said next. "Your pardon?"

Loee blinked sleepily back, implying she'd either been napping or should be. Gallie tucked her closer. "Is Kydd—I hope he's all right."

She'd seen the altercation then. While tempted to ask for details, finding the notion of the Uhthoffs at such odds hard to believe, Jenn merely nodded.

To her relief, Gallie tactfully changed the subject. "Have you seen Hettie? I've promised to babysit the twins while she helps today in the dairy, but there's no sign of them yet." Her pleasant face grew troubled. "Not a peep."

True, the village did seem quieter than normal. Though sunny of disposition, Elainn and Torre possessed exceptional lungs, attributes they used at full force every waking moment.

Aunt Sybb had taken to stuffing tuffs of wool into her ears when abed in the afternoon and likely wasn't alone.

The Emms' house toad appeared in the shadow of the doorway. ~Elder sister, this moon cycle I ate four evil nyphrit and laid eleven eggs. I matter to Marrowdell.~

Jenn gave an acknowledging nod, not about to engage in outright conversation with any toad in front of Gallie.

Who immediately took her nod for an answer. "You have seen them! Ancestors Blessed. I was getting worried. Where?"

"Yesterday," Jenn hastened to qualify. "Not today." She gave the toad a questioning look.

~They are asleep, elder sister. All of them.~ The house toad puffed slightly to express disapproval. ~Asleep on a blanket in the sun by the river, where they are exposed and undefended.~

A sunny blanket by the river sounded blissful—even more so

with a book or better still Bannan—but Jenn understood the little cousin's concern. Marrowdell was a safe place.

But also a wild one, full of unpredictable magic; even if one didn't count the occasional dragon—which she didn't and the little cousin shouldn't, Wisp being in charge of his kind—there were the efflet ready to fiercely defend their crops, if less nyphrit than before to be a threat.

Jenn felt a qualm about that. She'd put the wicked creatures to sleep while the house toads were away from Marrowdell, only to find out later—from Wisp—that the efflet and yling had seized the opportunity to avenge themselves on their helpless enemy. The nyphrit had almost been wiped out.

More would come to replace them, Wisp warned. How they'd arrive, her dragon didn't or wouldn't say, implying nyphrit had a worrisome ability to cross from the Verge—on their own or with the aid of something else.

A question on her list for Mistress Sand on her next visit. Right now, Gallie needed reassurance. "Have you checked the riverbank? It's lovely there this time of day. For those who might need an extra moment's rest," Jenn added meaningfully.

"Like sleepless parents." Gallie's eyes sparkled. "Thank you for the suggestion, Dear Heart." Shifting Loee to both arms, with a nod to Jenn, she headed up the path to find her wayward kinfolk.

Jenn crouched before the house toad. "Thank you, little cousin. You matter greatly to Marrowdell."

It gave her a slow, gratified blink before shuffling its bulk around to disappear back inside. With the house toad on watch, and the day lovely indeed, Jenn didn't bother closing the door behind it.

She accomplished five whole steps before encountering Old Master Jupp, out for his daily constitutional, bright scarf wrapped around his throat regardless the weather. As he'd left his silver horn at home, and was quite deaf without it, Jenn escaped the need to converse, pausing only to give the elderly man a smile and quick curtsy.

Almost there.

Around the fountain she went, pie in hand, pausing to shift the pie to her hip so she could dip her fingers in its sparkling water in thanks. The Uhthoffs' home in sight, she continued on and made it almost to the porch before Devins, in the house next door, stuck his head out his kitchen window. "Jenn, come take a look at this for me?"

"This" doubtless some improvement he'd made to the home he hoped to share, Roche now settled in Vorkoun. What use her opinion would be when it was the sister who'd share it he needed Jenn didn't know, and she'd no time to spare, but Devins looked so desperate she hesitated.

"Jenn! Quickly. Come here, please." Much to her surprise, Master Dusom practically bounced on his recently contested porch. He held open his door, gesturing almost frantically as if she must enter with all haste.

How unlike him—"I'll come by later," Jenn assured Devins. He'd accost Riss or Peggs next anyway, having developed a habit of consulting with as many as he could, except for Lorra Treff, who'd have no patience for it or insist things be done to her taste.

Devins gave her a wan smile, Master Dusom a distinctly worried look, and pulled his head back inside.

Stepping up on the porch, Jenn held forth the pie. "I've—"

"Yes, yes, and thank your sister." Master Dusom urged Jenn through the doorway with a hand on her back, closing the door behind them. "I've been hoping to get you here on your own," he went on in a low strained voice, most unlike the man she knew. "You've no idea how much I need your help, Jenn. Kydd's become persistent. Matters couldn't be worse."

So much for easing into questions with pie.

They didn't know. Couldn't possibly imagine, with the goodness in their hearts, the many and horrific ways magic could harm.

Or what he'd been before coming here.

Kydd Uhthoff would give anything to forget. He'd done his best to turn his back on a younger self who'd valued curiosity and scholarship over all else. Who'd listened to those who thought nothing of experimenting with the most despicable spells, eager for power to overturn their prince. To rule nature herself. Seduced, enthralled, his former self had wanted it all.

He'd been, Ancestors Weak and Wanton, trusting.

Being torn from his studies and exiled with his family had been his salvation, little as he'd thought it then. At least he'd had the great good sense to leave his darkest notes for Dusom to burn lest they be used against those he loved.

Lest those he loved ever learn how far down that shameful path he'd gone.

Marrowdell. Outside, that first sunset, he'd found himself studied by eyes in the trees and under the hedges. Heard whispers, as if what saw him in turn passed some judgment. Desperate for answers, he'd scoured the books he'd brought between the innumerable, wearying chores of setting up homes, instead—he knew later—of grieving Larell and Ponicce, crushed that terrible moment Dusom's wagon flipped as they fled bandits, Ancestors Dear and Departed, Wainn lying as still as death, his head bloody—

Heart's Blood, Dusom had never questioned why the bandits turned and galloped away as if for their lives instead of pressing their advantage.

Never knowing how their brains boiled in their skulls. Kydd remembered his rage as if it was but a moment old. Remembered how easily the murderous spell had come to his lips, the tokens to hand.

No one in Marrowdell must know what he'd done.

The wine soured in his mouth as memories sickened his stomach. He had to be gone from here.

Kydd bided his time. When Peggs took a pie outside for Jenn to take to his brother—a plan made in reckless haste by the ladies of the house, to whom any misfortune could be cured by food—he deliberately leaned back and closed his eyes.

Blessed Ancestors, he'd no need to feign exhaustion. Since the flood, his every bone ached with it and the very pretense of sleep felt a gift.

With a whisper of lace, Aunt Sybb rose and left the kitchen. Heading through the parlor to the front door to consult with Tir or get more of his tea, Kydd didn't care. The instant the curtain closed behind the lady, he was on his feet and outside in a flash.

Peggs sat with Jenn at her bench, their backs to him. To avoid the sisters' notice, he edged along the porch, keeping within the shade of the roses. Their scent clung to him, saturating and calm. *Trust*, it said. *Believe*.

He believed. No doubt of that. As did everyone who'd been rescued by invisible dragons then witnessed Jenn Nalynn's healing of the valley. Well, except for Lorra Treff, who stubbornly claimed all had been natural occurrences, the "dragons" being wind and her neighbors short on wits.

Trust? Not this day. Kydd covered his mouth and nose with a sleeve, forcing himself through, thorns grabbing for him like tiny fingers only to let go. Melusine's roses. Melusine, betrayed by magic to die in childbirth and now his Peggs, her eldest daughter, stood at risk of the same.

Free of the roses, temporarily shielded by the house, Kydd paused to straighten his shirt, combing fingers through his hair. If he ran like a madman again, someone kind would stop him. Marrowdell was so full of kindness it was nigh impossible to raise an alarm without it being smothered, like snuffing a candle before it lit your way to safety, and he'd—

This wasn't then, Kydd scolded himself. Lady Mahavar was correct. He'd no reason or right to despair. Now, Ancestors Prepared and Protected, there were others in Marrowdell with the experience and knowledge to appreciate the peril he feared. People who'd listen and believe. Bannan, the truthseer, prime among them.

And one, Jenn Nalynn, possessed of the power to counter it.

He must speak to her—alone—before she met with his brother. She'd never suspect Dusom's mind had been overcome by dark magic but Kydd was as certain of it as if he'd read the spell and gathered the tokens himself. Otherwise, the warm and loving brother he knew would never have grown so abruptly distant and aloof, refusing the company of his own flesh and blood.

Somehow, someone—something—had contaminated Marrowdell.

Heart's Blood, there'd been other signs. The tokens and spell sent to enslave the truthseer. The haunted mirror. Come to think of it—and he had in nightmares since—had the flood been natural—or the act of dark forces beyond the toad queen?

Kydd brushed a hand over his chest. The push hadn't hurt; the shock of it, of what it signified, continued to ache. Dusom was under attack—possibly coercion.

He had to save his brother. Jenn must.

The beekeeper crouched behind a row of beanpoles, moving as quickly as the moist soft soil permitted. If he could reach the Emms house before Jenn passed by—

"There you are, Jenn."

Gallie's cheerful voice froze Kydd in place. He listened in an agony of impatience as the two chatted, wincing to discover the older woman had witnessed his scuffle with Dusom, mentally urging Jenn to hurry.

To his dismay, he had to keep hiding, Gallie electing to walk by the garden to pick beans for Loee on her way to her daughter-in-law and her family. By the time he could raise his head, Jenn was past the fountain and Jupp, now talking, of all things, to Devins.

Before Kydd could think what to do next, other than shout across the width of the village, Dusom stepped out of his house, beckoning Jenn inside. As he'd refused to allow his own brother.

Kydd sank down on his haunches, rubbing his face with one hand. He was too late. Jenn was perceptive and cared for Dusom, but there was no telling what tale his brother, in his current state and under a foul influence, would tell her.

He needed someone who'd know the truth when he saw it.

Rising, Kydd looked to the commons and beyond. Bannan had to return soon. He'd—

A house toad appeared in his path. Before he could step around it, his nephew came through the beans, careful of the poles and tiny Delfinn, asleep in her carry sling. Wainn said, "Greetings, Uncle," as cheerfully as if they met daily in the Emms' vegetable patch.

And Kydd hadn't been hiding from sight.

Gazing at his nephew was like looking in a mirror to see who he himself might have been, the beekeeper thought, had he made better choices and far better friends. Wainn was younger, his face unlined, but they shared the Uhthoff high cheekbones, brows, and straight nose, and the tall, spare build. Both possessed the same unruly hair, though Wainn's had red-brown highlights like his mother's.

But where they truly differed?

Wainn glowed. He exuded joy and innocent wonder, as if constantly discovering the world. It was in some part true, for his brain had been damaged in the attack; for years, they'd worried he'd never learn to speak. Yet he did, and well. To this day, Wainn couldn't read; as if to compensate, with a glance he memorized any page shown to him—including the books of magic now pulped and gone—and could recite any passage on request.

After Wainn gave Jenn Nalynn a spell in return for a piece of pie they'd had a talk, he and Kydd, about which texts not to share in future. With no guarantee, Kydd knew, his nephew had understood or agreed.

Grown, Wainn was quiet and kind—with a disconcerting ability to be overlooked unless he chose otherwise—but to be near him was to feel your spirit lift and worries fade. Everyone in Marrowdell loved him.

And everyone, including his own family, Kydd thought wryly, had underestimated him until Wainn began to speak as Marrowdell, a channel for its magic. In hindsight, they shouldn't have been the least surprised when he proved to know what others didn't, or even that he'd loved Wen Treff in secret and fathered a turn-born child.

And now the remarkable young man stood gazing back at him with an unusually serious expression on his face.

"Greetings," Kydd replied cautiously. "Do you need my help, nephew? This isn't a good time—"

"TIME IS BREAKING," Wainn interrupted, which he never did, and his voice was hollow and grim and a stranger's. *"PAY ATTENTION."*

Marrowdell.

The beekeeper stilled, searching Wainn's face. "I am now. What do you mean, 'Time is breaking'?"

His nephew looked down at his baby. Looked up again with his glad and carefree smile and Kydd knew the moment was over. "Delfinn likes going for walks," Wainn assured him. "She sleeps until I stop. I'd best keep walking. Goodbye, Uncle." With that, he went back through the beans.

The house toad remained, staring up. Kydd let out a long breath. "I promise to pay attention," he said absently, knowing the creatures understood speech. "After I see to my brother—"

But Marrowdell wasn't done. Words drifted over the beans.

"HE'S NOT THE ONE AT RISK."

Bannan caught his balance and bowed low, buying time to school his expression. A terst turn-born here? A visit more than unexpected—such a presence threatened this part of the edge, possibly even his family. Worse, Mistress Sand appeared to be alone, without her little white dog, but, what was far more perilous, without another turn-born to counter her merest whim.

Angered, she could level mountains.

He let none of his dread show as he straightened, offering a smile of welcome. "Greetings, Mistress."

His heart sank when he saw her face, smileless and bleak. "Truthseer. Is this a place we can talk, na?" She tipped her head at the forester's hut behind him.

"Of course," he replied smoothly, fairly caught. Worse and worse. She must have seen him come out.

Instinctively, Bannan hid the means of opening the door, but Sand didn't appear to care. When he let her precede him, she evinced outward no interest in the interior, walking straight to the table to sit as if it were entirely normal to find a lovely room inside a ramshackle hut.

Maybe it was, to her. Maybe the terst turn-born maintained such safe places wherever they crossed into the edge. Hadn't he seen their preparations in Channen, complete with a society of people dedicated to protecting their secrets?

Ancestors Startled and Stunned, he'd bet Lila and Emon never imagined a resident of the Verge would be first to guest here. Thoughts racing, Bannan took the chair opposite. "Tea, Mistress?"

She shook her head, eyes bright. "All this, for our Sweetling, na?" A salacious chuckle. "An appreciation for her gift, na? A private place is—convenient."

Rather than lie, Bannan winked. Jenn had told him she'd asked the turn-born's permission before creating his crossing, and if Sand believed he'd built this hidden cottage as their love nest, well and good.

If only, he thought wistfully, it were.

Still, the matter of whether or not to tell his beloved was settled; beyond any doubt Sand would bring it up the next time they met, delighting to make Jenn blush.

No trace of delight in the eyes regarding him now. After that one light-hearted chuckle, the turn-born fell serious again—so grim Bannan felt a chill, a chill intensified when she spoke, low and pained. "We need your help, Truthseer. I am here to ask it."

He sat in the opposite chair, hands on the table. Risky, bargaining with the powerful and strange, but hadn't it gained him everything? "What can I do for you, Mistress?"

"One of us is lost. We want you to find him."

A lie, at least in part. Seeing it in her face, Bannan raised an eyebrow.

Her lips tightened, then she snorted. "We want you to find out why. Tooth crossed into Gordit, to conduct our business there—which isn't business of yours, Truthseer," sharply. "What is, na? Tooth failed to cross back when expected." A heavy pause. "As long as we live, we do what is expected."

Thus maintaining the tapestry of magic that, as best as the dragon and Jenn could explain, kept the Verge intact while strengthening the edge at the same time. How many turn-born did that take?

Not a good question to ponder, if they were down one already. But what could interfere with a terst turn-born? Jenn had told him about Symyd, of Shadesport. The scoundrel had babbled of secret knowledge granted by beings beneath the sea, boasting he could crack the glass of a turn-born's true self.

After her encounter with those beings, the spites, Jenn was firmly convinced Symyd was foolish and had lied, attempting to scare her.

The story had scared him, Bannan remembered. Enough that he'd marked the name, passing it to Lila along with Nonny's, the Eld owed compensation for the boat Jenn had taken out only to lose it to the toad queen.

His sister had barely raised a brow.

He focused on the real and present problem. "I know Gordit. A mining town." East of the former Marerrym Estate and its closest neighbor in those long-ago happier years of peace; since, it had been part of the contested territory known as the marches, where he'd fought a bloody, useless war for years.

Including in Gordit, where he'd lost good soldiers under his command; he'd no desire to return. "That's in Ansnor. This—where we are—is Vorkoun, in Rhoth."

Her shrug dismissed the existence of domains, borders, and probably war as well—and she had, he supposed, the right. Outside the Verge and edge, within his world, a terst turn-born couldn't and didn't exist.

Nor could Jenn Nalynn.

Sand tapped the tabletop, the sound a ring of glass. "Understand, truthseer. Until we learn what befell Tooth, we remain vulnerable to the same fate. Including" —she added like a dagger's thrust— "our Sweetling and tiny Delfinn. To take the risk to find out for ourselves, na?" A shrug. "We dare not."

It struck Bannan then that, for all her words to the contrary,

Mistress Sand had come prepared to take that risk if she hadn't found him. She wore what he recognized as miner's clothing, lacking only the hat with its lantern, unless she needed no light underground.

If he refused, she'd go herself. Not a decision her fellows would make, but Sand was capable of emotions they weren't. Catching the warning in her blue eyes, he chose not to press. Yet. "I'll discuss this with Jenn before I agree to look into the matter."

Another shrug. "As you should," Sand replied agreeably. "Our Sweetling's grown wise, na?" She stood. "Send the dragonlord with your answer, truthseer, but don't take too long." An experienced trader, her face showed only what she wished, a pleasant, noncommittal expression.

Until, for an instant, she let him see her fear.

Jenn stopped on the entryway rug, letting her eyes adjust from the bright sunlight to the strange gloom indoors, for Master Dusom had pulled the curtains over the windows, lighting lamps midday and wasting oil, which no one did.

Unless something needed to be hidden and it wasn't hard, the man having tossed out his own brother, to know from whom. Kydd. But what?

The person who knew took the pie from her hands, setting it precariously on the arm of a chair. "It's the books, Jenn."

She blinked. Ancestors Baffled and Bewildered. "'The books'?" she echoed.

Well, yes, this building was Marrowdell's library, home to most of its books as well as its school. Every child in the village took or had taken lessons from Master Dusom Uhthoff—from Roche to Alyssa—during the quiet between the first snowfall and planting—and in summer, once chores were done. The parlor would be set up with tables, barrels, and benches for however many showed up on a particular day, and the kitchen was next to it, behind a curtain, where waited snacks and drinks.

This house was their school because those in Endshere, being the last village on the Northward Road before the turn to Marrowdell and the Barrens beyond, had told Larell Uhthoff of this same house and how well-suited it would be for teaching, something she'd firmly intended to undertake.

Wouldn't their own children need lessons?

Larell died on the Northward Road, along with their youngest, their son seriously injured. Still, on reaching Marrowdell, Master Dusom quietly took up her quest, shelving his books and opening his home to every child within days of arriving.

Aunt Sybb said it was that or succumb to his grief, which did none of them any good. Later, Jenn came to understand that choice had faced everyone exiled to Marrowdell; they'd survived the first year and those following because each made the choice to move forward.

Going back being impossible.

As for books? By Larell's foresight, there were primers and early readers suited to young children. The rest, however, comprised the library of an academic of wide and varied interests, who'd been a professor in Avyo before the prince decreed those of Naalish heritage give up careers and belongings, take a settlers' portion, and head north till the road ended. By the hundreds of books carried on their wagon and that of his brother Kydd's, Master Dusom hadn't taken the prince seriously when it came to belongings.

To Marrowdell's great gain, for those books were the foundation of scholarship in the isolated village. Aunt Sybb brought more, every trip north, having lists from Master Dusom as well as from those in the village. If a question needed answering, a spark of curiosity encouragement, or simply if a book became loved beyond Frann Nall's ability to repair, he'd include the topic or title in a letter to the Lady Mahavar of Avyo, who'd take it as a personal quest to find the right volume.

Or as close to it as she could, Master Dusom's requests occasionally either too vague or too specific. But here? He knew where every volume was, be it on his many shelves or borrowed by a student or neighbor. Admittedly there'd been some confusion after the flood, with books scattered throughout the village after Wisp used his breezes to dry those touched by water, but everyone had helped sort and reshelve them.

Jenn glanced involuntarily at the shelves lining every wall. They were full and in good order, unlike her host. She'd planned to ask for some about trains, but time slipped past—

Unlike her host—she refocused, realizing what was wrong. Usually immaculate and dignified, Master Dusom's hair was disheveled and sweat beaded his brow. Dirt smudged his cheek, which was unshaven, and the buttons on his vest were in the wrong holes, as if he'd paid no attention to dressing.

He'd laid hands in violence on another person—his own brother—

This wasn't the teacher she'd respected and loved all her life. This was a stranger.

Jenn caught herself about to bolt from the house. She knew this upset feeling, as though the world tipped. She'd felt it the first time she'd seen her father cry—or that he'd let her see, for Radd Nalynn must have cried before.

On that day she'd grown up, at least in part, the part finally understanding how unfair she'd been to her father, to all of her elders, in holding to a childish belief they were never afraid or unsure or sad. To expect them to always offer her help and guidance—and never need hers.

Master Dusom deserved all respect and love. Today, he also deserved her help—and Jenn felt something else. Foreboding. If only her help would do, from all of Marrowdell?

His problem must concern magic. Magic of a kind he refused to share with his brother Kydd, who'd studied such things, or with Wainn, who was.

"Tell me what's happened," Jenn said gently.

A flash of relief lightened his face before it reset into anxious, worried lines, then Master Dusom put a finger to his lips. He pointed over their heads. "I'll have to show you," he whispered, then shook his head. "Or tell you—no. It's too incredible for words. You have to see for yourself. It's—the loft."

Said with an ominous inflection very like Aunt Sybb's when describing the sundry disreputable inns she was forced to use on her journeys to and from Marrowdell—though Bannan had informed her Endshere's, which was Palma Anan's, was a very nice place and of excellent repute, implying the others might be as well.

The point being, Aunt Sybb worried what might befall her or anyone traveling alone in such places, making the loft—which should be Master Dusom's sanctuary—something entirely different.

"Then I will." Jenn picked up the pie, keeping her voice brisk but low. "Let me take this to the kitchen, first, and put the kettle on for tea."

She'd a feeling they'd need it.

"Uncle, wait!"

Ancestors Untimely and Unwelcome. About to cross to Marrowdell and home, Bannan swore under his breath but stayed where he was. Werfol ran to him, boots kicking up rocks, such was his haste. Seeing his face, the truthseer crouched and opened his arms, braced to receive the bundle of unhappy boy without staggering. "What's wrong?" he asked.

Everything, it appeared, from Werfol's gasped list, starting with "why must you go" through "he hadn't learned enough and he promised to try harder" ending with the predictable "take me with you, they don't understand me."

Bannan rested his chin atop the boy's curls and sighed inwardly. "You know why I'm leaving, Dear Heart. My home is with Jenn in Marrowdell. You need practice more than lessons. And—" with a gentle squeeze "—Semyn needs you."

An angry mutter.

"Pardon?"

Werfol pulled back, regarding him with those glowing gold eyes. Dared him to lie. "Semyn has Dutton."

Ah. Bannan made a show of looking around. No sign of the guard. Wait, there, in the trees. A figure showed himself, then stepped back into the shadows.

The truthseer hid a smile. "How is Dutton to serve as your guard and companion, Werfol, if you continually sneak away from him?" He let himself frown. "It's unwise and unkind."

"And Dutton is unnecessary, Uncle." A stubborn tilt to that small chin. Lila had her hands full here. "He's going to Vorkoun with Semyn and Poppa. I want to stay with you. You can protect me. Better than anyone. Better than that new guard. Even Wisp—" An abrupt stop, like a hiccup, and a wary look from under a lock of hair.

"Wisp's been here?" Bannan resisted the impulse to use his deeper sight. The dragon was far too clever to be found unless he wished it—and disapproved of his door to Marrowdell, making any such visit suspect indeed.

"I glimpsed something that might have been Wisp," Werfol replied, the careful wording proof he'd at least learned how to tell an almost truth. "A few times." A more honest burst of betrayal. "When I called out, he didn't answer me, so it couldn't have been Wisp." Making it clear what the boy believed, if not a dragon's motives.

Heart's Blood, Wisp cared for Werfol. Why such disdain? Unless it was another dragon entirely—

"Please, Uncle," Werfol said very quietly, his face screwed up with misery. "You're the only person I can count on. Take me with you."

Hardly surprising, after the events just past, that the boy looked to him. Bannan pushed down a rush of affection. Werfol had to stay with his family. Had to learn to live with his gifts among those without, that most of all.

Standing, the truthseer took a step back. "Here is where you must be, Werfol. Here you'll be safe—providing you let those assigned serve you properly. By the Hearts of my Ancestors, I'll come as often as you truly need me." He circled his fingers over his heart. "However far we are apart—"

"Keep Us Close," Werfol finished, looking, if not happy, then appeased to be spoken to as an adult.

Which he wasn't, by many years yet, so Bannan knelt to take the boy in his arms once more, bestowing a kiss on his forehead, before sending him down the hill, watching until Dutton stepped oh-so-casually from the forest as if just arriving; a lesson for the wayward lad.

One could hope. Shaking his head, Bannan spun on his heel.

Time he went home and spoke to his love about a missing turn-born.

Master Dusom went first up the stairs, a lamp in his hand, walking on his tiptoes so Jenn did the same, setting her toes where he did, accustomed to the tendency of wooden steps to squeak in unpredictable places. Why silence mattered in an otherwise empty house was a question she really should have asked before this point; it being too late now, she did her utmost not to breathe loudly, which wasn't as easy as she'd thought.

Near the top he stopped and crouched, being a tall man, for the hatch above was closed. Passing Jenn the lamp, he looked down into her eyes, his wide and anxious. Seeing him swallow, she almost told him to stop.

Too late. He pulled the cord.

The hatch opened on well-oiled hinges, lifted by a pulley.

Jenn tensed.

When nothing else happened, she waited for Master Dusom to straighten and lead the way up the stairs. Waited.

And waited.

Abruptly it dawned on her the poor man was frozen in place, as if stuck to the stairs, and further movement was up to her.

Without a word, Jenn eased by him and stepped into the loft.

The Nalynn loft—where she'd slept with Peggs most of her life—was a large single room, as was that of the Emms and Bannan's, the peak of the roof forming the height of it, with a large window at one end. Uncle Horst's old cabin, now Hettie and Tadd's, lacked a loft high enough for more than storage, thus the building of an extra room had been a matter of some urgency once the twins arrived.

This was a grander space altogether.

A hallway led from the opening in the floor, defined by walls to either side, the lower half wood, the upper made from a variety of quilts, most, by their look, the work of Frann Nall, now Dear and Departed. Tall dark curtains formed doors, one set drawn back on quite a normal-looking bedroom, presumably the one once shared by Kydd and Wainn and possibly where Master Dusom now slept.

The other curtain remained closed.

Raising the lantern, Jenn walked to it. She eased the fabric aside with her free hand and stepped through.

The lantern's light shattered.

It coursed along threads like the finest of silks, glinting and glistening from threads spun overhead, from rafter to rafter, and such threads were yling-work.

Why would the shy little creatures be inside a house, let alone Master Dusom's bedroom? Those of Marrowdell lived in the old trees, the neyet.

Jenn raised the lantern. The yling hadn't only used threads to cross the ceiling, they'd used them to affix book-shaped bundles to the rafters. "Whenever did this start?" She found herself whispering, though any yling would be well able to hear, if not respond without the interpretation of a house toad.

More to the point, why hadn't one of them come down to greet her?

The answer, she guessed, had come to stand at her side. Master Dusom, having unstuck himself, dug fingers into his hair and pulled, explaining its condition. "I found this a few days after the flood. I tried to knock the journals free with a broom handle. Something objected." Holding out his hand, he showed her the puncture-like scar.

Heart's Blood. What if the yling had objected with a poisoned spear? "You mustn't do that again," Jenn warned.

A weary nod. "I didn't and won't, trust me."

From where she stood, Jenn counted eight bundles. Was that another in a corner? While they should all be relieved the yling hadn't grown similarly overprotective of the books downstairs, she'd no idea what to do next. She faced Master Dusom. "Kydd might—" Seeing him flinch, Jenn swallowed the rest.

He'd said journals, not books.

It wasn't hard, she thought, to guess whose.

Ancestors Witness, something had to be done. Master Dusom wasn't comfortable in his own home and, by the dust coating bedcovers, floor, and trunks, he'd not slept here since discovering he'd uninvited housemates. Jenn glanced around, looking for the Uhthoffs' house toad. The little cousins were able to communicate—after a fashion—with their smaller, more skittish brethren.

No sign of it. Well, that wasn't helpful. "Let's have our tea," she said brightly. Maybe they'd find the toad in the kitchen.

Master Dusom stared at her as if she'd proposed burning down the house. "'Tea'? At a time like this?"

"And pie," she replied firmly, taking his elbow. Kydd's journals weren't gone, merely elevated. This poor man needed a respite.

As did she, to consider what to do next.

The girl was startled. As such emotions played through her constantly when she visited with other people, Wisp had learned long ago which deserved his concern and possible intervention—

—and which meant simply she'd have a new story to tell him once back in their meadow.

He did enjoy her stories.

Not that he'd admit it.

Nor did he plan to tell the girl about his trips through Bannan's door. At first, to search for worthy prey, the giant bears gone to the

Barrens for the summer, always with stealth and care. To his dismay, he'd observed people being almost as sneaky. They'd repeatedly enter a small ruined building with tools and supplies. Curious, he'd flown in through the roof to see why.

Finding a growing kitchen and other comforts, he'd realized at once what it presaged.

Bannan made a den for Jenn Nalynn. A den in his part of the edge, not hers; a den with his people, not hers. Though angered, the dragon had let the building stand—for now.

Maybe it was time—

After he dealt with another, more immediate problem.

~We do not steal food.~

~But, Great Lord of Dragons . . . ~

When the youngling dragon the sei insisted he teach used that wheedling tone, it meant trouble of the annoying, petty sort. A grace that Imp—for the girl had granted it a name—plagued him here, not there; the silly creature was afraid of the boy, Werfol Westietas, since overhearing the young truthseer ask Wisp if he could keep it.

A request more appealing every time the fool got itself into mischief. As it had. Wisp snapped at the youngling's tail, fangs clipping a scale or two. ~We do not steal the villagers' food,~ he qualified.

Wings beat frantically, gaining distance, then the impudent creature bent its neck to look back. ~What of biscuits, Great Lord of Dragons?~

Explaining the difference between extras left neatly on a plate, available for the taking, and those still baking in an oven—that being what the fool had done, with the result of bent hinges, the Nahamm house toad justifiably furious, and the old soldier chasing the youngling with his sword—seemed overly tedious.

Wisp caught up with a single powerful beat and knocked into Imp, sending it tumbling as he roared. ~Biscuits are MINE!~

It recovered and, slowly, drew up to follow a respectful distance behind. ~What of cheese?~

Incorrigible creature! ~I haven't had a good meal of dragonflesh lately,~ Wisp suggested, oh-so-pleasantly.

The youngling promptly wheeled and flew off into the distance.

Learning, that was. Wisp would take it as a promising sign if there was any indication such lessons stuck inside that narrow skull.

He returned to his grassy nest to find it much reduced, rabbits taking advantage of the distraction of dragons.

Clever fluffs.

Blood still up, Wisp decided not to reclaim his due, instead launching himself skyward. He let himself glide within the rising air over the fields, easily able to watch for the girl's return—or the truth-seer's—from the heights.

Glumly unsurprised when the first arrival he glimpsed was Imp's, back, no doubt, to pester him again.

Maybe it *was* time for a taste of dragonflesh . . .

THREE

THE UHTHOFFS' HOUSE toad wasn't in the kitchen. Had Jenn taken a moment to think about it, she would have realized it would have accompanied Wainn, the little cousins most attached to him.

Ancestors Perplexed and Puzzled. Yling in a house. What next? Nyim in the fountain? "More tea?" she asked hurriedly, lifting the pot.

"Please." Master Dusom's cheeks held some color at last and, after a slow and fretful poke at the pie on his plate, he'd managed a bite. A second went in more promptly, Peggs' pie having that effect.

After pouring more tea in his cup, hers still full, Jenn slipped another piece on his now-empty plate. She sat, hands around her cup. Sunshine filled the little kitchen, a relief from the gloom in the larger room, and there were no signs the yling had been active here, though there were shelves of books built into the staircase to the loft—the Uhthoffs' larger home able to fit narrow stairs instead of the ladders of others. Books on gardens and cooking. A well-used set of Gallie Emms' helpful illustrated guides for new settlers, published in lower Rhoth under the pseudonym Elag M. Brock.

Seeing where she looked, Master Dusom shook his head. "Those are safe. They—" He stopped, his expressive face troubled. "—It's only Kydd's journals."

"I thought—" Jenn stopped, unsure it was her place.

"That my brother had hidden all his books in the hives?" A slow nod. "He did, quite thoroughly. What's stuck to my ceiling is something different." A fleeting grimness. "Kydd insisted I burn his journals before we left Avyo and I'd intended to, believe me, but—" he rubbed a hand over his face "—I couldn't, Jenn. They represented years of scholarship. Years of his work."

Making the items of such great interest to the yling about magic.

"I'd kept them—" Master Dusom continued, pushing his plate gently away "—tucked under a floorboard. Please understand, Jenn, it wasn't that I thought Kydd would ever want his journals again. I know he won't. But they were all that remained of a time of passion and effort and joy. Of a time before—" His voice trailed away. His fingers traced the wooden tabletop as if discovering it for the first time.

Or as if he remembered other tables and another life.

"Then Wisp took everything outside to dry," Jenn said, seeing what must have happened. The entire village—and those from Endshere—had pitched in to sort belongings. All had known to return any books here. Order had been, she recalled, less a concern than speed, everyone eager to go back to normal.

His cup rattled the plate when he set it down, making them both jump a little. With an apologetic grimace, Master Dusom moved it away, then sighed. "The journals were gone. I checked every stack of books as they came in but I couldn't raise a fuss about them, not without admitting to my brother what I'd done. Hadn't done." His voice turned somber. "With Kydd and Wainn fussing about the hives—about the books inside—I couldn't tell him, Jenn. And then I went upstairs. You saw."

The yling had found them first. "I'll do what I can about the yling," Jenn promised, though in lieu of a toad she'd have to ask Wisp for advice. "But you should tell Kydd, Master Dusom." Aunt Sybb being very clear about secrets and the poison they could create within families—and hadn't the secret of Melusine's death almost cost them Uncle Horst?

He couldn't quite smile. "Thank you, Dear Heart. You're right. I suppose I've been a coward, to wait so long. But—" He took a deep breath and gave her a look that wasn't happy at all, a look so full of warning it rattled her inside, like the cup and plate. "—the Kydd who wrote those journals isn't the man who married your sister."

Bannan waited until Werfol reached Dutton, the guard raising a hand in salute. Watched without moving until the pair disappeared down the path through the forest, leaving the edge, then stayed where he was several long moments more, one thought paramount. The boy mustn't see him cross.

Only the truthseer had seen Mistress Sand take the crossing higher up the talus slope, vanishing from sight between one step and the next, but Werfol well knew the possibility existed. After all, his uncle had some way of traveling to and from Marrowdell quickly. To no one's surprise, Werfol tried repeatedly to locate a crossing, determined to pass through. Failing each time, to Dutton's vast relief, while entertaining the little scree, who'd chime with laughter. Not helping, Bannan would have told them.

Nor did the events of this spring, he thought, jaw set.

According to Wisp and Scourge, the Westietas' crossing they—and the turn-born—used had been created by the sei, like the rest going from wherever in the edge they were located into the Verge. To a place in that magical realm which was usually the same, but not always—

Sei, according to Wisp, being forgetful.

Bannan had no idea where that crossing went, other than the Verge. A flesh and blood person like himself needed a being of magic to take them through—and to help them survive once they did.

But the toad queen, before her defeat, had flouted sei strictures. She'd dragged Werfol from here into her prison within the Verge. That the boy had been saved they owed to Roche's friend Edis Donovar—once an Ansnan soldier and now a creature of magic and the Verge—who'd also proved able to move through the edge at will.

Edis had brought Bannan and Roche back here after the queen took them, to later return for Werfol with him and Lila, saving them while he'd stayed for Jenn.

A worrying question, what else in the Verge could cross into this world where the sei didn't intend—one, Bannan decided, he'd like answered.

He'd his door, Jenn's gift. It would admit Werfol—once one of them took him through a first time, a day he knew, deep in his heart, that would and should come. For now he obeyed his sister's wish.

Access to Marrowdell? Ancestors Tricky and Tempted, there'd be no keeping the boy home then.

Time to go. The truthseer sprinted up the rock-strewn slope, heading for the spot near where the forest curved back up the mountainside, cupping the rock.

There, a little pile of scree. He paused to run his hands through his hair and straighten his jacket, smiling as he took that step, only to stagger as his foot landed in Marrowdell, as if the crossing—his crossing—didn't quite align where he'd been with where he was, or as if the unfelt journey through the Verge left its mark.

Somehow, the tiny lurch always made Jenn's accomplishment more miraculous.

He shaded his eyes, looking eagerly for her. Shrugged to find himself alone. She'd be at their home or in the village, a mere stretch of legs away—

—but there was no home.

No farm. No buildings in the distance. No village at all and Bannan looked deeper, seeking the truth in what had to be a lie, because this was Marrowdell. The Bone Hills rose, smooth and creamy, as he remembered they should. Scarred ridges bounded the valley but the river—

Wait, the river was wider, straighter—and there, where ruins should be—

Nothing changed to his deeper sight. By that measure, what he saw was as real as it was impossible. He stared in horrified disbelief at the pair of elaborate towers rising to either side of the cataract, joined by a massive colonnade shrouded in mist. Rooftops glinted with inset gems and gold—

The northernmost Ansnan temple to their stars. The Great Refuge of the North. Destroyed seventy-three years ago when the sei was pulled too far into the edge by the priests—priests he now saw, beyond any reason or sense, strolling along balconies—for as the sei writhed in pain, it had torn those towers down, scarring the land.

Bannan couldn't say what made him whirl around and leap back through his door, unless it was the fear that taking a single breath in this Marrowdell?

Might cost him his own.

Putting aside what Master Dusom implied about Kydd—for now—Jenn decided her duty was to deal with the yling, or rather find someone who could.

After saying her farewell, she hitched up her skirts and ran the rest of the way through the village to be sure no one else stopped her, though she had to pause to open the commons gate and the new calves thought it a wonderful game to try and crowd past as she closed it and then Wainn's old pony trotted up, confident she'd brought a wizened old apple despite having the last of those before the flood, so she must to give him a rub behind his hairy chin at least.

Then Jenn ran through the tall grass to the river gate, climbing the rails rather than tempt the calves who'd galloped behind her.

Keeping her skirt high, she passed through the shadow of the great oak, nodding a greeting, then splashed through the ford, and such was her need to reach her meadow and consult with her dragon the Tinker's Road seemed only four steps long, and the farmyard of her home took less than a breath to cross, putting her bare feet on the familiar path to Night's Edge.

Where she halted to check for smoke from their chimney, in hopes Bannan was home and waiting—but there wasn't, so he wasn't.

Yet.

Off she ran and "Wisp!" Jenn called the instant she burst into the open, though he'd know she came and from where.

Bits of grass rose in a spiral. A breeze found her ears. "Here. Here."

"Me too!" A breeze more like a gust and chill, Imp still learning how to speak aloud.

The spiral toppled and a growl followed, but it sounded more resigned than angry.

"Hello, Wisp. Hello, Imp." Jenn hesitated, not wanting to be rude, but she needed to converse with her dearest, most trusted friend, alone.

And, while Imp had mostly good intentions—other than a continued and deplorable interest in Wainn's blood—Wisp's student remained impetuous and prone to unpredictable acts, traits less than ideal in a creature as powerful as a dragon, even a young one.

Wisp knew her thought, as always. "Begone, Imp."

"But—Great Lord of—"

Nothing resigned in the roar that followed. "TO THE VERGE WITH YOU!"

Silence. Birds chirruped, as if they'd held their breath the instant before, and Jenn straightened her dress, giving her dragon time to compose himself. Little breezes assembled a pile of soft grass for her and she sat, relieved. "Thank you, Wisp. I would like a little privacy for what I'm about to—"

A *THUMP* as something invisible landed without grace next to her, followed by the buffeting of a frantic wind. "DANGER! Gone! WOE! Missing and gone! DANGER!"

Had Imp crossed to Vorkoun? Jenn rose to her knees, heart in her throat. "Bannan? Is that who you mean?" She'd lost the truthseer more than once, to her great dismay, and hoped never to go through the experience again.

"I told you to leave, fool!" Wisp showed himself, as he rarely did. He stood, aged silver and furious flame, a clawed foot pinning *something* to the ground. His wild violet eye found her, then glared down at his quarry. "Show yourself," he ordered, and there was nothing gentle in his tone. "Explain yourself," and that was advice deadly to ignore.

A smaller dragon came into view, white scales edged in orange, the same color, paler, in its eyes, though they held a hint of red at their heart. Whole and unscarred, unlike Wisp with his crippled left side and wizened left limbs, but there was no doubt who was greater.

Or who was terrified. Seeing Imp's eyes roll in panic, Jenn spoke quickly but gently, as she would to a calf. "You aren't in trouble, Imp. Please, just tell us. Is Bannan—is he all right?"

The eyes fixed on her as if finding a lifeline. "A TURN-BORN IS MISSING!"

She winced at the shout. Telling, that Wisp didn't correct the youngling. "Who?" Jenn asked, her mouth dry, for she'd favorites, in her heart. Ancestor's Blessed, let it not be Mistress Sand or Master Riverstone.

Wisp gave her a grim look. "Dearest Heart, terst turn-born disappear when it's their time—"

"Tooth," Imp interrupted, greatly daring given the claws at its neck. "The one called Sand was at the dragonlord's crossing. SHE SPOKE—TO ME." Wailed with such distressed confusion, Jenn felt some regret for her own offers of conversation. "I'm to warn YOU, Great and GraciOUs TURN-born! I AM warning you," the young dragon finished, giving a muffled squeal as those claws drew blood.

"Wisp," Jenn chided gently.

Disbelief in those violet eyes, but her dragon let go, though he made a point of licking his blood-tipped claw. Jenn might have protested except for Imp's worshipful gaze.

Dragons. Still. A terst turn-born missing? It seemed impossible—Imp must have misheard. "Imp. What exactly did Sand say to tell me? Her words, please."

Confronted, the youngling startled and promptly vanished, an ineffectual strategy given the conspicuous depression its body made in the grass.

Wisp snapped at the air. "Answer the turn-born. Or she'll turn you into a little cousin," he added slyly.

She wouldn't—couldn't—could she?

Imp began to speak, the air against her ear and cheek fluttering as if he trembled, and well he might, for the words were dreadful.

"'Tell Jenn Nalynn this, young dragon. One of us is missing. Tooth crossed into the edge and failed to return. Tell our Sweetling to come to me, to remain safe in the Verge until we learn what peril we face.'"

Jenn sank down in the grass, absently petting the rabbit nestled at her side. The creature knew it was safe from dragons.

She'd thought the turn-born were safe from, well, everything but themselves. How had Sand put it? A turn-born grew weary of the effort to remember flesh and blood, to hold shape and purpose. Ultimately, the effort ended and the turn-born emptied.

Did sad little piles of shark teeth mark where once stood a being of incalculable power? Whose mere wish shaped realms? Assuming the others concurred, for turn-born must agree.

She lifted her hands, willed them glass and pearl, imagined the glass cracking—

"Do not," said her dragon, with some alarm. "What Sand said—if we trust the youngling's memory—means only that Tooth is late. For all we know, he decided to cross elsewhere, live elsewhere a time."

Jenn raised her eyes to the shimmer where Wisp might be. "Has a turn-born ever done so?"

Hesitation, then honesty. "No. But there are other enclaves within the Verge."

This was news and unexpected. She perked up. "Do any live there now?"

"No."

Making Mistress Sand and her group of seven the sole turn-born of the Verge. Six. "What if Tooth doesn't come back?"

"More will be born." Wisp's voice held the impression of a shrug.

Well, yes, their own Delfinn was newly born and at the turn, but she wouldn't become a turn-born and into her power until her eighteenth birthday neared. Jenn wished she knew more of the terst—how they aged and grew—anything to help her now.

"I must speak with Mistress Sand," Jenn declared. "This instant." Jumping to her feet, she made for the gap in the old trees that marked the way to Wisp's little meadow and its crossing.

"You must *not*!" A chill breeze shoved at her, flipping her braid over her shoulder and turning her skirt into a sail, which was rude of Wisp, if utterly predictable. "You can't trust what the youngling says," her dragon warned, half frantic. "It makes mistakes. Or this is a trap!"

Jenn stopped and held out her hands. "But you'll come with me, won't you, dear Wisp? To keep me safe."

The breeze subsided, but Wisp wasn't done. "What of your truthseer?" he asked cleverly. "What if Bannan arrives to find you gone?"

"Imp will wait here to tell him what's happened. Won't you, Imp?" She looked around, unable to spot the youngling but quite sure it was nearby.

"I WILL!" came its uncomfortably shrill, loud voice. "I WILL!"

"Well, then." Jenn dusted off her skirt and gave a determined nod in the direction of Wisp's meadow. "We'll be off. If this is a misunderstanding and Tooth merely delayed, better to find out soon than worry long." That being one of Peggs' sayings and most applicable, she decided.

Her dragon's silence was as good as a sigh.

Alas, in her urgent desire to help the terst turn-born, Jenn Nalynn completely forgot why she'd come to see Wisp in the first place, that being to help Master Dusom with the yling inhabiting his bedroom.

She shouldn't have.

As Jenn ran through the commons, Kydd slipped onto his brother's porch, easing in through the door and closing it behind him.

Unchallenged, he stood a moment to let his eyes adjust to unexpected gloom in a place he'd lived so many years—

—and to fight the rush of memory. Regret and guilt twisted in his stomach. Sneaking into his brother's house was all too familiar. In Avyo, he'd entered by stealth countless times, preferring the silent hour pre-dawn. At first, he'd been after better food than a student's daily lot and, often as not, found a covered plate waiting thanks to Larell.

Then later, to his lasting shame, he'd come seeking whatever might work as a token for a spell, taking from his own. A thief. His family must have known. They hadn't said a word; perhaps they'd suspected him of a gambling habit or some other need—believed him too proud to ask for funds.

They hadn't known him, then or now.

Kydd blew out a silent breath, a shudder unpinning his muscles, and inhaled the homely scents of pie and freshly brewed tea. The kitchen. Beams of light led into it. His brother would be there, thanks to Jenn and Peggs.

Quick and sure, he crossed the room and was up the stair to the loft before he heard the first stir from below. No hint of damp or must, only a growing, unpleasant *pull*. As if the world tilted in the direction of Dusom's bedroom, the hall shrinking around him, forcing him on.

Heedless, now, of discovery, Kydd rushed to the curtain that was his brother's door and shoved it aside, determined to hunt out the dark tokens—

Stopped in his tracks by the prick of a tiny spear on the pulse in his throat.

The yling showed itself. Wings glimmered. The face beneath an acorn helmet was contorted with rage and Kydd knew himself about to die—if not why—

"Don't hurt him!" Dusom came charging down the hall, beams from his wildly swinging lantern careening from floor to ceiling. He seized Kydd's arm with his free hand to pull him back.

Kydd planted his feet. Took hold of the door frame and refused to budge as his astonished gaze took in a ceiling covered in strands of yling silk, fired by the lantern's light. Any more yling were in hiding. His eyes narrowed. And there was something else.

His journals!

By the number imprisoned above, the entire sum of his dark explorations were here, and what had his brother been thinking, to so taint their future home?

"It's all right," Dusom gasped, and it was unclear who it was he hoped to reassure.

Kydd barely heard, his journals impossibly *aware*, clamoring for his attention, wanting his touch. Ancestors Bloody and Bowed, by all he'd been taught it was impossible. They were inanimate—

Not, he thought numbly, in Marrowdell. Not after the wild magic spilled throughout the valley during and after the flood. The only wonder was that he hadn't sensed them sooner, unless he had, in his nightmares since—

The spear was withdrawn, reluctantly. The little warrior continued to hover in Kydd's face.

He dragged his head around to stare accusingly at his brother. "You promised to burn them. They were never to come with us."

The yling chirped angrily, as if in full agreement.

Dusom eased his bruising grip on Kydd's arm, sliding his hand up to the other's shoulder. He gave a sad little shrug. "I had them hidden for so long I'd almost forgotten, then the flood came and this happened—I'm sorry. I couldn't bear to let you in, to have you find out this way. I was wrong—"

None of that mattered. "But why?"

His brother's eyes filled. "I couldn't bear to destroy your years of scholarship."

"'Scholarship'?" With a bitter laugh, Kydd jerked free, slamming his back against the wall. The yling darted forward, spear ready. Did the creature know? How, even now, a lifetime later—and by the Bones of every Ancestor a better person than he'd been then—that dark knowledge pulled at him?

He'd feared contamination from without. Well, now he'd a name and face to put to it. His own. "I should never have come here," Kydd whispered. There was power written and drawn ready for use on those pages—and if it had been potent in Avyo?

Heart's Blood, he dared not imagine releasing any of it here, touched by the incalculable magic of the Verge.

But what if he did . . . ?

He shook his head violently. "I have to destroy them. Now." But as he went to go into the bedroom, the doorway filled with a horde of yling, spears raised to deny him. "Please. I must! Don't you understand?" he pleaded.

"They don't, Dear Heart. Any more than we understand them," Dusom told him, his voice strained but calm. "That's where Jenn's gone, to find help. Come," gently. "While we wait, let's to the kitchen and talk. There's pie."

No one knew the real danger here. "I can't stay," Kydd blurted out, backing down the hall. He put out a hand to fend off his brother, then turned and ran.

Having taken her dragon's crossing in his little meadow by his tiny crystal house—which he used rarely, the temperature inside almost never to his liking—once in the Verge, Jenn walked behind Wisp to his true home, though she wondered why he walked at all down the now-familiar narrow canyon—that being harder with only two good legs—instead of taking to the air. His steps, and hers, shattered crystal that bled purple as they died, so she did her best to avoid them. There were other tracks, shaped like hers, ahead of them.

Mistress Sand's?

There was but one way to find out.

Familiar yet different. Instead of the myriad and strange colors of the Verge, the sky above was filled with downward peaks, a mountain range poised to fall. It was only, Jenn tried to reassure herself, the Verge, ever fluid with perspective. Not that she doubted those were mountains, but they weren't about to crush them, and it was every bit as likely someone there thought they looked up at her. Did that mean she looked down at them?

Ancestors Witness, it was most confusing.

"Wisp," she began, having remembered her other duty as she walked. "Master Dusom has a problem—"

~Hush, Dear Heart.~ Wisp's ticklish, soundless speech was stern. ~This is no place to speak aloud.~

That being the only way Jenn knew how to talk, she closed her mouth.

The winding path led to Wisp's sanctuary, a place she'd been before and where she'd met Sand for the very first of their discussions of what a turn-born was, and wasn't. Which had, to Jenn's dismay, involved a great deal of shrugging, the terst turn-born unable to say what applied to her and what might not.

They were almost to the bend when Wisp spun about, wings outstretched to block her way. ~BEWARE!~

His shout came as a wall of mimrol struck, its silver frothed and sparkling, sweeping Jenn from her feet. Instinct had her abandon flesh for glass and pearl, her turn-born self better able to take being smashed against the sides of the canyon, a wise choice when she discovered swimming in mimrol to be nothing like water. The stuff was warm and viscous, clinging to her like sodden wool. She sank with its weight while being carried away—

Claws grabbed hold. Wisp plucked her free then, wings straining, hovering close to a vertical mass of boulders until she found holds for her hands and feet.

The canyon had become a gushing fall of mimrol pouring into abyssal depths, and she'd no idea why.

Or what to do now.

Bannan found himself back on the scree slope, shaded by a forest of mixed pine and neyet. Taking a deep, gasping breath, he struggled to comprehend what had just happened. Had his door taken him back in time? Ancestors Witness, since coming to Marrowdell, he'd seen incredible sights, ones he wouldn't have believed if not experienced himself.

This?

A confusion, it had to be.

His Marrowdell couldn't be . . . gone.

Heart pounding, Bannan aimed himself at his door and took that step once more.

Coward, to close his eyelids, but beyond him to do more than squint through a crack at first, then gradually open them until convinced.

Ancestors Blessed, he was back. Bannan drank in the sight of planted fields and tall hedges, of the village in the distance.

He couldn't help but check the ridge, relieved to see the ruins that should be there. He'd hallucinated, that was all. Wisp had sculpted the original refuge in the dirt for him and Tir. That's how he'd known.

Something more to tell Jenn, he decided, starting off briskly for their farm. Maybe there was something she could—

He stumbled over a barrier, hard and invisible. "Wisp?" The truthseer looked deeper, annoyed, only to relax. A dragon blocked his way, yes, but one far less intimidating. "Hello, Imp. What's this about?"

"I HAVE WORDS foR YOU!" the youngling bellowed, eyes bulging.

With a wince, Bannan gathered his patience. Words? Most likely a complaint from Wisp concerning his neglect of Jenn—and, while rather pleasant to think she'd missed him, it was none of the dragon's business.

Not that he stood any chance of convincing Wisp otherwise. "Use a softer voice, please, Imp. What words?" The truthseer kept his eyes on the path to the farm, wishing he'd his love's gift to shorten the way, and didn't pay attention until, "What did you say? No," when the literal creature began to repeat itself. "I heard you," he said grimly.

Sand had summoned Jenn to the Verge, passing on the message about Tooth.

But why?

Because they were short a turn-born? Because Sand needed an ally who'd take her side of things? "Where's Wisp?"

"The Great Lord of Dragons went with our turn-born."

Bannan supposed he should be grateful for that much.

Sand had told him to keep Jenn safe. He'd have known if she lied; it just hadn't been the whole truth. The terst turn-born had her own plan.

He found himself staring into the now-ominous shadowed gap beneath the old trees. He couldn't follow but—"I could send you after them," he mused aloud.

"NO! No, NO, no! I promised to stay with YOU, truthseer. Guard YOU!" The young dragon flung itself into the air, wings beating a gale at Bannan's head. "FoR BISCUITS!"

The last would be Imp's wishful thinking, the rest his beloved's determination to keep him safe—while keeping the youngling far from the terst turn-born.

If that's who waited in the Verge. Bannan rolled his shoulders to ease the tension building there. Ancestors Foiled and Flummoxed, he had to trust Jenn and Wisp to learn what they could—while he minded yet another youngster. "Stay with me, then," he told Imp. "And do as you're told or there'll be no biscuits."

"I WILL! I WILL!"

The truthseer waved a hand. "Shhh!"

The whisper that followed was almost too soft to be heard. "Biscuits!"

Shaking his head, Bannan headed for their empty home to wait.

A home not empty after all. A tall figure sat slumped on the porch step, face in his hands. Bannan hurried across the farmyard, oblivious to the healthy growth in their gardens and heady smell of summerberry flowers. What could have brought Kydd Uhthoff here, in obvious misery?

Heart's Blood, had something happened to Peggs? Her baby? Sinking to the step beside the beekeeper, Bannan couldn't form the words.

Kydd lifted his head. "Peggs is fine."

Reading the truth, Bannan sighed with relief. "Glad to hear it." He gave the other a keen look. "But you're not."

The beekeeper rubbed a hand over his face and sat up straight. "I—I didn't know where else to go." A grimace. "Some days Marrowdell's smaller than others."

A lie within a truth. Bannan schooled his face to hide an inner wince. "It can be that," he agreed blandly.

A perceptive look. Color rose in Kydd's cheeks and he ducked his head. "My apologies, truthseer." He met Bannan's gaze. "I find myself afflicted with old habits."

The truth. And interesting. "Why—"

"Biscuits? Biscuitsbiscuitsbiscuits?"

Kydd started, plainly able to hear Imp's plaintive whisper, and looked to Bannan, raising an eyebrow in question.

He'd no hesitation answering, Kydd bringing his scholar's passion to learn all he could of the valley's magical residents. Ancestors Wise and Wondering, who better to hear of his vision—or imagining—of Marrowdell-past? "I'm minding Wisp's student while Jenn's—"

"I GUARD YOU!"

The outraged bellow made both wince, tousling their hair and knocking over an empty bucket. "Jenn isn't here?" the beekeeper asked, plainly disappointed.

No more than he. "She's crossed to the Verge."

To his surprise, Kydd gave a quick nod, as if Jenn's departure made perfect sense. "I believe I know why she's gone. We need to talk." He glanced around the farmyard. "Alone."

No matter what had brought Jenn to her meadow, Imp's message had drawn her from it and Bannan only wished he'd crossed in time to talk to her first. His heart sank at this hint of a new problem.

"Come inside." But as he got to his feet, he was pushed back by a wildly beating, if unseen wing. He grabbed the nearest post. "You," he ordered, pointing at the exact spot in the air inhabited by the over-eager dragon, "wait outside. On guard."

The depth of woe in the faint "No biscuits?" brought a quirk to his lips despite the seriousness of the situation.

"I'll bring you—" They'd likely no biscuits, Jenn sensibly preferring to visit her sister's kitchen while he was away. Bannan thought quickly. "—something better. A piece of cheese." Surely they'd some left. "Once you've done your duty," he emphasized.

"I SHALL GUARD, TRUTHSEER!!"

Now to find out what Kydd Uhthoff thought he knew about Jenn.

Wisp set the girl down on a ridge, landing by her side. Below them, mimrol boiled and seethed, chewing at the rock, and he doubted his sanctuary would survive it.

Though it might, should this unreasonable river drain away.

"Something's wrong."

Her certainty chilled his heart. ~The Verge does change without warning, Dearest Heart,~ the dragon ventured.

"No. Things feel—different. Wiggly." She made a frustrated noise. "Stretchy. Wrong."

Experimentally, he closed his claws on the rock. It crumbled as rock should and always had.

"If the sei were upset . . . ?" She let her voice trail away.

The dragon shuddered. ~We'd know at once. All of us.~ And suffer for it.

"If it's not that—" She gave a soft sigh. "We must find Mistress Sand. Or any of the turn-born, of course."

Kindly said, but he knew she'd prefer the one she considered a friend, however unlikely and, in a dragon's opinion, dangerous that assumption was. ~Then we will,~ Wisp agreed, then hesitated. ~Can you? Find them? Not with your mother's gift,~ he added hastily. A magic she'd inherited, to summon what was lost, and there was no telling what would come forth should she unleash *that* in the Verge.

Her eyes widened. "Do you think I could?"

Wisp raised and lowered his wings in an approximation of that useful gesture, a shrug, he'd learned as a man. ~Better than I,~ he admitted. ~Turn-born leave few tracks and less scent.~ And anything with sense avoided them.

He waited patiently as Jenn closed her eyes, slowly turning her face one way, then the other for no apparent reason. Opening them again, she shook her head. "Surely Mistress Sand will find us. Imp said she wanted to see me."

Wisp showed a disparaging fang. ~Words I would not trust, Dearest Heart. The youngling curries favor. It is most—~ The dragon fell silent, abruptly aware the glorious warmth of the Verge was fading.

The light of the Verge faded and grew sly at the dimming, deepening shadows to confuse the senses, favoring hunters. It fell in time with night in the girl's world and was the sole reliable aspect of the Verge.

Now? This dimming shouldn't be happening—it was too early. Something *was* wrong.

Wisp wrapped a claw around the girl's tender arm. ~Become turn-born, Dearest Heart. We must leave.~

Before what hunted the dimming unwisely chose to test him.

Or her.

FOUR

SECURE IN WISP'S hold, Jenn tried to relax as her dragon flew swiftly and more or less straight—other than the period when she was quite certain they were upside down and another where she thought they went backward—to his chosen destination. She assumed that would be to the turn-born enclave and, frankly, wondered why they hadn't gone there immediately.

She stopped wondering as the dimming became complete, muting the vivid colors of the Verge into ominous mauves and grays and blacks. The air around them filled with sounds of an unpleasant nature. Roars and eager howls.

Screams and pitiful whimpers.

Landing anywhere, Jenn realized, was a very bad idea, be she turn-born or not, and she changed her mind to earnestly hope Wisp took them to a dragonish shelter. Ideally one without dragons already in residence, for much of what roared and howled circled closer, flying on similar wings.

As if in agreement, Wisp let out a blood-chilling roar of his own, startling Jenn, who clutched his good front leg.

There was, of a sudden, an immediate lack of other threatening sounds in their vicinity, which was a relief. At the same time, Jenn felt herself grow heavier and heavier, as if being in the sky was foreign to whatever she was here and her very essence fought to be free and on the ground. Despite his great strength, Wisp couldn't carry her turn-born self much longer.

She should return to flesh and blood—

Wisp's neck curled around midflight, bringing one wild violet eye to bear on her. ~Do not change now, Dearest Heart. We're about to land.~

For the life of her, Jenn couldn't see where they might, the landscape below of jagged rock where it wasn't a mass of thorn-encrusted tree things. To add to the risk, they were spotted by a pack of regrettably large furred things that howled hungrily up at them, things possessed of enormous claws on long arms, arms stretching out to grab them!

~There you are!~ Wisp exclaimed impatiently, angling his wings to send them in a steep dive.

Directly at the pack.

Jenn would have argued—

—but as they dropped, the pack and thorns and rocks shimmered. Changed.

Until below them appeared a quaint little village, so like Marrowdell she couldn't believe her eyes.

Though it troubled Semyn not to have the same memories of Marrowdell as Werfol—and of dragons in particular—there were, according to Momma, distinct advantages to not remembering magic outside the edge. For one thing, he couldn't be tricked into revealing what he honestly didn't know.

For another, how could he miss what he couldn't remember ever having, or enjoying, or even fearing?

Except he did.

Semyn kicked a pebble from the path, looking around quickly to be sure no one had seen. But no one paid attention. Everyone was busy getting the coach ready for the baron's trip to Vorkoun—one not, by Momma's firm direction, to be by stealth. Meaning the Westietas' coach had been pulled from storage yesterday to be cleaned and polished, and there'd be a full horse guard of four riding ahead and two behind who also, as it happened, needed their dress uniforms pulled from mothballs.

The team arrived, black coats gleaming and hoofs painted, their manes braided with Westietas' ribbons of gold, black, and teal, courtesy of his Great-Aunt Kinsel, who bred the best coach horses in Eastern Rhoth and was their nearest neighbor and family.

And who'd want more than anything to come along, but this trip was for the baron—

And his heir.

Semyn knew his role, now and to come. Nothing in it let him be a fool or foolish. Or act the child, for that matter. Not that he had complaints.

Well, maybe one or two.

But nothing, he told himself firmly, straightening his posture and walking without scuffing his boots, worth the mention of a person of nine years. Young for an acclaimed heir, if by no means atypical. The Barony of Nycharl had been laid on the shoulders of a daughter a day old, and that of Lippet—

Precedent aside, his acclamation was to have waited another three years, but when Poppa went to Channen for the good of Rhoth, their enemies had struck. Semyn had held the key to Vorkoun's seat in his hand, in Marrowdell, sent there as had he and Werfol, Momma preparing him to become baron should Poppa die and that had been—

He stopped to kick another pebble.

—the worst moment in his life.

He'd talked to Weed about it, his younger brother having been there and a truthseer and a truedreamer, which meant there was no hiding anything from Weed even if he wished. Not without preparation and practice, anyway, which they'd not had, then, and he'd no intention of ever hurting Werfol, who couldn't help what he was.

Difficult.

Their tutor, Namron Setac, understood. Without telling Momma, he'd gone to Avyo for more than a meeting with his group. He meant to obtain tokens, knowing a spell to let a person keep secrets from a truthseer, and willing to help Semyn.

He might not remember magic, the boy thought grimly. That didn't mean he wouldn't take advantage of it.

The reason he might need to do just that came running up the path, jacket open and hair a mess. Petrill, Weed's new guard, ran behind, but his brother had a good jump on the man. Semyn waited for him.

Weed slid to a stop and thrust out a bag. "Candies for the ride. You know how you get when it's dusty."

Semyn gave a grave nod of thanks, then, impulsively, pulled his brother into a tight hug. "Watch over Momma while we're gone," he whispered.

Comforted by Weed's curt nod, better than a blood oath from anyone else in the world.

Captain Ash had been tasked with the most recalcitrant—and valuable—of prisoners, those possessed of secrets they'd thought to take to their graves. Their faces blurred to a sameness in memory, the pattern unchanging, the result predictable. Refusing to confess when confronted with proof of his gift merely delayed the inevitable. His questions stripped away pretense and protection; there was no training, no drug his true sight couldn't overcome.

Bannan gave himself an inward shake as he poured Kydd a mug of tea. Ancestors Tedious and Tiresome, what had dredged that up? Yes, he'd had a storm of conflicted reactions to the hidden cottage, but this was far from the first time he'd pushed his past aside, nor would it be the last.

Easier to do in Marrowdell, land of peace. Easiest of all, were Jenn here, and there it was, he assured himself. Jenn's absence. Imp's message. Why wouldn't he be unsettled? Not to forget the illusion he'd faced on his first attempt to cross. Heart's Blood, there was no denying the shock of that.

As Kydd took the mug, his hands trembled.

A minute quiver, hard to spot and as quickly stopped—the sort of involuntary twitch made by the guilty. The truthseer went to stroke his beard, for an instant startled to feel a smooth chin.

Bannan bit his tongue, hard, thoroughly dismayed by the return of that old habit, chagrined, however briefly, to think Kydd guilty of anything but worry. His good friend was under great strain, understandably anxious about the birth and likely about what came after. Why, by the look of his wan face and bruised eyes, Peggs' husband hadn't had a solid sleep in weeks.

Making *him* the guilty party. How had he missed how troubled the other must have been? The extravagant blissful joy of his first summer with Jenn was no excuse.

Bannan made his tone easy and light, saying, truthfully, "Jenn left to visit her friends."

"She did," Kydd agreed quickly, for all the world as if grateful Bannan brought up the topic so soon. "Jenn seeks help for my brother. Creatures—yling—have infested his bedroom."

About to pour his own tea, Bannan froze. "Say that again?"

"You heard me," came the gloomy reply.

"Yling?" He smothered the urge to laugh, the beekeeper obviously serious. "Indoors?"

"And they won't leave," the other insisted. "Or tolerate interference." Kydd pulled down his collar to reveal an angry red dot over the artery pulsing in his throat.

The truthseer was well acquainted with yling spears. Kydd's tiny wound showed skill and restraint—a warning to take seriously. "Why not ask Wisp?" Or, for that matter, a house toad? At the thought, he looked around for his, not that he could speak with it in the edge.

But the little cousin was either absent or hidden. Had Dusom's absented itself? Not a good sign, if so.

"It's what Jenn told my brother," Kydd replied, his tone almost defensive.

Bannan finished pouring his own tea and sat in the second chair, crossing his ankles as he sat back. He didn't need to be Captain Ash to feel something awry here. The Kydd he knew, exhausted or not, should find Dusom's problem fascinating—would relish the opportunity to study Marrowdell's shyest inhabitants up close. "I confess to being at a loss," he said evenly. "The yling have been excellent neighbors. Friends, in their way." He pretended to study the wildflowers Jenn had put in a crock before their unused fireplace, his attention for the man beside him. "Why do you think they're in Dusom's house?"

Hesitation.

"You know." The truthseer gazed directly at Kydd, his deeper sight taking hold without his planning it, his eyes glimmering gold. "Why?"

"Your gift won't work on me unless I allow it, truthseer," the beekeeper shocked him by saying, his voice oddly hollow. "The first spell they taught was concealment from such as you. It took Marrowdell to expose what I am."

Spell? As Bannan's heart sank, Captain Ash surged up. "And what are you, Kydd Uhthoff?" he heard himself say in that cold, perilous tone. "You will answer."

"Yes. It's time I did." Kydd leaned forward, staring back at Bannan, eyes devoid of emotion. Or did they glisten with tears?

"I'm not who anyone here believes me to be."

There. Ancestors Blessed, the words were out and couldn't be unsaid. Kydd waited to feel a bone-shaking relief. Or sickening dread at the gold burning in Bannan's eyes, the unfamiliar chill in his voice. Even to feel impatience when the truthseer remained silent—

Anything but numb. Anything but this inability to move or speak or think, as if only the effort to sustain his long-held secrets had kept him alive in Marrowdell and once they were out—

Bannan set aside his mug, aiming his chair to face Kydd's as if preparing to interrogate a subject, yet the color of his eyes, their magic, faded to normal, and his expression held an unexpected— *undeserved*—compassion. "I believe you to be my friend," he said calmly. "Ancestors Witness, I believe," with emphasis, "we've the right to try and be better than we were. To leave our pasts behind and start new lives."

An offer, Kydd realized, his mouth going dry. Bannan gave him a chance to back away from revelation. Promised to continue to consider him the harmless beekeeper who'd somehow won Peggs' heart, the failed academic who'd studied magic as a curious subject amid others; promised to stay his friend.

For a heartbeat, he thought to accept, about to suck the truth back inside and let it rot there. Then Bannan's wording struck home. *To be better than we were.*

The truthseer had told him, not all but enough, what he'd been before Marrowdell. His man, Tir Half-face, had added more, late one night and in his cups, and Kydd abruptly knew he sat across from no friend, but the infamous Captain Ash.

Oh, the offer was sincere, he'd no doubt. But neither did Kydd miss the consequence of taking it. Should he choose the lie, he would forfeit this man's trust, meaning he would lose Jenn's—

—then lose Peggs.

He put down his mug, leaned back, and pressed his palms together, forefingers over his lips. Automatic, that posturing, the readiness to begin an offensive spell—when Kydd realized what he'd done, he hastily dropped his hands to his lap.

"I was—" Only the truth would save him. "I am a spellcaster, though I swear by the Bones of my Ancestors I haven't used that skill since coming to Marrowdell."

"What kind of spells?" And oh, the threat in that tense question.

"Harmless. At first." Kydd refused to look away. Knew better than flinch. "A practitioner in Avyo introduced me to others—we were a small group, eager to learn. Too eager," he qualified, feeling his blood grow cold as memories he'd suppressed flooded back. "We came to believe ourselves special. Worthy. The rightful heirs to magic. It's what we were called, the *Heirs*. We were taught to value only how much power we could hold." His hands cupped.

Noticing, Kydd rubbed his palms flat against his thighs. "I was good. So good I was about to be presented to the Mage Prime when Ordo sent us north." His lips twisted. "Ancestors Besotted and Blind, I couldn't have escaped them otherwise—at the time, I wouldn't have known to try."

Muscle flexed in Bannan's jaw but he remained silent. Waiting. As if aware there was more and worse to come.

"Don't think me young or misled. I knew full well the path I took," Kydd confessed with detached calm, part of him certain all of Captain Ash's subjects had felt this way hearing their darkest secrets vomit forth. "Even as the spells grew darker, I willingly learned the next and the next. I glimpsed glory ahead—raced to get there first. I cared nothing for the cost—"

"You killed."

Quiet, those words but Kydd winced as if struck by a fist. "No! Not then," he corrected. "Animals, yes. And we did harm to people, I admit. The spells of greatest importance to the Heirs were any to twist minds and wills."

"Like that sent here last winter by Glammis Lurgan, to enslave a truthseer. You recognized it."

The accusation hung between them like a drawn sword, hungry for blood. Seeing his fate in the blaze of gold-filled eyes, Kydd chose his next words with care. "I swear by my Ancestors I've done no harm to you or yours, truthseer."

The imagined sword didn't withdraw. "But you have killed."

"I—yes. Dusom believes the bandits who chased us to Marrowdell gave up the chase." Kydd summoned his courage. "That's not what happened. I'd brought tokens for a defensive spell. I didn't—" This time it wasn't Captain Ash who drew the truth from him, but the remembered horror of seeing Larell and her baby vanish beneath the wagon. "—I did. I wanted them to die. To pay."

Bannan sipped his tea. "And now you want to burn down your brother's house."

Heart's Blood, how had he sped to that? "I don't want to—it would be a last resort, if we can't get the yling to leave."

"Because they have something of yours."

Who *was* this man? Kydd nodded, now beyond surprise. "My journals from that time. Records of spells and lessons—more—" So much more. "The mages—our instructors—forbade us to take notes on pain of death—or worse." The thought of that worse made him shudder. "But I was reckless. Fearless. A fool. When the order exiling us came, I couldn't risk my journals being found in our wagons. Before we left Avyo, I gave them to Dusom to burn."

Another sip of tea. A cool look over the mug. "Why didn't he?"

"My dear innocent brother mistook them for a legacy of my scholarship, worthy of preservation." Kydd shivered inside. "It might not have been wholly his decision. Objects used for magic—just say it's possible my journals refused to let themselves be destroyed." And since the flood, had they scratched at his mind, demanding to be used again?

Speculation. Guilt. A fear he dared not share, so Kydd went on quickly, "Dusom brought them to Marrowdell but had the great good sense to hide them from me. I don't know what I'd have done—" He let out a breath. "Ancestors Crazed and Confounded, Bannan, I was trouble enough then. It remains a wonder to me they didn't vote to exile me to the Barrens."

"Then the yling found your journals and chose to guard them." Bannan pursed his lips, the gold dampening in his eyes once more as he pondered, and the beekeeper tried not to hold his breath. "From you," he concluded at last.

"I don't want them." *He did. He did. But why did he? How could he?* Kydd quashed the inner whimper, firmed his tone. "It's long past time they were destroyed, Bannan. Ancestors Witness, I hope without burning the house but I'll do whatever it takes. I swear it."

"What *more* did you write in them?"

"It doesn't matter—"

"I disagree. My parents were murdered by those able to use dark magic." Bannan held out a pleading hand, his face earnest. "By the Bones of our Ancestors, Kydd, tell me there's something in your journals to help me—help Lila—get justice."

Faces. Aliases. Meeting dates and locations. Notes and complaints. Nothing, he recalled, to point to any of the Heirs as responsible.

Nor exonerate them. Hadn't their leadership been zealous in their control, reacting with swift brutality against any who cast a spell without their approval? He found it hard to imagine that changing.

It didn't matter what he thought. What he'd recorded could well be the clues Bannan and his sister needed and, however desperately Kydd wanted to leave his past behind, his friend's pain demanded he not.

Not yet.

Try to be better. With the sense of standing before an abyss, he gave a nod. Bannan seized his hand, squeezing it with silent gratitude.

At least, Kydd told himself, he felt something other than numb at last.

Though sickening dread wasn't what he'd hoped.

Small homey buildings, with large round doors and small round windows, formed a circle around a tile-ringed fountain identical to that at the heart of Marrowdell. Paths crisscrossed the low brown-green turf, but Jenn saw no sign of gardens. What appeared to be statues of rough-hewn wood stood beside each round door, but there wasn't a tree in sight.

If this was a village, who lived in it? Wisp's landing had been as skillful as always, but she'd lost her balance during it and, as turn-born, almost tumbled into their fountain. In the process letting out a cry loud enough, surely, to draw attention.

But no one appeared.

Ancestors Perilous and Precipitous, she thought suddenly, had they scared everyone into hiding? Horrified, Jenn became flesh at once, smoothing her skirt. "Hello?" she ventured, turning slowly. "We won't hurt you."

This with a meaningful look at her dragon, who obligingly lowered his head. Which didn't remove his air of potent menace but at least, Jenn thought wryly, made him look less hungry, it being the dimming—

—except it wasn't, here. She looked up, confused, to find the sky of the Verge replaced by a shimmering bright dome, as if the village was roofed in sunlight. *How vastly clever.*

A clever dome with a jagged dragon-sized tear in it. Jenn glanced again at Wisp, who didn't appear the least guilt-ridden.

"We're sorry we broke your—roof," she said quickly. "We needed a safe place to spend the dimming."

Such as this, for the dome, now that she knew what to look for, extended to the ground and possibly into it on all sides. The outer rim wasn't round, as she might have expected, but more like the irregular edge of a puzzle piece. Jenn started to walk toward the closest side.

~I would not, Dear Heart. The terst will be unhappy if you crack their protection. More than we did coming through,~ her dragon added without a trace of guilt.

Terst? Overjoyed, Jenn smiled and spun around. "Oh, hello! Hello! My name is Jenn Nalynn. I know your kin, Mistress Sand and Master Riverstone. We're good friends. Won't you please come out?" For it felt, as she paid attention, that they were indeed not alone and were watched, possibly by many people.

A slow, rhythmic humming filled the air. Though Jenn couldn't tell from whence it came, she felt it hover over her skin. Not unpleasantly. More like the soothing tingle left by Aunt Sybb's prized cream—and when, on that thought, Jenn looked up?

The dome pulsed in time. Slowly, then with a rush, Wisp's tear closed itself until Jenn could no longer tell where it had been. Healed, rather than repaired, because that was the magic of the terst. Mistress Sand had told her, when they'd healed Uncle Horst's grievous wounds, and Jenn had decided then and there it was the best possible use of magic.

Silence again.

Aunt Sybb would say it was rude to ignore a visitor. Although, Jenn remembered in the nick of time, that wise lady had also impressed upon her and her sister the importance of granting others space and peace. Admittedly in a vain effort to have quiet time with her book, but the lesson applied, Jenn was sure, to people who'd had a foreign type of turn-born—with an exceptionally terrifying dragon—drop in uninvited.

She went to the fountain, curtsied, then dipped her fingers in the cool clear water, as she would at home. "Hearts of my Ancestors," Jenn whispered, "I am Beholden to be safe in this place and hope those here know I mean them no harm."

Adding her vow to leave, when that meant breaking the terst dome again, didn't seem prudent.

All at once, what she'd thought a featureless statue beside a door shimmered, becoming something else entirely.

A person.

Much as he regretted the dread-filled look on Kydd's face, Bannan didn't relent. How could he, finally with a chance at real information? A chance costing his friend dearly—Deliberately, he turned his back, walking toward the kettle as if to refresh his mug, choosing trust over suspicion.

But it wasn't the former student of dark magic who suddenly shook the farmhouse, toppling pots and pictures. "DANGERDANGERDANGER!" shrieked the dragon, the blast shattering the panes of window glass Bannan had had shipped from Endshere at no little expense.

He grabbed for a weapon, finding a pot handle. Felt more than saw Kydd come up beside him, poker in hand. "What's come?" the beekeeper whispered.

Something to scare a dragon—

Or—

Lowering the pot, Bannan went to the door and thrust it open, somehow not surprised to find Tir and Scourge paces from the porch. The former had his axes out, the latter rearing in outrage, while to his deeper sight Imp crouched before them on the porch, jaws agape, if thankfully flameless.

He'd best calm everyone down or Wisp would be out a student. The truthseer held up his hands. "These are friends, Imp. Let them pass."

At the "Let"—in hindsight, not the wisest word to use—Scourge plunged to the ground with a ground-shaking snarl, showing fangs dripping with dragon-killing venom.

Bloody Beast.

Imp scurried behind Bannan.

"Imp's been standing guard," the truthseer said quickly. "A little too well, perhaps."

Tir, like the kruar, had yet to stand down. "Against what, sir?" he demanded, pale blue eyes icy. Turning slowly, he surveyed the peaceful farmyard as if ready for a rush of Ansnan foot patrol and what did it say, that neither of them had left those instincts behind?

Kydd showed up with a plate containing not one but two pieces of cheese, one much larger than the other. Bannan took it with a grateful nod. "Friends," he repeated firmly. He dropped the smaller piece behind him, hearing a *snap*, then held out the plate.

Scourge's red-rimmed eyes shifted from the dragon to the overly generous chunk of cheese remaining. His fangs retreated, slowly, as his lips calmed. He came forward—Imp retreating—until his outstretched neck let him delicately take the cheese. "Idiot Beast," Bannan said gruffly.

A fetid hot breath in his ear. *"The only idiot cowers behind you."* But Scourge seemed content with the mild insult, unless it was the cheese.

Meanwhile Tir, seeing how matters stood, gave a shrug and slung his axes. "There'd better be biscuits," he growled as he passed Bannan on his way into the house. "Sir."

"'Biscuits?'" came a wistful echo.

Scourge snarled.

Imp fled the porch with a clumsy flap of wings, overturning the bucket again and the bench for the first time, perhaps concluding Bannan amply guarded and itself at greater risk.

Kydd stopped Bannan with a touch on his arm. "They followed me here," he whispered, eyes haunted. "Why?"

The truthseer took hold of the other's shoulders. "Friends," he asserted a third time, squeezing gently. "Who need one another, now more than ever. Who will understand and accept," he added, knowing what clouded Kydd's face.

For an instant, he feared Kydd would bolt—try to get to his journals first and destroy them—and Bannan readied himself to hold fast and stop him. It wasn't just the loss of whatever they contained of concern here. In any confrontation with the little cousins the man would lose, a man they all loved and who mattered to Marrowdell. More, it was clear, than he himself appreciated.

Kydd relaxed, shaking his head. "You're the most terrifying person I've ever met—and I don't mean Captain Ash."

Bannan made himself chuckle. "You haven't been with Tir when he's losing at 'stones. Come on."

He beckoned Kydd, who still seemed anxious, inside. When the truthseer glanced back to see what Scourge would do, he wasn't surprised to find the kruar standing in the shade of a tree, his grim gaze fixed on the roof.

Imp best mind his manners.

They found Tir already by the fire, a glass of brandy, not tea, in his hand, mask off to show the fullness of his scowl. "What's all this about, sir?" he growled.

"Why, we're planning a raid," Bannan informed him, grabbing two more glasses.

Kydd took his, shaking his head as he took the other seat. Tir splashed some of the last of the fine bottle into the beekeeper's glass, handing the remains to Bannan, who drew over a kitchen stool for himself. "Been a while," his old friend said, eyes alight with interest.

Heart's Blood, not long enough, Bannan told himself.

Then began to explain.

A terst! A person, Jenn decided on the spot, reassuringly like herself—when she was flesh—with bright red lips and cheeks, as well as curly black hair and sparkling blue eyes.

Except she—or he, because Jenn found nothing to advise her one way or the other, the terst dressed in a stiff jerkin over pants, the cloth like pressed twigs or straws—was plainly furious. Not, she realized at once, at her, for those blue eyes glared at Wisp, curled at her feet.

The dragon, unperturbed and entirely visible, let a whiff of steam drift idly from his nostrils.

"I apologize—" Jenn began.

A sharp gesture cut off the rest. ~This is their tool. This is their taker.~ Words inside her head, like Wisp's in the Verge, or Mistress Sand's, for that matter, when not practicing her Rhothan. The terst's glare shifted to Jenn. ~Now yours.~

The meaning was plain. The turn-born, Jenn knew, had ordered Wisp to collect turn-born babies from the terst, hunting any they'd tried to hide. She also knew—for Wisp had told her most and she'd surmised the rest—her dragon hadn't been happy nor had he been safe, in those days. Not that any had been safe from him; he'd wiped out a terst village because, as he'd said, he could harm them if not the turn-born.

The sei had dictated his terrible penance and declared it served. The terst opinion wasn't hers to debate, nor, Jenn realized all at once, would Wisp care or want her to intercede.

"We are not—" About to say "here for your babies," Jenn stopped, transfixed by the terst's long finger as it reached for her nose. She went a little cross-eyed, following its path, but didn't sense a threat.

The finger, possessed of an elongated nail much like a claw and painted bright green, came to rest between her eyes. It gave a light tap. ~Your mask is not our making.~

Said very much as Lorra Treff would disparage the work of a novice potter at Endshere's market, and Jenn stiffened, offended for her house toad who'd done a remarkable job to come up with a mask for her under difficult circumstances.

And had swallowed a moth, at great risk, to do so.

The finger arched over her brow then stroked the side of her face, leaving a chill where it passed. Finally, the terst took her chin between thumb and forefinger, tilting Jenn's face this way and that as if hunting for flaws.

Ancestors Witness, she'd had more than enough touching and holding, given terst had refused to make her a mask in the first place when approached by Mistress Sand. Jenn pulled free. "I wear this out of courtesy," she said sharply, reminding the terst, should they need reminding, that without a mask to hide the light within her they would be blinded.

No need to tell them she couldn't take hers off.

The terst, who was her height though broader, gave a neat little bow. The effect was spoiled when a thick black lock of hair caught on a little pin, to be freed with a too-impatient grab and telling wince.

Cynd's habit, her hair regularly caught on the straight pins she tucked on her sleeve to be handy, and Jenn grew slightly more at ease.

"Your village is lovely," she complimented, feeling it time for better manners. "And your buildings are—remarkable." Which they were, distinctly so, for on closer inspection Jenn had seen the walls and roofs weren't made of wood or stone, but consisted of cunningly fitted metal clockworks. Even the round doors were of metal gears.

The terst made a rude noise. ~This, na?~ The finger with its painted nail lifted and flicked at the ring of buildings. ~A disgusting place, unworthy of notice.~ A *tsk* like Mistress Sand made with her tongue.

Wisp's snout rose the tiniest bit. Noticing, Jenn swallowed her immediate disagreement. Ancestors Posturing and Pretentious. The terst seemed as bad as Roche had been, exaggerating matters and telling untruths. She made a wild stab at a response. "I don't know how you can stand to live here."

The terst's smile was sudden and alarming, teeth studded with dark flecks of stone and the front pair filed to points. ~It's hard on us all.~ Hands clapped.

The rest of the statues shimmered to life. Within heartbeats, Jenn stood in the midst of what she guessed to be the entire population of the village.

There were twenty-three terst, varied in age and size. All wore stiff pants and tunics made of straw, like the one who'd greeted Jenn, and, like the first, had pins affixed to their tunics below their right shoulders.

Pins that differed from one another, perhaps individual taste or to signify whatever terst needed to share. They were comprised of clock parts, shiny and bright as if new. Seeing so many, Jenn thought of Riss Nahamm, who kept a box of such parts and planned, one day, to surprise her uncle by repairing the treasured heirloom clock he'd brought from Avyo.

Admittedly a challenge, for on arriving in Marrowdell, Master Jupp had taken the metal tip of his cane to the clock's insides, but Riss was determined, and more parts would help. She'd ask the terst—

Heart's Blood. What if their pins were like Melusine's? Which she really shouldn't have left with Peggs, given the wishing in mimrol on the back, but there was nothing to be done about that until home again. She'd trust her sister's abundant good sense in the matter.

But if the terst pins were magic, what might they do?

Thoughts flying through Jenn's head, the terst studying her as earnestly as she studied them.

The terst wore shoes, complete with shiny buckles Aunt Sybb would approve, and Jenn's bare toes curled self-consciously. Several terst had soft scarves around their necks or hair, and those differed widely in color. Some terst appeared female, the elder of those possessed of generous matronly curves reminding her of Mistress Sand.

Those who appeared not to be were beardless, like Master River-stone, and there were other similarities.

So many, in fact, that had she not seen the terst turn-born as other than flesh and known them only by the features displayed on their masks and the coloring they remembered for themselves, she'd have believed them born here.

A small face peered from behind an adult, to be quickly pushed back. There were more and, to Jenn's dismay, it was plain the terst hid their children from her.

Or from her dragon.

Regardless, it was a sad state of affairs, if understandable. She gave a little sigh, unsure how to proceed.

~Demand your rights as turn-born, Dear Heart,~ Wisp suggested slyly. ~Terst cannot refuse you.~

Well, she wasn't about to demand or ask for anything, other than an introduction. "My name is Jenn Nalynn. I'm from—"

~Marrowdell,~ finished an older terst, stepping forward.

"They've been there for weeks. I say leave'm be." Tir spat eloquently into the dirt before the porch step. "Wait for Jenn, sir. Let her fix the wee beasties."

Bannan's house toad seemed to agree, taking a post under the bench, limpid brown eyes bulging more than normal.

Kydd rubbed a hand over his face, then glanced at Bannan. "Much as I want this over and done, Tir's right," he said heavily.

"Don't recall asking," the former soldier retorted with a glower.

The beekeeper actually grinned. "No need to thank me." He'd reverted to his former self during their discussion of how to free his journals from the silk clutches of an unknown number of armed yling, as if sharing his dark past a second time somehow helped.

Unless it was Tir's assertion they'd each had a turn as blithering idiots before learning to shave and did Kydd have a spell to cure flatulence? Assured he did not, the former soldier had cursed cheerfully, then suggested they sit outside. Something about Devins' experiment with home brew and a lingering result.

A bald-faced liar, mask or no, was Tir, but nothing could have broken through the beekeeper's anguished guilt faster. Bannan was grateful.

Among a mix of other feelings, the most important his growing impatience to get those journals to Lila. Their hunt wasn't for justice alone. There were present-day threats, including the likes of Glammis Lurgan, who'd thus far eluded Lila's pursuit, thwarting her efforts to identify the *collector* who'd paid Lurgan to have Bannan—and her—kidnapped.

Mistress Sand hadn't kidnapped Jenn, but would, Bannan greatly feared, keep his beloved preoccupied in the Verge until he resolved this business of the missing terst turn-born. A complication Kydd didn't need to know, and Tir? The truthseer winced inwardly. Odds were his old friend would tie him up and sit on him, all while lecturing him—for his own good, of course. Possibly after knocking him out with whatever was handiest.

No. He'd take the journals to Lila as quickly as possible, then leave for Gordit.

Ancestors Witness, the first part of the plan was straightforward, despite Tir's fussing. Get in, grab the journals, get out. Without being stabbed by a poisoned spear—

—or waking the baby.

Neither Tir nor Kydd would let him go alone. Together it was, and, while Bannan's deeper sight would let him spy the number and location of the yling guarding Dusom's ceiling, the others were blind to them. Except at the turn, when the light of the Verge would expose the little beings, so that was their intention, to rush into the bedroom at that moment.

And, Ancestors Harried and Hopeful, trust the yling to be unwilling to cause them serious harm.

It would help if the yling who'd been Bannan's companion and helpmate in Channen was with those in the loft—not that he'd reason to believe it would intervene for them nor, the truthseer thought ruefully, was he sure he could tell it apart from the rest.

Tir and Kydd continued bickering and Bannan roused himself. "We can't wait for Jenn."

"Yessir." Amazing how much doubt Tir instilled in two syllables.

Bannan eyed his house toad with regret. He'd nipped out to ask Scourge to talk to it on their behalf—bringing the last of their cheese for inducement—but the bloody beast had vanished.

Bannan stirred. "We move just before full sunset," he reminded the others as much as himself.

When, if this were a story, Jenn would appear in the nick of time strolling down her path—running, he could wish, to be with him as quickly as possible. She'd only to want the distance to disappear and it would.

Ancestors Blessed and Beloved, a man could die happy, knowing such love. Not that he'd any plan to die, especially on the spear of an yling acting in what it would consider the just defense of Marrowdell.

Against Kydd, whose own plans to keep his past from tainting his present had been thwarted by the kindness of a brother, and who quite possibly posed the greater threat.

Tir grumbled under his breath, his friend likely reasoning along similar lines but unwilling to speak.

"We should eat," Bannan announced, getting to his feet. Not that he'd an appetite—nor had any idea what was in the cupboards—but it was a soldier's wisdom, to fill stomachs while peace remained.

And a friend's, to take care of his own.

Appetite lacking, Kydd pushed his plate to Tir, who scooped the mass of scrambled egg into his ruined mouth with practiced dexterity, not losing a morsel or sight of him.

The former soldier had strikingly cold pale blue eyes, framed by lines baked into his tanned skin; the beekeeper held himself steady under that grim regard. It ended only when Tir, finished, got up to settle in a chair and apparently fall asleep.

If it came to the worst, Kydd thought, if they came to believe him too dangerous to live, Bannan would hesitate, torn by thoughts of Jenn and Peggs.

Tir would not. It made the pair more dangerous than either alone, but he'd no way of separating them. Here.

Then where? As Bannan readied for their assault on Dusom's loft, Kydd scraped the dishes, keeping his tea, though he felt drowned in the stuff. He examined the thought cautiously. The truthseer would take the journals through his magic door to Vorkoun—

No one can have us but you—NO ONE!

The denial made Kydd tremble inside, its growing force a warning. He took a real swallow, trying in vain to warm an inner chill resident since he'd discovered his cursed journals still existed, were—Heart's Blood—still in reach, with all they had to offer—*wanted* to offer—

No. He was better than that. Must be better than that. A conviction straightening Kydd's shoulders and firming his voice as he spoke.

"I'm coming with you, Bannan. Not just to Dusom's. Afterward. Through your door to Vorkoun."

The terst turn-born, having access to the edge and the societies found there, furnished their home with exquisite items, items someone like Jenn recognized even if from a distant land. A chair, after all, was a chair.

Not here. Jenn did her utmost not to squirm, for her chair—as she charitably called it—would *ticktocktick* in disapproval. Much like Aunt Sybb, really, if that dear lady was a squat cylinder of movable parts—but unlike Aunt Sybb, who was reliable above all else, if Jenn stood? Her terst chair would abandon its job and toddle off to click itself to the table.

She knew, being sat on her second.

Appearances everywhere were deceptive and changing and mechanical. The pins, Jenn thought ruefully, should have warned her.

What the terst wore flowed like fabric, so wasn't straw, and that was the least of it. The rest of the furnishings weren't furniture—except for the table, which seemed a sort of mother figure. Many and myriad little clockwork figures romped around the room, when not attached to the table, able to move because each contained a bubble or tube of mimrol, reminding her of the magical artifices sold in Channen's Shadow District.

Mimrol the Verge had in plenty; the mystery was where the terst obtained such fine and detailed metal components—or metal at all, the ever-changing Verge hardly the place for a mine or mill.

The clockworks seemed of no obvious use, other than those temporarily combined into opinionated chairs and, yes, the motherly table; those Jenn was able to study looked as if someone had shaken rods and gears and springs in a bag then attached the resulting jumble together to see the result.

One couldn't move properly, *whirring* miserably in its spot.

She might have thought them toys, but their motion wasn't random. It took a while for several to *tiptap* on their little rod legs or roll, but eventually the majority came to a halt surrounding Wisp, who curled on the floor with his eyes mostly shut as if bored or asleep.

Which he wasn't, of course. Jenn could just make out the gleam of white-hot flames flickering between his—*mostly*—closed jaws, and really hoped the terst weren't planning something they'd regret.

Other clockworks climbed walls, stopping to hang for a while or drop without warning, making it difficult indeed for Jenn to focus on the dry monotone of the three terst elders who'd accompanied her indoors.

Not, Jenn thought, that there was a door as such, it being more a shimmer—

~—to avoid the dimming, Jenn Nalynn of Marrowdell.~

She nodded hastily. Unlike terst turn-born, who'd but the memory of mouths after all, the terst spoke aloud. They'd told her their names, complex to her ear and remarkably long; she feared she'd misspeak them if she tried so wouldn't. To keep the three straight, she thought of them as "Ollaha," "Mengeeo," and "Ro."

"Yes. Thank you again for sheltering us. When the dimming ends, we'll happily leave—more carefully," she added, that likely a concern.

The three exchanged looks. ~It may never end, Jenn Nalynn of Marrowdell,~ Ro said. He was the taller and older of the two male terst, with thick red hair.

~In the Perfect Before, Terst Were Safe,~ Mengeeo intoned.

~'In the Perfect Before,'~ the other two echoed, adding, ~All Stayed Where All Should.~

They'd intoned, echoed, and added those words several times, an unhelpful punctuation to what at best was a stilted conversation. She'd yet to get a straight answer as to how they'd known she came from Marrowdell, let alone that Marrowdell existed.

She guessed the "Perfect Before" referred to the time before the sei pulled the terst world into hers, creating Verge and edge. A time, according to her dragon, generations ago for most creatures of the Verge, including the terst, so how could these terst know it was perfect?

They couldn't, a truth which didn't stop them fervently believing it a time of safety and stability. Aunt Sybb said anyone who longed for the golden days of yesteryear hadn't done those dishes, her way of saying everyone's version of the past differed and not all people had good ones.

She'd also said people had a right to their beliefs, especially those of comfort to them and no harm to others, and Jenn tried to be patient. Even if the terst sayings reminded her of Old Master Jupp, who, when overtired, would become distressed and drone, "Ordo doesn't deserve to be anyone's Blessed Ancestor. Feed his bones to the fish, I say!" over and over, unable to stop on his own unless distracted with a warm drink and blanket.

Options she didn't have. Jenn sighed to herself. To complicate matters, she couldn't be sure if Ro told the truth when not intoning or echoing.

Yes, Wisp had warned her, often, that turn-born weren't always truthful, but Ancestors Treacherous and Tricky, it would have helped to know terst almost never were—at least before engaging in an important conversation with three of them.

Their lies, however, followed a pattern of sorts. If something was good, like their village, they called it dreadful. If something was bad, they tended to praise it. Unless it came to dragons or turn-born, in which case they made their true feelings clear, though what they thought of her she'd yet to discern. Bemusement, perhaps.

The terst also, she suspected, enjoyed riddles; if not for the situation, Jenn might have enjoyed the challenge, being fond herself.

Bannan would be better at all this, she'd no doubt.

Time to move matters along, even if the terst thought her contrary and rude. Better that than Wisp, who'd begun to glare at the clockworks around him, burn their house down. "When the dimming ends," she asserted firmly, "we must seek out Mistress Sand. One of the turn-born—"

Mengeeo scowled, baring her filed teeth. ~The Cursed.~

~In the Perfect Before, None Were Cursed,~ said Ro. For a change, the other two remained silent, their lips tight.

Because the terst's "Perfect Before" would have been the last time free of turn-born, when no baby born at sunset was forever lost to their family. Such loss, without choice or recourse, had to be the worst thing a parent could face.

Deplorable. Maybe unnecessary, Jenn thought abruptly. She was proof a turn-born could grow up within their own family and be the better for it—a point she'd raise with Mistress Sand. The terst hadn't been offered the chance. They deserved it—

Once the terst turn-borns' problem was resolved. "A person I care about is missing," she said. "I must help find him."

~The taken and gone and forgotten,~ this from Ollaha, the second male. He and Mengeeo weren't alike yet were, both having scars like stitches along their left cheek and jawline, as well as a row around each wrist.

They didn't, as far as Jenn had seen, nod or shake their heads, preferring to use the painted nail of their forefinger to draw in the air. Now all three stroked a long line followed by a slash across and she'd no idea what it signified.

Another round of "In the Perfect Before, Terst Were Happy" followed.

When they were done, Jenn forged ahead, determined to explain what mattered to her and should to them. That the Verge depended on the terst turn-born to moderate its wild magic. That a risk to them was a risk to the Verge—and so to the edge and on to the magical land beyond either that had spawned the sei and everything else here in the first place.

Including the terst.

And her dragon, who remained curled and still. Despite Jenn's frequent and urgent looks in his direction, Wisp offered neither comment nor suggestion, apparently ignoring her.

He didn't, though.

The girl's great heart struggled. Beyond a dragon to ease it. Having experienced Marrowdell, Wisp suspected the problem was that Jenn Nalynn's expectation of family and proper behavior was in no way the terst's.

Who were more like the turn-born they feared and reviled than they'd ever admit. Worse, in some ways. Ordinary terst lacked the power to impact reality, but they'd gladly cheat a little cousin. As for their villages? This place?

Lies. Illusion. Their safety built on pretense such as the fakery of their mechanical pets and no safety at all. He'd proved that to many of them, during his years prying out the turn-born brats they didn't willingly provide.

Sand among them.

Still, since the end of their "The Perfect Before"—having been there, Wisp enjoyed the irony—the terst had made their place in the Verge. The terst built roads like the girl's and buildings like these.

Temporary and movable, to trick hunters, but their kaliia farms were impressive in scope.

If deadly to intruders.

Dragons, as a rule, left the terst alone. Younglings couldn't see through their illusions; those who could—and lived long enough—learned not to disturb what turn-born valued. The turn-born viewed the terst as a source of future replacements, making them crops.

Not that terst viewed themselves thus.

Wisp spat a lick of flame, darkly amused when the little mechanicals—doubtless intent on caging him—scurried away so quickly parts fell off.

There were, of course, two living terst turn-born who remembered family as the girl did. Riverstone, though his memories were vague and unhappy.

Sand, however—

Not his fault, Wisp reminded himself. The terst who'd kept their turn-born daughter until half grown had been sneaky, enlisting little cousins, moving her from village to village. While he'd languished under a kitchen floor, forgotten.

Hadn't eaten her dog.

As a moment of restraint, hardly memorable, though the dog likely remembered, seeing how it avoided him.

Wisp snorted to himself. The beast owed him its continued unnatural existence. Miserable and new to her power, Sand had made her ridiculous wish to preserve the dog's life just in time to save it from his jaws.

A snack missed.

An enmity grown. Sand already hated him for taking her from her family then destroying her village as a lesson, though he'd been commanded by the turn-born. Almost eating her pet had turned her hate into loathing, yet he'd only been true to his nature.

Wisp understood more, now. Sand could hate because she remembered love. It had led her to befriend the girl's mother and dote upon the villagers. Riverstone, who remembered wanting to be loved, had done the same.

Confusing the other terst turn-born, whose fondness for Marrowdell's inhabitants resembled Imp's for biscuits.

Wisp listened as Jenn changed tactics, it apparently having occurred to her the terst might like to meet the children they'd lost. "Let me bring Mistress Sand here," she offered. "Surely you—"

Fingers scratched the air, unhappy terst like nyphrit in their desire to claw, though too civilized to attack.

Or aware he watched.

Or afraid, Wisp thought more cheerfully, of the girl. Who'd never hurt them, but he'd not tell them.

Still. ~Despite prediction, this dimming is over,~ he informed Jenn, rising to his good legs. ~It's time for us to leave.~

She stood, looking relieved to eyes that knew her. "Thank you for—" She paused very briefly, in Wisp's opinion stuck for anything the terst had done worth gratitude, then said, "—the chance to meet you. I've wondered what you were like."

~While we know your kind, Jenn Nalynn of Marrowdell, very well,~ replied the older terst, his gesturing amused. ~Your world is no mystery to us. Any terst can step into it. We are familiar with your domains. Your politics.~

Terst could cross into the edge and back? This was news even to a dragon of Wisp's age and experience. Alarmed, he sank back down. ~It might be a lie,~ he warned. ~Ask them why they cross, Dear Heart.~

Where they went, so long as not to Marrowdell or where the young truthseer lived, Wisp didn't care at all.

An opinion he'd change.

FIVE

*T*ERST, VISIT THE edge?

They'd healing powers, Jenn knew. Were crafters of masks and these devices and doubtless other things. Above all else, she'd seen they were masters of illusion and misdirection, making it not only possible a terst could walk more easily among her people than she among theirs—

—but likely. "Do you tell people what you are? Where you're from?"

She didn't need Wisp to tell her the terst found this hilarious; their fingers wiggled in a paroxysm of what had to be mirth and their tongues stuck out. Mannerisms certain to be noticed and remarked upon in her world, perhaps the reason the terst turn-born didn't perform them—or hadn't in front of her.

Unless they hadn't learned them in the first place, torn from their kind too young, leading Jenn to wonder next what more they didn't know about the terst, for surely if Mistress Sand knew the terst crossed into the edge, she'd have said—warned them—

As if sensing her incredulity, Ro stopped moving. Shimmered.

All at once, standing in front of her was Rhonnda Taff, the artisan she'd met in Channen's Shadow District. She'd painted tattoos that appeared to move—now Jenn had to ask herself if those had been illusions, too.

Ancestors Stunned and Startled, Jenn supposed this did clarify where the terst obtained parts for their pins and devices, the latter mostly clinging to walls—or festooning the table—after Wisp's little display.

Her wise dragon, questioning their motives. "So you cross to my world just to get these?" Jenn gestured at the hapless device quivering near her feet, unable to retreat with the others.

~In the Perfect Before Terst Had Everything,~ Ro intoned. ~Here We Have Nothing.~

~The Perfect Before,~ echoed the others.

She took it for agreement, but that meant the terst, unlike dragons and kruar, were able to cross with more than themselves.

And it was one thing to bring little gears and tubes home with them, but what did they trade in return? Jenn couldn't help but think of nyphrit, of other fell and perilous creatures in the Verge—then stopped. Surely the terst traded their work for what they needed, as people did.

As, she swallowed, *people*. How many terst went to the edge—how would anyone know?

Mengeeo pointed at her. ~Why do you?~

Avoiding her question, that was, aiming it back at her. Jenn didn't allow herself to be aggravated. "I've explained that. To visit my friend. To help another, if I can."

~Turn-born lie.~

Ancestors Tattle and Tale. Terst had, she decided, no sense of irony. Unless their distrust and disdain—their hatred and loathing—was the real reason the terst crossed into the edge. Were they spying on the terst turn-born?

Heart's Blood, had the terst something to do with Tooth's disappearance?

At the awful thought, the air chilled, and Jenn concentrated with desperate speed on pots and diapers.

The air warmed again. If the terst noticed—or cared—they gave no sign of it.

Jenn composed herself—and would have sat to emphasize her

composure had her second chair not abandoned her to cozy up to the table. "I don't lie," she countered as calmly as she could, fighting the temptation to wish them all to be truthful, as she had poor Roche, who—on his own—had found a home and a place far from Marrowdell.

~Your existence is a lie,~ Ollaha told her. ~Your appearance now is a lie.~

Really, the terst sounded like Cheffy when teased by his older sister, a mix of petulant and petty.

If the terst wouldn't answer a direct question, maybe she'd learn more by, as Bannan put it, coming at the issue sideways. "Why bother with my world?" she asked, keeping her voice light. "I'd have thought you'd cross into your own."

The terst closed their hands into fists, tucked those into armpits, whirled, and marched out of the building. Their devices were equally offended. The encumbered table rose on two legs and reshaped itself to walk, while those on walls dropped to the floor, the lot following their owners with a furious *clatter* and *whirr*.

Those that could move, anyway.

Frustrated, Jenn crouched near her dragon. "What did I say?"

Bannan frowned at Kydd. "Impossible. You can't survive the Verge."

The beekeeper raised an eyebrow. "I can. In my journals—I've a spell to temporarily blind a person to magic—"

"Won't need one," Tir interrupted, eyes still closed. "I'll knock you senseless."

They'd gear spread over the table. Avoiding Kydd's expectant look, Bannan busied himself with it, absently deciding Tir's helmet would be the most useful and Jenn's ladle the least. "You'd leave Peggs, now?" he asked. Cruel, that question, but one to ask. "Why?"

"Not for long—I can't be gone—she'll be fine—" Kydd abruptly sounded like a man arguing with himself, a man losing. "I'm the only one who can decipher my writings," he finished in a rush. "I have to go."

It *felt* like the truth. Heart's Blood, annoying to believe and not at the same time.

Didn't matter, Bannan decided. He set aside the ladle. Pretended to give serious consideration to a long-handled fork. "The baron's a master code-breaker—"

"It's not code. The pages are—" Kydd stopped, leaning forward. The side of his face was caught in the sunbeam coming through the open window; his expression was stark. "The pages are attuned to me. Anyone else who tries to read them, even after so long, I fear—I know—will be at risk."

Lila—Bannan froze in place, but before he could ask, Tir's eyes popped open to glare at the beekeeper and he snapped, "Risk of what, itchy fingers?"

"A coma," Kydd replied grimly. "Unto death. A precaution—"

"Heart's Blood, and you're telling us now?" Tir surged to his feet, arms flailing, and just as well his axes were outside on the porch. "Magical pins and now books!? Never did trust books," he muttered darkly, if less than truthfully, being fond of mystery stories. Louder and very clear, "I say we burn the lot and be done."

Magical pin? He'd missed something—

"Yes! Yes! Ancestors Witness, we must!" Kydd blurted out. "Burn them! There's nothing good to come of them here. I swear it."

Tir lowered his arms, looking confused. He'd be angry next, and Bannan didn't blame him. Or Kydd, who he now feared struggled against a powerful—and, yes, magical—temptation, at times beyond his control.

The yling must have known—or had Marrowdell itself?

Bannan put down the poker. Held up his open hands for peace, giving Tir a look. "Which is it, Kydd? A moment ago you offered to cross with me, to read for us—"

"Ancestors Dire and Desperate—you can't!" The protest came from the open doorway where Peggs Uhthoff stood.

Holding a bundle of nine leather-bound journals.

Wisp raised his head. ~You annoyed them with the truth, Dearest Heart. Terst can no more cross to where they came from than you leave the edge. The sei sealed the way.~ A pensive snarl. ~The Verge is better. Terst are fools.~

The device on the floor gave a faint *ticktick* of protest, and Wisp smacked it with his good foot, leaving a flattened pile of gears and pieces amid a silver puddle of mimrol.

They weren't fools, Jenn thought. From what little she'd seen of the terst, to them the Verge was a place where they hid under protective domes and lost children, though she dearly hoped there were more and happier aspects to their lives.

Crouching, Jenn sorted out the intact bits and looked for a place to put them, deciding a spot near the wall would be best. She'd have taken them for Riss, but it didn't feel right, not to have asked.

She sank down to sit by her dragon. "You remember it?" she asked gently, astonished anew. "That 'before' place?" Wisp was ancient but the sei had reached from that world to hers to create the Verge and edge over four hundred years ago.

A gleam in the wild violet eye aimed her way. ~Boring and dull, I assure you, replete with rules to govern everything that lived. I was among the first to seek this new realm, to soar in its sky and breathe in its magic. I would never wish to return.~

"I wouldn't want you to," Jenn asserted stoutly, dismayed at the mere thought of her dragon leaving. "Not ever!"

~Then I won't,~ Wisp told her and she'd the feeling he was pleased.

She gathered her skirts around her shins, hugging her knees to her chest. "What do we do now?"

~Now, since the dimming is over, we will go to the turn-born's enclave.~

He sounded more confident that she felt. "According to the terst, it might never end."

A snort.

Ancestors Tricky and Trapped, she didn't believe the terst either, but—"Something's not right, Wisp," Jenn insisted. "I—I feel it." As if spots of weakness grew in the layers of turn-born expectations weaving through the Verge, the way Devins' bony elbows wore holes in his shirts. Holes that needed patching before neglect made them worse—but here? She'd no idea where or how or if she even dared try. "I need Mistress Sand," Jenn decided, sure of that much.

Wisp stretched his neck until his snout almost touched her bare toes and she felt the banked heat of his breath. ~I will get you to her, Dear Heart.~

Her bold, brave dragon would try.

Alas, she wasn't at all sure he could.

Peggs sat in their best chair, journals balanced on her bulge and kept there by a white-knuckled grip warning against any attempt to relieve her of that burden. Dusom sat in the other chair looking unusually haggard, while Kydd perched on a stool facing both, his gaze fixed on the floor. The warmed pie Dusom had brought—Peggs saying curtly her aunt and father were better able to feed themselves than the three grown men in front of her—waited on the oven, no one ready to eat.

Kydd's wife had arrived with his entire family, Wainn on the rug by the cookstove, Delfinn cradled in his lap, her dark eyes wide open. They'd had an unexpected escort right to the door, Scourge waiting at the ford to prance alongside. Realizing why the beast had deserted, Bannan was grateful beyond words. Imp had tasted Wainn's blood; the youngling couldn't, according to Wisp, help but lust for more.

Once the young father was safely settled inside, Bannan's house toad came to lean against Wainn's foot, taking its turn as guard. Meanwhile Tir, the coward, eased out the door when the truthseer wasn't looking, leaving him to play host.

"Are you sure?" Bannan repeated, holding up the kettle.

Peggs shook her head. "Thank you, but no." Her gaze never left her husband's bent head, her expression one of intense focus, as if she knew there was an answer and a reason and path forward. She'd only to find it.

Ancestors Tested and Tried, Bannan scolded himself, if anyone could, it would be Peggs. Who'd helped with the wishing to transform the dragon into a man. Been the first to know and accept Jenn's transformation to turn-born. Magic wouldn't frighten her.

She was here to fight for her family.

Putting down the kettle, the truthseer went to stand beside the ladder to the loft, a spot letting him watch every face but Wainn's. He rested his arm on a rung then said bluntly, "The journals contain dark spells—magic Kydd learned and practiced in Avyo."

Kydd looked up, profoundly shocked. His gaze shot to Peggs. "I—" He stopped, likely lost for anything to add to that.

She dipped her head. "We thought as much. Didn't we, Dusom?"

Dusom gave a tiny nod, his lips in a tight line.

"You shouldn't touch them," the beekeeper erupted, hands holding the stool as if only that grip kept him from leaping up to take the journals from her. "They've power of their own—they're dangerous, Peggs!"

"Ancestors Foolish and Failed, it's my fault they're even here," the elder Uhthoff said despairingly. He clasped his hands together, leaned forward on his elbows. "I'm sorry, Dear Heart," he told his brother, then looked at Peggs.

If anything, she tightened her grip. "The yling gave them to me to hold, no one else."

"About that," Bannan began, consumed with curiosity. As far as he knew, Peggs had no contact with Marrowdell's wild inhabitants, other than giving pebbles to toads like the rest of the villagers.

"We went upstairs with Peggs," Wainn piped in cheerfully. "We talked to them."

Everyone but Peggs turned to look at him.

Wainn looked peaceful. His daughter—Wen's daughter—stared back, eyes unblinking, her expression serious. The little silver disk she wore caught the light and it was no mere trinket, but a heart compass tied to her mother, acclaimed as the toads' new queen and living in the Verge. Bannan's breath caught in his throat.

Then Delfinn snuggled into her father's arms, giving a tiny blissful burp, a baby again and unaware.

"They wouldn't let me have them, in case I saw the bad words," Wainn continued calmly, as if it didn't matter that his uncle blanched. "They were happy Peggs took them. They don't—" this to Dusom "—like it in the loft, Father. It's not your fault. You snore."

Confronted by such an ordinary complaint, the elder Uhthoff puffed his cheeks then let the air out slowly, his face filling with rueful wonder. "I trust," he said diplomatically, "they've left?"

"MARROWDELL STILL WATCHES." This in a voice not Wainn's at all and none of them mistook it for anything but a warning. Having startled them, the young man ducked his head to kiss his daughter's, looking up again with his easy, ordinary smile.

"So, Dearest Heart," Peggs said to Kydd, her tone brittle but firm. "What's all this about crossing to Vorkoun?"

The cavalcade returning Baron Emon Westietas and his newly minted heir to their city arrived in Vorkoun after the day's busyness had subsided, but before outdoor patios and terraces came alive with lights and music, it being, as Momma put it, prudent not to attract undue attention.

Prince Ordo Arselical of Rhoth was still unhappy with his baron, dictating terms for his banishment from the House of Keys in Avyo that forbade political activity of any sort, anywhere; a ban which absolutely made Poppa showing his face to those more loyal to baron than prince in Vorkoun a serious offense.

Not, Semyn knew, that the prince actually cared. Vorkoun was so far from Avyo's concerns—other than as a token to play—he judged it unlikely Ordo could name a street in it, which was foolish. Poppa taught the importance of knowing places as well as people, the two intertwined, and map study was one of Semyn's favorites, as it was Werfol's.

The fancy coach was designed to impress onlookers while protecting its passengers from any with ill intent, making strength more critical than comfort. Semyn sat on the backward-facing bench squeezed between Dutton and Elsa Lowin, a guard added to the heir's protection, everyone bouncing haplessly on the run down the lesser road to the even less well-maintained lower one through the valley.

When they finally reached the flat and smoother road—come from Weken and northern Rhoth, to cross the Hilip River and hence into Vorkoun proper—the driver sped up, adding more force to the jostling in her eagerness to reach the city.

His shoulders and one knee well bruised by the guards' armor, Semyn didn't complain; his father, across from him, sat squeezed between his personal guards, Vin Macle and Ally Ennan, and looked equally uncomfortable. After a particularly violent bounce, when despite strong grips on the straps the guards couldn't keep from bashing into them, his father winked and made a face, so Semyn did the same.

It left a good feeling.

Not better than having his brother with him—Weed would have made a game of it and doubtless found some clever way to brace themselves to prevent the worst bruises—but good. There was a special warmth in how Poppa winked, in how he—a baron and the most important person in east Rhoth and possibly the entire domain—acknowledged they shared the necessary discomfort of this journey.

And its risk. The living barrier of armored guards made that aspect perfectly clear and, so thinking, Semyn was glad Werfol had stayed home, watched by Cheek and Scatterwit, Poppa's crows, from their nest.

If only he'd been able to remember home included the edge and magic, potent risks of themselves.

This was a terst road? Jenn regarded the dimpled length of brown embedded stone dubiously. A road, in her experience, shouldn't be narrower than any path in Marrowdell—let alone the Tinkers Road, which was wide enough for a good-sized wagon and someone to walk alongside, if not, admittedly, as wide as roads in more civilized places such as Channen.

The terst were back to hiding as wooden statues, a sign they were done talking to her and wouldn't so much as say goodbye—which was discourteous, but what she deserved, Jenn sighed to herself. After all, she'd upset them.

And wouldn't miss more rounds of *The Perfect Before*, so there was that.

According to her dragon, who'd brought her to the rim of the village dome, terst roads like this weren't for terst, but to guide their cows.

Jenn kept her voice low. "Where are the cows?"

~On the roads,~ Wisp informed her with an amused glint in his wild violet eye. ~Those who stray are eaten.~ This in a tone suggesting he'd tasted his share and wouldn't mind another. ~The roads provide safe passage for them and will for you.~

Finally. Caring for their livestock was the first familiar thing about the terst, a relief, Jenn admitted to herself.

Plus, knowing cows as she did, keeping them to roads would let the terst collect as much of their dung as possible, not that she'd seen terst gardens but they must, she reasoned, have some. Master Dusom taught that the material was also valued in southern climes such as the deserts of Eldad, being used to seal baskets and walls where clay wasn't available, and to smooth floors.

The terst floors had been very smooth, come to think of it. Which she did, almost missing what her dragon said next. "'Cut a hole'?" Jenn echoed, dismayed. "Wisp, we promised not to make any more."

~You promised, Dear Heart, ~ her dragon pointed out with reprehensible precision. ~Fear not, the terst didn't believe you.~

Slightly insulted, Jenn glanced over her shoulder at the nearest statue. Without features, she couldn't tell who it was or if who it was glanced back, terst continuing to prove a frustration, if she were honest, and difficult to comprehend. She hadn't a saying from Aunt Sybb to help, other than the dear lady's blanket assertion that getting a job started was the greater effort.

Meaning, if they had to make a hole, best do it. "Please make it as small as you can, Wisp," she told him, to salve her conscience, if not at all his.

This time, she was able to see how her dragon parted the terst illusion. Extending his good front leg, Wisp used a single needle-sharp clawtip as she would a knife, slicing down. As she'd asked, the slice was small, so she had to bend over and twist to follow him through the gap.

By the sudden aggrieved *hum* from behind, the terst saw to healing it immediately, sealing them out.

Jenn hardly paid attention, for once outside she found herself back in the Verge, beneath a sky blazing with color and wide as a sky should be, though mountains floated sideways and a river of mimrol flowed past to her upper left.

What mattered was the light was bright again, marking a safer time, and Jenn gladly stayed flesh and blood as she followed Wisp, the pair walking what turned out to be an ordinary, if narrow, road of packed dirt.

A road soon scored with knee-deep ruts about the length of her forearm apart, as if used by a too-heavy, too-skinny wagon, forcing Jenn to walk on the rise between. Setting her bare feet carefully one before the other made her tip from side to side; keeping her balance took most of her concentration.

Which was why she bumped into Wisp when he stopped without warning. He steadied her with a curl of his tail, swinging his head around to regard her. ~Cows.~

Ancestors Blessed! She'd hoped to see the terst version, not that she expected they'd resemble Marrowdell's docile bovines, but cows were, in her experience, gentle and curious animals—not to mention Devins, who longed to acquire a new calf or two to enrich their stock, would be very interested in such foreign versions—

Jenn eagerly craned her neck to look past her dragon.

Only to duck behind him. "Those?" It came out a squeak, one

she felt justified. Ancestors Terrified and Trembling, the terst cows were the tall monsters with enormous claws on the ends of long arms, the same monsters who'd tried to grab them from the air, and the only thing possibly more menacing than one of them?

Was the whole herd turning to look her way.

They'd tea, after all, that sovereign ritual to calm nerves and lower temperatures, though glancing at Kydd and Peggs, Bannan doubted there was enough in Marrowdell to do the trick.

Tir had slunk back in and nipped a chunk of the pie. He sat on his heels in a corner, sipping what wasn't tea, eyes bright with amusement.

Tempting to join him.

When the time came for Delfinn to visit Hettie for her next meal, something she announced loudly for such a tiny babe, Wainn stood with Dusom to take their leave. Dusom took Bannan's hand, in lieu of approaching his brother, still locked in argument, leaning close to say a fervent, "Keep them safe."

Wainn gave the truthseer an unusually somber look, but all he said was, "It's time to go."

Heart's Blood, it might have been—probably was—literally that time as far as Delfinn was concerned, but Bannan hesitated, searching Wainn's calm face for a sign this was Marrowdell urging for him to cross this very minute—

—the question to answer being did he go alone with the journals, or take Kydd?

Something Peggs adamantly opposed. Along with Kydd's suggestion he use a blinding spell on himself, and Bannan had to agree, the whole business of magic felt fraught with—

Consequences. Thinking the word, Bannan thought of Jenn and smiled involuntarily.

Wainn smiled back. "Imp won't attack me," he said, to the truthseer's instant shame. He'd forgotten that threat.

"I'll see if Scourge . . ." Bannan let the offer trail away, seeing how Wainn gazed fondly down at his daughter and Delfinn gazed fondly back.

The young dragon feared turn-born. Not that tiny Delfinn had that power yet, nor would until her eighteenth birthday, but Imp wasn't, as Wisp put it, the brightest of students, and it wasn't, Bannan thought more cheerfully, beyond its teacher to encourage that healthy fear.

To be sure, he saw them out the door and farmyard and, once the three were on the Tinkers Road, Bannan turned and used his deeper sight to check his roof for dragons.

There. Draped bonelessly over the peak, Imp basked in the sunshine, its eyes half closed, and a less threatening sight was hard to imagine. *Still.* Without Wisp in Marrowdell, given the distrust Scourge and the toad held toward the young dragon, this wasn't a problem to leave on the loose.

"Imp!" Bannan called.

Eyes shot open. The dragon scrabbled frantically, barely managing not to slide down the roof, and a tremulous breeze found the truthseer's ear. "I was on guard," Imp asserted weakly. "Guarding."

Worse than a new recruit. Tir would have its head, Bannan thought, amused; a feeling he kept from his voice. "I no longer require a guard, Imp. I'm about to leave Marrowdell and cross into Vorkoun. While I'm gone, I've an important task for you."

Imp reared its head. "You can't leave! If you go—" it wailed, seizing on what mattered to it "—the kruar will ambush and kill me! IT HATES ME!"

"Which is why," Bannan said quickly, holding in a wince, "I want you to cross into the Verge and find Jenn Nalynn and Wisp. They'll protect you," he added.

It tensed, suspicion in every line of its body. "The Great Lord of Dragons won't be happy if I abandon my post. HE will KILL ME!"

"Jenn won't let him," the truthseer soothed. "And you've no post to abandon. I won't be here." He could almost see the thoughts work their agonizingly slow way through that narrow skull, a passage leading to who knew what conclusion, and found a new sympathy for Wisp, forced to instruct this flighty creature. "I'm sure Jenn will reward you with biscuits."

Imp sidled down the roof, knocking a few shingles awry, to lean over the edge, its gaze locked on Bannan. "Is that a promise, truthseer?" Its head twisted from side to side, as if it needed multiple views of his face. "Is it?"

With a silent apology to his beloved, Bannan circled his hands over his heart. "By the Hearts of my Blessed Ancestors, I promise Jenn Nalynn will give you biscuits. If you find her."

With a joyful flap of wings, Imp lifted into the air then spiraled away into the distance. "I WILL! I WILL!" Fainter, but still clear, "BISCUITS . . . biscuits . . . biscuits!"

Shaking his head, Bannan went back inside, stopping just inside the door.

"—not upset," Peggs said fiercely, her voice rising. "I'm sensible and I'm reasonable—qualities you no longer exhibit, Dearest Heart, despite doing so in abundance until today! Ancestors Cursed and Confounded, are these—" she rocked the journals on her bulge "—to blame?"

Kydd covered his face with his hands and nodded, mute and overcome. Bannan took a cautious step closer.

Peggs chewed her lower lip, then looked up at Bannan, her decision clearly made. "We dare not burn them here."

She'd seen what happened when tokens were set afire in Marrowdell. The truthseer gave a little bow. "A wise precaution," he acknowledged. As was, he'd decided, taking Kydd with him, if reading the journals posed the slightest risk to Lila or Emon—or anyone else.

Making it the worst idea to take the bundle and sprint to his door, despite its appeal. He'd have to convince—

Tir spoke up. "Let me take them down the road, sir. They'd start a fine bonfire."

The beekeeper's hands dropped and he shook his head. "They won't let you," he warned hoarsely. "They'll summon bandits—or bears!" He looked at Peggs. "You're right. They must leave Marrowdell—but it must be in the hands of those who understand the danger they pose. Who will destroy them with every precaution taken." His voice gentled. "Dearest Heart, we can't let Bannan do this alone."

"Ancestors Bloody and Bowed," Peggs muttered. "Fine time for my sister to go gallivanting."

Giving in, that was, and Kydd slipped from the chair to kneel at her feet, hands on her knees. Seeing the worship in his face, Bannan turned away.

To find Tir raising his cup, as if he'd won a bet.

When her dragon didn't seize her and launch into the air—and, more significantly, when the monsters filling the crossroads ahead huffed and looked away again, disinterested—Jenn took a decidedly shaky breath. "Are we safe?" she whispered, that being the most pressing question.

Wisp, still visible, yawned widely. Of course, dragons didn't yawn, making this show of fangs and the glowing heat deep in his mouth a display of his might.

Not, she noted wryly, an answer.

Nor was running back to the terst village, which, now that she glanced back to check, had disappeared again. Other than the way the cow road ended abruptly at what looked like a rocky cliff.

She made herself study the herd. Only eight, which would be more reassuring had each not been three times Wisp's size—let alone the dismaying reach of those huge arms, for they didn't go just on all fours. Seven stood erect on legs thicker than she was, waving hands possessed of three formidable claws, each as long as her forearm.

A terst cow turned and, with a single swipe of its hand, neatly collected the head of a tall plant.

Kaliia! Here growing the height of a goodly tree back in Marrowdell, with heads loaded with grain, and how had she missed that rows of it lined the road, a field curving up to the sky? Another terst illusion.

The cow pushed its prize into a gaping mouth full of small, peglike teeth, munching with every sign of delight. Teeth smaller than those of Himself, the Ropps' bull, and really, Jenn thought determinedly, hardly threatening at all.

Only to freeze again when the nearest cow swung down its big head to aim a small rheumy eye at them, an eye full of suspicion despite its size. It nudged a neighbor, who began sniffing the air in her direction. When a third renewed its attention to her, Jenn took a step back. "Wisp—"

~I'll move them from our path, Dear Heart.~ With no other warning, her dragon roared! Flame spewed from his mouth, licking at the feet of the great beasts ahead of them, and Jenn might have objected there was no call to scare them—

But the terst cows didn't stampede. Not exactly, she corrected to herself, fascinated, for using their powerful arms and hands, the beasts burrowed under the kaliia field, digging with such ferocious speed the last disappeared within seconds, leaving a choking cloud of fine dirt behind.

As well as huge deposits of fresh smelly dung, and Jenn pinched her nose.

~That would be why kruar loathe cows,~ Wisp informed her cheerfully. ~Including yours.~

While their cows didn't make such a—generous—mess, Jenn understood the feeling. "Where did they go?" she asked. The kaliia was a dense forest of stalks, but it strained credulity for creatures so large to simply vanish without a mound or tipped plant to be seen, though it did imply a daintiness Marrowdell's cows could stand to learn—

~Down. Away. It is how they elude the efflet, who are no more tolerant here than in the edge. And dragons.~ A moment's pause. ~Also kruar. Much as they dislike the smell of cow, their younglings grow desperate at times.~ With a touch of smug.

Feeling a rush of sympathy for the besieged terst cows, Jenn tried without success to spot any sign of efflet, curious if those of the Verge were different somehow. Though by what her dragon said, they remained the protectors of the kaliia here as well, and she'd not risk offending them.

Nose pinched, for once she'd felt no danger she'd become flesh again, she stayed with her dragon as he skirted the herd's odorous deposits.

Neither saw the terst cows poke their great heads from the ground, for the beasts, like dragons and some little cousins, possessed the ability to bend light around themselves. Nor noticed how, once sure they were safe, the herd shimmered back into view and climbed onto the road to resume their rudely interrupted grazing.

Most of all, neither dragon nor girl noticed the pair of terst cows who didn't graze, instead staring intently after them.

For Jenn's part, her lack of attention to cows had to do with her delight at discovering a crossroad unlike any she'd seen on a map. Roads entering from her left and right made tight bends to join the one they were on, while that bent as well, linking all around a fat half-circle.

Why, such an arrangement, if used by wagons, would keep traffic flowing with no one needing to stop and wait. Did terst cows need to keep moving? Or were they thus, she suddenly envisioned, kept from meeting face to face, like the silly calves who'd start to butt heads and forget where they were to go?

Wisp took the branch of road that went left. It began to rise, steeply. Not that in the Verge such a slope mattered. Her dragon drove in his ample sharp claws, using beats of his wings as needed.

Jenn lifted her foot and planted it at a right angle to her body, shifting her balance. The cliff face became what was perfectly level and flat—unless she glanced behind and down to see the road below, or noticed how her skirt stuck out.

At the notion, she did glance that way, utterly failing to see the pair of terst cows were now quite close behind her, for they shimmered and vanished before she could.

"How far is it, Wisp?" she asked after a while. "To the enclave." It seemed a reasonable question, the Verge prone to change.

Wisp paused and raised his snout, nostrils flared, then resumed climbing. ~Further than it was,~ he told her.

Which was unsettling, though hardly unexpected, there having been very little ordinary about this particular trip. *Ordinary.* Jenn's lips quirked up. Ancestors Bemused and Befuddled, what a word to think about the Verge, where nothing was ordinary, ever, at all. She'd have to tell Peggs—

~We're here.~

They certainly were. Without the warning, Jenn's next step would have sent her smack into the blue crystal wall around the turn-born enclave, which clearly wasn't *further* in any sense, and how had her dragon made such a mistake?

Wisp snarled softly. ~What did you do, Dear Heart?~

"Nothing," she replied wonderingly, reaching out to touch the wall and be reassured it really was there. "Nothing at all." She met her dragon's worried gaze. "What's going on?"

Neither saw the shimmer marking where the two terst cows curled up against the wall, nor heard their silent sighs of longing.

Kydd walked his beloved home, grateful the Tinkers Road had been well raked and smoothed, grateful the sun shone, still, and presumably the air was warm, though he'd no thought for any sensation but the hand in his and no care but to see Peggs safely to her family.

Especially hearing how she panted, though walking slowly, and if he'd dared suggest it, he'd have run to the village and returned with Davi's cart even if he had to pull it himself, but he had, the beekeeper thought sorrowfully, squandered his right to suggest anything at all.

"I'm not going to break," Peggs assured him, a reassurance tempered by how she puffed out the words. "This massive babe of ours takes up space, that's all, and leaves me barely enough to fill my lungs. Or pee," she added pensively, eyeing the forest to one side.

"Do you need to stop?" he asked at once. "We can stop." He hoped beyond the shade of the old trees, who'd a temper made worse since the flood.

Her hand gave his a squeeze and she cast him a fond smile. "Not before home, Dearest Heart. I used Bannan's privy. That said, we drank a goodly amount of tea, so best we hurry on."

A few steps later, Kydd blurted, "I thought this impossible."

Peggs put her free hand on her stomach. "Then you weren't paying attention."

He brought up the hand he held, tenderly kissing her fingers. "Not that. Well, yes that. I am old, you know." Years older, during which he'd seen Peggs Nalynn grow from a toddler to this glorious accomplished woman, as far beyond his reach as the stars.

Or so he'd believed.

She puffed a laugh. "Not so old, obviously."

They bantered to avoid the topic that would see her home and him away, every argument and tear spent. Peggs, of all Marrowdell, possibly better than he, understood the risk he took.

If not the how. Sure enough, when they paused to rest and tie up her skirts—it presently impossible for Kydd to carry her in his arms across the ford as he'd done often and with joy—Peggs became still, gazing at the village on the other side of the river. "You're sure Aunt Sybb will have what you need. The tokens for this blinding spell?"

"A temporary blindness, to magic alone," Kydd reminded her, not that he'd reason for confidence. Over twenty years since he'd cast a proper spell and he'd need to read those cursed journals to check the words. But the ingredients for this one he couldn't forget, for they were as harmless as they were, for a young student, hilariously awkward to obtain and use. Items that truly defined the "don't look at this" of the spell. "Whatever Aunt Sybb doesn't have, Riss should." Or Lorra, but she'd be far too quick to guess.

As always.

Finished, Peggs gave her skirt a tug to test it, then looked up at him. Her eyes were beautiful, huge and soulful, like gazing into a starlit night; he'd yet to come close to the color in paint, not for lack of effort.

Their shape he could sketch in his sleep, along with her full and loving lips. He bent for a taste.

To meet a finger. "Dearest Heart," he pleaded against it. Kissed it and the warmth of her palm, then started nibbling her sweet, strong wrist.

Peggs choked out a laugh and grabbed him by the ears. "I'm not your supper," she chastised fondly, planting a wonderful firm kiss on his mouth which was, in Kydd's delighted opinion, as good as a meal. "Ancestors Blessed," she huffed when they were done, breathless for another reason.

And abruptly giggled. "You woke the little beast!"

Kydd put his hand over the newly active spot, his gaze lifting to meet hers. "Hearts of our Ancestors," he begged in an anguished whisper. "I pray you not break my heart."

Peggs laid her hand over his. "By their Bones, do not break mine."

"If it'll work fer him, it'll work fer me. Sir. Just say'n."

Bannan hung the cleaned mugs on their hooks. "No."

"You'll need me there, not here, and ye know it."

Tir being reasonable was almost as bad as the man when he wasn't—no, this was worse. It made it impossible to swear at him.

Almost. "Ancestors Obtuse and Obstinate, what I need is for you to be quiet and let me think."

"Nothing to think about, sir," cheerfully.

Oh, but there was. Starting with the vision—real or imagined—he'd faced on his first assay through his door and what it might mean. Or not.

And the fact the door was his, a magical gift from the love of his life, meant to help him stay in touch with his family, not—

Not to facilitate whatever grim result came of Kydd, his journals, and the knowledge in the poor beekeeper's head, for Bannan was under no illusion what Lila would want to do with all three.

"Jenn gave it rules," he said at last.

"Aie. That only you or Jenn can take another through. Sensible, sir. Don't want an enemy popping in back of the baron's estate."

Trust someone who'd served in the marches, where ambush had been the tactic of choice on both sides, to think of that nightmare. Hooking his foot under a kitchen chair, Bannan slid it around and sat with his arms crossed over the back to face his old friend. "There's another rule," he said, resting his chin on his arm. "No one of ill intent may cross."

"What happens to'm, then?"

Bannan blinked. Jenn hadn't said, other than to intimate it was simply a question of the door not opening at all.

Did she even know?

His companion raised both eyebrows. "Like that, is it?" he growled. "Then how do you think to pass, sir, seeing you're already half on the hunt and grim?"

Was he? Bannan straightened with a frown. Tir's insights were often uncomfortable and rarely wrong—but in this case? He relaxed. "Not for revenge. Mistress Sand gave me a mission." The truthseer told his friend about the missing turn-born, Tir's scowl darkening apace. He finished with, "I didn't give my word."

"Heart's Blood, you didn't have to," the other observed roughly. "A threat to Jenn and the wee babe?" His eyes flashed. "But Gordit, sir? That foul, foul place—" Tir's voice cracked, failed him.

For good reason. Their patrol had taken shelter deep in a collapsed shaft of the mine overlooking the town, Captain Ash under orders to "interview" a group of high-level prisoners. They'd been discovered, pinned there by roving Ansnan soldiers—

—lost four, one to an arrow, one crushed by falling debris, and two to the strange wasting sickness afflicting them all by the end and had that been a spell? Past time to ask, Bannan thought grimly. Past time.

"Settles it. I come with you. Sir." The last with a decisive nod.

"Like Vorkoun, Gordit is again at peace." Or should be. Bannan managed a smile. "I need you, my old—my most trusted—friend, to guard my back, as you've done times without count." He let his smile fade. "You know the situation. Kydd suffers. Marrowdell protests. Let alone Peggs about to give birth at any moment. Those spell books have to go to Lila as soon as possible—and," hard as it was to admit, "I've no idea when Jenn will return."

He refused to think she wouldn't, that the other turn-born could sway her into staying with them. But Jenn linger overlong to help?

That he believed. "Ancestors Tried and Trusted. Tell me I can depend on you. Please."

A fierce look.

He waited, chin back on his arm, regarding his friend.

Who resembled a kettle about to boil, his scarred head growing redder and redder until finally Tir exploded, swearing inventively and with feeling for several minutes before gasping to a stop.

Bannan tipped his head in question.

"Yes. Yes, SIR, I'll stay bloody put—but I won't be kept in the dark, not again."

Hadn't forgiven him for leaving with Jenn in search of Emon this winter past, barely making it home alive. The truthseer said gravely, "I'll send messages this time."

Tir lowered his head and glowered. "The first best be you've made it through or I'll send the Bloody Beast to rip up your good leg. Sir."

"I'll be with the family." With a grin, Bannan circled his heart with his fingers. "But I swear on the Bones of my Ancestors to let you know," he vowed, blithely sure sending a soothing message would be the easiest task he'd face.

Vorkoun hadn't stayed as memories promised. *Don't be such a child*, Semyn scolded himself, mimicking the tones of a tutor long gone and unlamented, but it wasn't a childish regret. He caught flickers of the same dismay in Poppa's face as the coach rumbled along the mostly empty overpass, crossing the heart of the northern half of the city.

Towers and terraces lined either side, many of those once belonging to friends and supporters freshly reapportioned to those of less clear allegiance. Dutifully, Semyn set himself to making new memories, focusing on the new flags and ribbons, even the flowers on display—for such were signals in themselves. He'd make notes tonight and, once home again, a map of them all.

One such changed place would be the Westietas Tower, out of sight on the far bank of the Lilem, now belonging to the Gerhen of Ansnor. It stood at the end of a winding stone pavement that rose higher than any flood, and the top three floors had held their apartment and been home. Those of their neighbors, home to playmates and cousins—

Semyn aimed his eyes forward, his mind ahead. They sped to a meeting, and, as heir, he would be expected to speak. When spoken to, in strange company, Momma had cautioned, going on at length to remind him—without need, so Semyn understood it was for her own comfort—how easily words became traps and how treason hid behind smiles—

—until Poppa had interceded with his warm laugh and a hug for them both.

Scared? Werfol had signed at him behind their parents' backs, and Semyn had replied with the truth. *We all are.*

The overpass twisted through the towers, then came the point it curled back on itself to begin its journey down, dipping so sharply the driver applied brakes as well as reining in her team and there were surprised oaths from the horse guard following behind.

The coach passed into a region of cool shadow and bright bars of sunlight. Businesses crowded close, taking advantage of how traffic need slow through what became a tunnel, but Momma had judged correctly and most were shuttered for the dinner hour. Being Vorkoun, openings in the street bed above and below let through not only light but the wastewater to flush away whatever wasn't to mar the lives of those above, making the air redolent here and rank near the cesspools lower down.

The saying was, you could tell a newcomer to Vorkoun by the scented satchels they shoved over their noses. Semyn, having grown up here, simply breathed through his mouth and paid the stench no mind. Worse below, regardless, and they'd not be—

The coach made a turn he hadn't expected. "The Candlas Bridge," Dutton announced quietly, grim and not surprised.

The Candlas went to only one place, the Ansnan half of Vorkoun—Mondir.

A significant deviation from Momma's careful plan. Semyn raised a questioning eyebrow at his father.

Who winked again.

Oddly cheered, the boy leaned over Dutton to press his nose to the window. At first, all he saw was a high stone rail, its pillar lanterns yet to be lit. Then the tenor of hoofbeats shifted, as did the sound of the wheels, as they came onto the wooden bed of the magnificent bridge. Less clatter, more hollow thud, not that the Candlas was in any way fragile, built ninety years earlier and having survived floods in each.

There. A gleam showed in the gaps. The flashing white of ships and sails. The clustered flags along the far shore. "The Lilem," he breathed.

More than a river. The trade the Lilem carried was the lifeblood of this, the greatest eastern city; its water formed the newly reset border between domains now at peace. That the Lilem cared nothing for the doings of people, tearing away buildings, sinking boats, and drowning any who underestimated it, like the poor souls swept away this spring, only made it a more potent symbol.

As for symbols, the Eld train would need a new bridge to carry it into northern Ansnor, Poppa adamant Vorkoun not lose any such critical structures and keen to learn more about Eld engineering.

Semyn feasted his eyes as they crossed the Lilem. His father, also taken by the sight, pointed out an eagle perched on a lantern, a large fish in its talons. A moment like their lives before, this trip an ordinary occurrence and perfectly safe.

Until the coach passed onto cobblestone again and drove into a cloud black as night and full of screams.

He didn't know what was happening, was the sorry, pained truth, and Wisp did his utmost not to reveal his frustration to the girl.

Nor his fear—for what bit and clawed him inside, as if he'd swallowed a nyphrit of ice, was the closest he'd ever come to the feeling. Not liking it, Wisp paced along the wall, looking for the gate. The girl followed.

They returned to where they'd started, marked by the handprint of blue tears left by the crystal cracked by her touch, however gentle, without sign of the opening or the gate to close it, and he knew without taking flight that the wall continued, roofing the enclave and keeping them out.

Or whatever the terst turn-born feared out. Where the girl was, and Wisp's fear intensified. ~We must return to Marrowdell. Let Sand seek you there.~

"Wait." She stooped then stood. "Look, Wisp."

In her cupped hands rested a miniature dragon of emerald green—no hatchling, ready to try its first tooth on anything that moved, but a dragon full grown, if misshapen.

The sei seeming. What it wore or became in order to cause trouble in his life, and Wisp was dismayed to see a being this powerful so reduced.

He showed his fangs. ~What happened to you?~ If it lasted, it was surely an improvement—

~FIX THIS!~

Well, it hadn't lost the ability to shout. The dragon briefly wished for Scourge's to roll his eyes.

"Fix what?" the girl asked, her face gone white. "What's wrong?"

Excellent questions. Would they understand the answers?

The sei-dragon wrapped its claws around her thumb, staring up into her face. ~FIX WHAT YOU HAVE BROKEN.~

With that less than helpful reply, it grew and grew until the girl dropped it with a cry. Kept growing, until its shadow covered the sky.

Gone, all at once.

Insufferable creature.

"What I've broken?" Her voice was faint. Grew stronger. "I've done nothing—Wisp, what does it mean? What could I have—" Her hands covered her mouth and her lovely eyes went wide.

She guessed. As did he, and the dragon took no satisfaction from it. ~Bannan's door.~

Her hands lowered. They trembled. "I thought—I asked—Wisp, what have I done?"

He gave a little shake to settle his wings. ~What your heart wanted,~ he reminded her, that being the truth, however hurtful, then paused, catching a hint of unexpected warmth, a whisper that said *terst* to his well-honed instincts.

Anywhere but here, he might have thought *cow*, but here lived the turn-born who were terst, and whom the girl wished to find.

So he concluded the hint and whisper simply meant one or more of them spied on them, and wasn't pleased. ~Come,~ he said grimly. ~We will find the way in and find your turn-born. Perhaps Sand will give us proper answers.~

Not that he'd count on it.

SIX

WAS HER DRAGON right? Wisp's accusation stung, but it was true, time and again she'd let her heart lead her head. She'd turned him into a man—drained Marrowdell's river—what if her crossing for Bannan was why the Verge felt wiggly?

How was she to do better?

Consumed by her thoughts, Jenn followed Wisp along the blue wall as he continued to hunt an entrance, arms carefully at her sides. Her dragon hadn't offered to smash his way through the fragile stuff. Jenn didn't need her sense of the turn-borns' expectation for protection and privacy holding the wall in place to know it would be wrong. The crystal of the wall was alive, doing what it considered its duty. They'd find a door rather than harm it.

As for her, well, she was alive, though turn-born and sei and sometimes of glass, and did her best, though knowing her duty at any given moment was, Jenn decided, often a difficulty.

And, as Wisp said, she was a person with a passionate heart that yes, did lead her on—

Was that such a bad thing?

Jenn pressed her hand over her heart, feeling its steady, reassuring *thud-thump*—even if it was but her memory making it real—and knew it wasn't. It was her heart, her compassion and capacity for love, that had led her to grant Frann Nall's final wish and save the wounded sei—though she did regret making rabbits of the nyphrit who likely hadn't wanted to be—the point being, when she'd followed her heart, much of what she'd accomplished was decidedly good, including to restore her dear Wisp.

Listening to her heart made her the person she was and, Jenn vowed then and there, she would try to be, always. Roses and tears and wishes. Kindness and love and laughter.

Along with, she promised Wisp and herself silently, a greater consideration of potential consequence.

Back at her handprint on the wall, Jenn gave a little nod. "We need to let them know we're here."

~Unless they do know and ignore us,~ replied her cynical dragon.

"I'm sure that's not the case," she said, which was more a hope than certainty. Sand and Riverstone wouldn't; she couldn't say the same for the others.

The task of being noticed was more difficult than she'd imagined. Knocking on the crystal would shatter it. Shouting—roaring, in Wisp's case—attracted the attention of a trio of kruar who bolted upon attracting theirs—and there was simply no wish safe to make.

At least, Jenn had yet to think of one. Nor did she know why the terst turn-born wouldn't let them in—"What are they afraid of?" she'd asked more than once. Her dragon had no answer to give, being equally perplexed.

"Do you believe the terst?" she asked suddenly. "That they cross into the edge?"

~They lied, Dear Heart. It's what terst do.~

She dug her toes in the not-alive sand. "They knew I came from Marrowdell."

A huff. ~Terst talk to little cousins. Little cousins,~ darkly, ~prattle about everything.~

She thought this unfair to house toads, who'd proved capable of great discretion and secrecy. About, Jenn conceded, their own affairs and perhaps less so about others', but still—

"Say that's so," Jenn said stubbornly. "It doesn't explain how a terst could be the artisan I met in Channen. Ancestors Confuddled and Confusing, it was the same person. I swear it, Wisp. How is that possible unless the terst do cross?"

She held her breath, hoping against hope Wisp had an answer. She wasn't ready to think of terst pretending to be this person or that at whim. Not ready at all. Was she to suspect every stranger she met? Or had met?

Alas, her wise dragon hesitated an instant too long before replying, ~All I know, Dear Heart, is that terst lie.~ Another pause. ~While I appreciate your curiosity, I would not mention our time with the terst to the turn-born. Their relationship is not a happy one.~

Jenn shuddered inwardly. "I promise." She'd wait and find a better moment than now, when the turn-born were already upset.

Admitting defeat, she leaned gently against the wall, her bare legs outstretched on warm sand, the dent where Wisp lay curled nearby. Since her dragon stayed alert and on guard, she chose to be flesh and blood, to remember heartbeats and pulses, breaths and swallowing, for forgetting what one was led to not being at all.

Which hadn't, she told herself firmly, happened to Mistress Sand. Who'd asked her to come, in the message Imp delivered, and it wasn't possible she'd ask only to—to—

Jenn sighed.

Close by, the terst cows lifted their heads and sighed with her, not that she or her dragon noticed.

~Are you ready to go home, Dear Heart?~

"Not yet." Though she was, most thoroughly and abundantly ready for an entire litany of reasons, but she mustn't abandon the terst turn-born.

Or ignore the sei. "If I broke something in the Verge," she mused aloud, still finding it hard to believe she could or had—but anything, she'd learned, was possible, "and if that something was broken because I made Bannan's door, that means I must close it again." Assuming she could. Though if the Verge stayed wiggly once she'd closed it, proving it hadn't been Bannan's door, did she open it again?

Close it first, she decided.

Sand shifted, Wisp getting to his feet. ~The crossing from the Verge to the young truthseer's part of the edge isn't far. Wasn't,~ her dragon qualified, both of them newly aware the Verge was less reliable than usual. ~If you wish, Dear Heart, I will take you there,~ with confidence. ~And stand with you,~ that with unexpected force.

Did he think Bannan would try to stop her? Her love would regret the loss of his access to his family, as would she, but—then she realized what worried her dragon wasn't Bannan at all. "You're worried about the baroness."

~They've built a home for you, in their part of the edge. A home—or a trap!~ This with a snarl.

A snarl Jenn ignored, stunned to hear of a home near the Westietas, which had to be for her and Bannan, which meant they'd have a second, for of course they'd keep theirs in Marrowdell, and now she was supposed to destroy that crossing and lose it?

She hadn't even seen it.

Ancestors Forthright and Fateful, she'd see it now—and make sure Bannan was with her, ready to return to Marrowdell when—

If—

WHEN, Jenn told herself firmly, she closed his door.

"Take me to the crossing, please, Wisp."

She'd decide what to do once in Vorkoun.

The pair of terst cows roused and padded along behind, unseen and unremarked. The youngest of the herd, ready and eager to imprint on a new leader, they answered only to their great and growing love for the one they would follow the rest of their lives.

Jenn Nalynn.

Wishings or spells or exhortations to the Celestials, whatever you called the act of summoning magic to a desired use, required the same elements: certain words said correctly and tokens, typically three in number and specific in nature.

Kydd's masters in Avyo taught that the proper tokens mattered most to success, since they served as the physical means of focus. In Kydd's carefully unvoiced opinion, it had more to do with such objects being rare, expensive, and often difficult to obtain, making it a waste for a student to squander them in oft-failed practice.

These?

Precious in other ways. Kydd sat with Peggs on the porch, going through their basket of finds, discarding any of doubt. He held up the next. "You're sure Aunt Sybb won't miss her garters?"

"Ancestors Sweaty and Steamed, not in summer." A mischievous smile lit Peggs' face, serious till now. "Besides, Aunt Sybb is convinced our house toad makes off with anything misplaced. It's kept Jenn and me out of trouble before now."

Putting the garters in his satchel, Kydd looked in the basket, then determinedly picked up what might have been a stout cotton sling, if not trimmed with lace and embroidered with a flowery "P." He felt himself blush.

"Dearest Heart, we've been married almost a year and you've washed worse than that," Peggs teased, chuckling at his face. "I won't have courses again until after our baby's born. When I'll sew another."

He kissed her cheek in surrender. Into the satchel it went.

If the previous tokens were items "not meant to be seen," the last token was meant to represent the opposite, "seen at the declared moment." Peggs reached into her bosom to produce Jenn's pin.

Kydd shook his head. "This—this isn't right."

"We can't ask Hettie for her wedding circlet," she replied reasonably. "She plans to pass it on to her children. After all, it's very fine—and silver. Unless you've changed your mind about mine?"

"Never," he said firmly. Her wedding circlet had been Melusine's, her and Jenn's mother, a priceless heirloom for a family with all too few.

"Then this it is." Peggs held up the antique pin, formed as a triplet of flowers. "Jenn told me Aunt Sybb waited for just the right moment to give this to her—to show her. That moment was today. Isn't that what you need? The moment seen?"

The heart of the spell. Peggs was, he decided—and not for the first time—more perceptive than any of his so-called teachers, but

Kydd couldn't help a final objection. "Your sister left it with you for safekeeping. What I use will be consumed when I cast the spell. We shouldn't take it without asking."

"Ancestors Blessed and Beloved, I know my sister. Jenn would want you—and Bannan—kept safe above all else."

How could he argue with that?

Though had Kydd not then taken Peggs in his arms, to kiss and be kissed with quite desperate warmth, this being their farewell—for now, they prayed—then to press his lips to the bulge of their baby-to-come?

He might have noticed the writing on the pin before putting it in his satchel. Writing of mimrol and magic, that changed, for the beat of a heart, to read . . .

"*Our lost spellcaster. Excellent. Go find them. Go!*"

Between Gordit and Lila, he'd be gone a while, no help for it. Bannan prepared himself. He wrote Jenn a letter. Three, in fact, vital details occurring to him only after folding each sheet of paper to put in one of their few envelopes.

He wrote about Kydd and the found-again journals, glossing over the family dispute—Jenn would hear about that from Peggs—while giving her what she needed to not judge Kydd harshly. The beekeeper wasn't the only one in Marrowdell desperate to leave his past behind and make a new future.

He wrote the details of his meeting with Mistress Sand, every word and nuance recalled precisely—a training he'd not thought to employ here—because Jenn had to know and he'd not trust Imp's memory. What she did with that knowledge would be up to her. And her dragon.

Last, after several false starts and hesitations, Bannan wrote about the vision he'd experienced, of a much older Marrowdell. He didn't add it might mean nothing. Deep in his heart he knew it did and it meant nothing good. If this next crossing saw them lost in the Verge or trapped in far-off Vorkoun—

—Jenn would be their only hope of getting home again.

Ancestors Blessed, if I could, I'd have waited . . . I love you . . . Be careful . . .

Keep Us Close said them all and best.

Letters left in sight, packing done, Bannan hung the key he'd found in the ruins of his family home on its string around his neck, comforted by its faint *Larmensu* of recognition and even more by its meaning. If a Larmensu called for help while holding the key, there were those in Vorkoun gifted by his father with coins bespelled to sound the alarm. They'd come in aid.

He'd pass the key to his elder nephew some day; he'd trust Semyn to decide if he should carry it or his brother, who thus far had been in more danger.

Was this journey dangerous?

Bannan looked around the loft. The sun had reached the Bone Hills, sending soft rays of light through the window and across the bed. It found the tall headboard and linens he'd brought to Marrowdell. They'd quilts folded in a trunk downstairs, gifts from the villagers tucked away for the season. Jenn had embroidered cases for their pillows and sewn curtains they left open, loving the warm summer air.

And to let moths come and go as they wished. His house toad stayed downstairs, concerned with guarding the door and windows. Jenn's? Always a question, but often as not it was in the barn, toads valuing buildings.

As for her dragon? Wisp had the good manners and prudence to use the door unless an emergency—or what he deemed as one—when he'd pass at whim through the shingles and wood of the ceiling or fly up through the floor. Skills he'd thankfully yet to pass on to his student, who might be too young to learn. In Bannan's opinion, it was more likely Imp's utter lack of discretion.

He eyed the rafters. "You there, Wisp?"

Nothing. Just as well. His worry lessened, to think Jenn had her dragon.

The truthseer grimaced. Of course, by this time, she'd have Imp with her as well, and he owed his beloved an apology for that. As for what the youngling would tell her—?

Heart's Blood, he'd have preferred she learned from him or his letter about the journals, let alone Kydd, but—

A rhythmic *thudding*. Bannan went to the window overlooking the farmyard to see the beekeeper, whose return he'd anticipated, riding into the farmyard bareback—on Scourge? There was a surprise. To Kydd as well, apparently, for the man's face was white as a sheet while the kruar's tail was flagged and his head high—pleased with himself, that was.

Two more riders came pounding up the road and into the yard—the Anan sisters in pursuit, not that they'd a chance of catching Scourge.

The question was, why?

Grabbing his pack, Bannan rushed to the ladder, hearing Tir's predictable—and furious—shout.

"BLOODY BEAST!!"

Someone pressed a cloth over Semyn's mouth and nose. It smelled, of all things, like fresh bread and home, so he took over holding it, guessing it a protection. One that had best work, for the coach had filled with a sort of mist—an attack, without doubt, and he'd memorized a regrettably long list of gases and powders along with their effects on a person—

"Out, lad."

He did what he could to help, though when Dutton took hold—for no one else in the coach had that depth of voice or size—things moved whether they wished to or not. In short order Semyn found himself through the door, steadied in pitch darkness to stand on what felt like cobblestones when he tested the footing. "Father," he said, making it an order.

"Aie."

Another took Dutton's place at Semyn's side with a muffled, "Lowin, sir." Hearing a sword drawn, the boy pulled out his eating knife, though weapons were of little use until they could see a target.

Their guards were the finest in Rhoth—and beyond, according to Momma, who'd trained most and tested the rest. Semyn felt the proof of it in the hushed, sure movements around him. He didn't need to see to know they'd formed a wall around him, as they'd do for Poppa—and hopefully already done, because Baron Westietas would be the prize here.

Others would range out from the point of attack, establishing a perimeter. They'd wait for a command before engaging their enemy, prudence when that enemy was well hidden, but would respond at need with deadly force.

Young as he was, Semyn had seen men die in battle. He and Werfol had been pursued up the Northward Road to Marrowdell last winter and almost perished. As these guards did now, Tir Half-face had stood between them and those who'd wished harm. In fact, he'd proved himself so capable—and knew so many family secrets—Momma hadn't been happy he'd taken service with the Lady Mahavar rather than with her.

Also disappointing Weed, who'd grumbled and railed for days, though not where Momma could hear.

But Semyn thought he understood, not that he offered his opinion. Tir, like their Uncle Bannan, had surely seen enough blood and war. Escorting Aunt Sybb—who was kind and generous—to and from Marrowdell was not only important work but would be a pleasant and deserved rest indeed.

"Keep the cloth in place." A whisper in his ear, barely audible, but a thrill went through Semyn at the sound of Poppa's voice. "At two, close your eyes tight." His father's arm went around him, pulling him against his chest. A finger tapped. Once. A second time—

Semyn closed his eyes.

A third—

Light burned against his eyelids as the *TWHUMP!* of a contained explosion nearby sent a tremor through the ground, Poppa holding him steady. A familiar sound to someone who'd spent as much time in their father's workshop as Semyn, and he took heart. They'd prepared for whatever this was—been ready—

"Safe, for now," Poppa said confidently, giving Semyn a squeeze before letting him go. "Stay with Dutton."

Semyn opened his eyes to find the terrifying black cloud dissipated, and lowered his cloth, tucking it away for safekeeping.

The cloud, oddly enough, hadn't thinned or blown away. The explosion—or some component distributed by its force—had shattered it, bits of black drifting down like palm-sized pieces of ash to melt when they hit the honest stones of the roadway. Seeing the guards hastily brush off any that touched them or the still-agitated horses, Semyn did the same.

Poppa, meanwhile, collected some in one of the vials he typically carried, calmly pushing in the stopper. Implying more to be learned from what happened; Semyn immediately paid closer attention to the stuff, crouching to watch a piece melt.

It didn't, exactly. Not like ice. Instead, it kept shattering until what remained was a dust so fine it blew away with his next breath.

Nothing did that. Nothing normal, he reminded himself as he stood, making this a magical attack.

And the cloth in his pocket a counter to it. On that thought, Semyn made sure it was secure.

Dutton, who stood by watching their surroundings, glanced at him when he did this and nodded in approval, his cloth in his belt. Ancestors Sneaky and Sly, his guard had received a fuller briefing.

Semyn smiled Momma's smile at him and wariness entered Dutton's expression, for he knew Momma well.

Time for some answers.

"Something's up," Emo Anan said grimly. "We want to know what."

Tir nodded vigorously.

Ancestors Smitten and Salacious, the sisters—particularly the elder, Emo—could have said the sun had already set and his friend would nod. Vigorously. A toss in the river might have helped, but the water was too warm to provide the shock Bannan urgently wished he could provide.

The sisters' presence most unhelpful.

Matched pairs of dark brown eyes regarded him. "Why did the beekeeper run from us, if there wasn't?" This from the younger, Elsinore.

Kydd, shaken from riding Scourge—and how that transpired, Bannan would love to know, the kruar detesting anyone else on his back—glared at the young women. "You're new to Marrowdell," he said stiffly. "Do not expect to understand it—nor to deserve explanations."

"Now, now," Tir piped up, his bright eyes unable to decide whom to ogle; to be fair, he did appear most entranced by the sisters' well-worn weapons. "Why don't we go inside and have something to drink?"

The suggestion earned him a glower from Emo. "Upset the cows he did, riding through their pasture like a bloody fool."

Her sister nodded. "We'll have to introduce ourselves all over again tomorrow. Hope they've calmed—"

"You could see I was in a hurry," Kydd snapped. "You got in my way—"

"Terrible manners, that," Tir interrupted, smoothly not taking sides. "Cookies, perhaps?"

Incorrigible optimist. Bannan gave a little cough. "I'm sure you've other preparations before you take the extra stock to their summer grazing." A reminder to Tir that the ladies he found irresistible were leaving and soon. "To our benefit—and I freely admit of great worry to all in Marrowdell until you came and offered to take on this trust. Ancestors Blessed, we are Beholden to you, Emo and Elsinore Anan." Having said this in his best imitation of his baron brother-in-law, Bannan bowed deeply, sweeping his fingertips over the packed earth in the finest Avyo style.

Catching his very broad hint, Kydd bowed as well. Tir nodded. Vigorously.

Their courtesy had the desired result. When the truthseer rose to face them again, the sisters had lost their grim look, seeming pleased and was that a little flustered? "Devins needed help," Elsinore said quickly.

Her sister, not to be left out, chimed in, "Happy to do it. I enjoy working with cattle."

Emo dropped a hand to her knife hilt. "I'll bring Devins the pelt of any bear what tries to tangle with them. It'll make a fine rug."

"I'll be finding the best grass—"

"I'll be—"

Scourge snarled.

The sisters' horses—who'd courageously endured the proximity of a predator—shied in unison, making their riders grab for their reins. Soothing her mount, Emo glared at the kruar. "Ye'd make a fine pelt."

Lips pulled back to show decidedly unhorse-like teeth. Before matters worsened, Scourge as ready to answer insult as Tir to race to some imagined rescue, Bannan raised his voice. "Peace! All of you." With a quelling look at his own mount.

Who huffed and perked his ears like a happy pony.

Idiot. "What's going on, Emo and Elsinore, is a project Kydd needs done before he becomes a father," Bannan told them. "I'm sure you understand the urgency of that. We'd appreciate it if you would tell Peggs he's arrived and all's well. And Devins," he suggested blandly. "I imagine he's wondering where you went."

Rather than be embarrassed, the two eyed each other over their horses' backs, as if the mention of Devins—or was it fatherhood?—added fuel to their competition and nothing else mattered. They mounted, gave distracted farewells, and were off that instant, Tir gazing after them glumly. "There are two of them," Bannan pointed out.

Scourge rumbled, amused. A sly little breeze added, "The more the better."

"No romance in your hearts," Tir accused. "Either of you."

And no time for anything but what Kydd brought in the satchel over his shoulder.

Catching Bannan's look, the beekeeper gave a curt nod. "I'm ready to cast the spell."

Since becoming turn-born, Jenn had crossed into the Verge through the Spine—that visible portion of the trapped mad sei who held the edge together—and inside a drop of mimrol—falling as rain into Channen's Shadow District while riding a kruar, Bannan with her on his own mount—and thought those two experiences encompassed the strangest there could be—

—until being swallowed by the toad queen, who'd a mutable crossing *inside* her body, making that passage unpleasant in the extreme.

This—"You're sure?"

Her dragon clung to a rock protruding over what appeared to be a small cave. A cave within a pile of rocks, one of several openings, in fact, and had Jenn found a cave like this in Marrowdell, she'd have run to Uncle Horst, who knew about bears and other dangers, to have him check it before setting a toe inside.

And, Jenn decided, unable to make out anything in the darkness within, she'd bring a lantern.

Wisp dropped down beside her, snapping closed his wings. ~This is the crossing, Dear Heart.~ He sounded puzzled. ~Do you not feel it?~

Heart's Blood, what she felt was a reasonable trepidation concerning the wisdom of entering an unknown cave with who knew what lurking inside.

It not seeming the moment to try and explain to her dragon— again—that she'd a great deal more to learn about her abilities as a turn-born, especially when Wisp persisted in believing her entirely capable and the best of them—Jenn pointed at the black maw looming in front of her. "It doesn't look safe."

Her gallant dragon gave her a startled look out of a wild violet eye, then eased his long neck in reach of her hand. Once she'd gingerly placed her fingers between a pair of razor-sharp spines, he said gently, ~We will go together.~

So they did, unaware the terst cows stopped following and covered their heads with their great arms.

As turn-born, Jenn walked beside her dragon, greatly heartened, though part of her feared her touch might hinder his response to any attack and she'd have to be ready to let go.

But nothing attacked. Nothing happened at all except the sensation of taking a step . . .

. . . her foot sank into a snowdrift.

Which couldn't be right, for it was summer in all of the northern domains, and most assuredly in Vorkoun, but Jenn stared down at snow—

A hot breeze in her ear. "Wrong! Wrong!"

—then up to see blackened stumps jutting up from more snow, where there should be summer and lush forest. "You're right, Wisp," Jenn agreed numbly. "This isn't where—"

"IT IS!" He snatched at her, drove them both back that step . . .

. . . out of the cave.

Jenn struggled free, becoming flesh and blood to be sure Wisp's haste hadn't left holes in her clothes.

~WRONG!~ Wisp roared.

Heart's Blood, she certainly agreed with him. "You needn't shout, Wisp," she scolded, still flustered. "It wasn't me."

A pause laden with meaning.

The terst cows peered from under their arms, mouths agape.

"It wasn't," Jenn insisted. "I thought you were taking me to Bannan's family." Not that she'd accuse her dragon of deliberately misleading her, but, Ancestors Warped and Wracked, wherever they'd gone hadn't been there, and Wisp was capable of being overprotective.

"Where did we go?" she asked, suddenly wondering if they'd traveled to the Barrens, rumored to be winter year-round. Though there weren't trees, burnt or otherwise, that far north, and—

Wisp showed himself. Sat before her, a wing out for support, his snout angled down in severe disapproval, and Jenn couldn't imagine why.

Until her dragon said, ~We went where you asked to go, Dear Heart. To Bannan's family. That was the Westietas Estate.~

The words were an ancient Naalish—he remained fluent. The objects waited on the smoothed wood of a kitchen table—tokens, he now thought of them, no longer embarrassed. The too-curious had departed—he was safe, with those aware on watch.

He wasn't, Kydd discovered with something akin to shock, afraid. *He should be.* Though the spell he would attempt was trivial compared to the rest in the journal, numbered one, under his hand—

It was a magic not used in Marrowdell before.

"Could knock you senseless." Tir sat down, careful not to touch anything on the table. "Just say'n'."

Well meant, the offer, for all its gruffness, and Kydd half smiled. "If this doesn't work, I give you leave." He looked up at Bannan. "I'll need that."

The truthseer stood with Jenn's pin between his fingers, turning it over thoughtfully. Kydd had been as surprised as the others to discover the inscription to Melusine on the pin—and as sorry to cause the loss of such a precious item but—"We've nothing else to use," he said finally.

"And past time it was gone," grumbled Tir, who'd made his opinion of Aunt Sybb's gift plain. "Naught good comes of magic-touched things."

The truthseer wore a string around his neck; whatever hung from it lay beneath his shirt. He flattened his free hand over it. "Some does," he said mildly, rousing Kydd's curiosity.

Not Tir's, the beekeeper noticed, meaning a secret shared. He nodded, accepting the point. "In my day it wasn't uncommon to see a family's wish for a child's joy given a—push—if they could afford it." Nor uncommon for student spellcasters to be involved, not that Kydd recognized this work. "Such a wishing would end after an agreed-upon time."

Or sooner, if the student needed an extra commission.

"It served its purpose." Bannan's eyes flashed gold then returned to their warm amber. "The mimrol is worn and thin. From what I see, it's harmless," he concluded, handing the pin to Kydd.

Mimrol—the word wasn't in his journals or known to his teachers, who'd referred to the wildly expensive metal in the manner of the Naalish, calling it Silver Tears. Kydd found himself treasuring a name that wasn't of then and there. "The mimrol's purpose would have been to add potency to the original wishing. That was the result when we were given any to use," he expanded, seeing Bannan about to disagree. "Ancestors Witness, the stuff was rare and grudgingly shared. My only concern is that I'll destroy something precious to Jenn."

"Rest your mind on that," Tir said. "The gaud worried her and she wanted sir, here, to take a look to see if it should."

Kydd raised an eyebrow at the truthseer, who grimaced then shrugged. "I'm sure Jenn will understand." The smallest frown. "Will the mimrol in it alter your spell?"

His turn to make a face. "If I thought it remained potent, I'd be grateful. It's been a long time." Setting the pin with the other tokens, he went to open the journal—

Bannan's house toad leapt onto the table and slammed a clawed foot over the pin.

Tir swore. Kydd grabbed the journal.

While Bannan gave his toad a considering look.

It crouched lower to stare at Kydd. As if Marrowdell forbade him to leave despite wanting him gone—was this about Peggs? For an instant, Kydd wavered, doubting his choice.

Unseen, the words in mimrol changed to read . . .

"GO! We Demand You Go!"

The house toad bared its startling teeth.

Kydd blinked. "We have to go," he heard himself say. "I must do this."

"Not until we learn what's upset my guardian," Bannan countered. Going to the open door, he called, loudly, "Scourge! Come here!"

"What?" Kydd turned to Tir.

The former soldier eyed the toad, then shrugged. "You'll see. Or not," this with a snort.

A pause, then with more force. "Cheese, you idiot!"

What was he thinking? The beekeeper dropped the journal on the stool as if it burned his fingers. Why was he still here? Why wasn't he with Peggs?

But as Bannan summoned the kruar and the toad guarded the pin, as Tir rummaged on a shelf and Kydd stood frozen, words reformed, hidden by a clawed foot.

"Do as you're told. Cast the spell and GO!"

He picked up the journal without another thought, pressing it over his heart.

~Greetings, Sweetling.~

The terst cows burrowed hurriedly under a rock as Jenn whirled at that most-welcome voice in her head. "Mistress!" She ran the few steps between them, throwing her arms around the terst turn-born. "You're all right!"

Though the other felt smaller somehow and changed, and worrying, that Sand reverted to speaking as the terst, as if on guard. Pushing back a little, Jenn searched her friend's face—or its mask, not that the two weren't the same, here—finding tense lines around Sand's mouth and the twinkle missing from her sharp blue eyes. "No sign of Tooth?" she asked, guessing the reason and sorry for it.

Sand clicked her tongue, then worked her strong arm through Jenn's, using that hold to tug her away from the cave. ~Come along. We've things to talk about, Sweetling, and this is no good place, na?~

~It's the crossing to the edge of Bannan's family,~ Wisp said, with almost a snarl. ~Of the young truthseer.~

"No. It isn't, Wisp." Jenn resisted Sand's pull to protest. "We tried. Through there was winter," this to the turn-born as she tried to explain what made no sense. "The forest wasn't there—it had to be the Barrens," she concluded, not that she'd proof, but, Ancestors Decided and Determined, they hadn't stepped into the Westietas Estate.

They couldn't have—

Sand turned her head to stare into the cave mouth, and her expression settled into something forbidding and cold, as if becoming part of that icy place. ~And the next time? You tried again, na?~

Well, of course they hadn't—

Wisp snorted. ~You interrupted us.~

With a little shiver, Sand collected herself. ~Leave it for now, Sweetling. Come into our home and we'll discuss what's to—~

The surface beneath them shook.

And from the ground poured dragons.

Bannan's house toad, according to Scourge's surly rendering, refused to permit magic in the kitchen or anywhere else under its charge, so not the loft, the porch, nor, it turned out, the farmyard, its tree, the barn, nor—to Tir's consternation—the privy, meaning not anywhere here, a declaration reinforced by the little cousin's implacable stare and Scourge's snort of agreement.

Ancestors Careless and Incautious, how close had they come to a dreadful mistake? A wizard had lived here once. Now this was the home of someone who was magic first and foremost—"We are beholden to you, little cousin," Bannan said warmly and with a shiver of dread, hands circled over his heart.

"As I've been say'n' all this time," Tir pointed out. "Spells probably leave soot—or a nasty stink. Nothing," he added darkly, "you want in your house. Sir."

The truthseer winced, their belongings barely restored after the upheaval from the flood.

Kydd gave a weary nod. "Then where, if not here?"

The former soldier scratched under his mask. "Best be close by. Unless you know how long yon spell will last?"

A flash from the beekeeper's eyes. Pride? Brilliant, driven, accomplished in what wasn't to be shared, there'd have been a time Kydd rejoiced in his forbidden knowledge.

No, that was fear. "I've the place. Not far," Bannan said, for there was, in truth, but one place left.

Leaving the house toad on guard at the door, the three took everything up the short path to the meadow called Night's Edge.

Scourge pranced along, distrustful by nature but mostly, the truthseer guessed, out of morbid curiosity.

The kruar brought his opinions, of course. When Bannan spread a flour sack on the grass, a chill breeze nipped his ear. "Not there!" A hoof raked the cloth aside.

Idiot Beast. Bannan snatched up the cloth, which he'd laid conveniently at the threshold of his door, the door Jenn had made so anyone who'd used it once could find it again simply by *knowing.* Not that he needed that peculiar sensation. Standing at that spot, you saw the tip of a Bone Hill to the west, the chimney of their home to the east, and the ruins—

He'd known where he was, that was all, and thought to save Kydd, once blind, needless steps. Wondering what bothered Scourge, the truthseer looked deeper at the spot—seeing ash and flame instead of summer grass and flowers.

A scar he'd seen before. Heart's Blood, Jenn had made his door where she'd done the wishing to turn her dragon into a man. If the house toad refused to let a spell be cast in the house, there was no telling the consequence if they added another spell to *that* memory, though how ground remembered was a question—

To ask later. "Over here," he announced briskly, as if moving steps away to a seemingly identical spot in the lovely meadow had been his idea all along.

Scourge snorted.

Wordless through all this, Kydd came and laid his satchel on one end of the sack, taking out his tokens. He carefully set down Aunt Sybb's purloined garter—Bannan planned to ask Lila for a replacement before the august lady missed it—Peggs' moon cup—he'd not commented, seeing Kydd's blush—and Jenn's pin.

All three items from women of the Nalynn line—coincidence or significant? Only Marrowdell, Bannan thought ruefully, would make him ask. Then again, he'd had a hard few lessons about magic and magical things since last autumn, including that such questions might be necessary.

"Does it matter," he spoke abruptly, "that everything comes from one family?"

Journal in his hands, Kydd tilted his head as if surprised. "They do, don't they," he mused aloud, then shook his head. "Often as not, tokens come from the same source—or through it. Not just one house or family. The same merchant. Or collector."

"'Collector.'" Bannan leapt on the word. "Like Glammis Lurgan?"

Kydd shrugged. "I didn't know the name when you first told me, my friend. I don't know it now. Nor did I recognize the source of the tokens in the wishing—the spell—you showed me this winter."

"You knew what it was for, quick enough," Tir accused. "Ancestors Foul and Fiendish, you've done the same!"

"No more!" Kydd glared at Tir.

Who glowered back, breathing heavy.

Bees flew around them. A butterfly settled on a stalk, its wings primly together, and Bannan took its advice. "Enough," he said mildly. "To the business at hand." Having kept the journals, he brought out the volume Kydd had identified. "What more do you need, Kydd?"

"Nothing. Thank you." Taking the book, the beekeeper opened it to a page near the beginning. From where he stood, Bannan couldn't read any of the text, not that he'd try given Kydd's assertion of the risk, but sketches caught his eye. Clearly Kydd had been an artist long before Marrowdell. Drawings littered the pages, crowding margins, and while some were of equipment or objects?

A few were faces—faces Bannan intended to examine, and closely, the first chance he had.

Sitting cross-legged on the grass, Kydd set the open journal on his knees. He hunched over it, mouthing a series of words over and over, then shut it. Deliberately, with a hint of defiance in his glance up at the truthseer, he put the journal in his satchel.

The other eight weighed down Bannan's pack, but, Ancestors Witness, for all he knew of spell casting, actually carrying the words might help their potency. He gave a short nod, hearing Tir mutter in protest.

Kydd Uhthoff passed his hand over the garter and it flashed into white-hot flame, dying at once to leave a tidy pile of glittering ash, the object consumed.

"Heart's Blood," gasped Tir.

He did the same for the moon cup, but when Kydd reached the last item, Jenn's pin, the flame caught only to flicker and die. "Ancestors Stubborn and Sly," Kydd muttered as, with a frown, he passed his hand over it a second time.

The pin took on a sparkle, gleaming as if freshly polished—or was it more than that?

Bannan used his deeper sight. The pin, metal and gems, held a flickering brilliance as if they'd kept the flame, a menacing glow—

Why had he thought that? The truthseer shook off the vision. "Do you need another token?"

"No. It's part of the spell now," Kydd replied absently. He picked up the pin, Bannan thought reluctantly, and laid it on his palm. Holding his upturned hand over the ashes of garter and cup, those lifted of their own accord, coming together to hover over the pin.

Kydd spoke, the words gibberish to Bannan's ear—

The ash vanished. Melusine's pin remained, though dulled. The beekeeper tucked it deep in a pocket.

"Well? Did it work?" Tir demanded.

Kydd looked up at them, his eyes blank and milky white, blood spewing from his mouth.

While the words in mimrol, hidden in his pocket, briefly changed themselves to read . . .

"Very good. We see all now."

After a moment's startled dancing back and forth, to be sure none touched her bare feet—though Jenn had changed to glass and pearl at once—she stopped and stared about in wonder.

The dragons, of more sizes and colors than she'd ever seen, launched from the ground to the sky, forming an immense funnel above them.

Above Wisp, Jenn realized as her dragon mantled his wings and roared in what wasn't quite a challenge but most certainly a caution, should any of these new arrivals think to pose a threat.

~Why are they here, na?~ Sand asked in a hushed tone, proving even a mighty turn-born could be impressed.

Stretching his great neck, Wisp canted his head to look up. ~They are afraid,~ he concluded, his tone strangely free of derision. As perhaps was her dragon, Jenn thought suddenly. ~They demand we fix what's broken.~

Sand shrugged. ~As the kruar have and next we'll have the toads' new queen yipping at the door again, and for what, na?~ This peevishly. ~Think we can do a thing, na? Think we dare, na?~

Questions echoing all too closely those Jenn had had after the sei dragon demanded the same of her. And before, for that matter, the entire business of being turn-born and powerful hemmed by more constraint than Aunt Sybb's corsets. Which that fine lady left in her trunks, corsets hardly garments for rugged travel nor, their aunt asserted, would anyone in Marrowdell note their absence.

In that she'd been only partially right, for Frann, Ancestors Dear and Departed, and Lorra would squeeze themselves into their antique and oft-mended corsets for any social event of significance, which in Marrowdell ranged from the Midwinter Beholding—when everyone wore coats—to summer quilting fests where extra clothing was, to be frank, a hindrance.

According to Hettie, who'd heard it from her stepmother Covie, on three separate occasions Lorra had fainted before sewing a stitch and had to be carried out to a cool resting spot under a tree, there to wait for her supper.

Not an approach, Aunt Sybb warned, suited to a proper lady. Though she'd smiled a little smile and never once accused Lorra—who did work hard on what she thought important—of using her corset as an excuse.

Jenn pulled her thoughts to here and now, and the dizzying whirl of dragons overhead. And deafening, that many wings and heavy breaths adding up to a great deal of noise—

~BE DONE!~ Wisp roared, out of patience.

The dragons disappeared. Unseen, the pair of terst cows eased their heads from their burrow to regard their new leader, the turn-born who ruled their ancient foe, with amazement and vast pride—

—only to quickly duck again, for a dragon remained, one with white scales rimmed in orange, circling as if it had forgotten what do to next. Or was distracted, for of those looking up, only the terst cows saw the single white moth clinging to the dragon's nostril and only they knew it for what it was.

Sei.

The terst cows, not being fools, huddled close together and closed their eyes, to prove they would not interfere with a god.

Unlike their leader, who dared to shout, "Heart's Blood! Imp?!" Jenn frowned, disturbed the young dragon hadn't stayed where she'd asked it to—waiting for Bannan in Marrowdell—then lost her frown in a flood of relief. "You've news from Bannan? Tell me," she continued to shout. "Quickly!"

Too late, Jenn remembered she shouldn't shout at Imp, who would panic—sure enough, off he fled.

Fortunately, Wisp was already in motion. He caught the youngling midflight, knocking it out of the air to land at Jenn's feet.

The moth fluttered up and away, unnoticed by any but the terst cows who, believing the sei scared by their leader's shouts, quivered with fierce joy.

An anxious orange eye gazed up at Jenn. ~The truthseer promised you'd give me biscuits.~

A claim she didn't doubt for an instant, though how she was to manage it in the Verge was a problem. Perhaps Mistress Sand, who stood watching all this in frigid silence, might. "Of course I will, as soon as I'm able," Jenn assured the dragon. "I'm glad Bannan's well and sent you after us. Thank you, Imp."

~He sent me to find you but I couldn't.~ Imp shuddered. ~I couldn't find you or the Great Lord of Dragons. I WAS LOST!~ A wail.

~The Verge has been misbehaving,~ Wisp replied magnanimously. ~How did you find us?~

It brightened. ~The sei ordered all dragons to follow it. So I did and found you!~

Jenn exchanged a look with Mistress Sand. The sei had ordered Wisp to teach Imp how to behave in Marrowdell. Clearly the youngling was of interest to them here as well, but why?

Then Imp said what drove all thoughts of the sei from her mind. ~I can't say if the truthseer is well or not, Most Gracious Turn-Born. I don't know.~

Jenn took a slow breath, refusing to panic. Literal to a fault, Imp might have taken her question as asking how Bannan was at this very instant—

Wisp snapped his jaws. ~Tell us what you do know, fool, and quickly!~

The young dragon flinched. ~I know the yling gave your sister the books of dark magic to hold.~ A decidedly wistful blink. ~The sister who bakes biscuits.~

As if she'd another! A numb part of Jenn supposed it was possible Imp couldn't count.

The rest of her felt ready to explode. "Why would they give Kydd's journals to Peggs?" Not to mention why would Peggs climb to Dusom's loft in the first place, given she struggled with the steps on their porch, and slept with their aunt on the main floor, the ladder beyond her for the past weeks.

~I don't know. I can't speak to yling, oh most glorious and merciful of turn-born. Only little cousins can——~

Wisp snarled with impatience.

Imp erupted in a spurt of words, ~I obeyed the truthseer! He sent me to find you! To tell you! I heard them. I heard them all, every word. The bad books can't stay in Marrowdell. The wizard is to blind himself and then the truthseer and the wizard will cross to take the bad books to the truthseer's sister in Vorkoun. The scary one.~ With an undertone suggesting firsthand acquaintance with the baroness—who could admittedly terrify—this followed by a quick, anxious look at Mistress Sand, who'd remained ominously silent. ~The truthseer promised you'd protect me. From the kruar. From everything!~ The young dragon stopped, trembling and quite overdone.

"I will, Imp," Jenn heard herself say. "It's all right."

But nothing was.

Ancestors Frantic and Fearful, where did she even begin? Bannan taking Kydd through his door? She'd warned him those without magic couldn't survive—and that was before she'd come to the Verge and discovered the trouble she might have caused by creating the door in the first place. What was Bannan thinking?

That Marrowdell wanted the journals gone she could see, but bringing them to Lila?

And why had Imp called Kydd Uhthoff a wizard? She'd only heard the word used for Crumlin Tralee, who hadn't been a good person in any sense and now lived in a box for his crimes. Kydd was good in every sense, as well as gentle and shy. Why, it had taken him years to gain the courage to confess his love to Peggs—and a great many pies.

And blind? Imp had to have misheard.

Jenn wanted to stamp her foot. Things were speeding along too quickly to make any sense, much like Imp's speech. She needed Peggs. Her sister was the most reasonable and pragmatic person she knew, able to make sense of anything, including magic.

Including, Jenn's lips twitched, her.

Yet if Imp could be believed, Peggs was a willing part of this. Ancestors Baffled and Bewildered, while her sister deserved her trust, not her fretting, why would she agree to Kydd attempting the Verge? She hadn't let him ride to Endshere, this close to the birth.

Sand grunted. ~Nothing's right,~ she announced, clearly of the same mind. ~Standing out here won't improve matters.~

No, it wouldn't. Jenn shot the dark, menacing cave an anxious look, then a determined one. "Imp said Bannan plans to cross—he may be in the Westietas Estate by now. I have to get there. I have to send him—and Kydd—back to Marrowdell so I can close his door." And not leave them stranded, days away from home, a consequence she'd rather not have to explain to her pregnant sister.

The terst turn-born's eyebrows rose. ~Close it, na?~ She made that *tsk* sound against her teeth. ~Hasty to meddle with what's done and works. Hasty and perilous. Come with me to the enclave. Let us help you decide, Sweetling, before you do more harm. If you have,~ with a wink meant to be reassuring.

It wasn't. Jenn's heart sank. If Sand wasn't sure, how could she be? "With Wisp," she agreed at last. "And Imp," when that dragon whimpered at being left.

Sand rolled her eyes but didn't argue.

The terst cows waited until the others were moving before following behind as they must. They halted when both dragons paused to sniff the air. The elder indicated the terst turn-born and the dragons continued on, unaware of their mistake.

And onward marched the terst cows, content it was so.

PAIN! At the searing burst of it, he'd bitten through his tongue, filling his mouth with blood. Without sight, he dared not—

A callused hand found his, brought it to touch grass. Kydd leaned over and spat, gratitude a dim warmth when he was so cold. So very cold. A side effect of the spell, he told himself. That was all. He should have remembered the cost. Been better prepared.

Words he'd inadvertently said aloud, for a question followed quickly. "Prepared how?"

Bannan's voice. Wiping his lips on a cloth pressed into his hand, Kydd aimed his face toward the truthseer. "This will pass." The words came out as regrettable gasps, forced through violent shivers; he rubbed his arms, impatient with his weakness. "Help me stand."

Hands eased him to his feet. Put his satchel over his shoulder—by its weight, his journal was inside, a return he hadn't been certain would happen nor, were he honest, truly wanted. Its closeness made his skin crawl.

The flour sack came over next, offering some comfort. "Tir's right," Kydd stated. "We can't count on this lasting."

Hearts of his Ancestors, let it not last.

A grip on his wrist. "You said blind to magic," Bannan protested, low and quick, his voice full of remorse. "Not to everything. What went wrong? The pin?"

Marrowdell. Why hadn't he realized—Kydd shook his head, feeling the shivers abate in his body, if not his heart. Too late now.

"Which way?" He pulled his arm gently. "I've you for eyes, my friend." And every reason to leave. "The spell will dissipate once we're in Vorkoun and leave the edge." Unless he'd made a mistake in the casting of it. Unless—

"If'n it doesn't, all this will be for naught," Tir said bluntly. "You know I'm right, sir. If Kydd can't read yon books for you—forgive my saying so, Kydd—what good is he?"

Kydd made himself chuckle. "I'm very good, Tir Half-face. Trust me when I say I'll have my sight back."

As the lie slipped out, he'd never been so glad the truthseer couldn't read him.

Semyn found himself hustled back into the coach with his father and their guards, postponing any opportunity to grill his guard as to Momma's plans. The horses, glad to leave this frightening spot, pulled with such enthusiasm the conveyance clattered and bounced its way along the road, slowing only for turns.

Turns Semyn matched against the map in his head, certain of their destination well before the driver pulled her team to a stop.

The Great Ossuary of Vorkoun.

There were many, all home to the Blessed Bones of Ancestors, and most older, for this had been built when Ansnor ceded their half of the city to Vorkoun to administer, a time of civil cooperation and mutual progress.

The first thing the Rhothans had felt necessary to do was built a sacred space in the middle of it.

The Ansnan reaction wasn't in any record Semyn had read of the era; he suspected it had been a mix of polite scorn and some confusion. Those of Ansnor considered bones useful fertilizer—or as tokens, that disrespectful and illicit trade. Perhaps that was why they'd gifted a major abattoir to the Rhothan priesthood to repurpose.

He would, Semyn suddenly thought, ask Master Setac for some Ansnan comedies.

History aside, the Great Ossuary was, despite its name, a restrained and dignified sanctuary, where living descendants communed with the carefully stored remains of their ancestors, paying well to join them in turn. While the prince's treaty made no specific mention or promise, Semyn was well aware Rhothans—most of them—blithely expected their bones to be safe forever.

Forever, Momma would say, was the purview of Blessed Ancestors or Ansnan Celestials or whomever you worshipped. Today and tomorrow were what rested in living hands.

The coach entered the portico in front of the ossuary, passing between tall columns engraved with symbols of reverence. To Rhothans, Semyn reminded himself as he got out to wait beside the nearest, with its depictions of skulls and other bones surrounded by an uncanny abundance of grapes—

—and stars.

Stars the Ansnans worshipped, cremating their dead to make

room for the living beneath the sky, to be judged by the Celestials. Ancestors Unjust and Unthinking, how these columns must repulse those living here now.

Had that been the builders' intention all along? This blatant disrespect? Other ossuaries—including the Westietas'—were simple and classic. Some were ornate and breathtaking, but nothing like this. Why?

Questions Semyn wanted answered. Momma taught that forcing their ways on others—who had their own, important ones—never ended well for either. He'd understand if the inhabitants of Mondir insisted the columns come down—but what if they next asked for the Blessed Bones to be packed up and removed from what was again their city?

Coming to stand by him, Poppa noted his focus. "What do you think of them?"

"They were meant to offend and still do," Semyn replied without pausing to consider his words.

Before he could take them back or rephrase, Poppa chuckled and put a hand on his shoulder. He leaned close. "That's why I've ordered the priests to give me a price on cladding them with stone or wood—something natural and neutral. Not this—" He made a face, leaving the right word to his heir.

"Pretentious?" Semyn suggested at once. He carefully didn't smile, but Ancestors Blessed, how Poppa's solution resonated in his heart. Power used to benefit everyone, not just a few.

And, being his father's son, Semyn Westietas understood something else. He was on this trip for more than as a show of the heir at meetings; he was to learn what wasn't in books.

"They're ready inside, m'lords," Macle told them. He looked up the street then down, checking vantage points. "We'd like you off the street, m'lords."

Semyn brushed the front of his coat and had to trust his hair was in good order. Initial impressions mattered, whoever *they* might be.

Especially if they knew who'd just attacked Vorkoun's baron and his heir with magic.

Acutely conscious of Kydd's hand on his shoulder, what it meant, Bannan took the six steps required to stand where his next would send them elsewhere, the beekeeper matching his strides, then stopped, overwhelmed by uncertainty. *What was he thinking—*

"Bannan?" Kydd asked quietly.

"Sir has his doubts," Tir piped in, too perceptive as always. His oldest friend had refused to be left behind, probably expecting to guide Kydd back to the village after their effort failed. "There are rules," he warned.

"I swear on the Bones of my Ancestors, I have no ill intentions," the beekeeper said at once.

Bannan clapped his hand over Kydd's briefly. "It's not you. It's—" He'd meant to tell his friends about the curious behavior of the crossing. Had foolishly delayed, unsure till this instant if it mattered in view of all else and now what could he say? *Sorry you blinded yourself, but we can't risk it, because I think I had a vision of Marrowdell-past.*

The very thought was ludicrous. They'd step through and leave the edge—no, go to the hidden cottage to signal his sister using Emon's device—

A breeze found his ear. "Send me first." Scourge tossed his giant head.

"We go together," the truthseer said firmly. He flattened his free hand against the kruar's hot neck, made sure of Kydd's grip, then shot a look at Tir.

Who scowled his displeasure but nodded. He'd stay at the farm to tell Jenn where they'd gone and why. He wasn't to try and stop her following.

Heart's Blood, nothing, Bannan thought with an inner thrill, could.

Kruar, truthseer, and beekeeper stepped forward together...

Into chaos!

"WHAT HAVE YOU DO—!!" Scourge's furious bellow was ripped

away by a wind threatening to knock Bannan and Kydd from their feet, a wind whipping twigs and leaves to strike them and kicking up dust—

—as blind as the beekeeper, Bannan held his friend, pressing them both to the kruar's massive side. "We have to go back," he shouted. "Try again!!"

They must, for this had to be another vision of the past and gone. A past Bannan greatly feared he knew something about. The last time a windstorm like this had hit Vorkoun, his mother's mother had been a little girl, a terrified witness to the destruction of buildings— to forests flattened—

"Turn around—cross to Marrowdell!" He hammered on Scourge's shoulder. "TURN!" Heart's Blood, they couldn't take much more of this—

To his relief, he felt the mighty kruar ease backward, step by slow step. Wisely so, Bannan realized at once, for if Scourge had turned as he'd ordered? They'd have been exposed and blown who knew where.

Scourge would be insufferable for years.

Bannan desperately hoped so, for a single step had brought them here. A single step should have taken them back, and as they retreated by three, then four, the truthseer feared they were lost. Keeping a tight hold on Kydd, he stayed with the kruar, the great beast's strength and senses their only hope of escape, trusting Scourge knew where he took them.

The wind stopped. Bannan rubbed grit from his eyes, squinting to see.

Marrowdell! They were back in the meadow. Which meant they'd made two passages through the Verge—however undetectable—in quick succession. He checked on Kydd.

The beekeeper stood on his own, satchel over his shoulder, windblown and filthy but otherwise whole. He kept his eyes closed but, as if aware of Bannan's scrutiny, gave a wry smile. "Is it always like that?"

"Ancestors Blessed," the truthseer said, beyond grateful the spell had worked. "No, that was a first."

"Better be the last." After the searing heat of that dark warning, Scourge shook himself from nose to tail, spewing dust and making both men choke.

"What do you mean?" Bannan demanded once the air cleared.

"I was in that storm." Sweat stained his flanks and neck, a rare sign of stress. "It happened before your father was born and we shouldn't have been *then*." Darker and suspicious. "How came we to be?"

Kydd's head rose, eyelids rising over the milky white blankness of his eyes. He barely breathed the words, "A shift of time."

It hadn't been real—"An illusion," Bannan countered. "Or a similar storm is happening there, now." Heart's Blood, he hoped not.

But if it had been real, thoughts tumbling as if he fell down a cliff, the dust on their clothes and hair, what they'd experienced, were from a moment long gone. Forests had regrown, since. Towers rebuilt.

Generations passed.

Otherwise—Vorkoun—his family—they couldn't have been erased—

"I saw Marrowdell's past when I first made to come home. This—" for no reason and every one possible he kicked the grass and threw up his arms "—Marrowdell was here the second time. We try again," he heard himself say in a stranger's voice. "We cross—"

Scourge reared, slamming his hooves to shake the ground. Rabbits fled. "NO!"

The truthseer stood his ground. "I have to know they're still there. My family—"

The kruar's head lowered, lips pulled back from fangs in threat, yet the breeze in Bannan's ears was soft as down. "Mine."

Ancestors Inconvenient and Insane, *now* the Bloody Beast turned sentimental? Bannan leaned his forehead near one red-rimmed eye, rubbing that spot under the chin Scourge couldn't reach. "We see anything but what we should see, we—"*retreat* wasn't a word that sat well with his companion "—withdraw and come up with another plan. What say you, Kydd?" This would be the beekeeper's third trip through the Verge; he'd know the risk of madness grew with each.

"That we've no choice. We must go. Now."

And while it was the answer Bannan wanted to hear, the eagerness in Kydd's voice gave him pause. With a final pat on Scourge's great neck, he stepped back to study the blind beekeeper. "Whatever's happening, Kydd, the magic of the Verge isn't for us," he warned. "This crossing is Jenn's gift—never forget that."

A graceful bow. "I understand."

Did he? Or did the former student of magic see only the potential to cross to a different time as well as place?

Was it possible?

Bannan looked to the Bone Hills. The body of the sei who held the edge and Verge together and, Heart's Blood, it wasn't invulnerable. He'd met the agony-filled gaze of an eye spilling tears like enormous pearls. He'd stood by a body more mountain than flesh, its still-living flesh torn and consumed by nyphrit since the Ansnan refuge fell.

Until Jenn Nalynn had saved the sei. Saved them all.

If—*if*—possible, Bannan forced himself to finish the thought, palms sweating and heart heavy in his chest, what might it do to the sei?

He couldn't reach Jenn, other than with stale words and an incompetent dragon. Help would only be found by moving forward, to take his now-treacherous door and hope beyond hope this time Lila was on the other side.

Bannan seized Kydd's elbow and they took the step together, Scourge's roar of protest ringing in their ears.

Jenn Nalynn sat with Sand, Riverstone, Fieldstone, Flint, and Clay at a broad table in a space new to her: the terst turn-borns' kitchen. Before, when invited indoors, she'd been hosted in their version of a parlor, full of artworks collected from the far reaches of the edge, though it had seemed also a workroom, for there'd been tools on tables as well, each turn-born adept at their own craft.

A deliberate choice, Jenn thought, displeased, for it was unkind as well. Wisp had served as a drudge in this same kitchen before coming to Marrowdell to be her friend—not that he'd started off meaning to be her friend, having orders from the sei to kill her should she venture beyond the edge, but friendship had happened to them both and both, she knew, were glad of it.

It helped that Wisp appeared in no way discomfited by Mistress Sand's invitation to enter a building not willingly host to dragons until today. He'd limped proudly beside Jenn, through the gate the turn-born made reappear, and curled on the rug vacated instantly by Kaj, Sand's little white dog.

Imp, on the other hand, hadn't stopped shaking; Mistress Sand had finally suggested it hide under the counter. A suggestion the youngling took to heart, squeezing into the small space until you wouldn't guess a dragon was there at all, except Kaj sat at attention in front, teeth showing in threat as if here was a foe more his size.

While the terst cows, who'd followed their leader and walked in last of all, wandered away to explore the interior of a place unlike any they'd seen before.

Ignoring the dragons and dog, unaware of the cows, Riverstone poured an amber liquid into thumb-sized glasses, themselves beautiful, but it was the contents that mattered and he made sure to pass one to Jenn as well as the others, taking the last himself.

The liquid was the beer they brewed in the Verge from kaliia grown in Marrowdell, a beverage combining the sources of what they were, one that satisfied turn-born like no other. The scant portions were, Jenn decided, because the terst turn-born rationed what they had left the way the villagers were careful with flour, it being early summer and the next harvest moons away.

Yet this sharing felt solemn, almost grim, feelings the terst turn-born let show on their faces; Jenn barely tasted the beer. This wasn't just what was happening in the Verge and whatever part her actions might have played, but about a dreadful loss to this group, this family.

Maybe more than one, by the empty chair where Chalk should be. Where was he? Not, Jenn decided, a question to ask directly, for the terst turn-born were rarely direct and she couldn't bear even a well-meaning lie.

When everyone set down their emptied glass, before Mistress Sand could speak, Jenn did. "How can I help you?" she asked, her voice quiet and respectful.

Perhaps a broader question and offer than they'd expected, for Mistress Sand was startled into a brief little smile. ~Always our Sweetling is generous, na?~ She looked to the other turn-born. ~Easy to forget, for we are not.~

Wisp gave an amused snort. Having met the terst—the kind of person these turn-born remembered being and were, if she were honest—Jenn couldn't bring herself to send him a quelling look. "But you are generous," she countered, knowing these individuals rather better. "To me. To Marrowdell. We're friends and we help one another."

Against the terst, if need be, though she was far from ready to bring up the topic.

Clay's bushy eyebrows met in an expressive frown, his dimples deep lines of woe. ~We've no friends.~ She felt the press of air grown heavy with anger. ~Only those who hate us.~

Jenn bit her tongue. Sadly, Clay wasn't entirely wrong.

The ill feeling eased, one or more of the others in *disagreement*. Sand clicked her tongue, explaining who, Jenn judged, relieved. ~We're under attack, it's true, but not by our Sweetling.~

~Her work, na?~ Quiet, from Fieldstone, sitting across from her. Perilous, his tone, and Wisp raised his head in warning.

The turn-born glared back, his features the most like the terst Jenn had met, and suddenly he looked as much a stranger. For the first time she doubted every face showed to her, for were the terst not gifted at illusion?

Ancestors Blind and Befuddled, she scolded herself. Masks weren't mutable, not even hers. More importantly, she knew Fieldstone as Davi's friend, the two working the forge together as often as harvest allowed, laughing so loud Lorra would try—and fail—to shush them. And last year he'd helped Anton repair the cows' feed trough, and this year he'd held Delfinn as if a treasure, so she wasn't to think otherwise, that was all.

"The Verge isn't right," Jenn said, looking Fieldstone in the eye but ever-so-careful in her choice of words. She wasn't about to take blame for everything wrong, not when she'd no idea what was. "You must sense it too." They didn't react outwardly, but the air went oddly still. Answer, she decided, enough.

"The dragons and kruar asked us to fix what is broken," Jenn continued, aware adding the sei to the list would alarm the terst turn-born further and quite possibly, knowing them as she did, incite an unproductive panic best avoided. "I fear they mean the crossing I made for Bannan, between Marrowdell and the Westietas Estate. It takes a—a shortcut through the Verge. If it's at fault, I must close it." There, she'd said it.

To her dismay, Riverstone made a dismissive gesture. ~We agreed to it, did we not, na?~

~An expectation is not simply unmade, Sweetling,~ Sand said heavily, Clay nodding. ~To attempt it?~ A shrug. ~The result would be unpredictable. Likely destructive elsewhere. Leave it be is our advice.~

Jenn would have been relieved, but the terst turn-born weren't, she knew, infallible. Nor were the sei, when it came to it, nor did they always make sense. A nuisance—

—worse, when the consequences were this dire. Involuntarily she glanced at the empty chairs at the table.

Mistress Sand noticed. ~Chalk crossed to look for Tooth.~

Alone? It wasn't her place to question what they did, but surely—

~While you hide here,~ her dragon accused.

~HOW DARE YOU!~ Clay erupted, rising with fists on the table. Fieldstone lurched to his feet. The two glared at the dragon, expectations forming—

DENIED! Jenn defended Wisp without hesitation, her dragon on his good feet with flame boiling in his open mouth—

Kaj barked, Imp having dared stick out its snout, and there was no telling what might have happened next—

Sand reached over and touched Jenn's wrist, a second *DENIAL* cutting apart whatever Fieldstone and/or Clay intended. ~Do we fight among ourselves, na?~ she scolded softly. ~The dragon lord is correct to say we are in hiding, but we should take no shame from that. Are we not afraid, na?~

The two sank down in their chairs. Wisp, blood still up, snarled at them before closing his terrible jaws and subsiding.

Imp retreated, the little dog looking proud.

Thoroughly shaken by the conflict, by how close they'd come to what couldn't be undone, Jenn put her hand over Sand's and squeezed gently, seeking as well as offering comfort. Families fought amongst themselves—hadn't their mother been driven from hers?—but she'd never experienced anything like this, never felt, in the aftermath, what Aunt Sybb called a grief deeper than loss.

Until now. Jenn felt tears spill, ice cold, down her cheeks. Grief tinged with betrayal. Sadness spiked with anger that they'd DARE harm Wisp—

None of it what she wanted to feel or should.

She looked to the terst turn-born and found her voice, or what she could of it through the tightness in her throat. "I'm very sorry you're afraid. By the Hearts of my Ancestors—I implore you—tell me how I can fix this—"

Which would have been a fine and upstanding thing to say if her last word hadn't ended in a sob.

Kydd fell hard on his hands and knees, landing on rounded stones, and dared not move until he could see his surroundings. The blindness spell would dissipate any moment—Mage Elect Daisy had been clear on its brevity, aiming her long finger at Dove, the first of them to try the spell and nervous as her namesake—

"—right?" Bannan's concern pulled him from the past.

Kydd made to nod, stopped when his head spun. Felt strong hands under his arms, lifting him to stand, and gratefully accepted the shoulder offered as support. "Did we—?" A pointless question. Heirs were taught to dispassionately assess their condition; his limits were familiar and well-tested. He knew how much each trip through the door had cost him.

And that he mustn't attempt another too soon. Peggs deserved better—

"We made it." The truthseer started them moving, his practiced ease with what had to be an awkward and heavy burden, for Kydd stumbled more than stepped, a reminder of who he'd been. What he'd been. A soldier who'd seen battle.

A man not to be underestimated.

A dear and valued friend, Kydd told himself fiercely, denying the other voice in his head, the one emboldened by the proximity of his journals and not, under any circumstances, to be heeded. "Thank you," he said aloud. Blinked over and over, fighting to make out anything but black. *Nothing.*

"The sun's set." Bannan's matter-of-fact statement helped. "Bit of a slope here." A soft grunt of effort as the truthseer took more of Kydd's weight as he edged downward. The ground leveled. "A few more steps."

Kydd lost count, but it wasn't, in fact, long before Bannan propped him gently against what felt like a log pile, only to collect him a moment later and lead him forward. The scents of pine and fern receded. He smelled a faint tang of soap as his feet found themselves no longer on uneven ground but a floor.

"Where are we?"

"A safe place." Taking Kydd's hand, Bannan drew it to the back of a chair, at the same time taking the satchel from the beekeeper's shoulder. Kydd swallowed a protest. "Rest here," his friend urged.

"I'll let Lila know we're here." Of all things, a chuckle. "You'll be a surprise. She'll expect Jenn."

The chair was made of smooth wood, with a goodly cushion on the seat, and, reaching out, Kydd found the table he'd half expected beside him. A kitchen. Making this a dwelling, and nothing of the kind had been in any of Jenn's stories of the Westietas Estate. Of where the edge touched it, he corrected himself, the limit of her existence. To those who loved her, that dire caution bore remembering, always.

He listened intently to Bannan's footfalls, learning what he could about this "safe place." Four quick steps, the last two muffled by carpet. A pause, then a series of little clicks as if the truthseer tapped small pieces of metal together, followed by an amused huff of breath. The truthseer was in a good mood—or better one. "Now to see if Emon is as clever as we all think he is."

More steps, the slide of chair legs on the floor, a settling as Bannan sat across from him. "We're a fine pair," he commented wryly. A slap, and Kydd smelled dust. They were coated in it, a reminder they'd *been* in the past.

The potential closed his throat, sped his heartbeat, and he wanted in that instant to ask for his satchel back, with its journal—to demand the rest from Bannan's pack. Mistrusting the reason, the beekeeper gripped the table edge and gave a little nod. "Ancestors Witness, I'm glad of a respite."

"And earned it. I've lit a lamp," Bannan added a little too casually. "It's in the middle of the table."

Not *can you see?* No *you said this was temporary.* The truthseer either knew or began to suspect something gone awry with the spell.

Yet did him the kindness of patience regardless. And was that a hint of gray in the darkness? Encouraged, Kydd smiled. Not one of his better efforts, but the attempt mattered, as did this man. "There's danger to my journals beyond their magic, Bannan," he warned, then said what he should have much earlier. "Merely possessing such knowledge means imprisonment without trial or recourse."

A chuckle with real warmth. "Rest easy, my friend. Ordo's minions aren't welcome here."

"True, little brother."

Kydd's head snapped around. He strained to make out the source of that soft, steely voice, but didn't need to see to know Baroness Lila Marerrym Larmensu Westietas had joined them. Automatically he rose from his seat and made to bow, forced to grab the table as the floor swayed under him. "My lady," he managed before accepting Bannan's help back to his seat.

While within his pocket words of mimrol flickered and changed to read . . .

"*The truedreamer. Well done, Spellcaster. Well done.*"

The girl's upset made Wisp desperate to bite something—preferably everything but her in this horrible room, a place he'd seen most often through cracks in the floor.

Being on top was, in his opinion, no improvement whatsoever.

But her great heart was accomplishing what fangs and fire couldn't. Her remorse, her sincere desire to help softened the terst turn-born, who, much to the dragon's surprise, seemed as intent now on comforting Jenn Nalynn as a heartbeat ago wanting him dead, even Clay coming to join Riverstone and Sand to enfold the girl in their arms.

He didn't need to understand, Wisp reminded himself, to use the moment. ~What happened to the others?~ he asked rather than demanded, though deep inside was his own fear. *Was there risk to her?*

Done patting and soothing the girl, the turn-born looked at him, none kindly. He gazed back serenely, a dragon having far more patience.

"We've interest in a mine," the one filled with clay responded at last, speaking as the girl for the first time. "It lies near a town called Gordit, in Ansnor. Tooth and Chalk are the ones involved with it."

Sand sniffed. "A hole in the ground."

"A promising source of gems favored by those in Eldad," this from Riverstone, also aloud. "Important to our trade there."

The girl brushed away her tears, eyes asparkle. "You go to Eldad?" She subsided at once. "I'm sorry. I just—I didn't think you did."

She'd been there, the dragon knew. Ripped away from him by the toad queen and sent, she'd confided, to where turn-born had been forbidden to ever return.

Before hearing her tale of the Bay of Shades, he'd been content to cross to familiar places, prudently wary of surprises. Wisp permitted himself an inward sigh. From the longing on the girl's face, he'd best become familiar with more.

"We go many places, Sweetling," Sand said, as if to taunt him. "Places better than holes. Places where we don't go missing, na?" This sharply, and her glare was for Clay. "Tooth was to cross back with Chalk. They were separated at the train—"

"'Train'?" The girl's eyes widened and her dragon glumly added *train* to his list of what to learn.

"Inside the mine," Riverstone clarified. "Chalk arrived here. Tooth did not."

Jenn nodded her understanding. "Then Chalk crossed back to find him."

"And has not returned. Do you see now why we hide, na?"

~We do not,~ Wisp snapped, out of patience. ~A threat to you anywhere in the edge means nothing in the Verge. Or are you not as all-powerful here as you think? Have you done nothing to save yourselves?~ *And protect the girl?*

He might have died then and there, such was the turn-borns' fury at his insolence, but Sand made a mistake.

"Of course we have, fool dragon. I've sent the truthseer to find out."

The girl paled. "What?!"

SEVEN

POWER SURGED AND flexed, intentions twisted and tore, and for a dreadful instant Jenn didn't care, enraged beyond measure by the gall of the terst turn-born, to send her beloved in harm's way for their own selfish reasons.

Had they waited to ask her—

Abruptly, her rage died, not that she was happy with Sand, for she wasn't, at all, but because Jenn realized had they asked, why, she would have talked to Bannan and together they'd have looked for Tooth and Chalk—who'd disappeared despite being turn-born, so mightn't she?

A fear she saw in her dragon's sober gaze. In Sand's sorrowful look and the anxiousness of Riverstone and Clay, in how Fieldstone knocked over a glass and Flint lunged clumsily to catch it.

She found herself flesh and blood and a deep shaky breath, where an instant before she'd been glass and pearl and pain. Pulling out her chair, Jenn sat back down at the kitchen table. "Might there be tea?"

~And biscuits?~ faint yet oh-so-daring.

Sand arched a disbelieving brow at the shadow beneath the counter, then gave her great laugh.

Jenn found herself smiling. "When we get home, Imp," she promised, the terst turn-born as far as she knew not bakers. "Where we'll go," she said next and quite firmly, "once I'm sure Bannan is safe and there as well."

And she'd have made it a wish, but threads of magic continued to pull and tug at one another like knitting about to unravel. Adding another would be foolish indeed.

"We've a tin of sweets," Clay said gruffly, then flashed her his quick little smile, with those deep dimples, as if to apologize for earlier. "They'll do with tea."

"Not so well as your sister's pie," Riverstone put in over his shoulder, having gone to a cupboard to pull out a pot and mugs.

Ancestors Comforted and Calming, when troubles felt too big to handle, Aunt Sybb said, first handle what fit your hand. Though she'd been referring to the enormous soggy mass of laundry pulled through the garden soil when one of Devins' calves got loose and somehow tangled itself in the line, it had been the right choice here and now.

"I'll let Peggs know you'd enjoy another," she told them.

Fieldstone shook his head. "Sweets and tea won't do." He patted his stomach. "When did you last eat, Sweetling, na?"

Jenn blinked. She'd had that bite of pie with Master Dusom, if not a full supper. Had she eaten since? Her stomach growled in answer. "I can't delay—" she protested. "Bannan—"

"Can find his own food." Sand gave her a sharp look. "What did I tell you about ignoring the flesh, Sweetling, na?"

That the body she remembered and absolutely must keep remembering would fail if she neglected its needs. Jenn sighed. "Perhaps I should have something."

Fieldstone and Clay brightened, apparently ready for a bigger meal themselves, and got busy at the counter. Any other time Jenn would have been curious, but she'd no time to waste. "A small something. We have to go—"

"There's no rush, Sweetling, if it's your truthseer to find. He told me he'd be going first to Marrowdell to talk over my request with you."

Putting, Jenn thought glumly, her in the wrong for not being there to be talked to—except she hadn't been there because Mistress

Sand had summoned her here. Poor timing? Coincidence? She'd think so, except terst turn-born left nothing to chance.

"You not being there," Sand matter-of-factly continued, "why, I'd think that means your Bannan's gone ahead to Gordit, and that's—" a tsk of tongue to teeth "—well, Sweetling, no telling how long a trip ahorseback that is, most being outside the edge."

Her heart sank. Sand was right. Bannan would have started the trip, and it was an excellent point, one that should have occurred to her, that he'd travel where she couldn't.

Crossing back and forth shouldn't make her forget the reality of the wider world, Jenn scolded herself. She'd maps. The Westietas Estate was west of Vorkoun, Ansnor to the east of that city, putting Bannan's travel at a day if not longer.

Might he take a carriage? Were carriages faster?

Aunt Sybb would know. Her own lack of practical knowledge— Jenn paused mid-thought, catching the lift of Wisp's head. A warning?

"What is it?" Though sorely tempted, Jenn didn't add "now."

~We can't leave regardless, Dear Heart. The dimming has begun. We must not venture forth until it ends.~

"The next dimming? Impossible! It's the middle of the day!" Riverstone put his hand to the wall, giving a start, and looked to Sand. "The dragon's right."

~Of course I am.~ An annoyed snarl.

The others frowned. "How is this possible?" Clay asked.

The rest voiced opinions; Jenn tried to make herself smaller. Should she tell them about the sei? It had looked shrunken in size and upset, but the latter was her interpretation and wholly untrustworthy when it came to such beings.

So maybe not.

As for her suspicions about the terst? She'd no proof they crossed into the edge, though if they did, she'd a sinking feeling the turn-born would immediately assume it was to spy on them. And this wasn't the moment to bring up sundered families and hatreds, the peace here fragile and the terst turn-born making her supper.

Jenn studied her folded hands, having decided. She'd keep silent a while longer, though it was beginning to seem more and more likely that what might be broken in the Verge—

Was time itself.

Lila had come alone, looking, as Bannan thought, to find Jenn Nalynn with him and eager to renew their acquaintance. And no doubt to gauge her reaction to what had been a significant amount of construction and cost designed to encourage his love to spend time within Lila's influence.

And care. His sister chose what face she showed others, but he saw through them all. Something had happened between Lila and Jenn during their brief ride over Channen's rooftops, a bond forged. Not that he'd ever ask, but to the truthseer it was plain his dear sister hadn't expected it, nor did she quite know what to do about it.

Jenn had that effect on people.

As for Kydd Uhthoff? Lila kept testing his claim to blindness, moving the lamp, waving her hand before his face, once aiming her knife at his eye.

She couldn't help it, nor was Bannan about to suggest she stop. By the taut lines on Kydd's face, this wasn't the outcome he'd anticipated from his spell, and while it might been lack of practice?

Bannan feared some kind of interference. "We should take Kydd to the house. Is Roche at home?"

"He's a class in Vorkoun and stays with friends." Lila, who'd turned a chair and sat, chin on folded arms, to study Kydd, glanced up. "Why not stay here?" Contained, that meant, and hidden.

"Because," the beekeeper answered quietly, "Bannan thinks the magic of Marrowdell, of the edge, might have affected my blinding spell." His lips twisted. "I find I share that concern."

Lila rested a fingertip on the stack of journals on the table between them. "And without sight, you can't read these for me."

A courteous nod. "I trust I needn't repeat my warning not to make the attempt yourself, my lady, nor to allow another."

Green eyes flashed with irritation, but Lila, to Bannan's relief, merely said, "'On pain of death.' I heard you." She managed to instill the three words with a warning of her own. *It had better be true.*

Bannan patted dust from his shirt. "A bath and fresh clothes would be most welcome. Oh, and Dauntless." There being no sign Scourge had followed them here, and he could only hope it was because the kruar was furious with him and not trapped in some— what had Kydd called it?—shift of time.

"Leaving us so soon?" Lila asked, a brow arched. Not pleased, his sister.

"I've promised to check on a friend." He put his hand, lightly, on Kydd's shoulder. "We can't keep our father-to-be here any longer than necessary."

The first earned him a sharp look, but, when she turned to Kydd, her gaze softened. "I'm grateful to you coming at such a time, Kydd." Lila rose from her chair to go to the signaling device, tapping quickly. "I've alerted the staff." Easily reading his face, she continued blandly, "People I trust with the lives of my sons. And with yours. We'll make this as quick as we can. If need be—" oh the reluctance in *that*, Lila without doubt wild with impatience to know what the journals held. "—I'll store your gift securely until you can return to assist with it."

"Ancestors Blessed. I'm beholden, my lady, for such consideration." Kydd rubbed a hand over his face, smearing the dust. "But much as I want to be with Peggs, should be with her—I must confess I fear to use your door, Bannan, until I've regained the strength lost in my recent passage through it."

Prudent of the man, not to mention they'd made three crossings or what had happened. He owed the beekeeper for that.

Lila looked a question.

Bannan shrugged. "We've a lot to talk about and little time for it. Kydd will brief you. I can't tarry. Even on Dauntless, I'll be riding all night."

His sister's lips curved in a secretive smile. "You won't need a kruar to reach Gordit, little brother. Or all night."

Bannan's turn to raise eyebrows.

"I've a new ally. Come," this as the knock on the door announced the arrival of aid. "Let's get Kydd to the house, then I'll answer—" a wicked grin "—almost all of your questions."

Unseen or noted, on the pin that had traveled from Avyo to Marrowdell and crossed to Vorkoun; passed from a mother's hand to a daughter's to a friend's and to granddaughters' to be used for a spell and kept in a pocket, on this far-reaching pin letters of mimrol changed for an instant, to read . . .

"Find them all, Spellcaster. Find them all!"

Trays of curds and crisps, traditional Ansnan fare complete with the required dish of salt to cut the heat, sat untouched alongside assorted Rhothan delicacies, the Baron Westietas having opened the meeting by saying, grimly, "My son and I were attacked on the way here. Someone here is responsible."

After that, matters became less than mannerly.

He wished Weed were here, Semyn thought. Of those gathered and shouting at this long table, one or some were liars.

Five Rhothans lined the left side, starting with Chancellor Rober Milne of Vorkoun, its most senior administrator and close friend of the Westietas; a comforting and respected presence sat next to the heir. Past Milne were Netej Hase and Sher Moreau, who controlled, between them, the major foundries—women who shared, according to Momma, pragmatically short memories where it concerned business setbacks.

Long ones, when it came to the war, the treaty, and Ansnans in general. Moreau had fought in the marches. Hase, until taking over her family's foundry, had been a warden who'd overseen Ansnan prisoners of war. They'd have opinions they'd gladly express at this meeting, given the opportunity. Loudly.

Poppa wasn't worried. He'd confided in Semyn he'd rather have those who'd try to poke holes in his proposal, than witless nodding.

No danger of that with this group.

Beside Moreau sat Jellicoe Dee, ably representing warehouse owners—a task apparently tantamount to herding squirrels. Past her, completing the Rhothan delegation, was Kluet Gore, in charge of Vorkoun's waterworks, including piers and bridgework. A straightforward and honest, if crude, individual—and family friend—Gore struggled not to squirm at his proximity to the priests.

When they'd lived in Vorkoun, Gore would take Semyn and Werfol to a sheltered pier by the waterworks to hang baited lines in the Lilem. If the fish weren't biting, Gore would regale them with stories to make them laugh and share his lunch.

A year and a half of turmoil and change since they'd last done it; Semyn doubted there'd be a next. The world, as Momma said, had turned.

Ansnans filled the right side of the table, five representing varied interests, plus two odemini to bring their number to a fortunate seven. The dolls perched on stools to either side of Elder Idat Cotalen of Gordit, leader of the Ansnan delegation. The Rhothan group hadn't one; it understood Chancellor Milne would report today's results to all and sundry who asked.

The elder was a person Poppa said to watch. Momma called Cotalen a thorn in the side of progress. In person Cotalen more resembled a wilted onion stalk. Semyn dutifully kept an eye on the Ansnan, careful not to appear too interested.

The elder sat between staff he'd brought with him: to his right, his chief accountant, Neb Carde, to his left, his scribe Seter Kilsyth. On the surface, it was unusual to have more delegates from a small town like Gordit at this meeting than from Mondir, Ansnor's capital, but Mondir's newly rebuilt administration remained in a state of— how had their tutor politely phrased it? Semyn nodded to himself. *Constructive disarray.*

While Gordit was presently the wealthiest and most stable of Mondir's closer neighbors, center of a mining district and, being on the proposed new rail line, set to become wealthier still.

Something Cotalen would know, making his being a *thorn* a puzzle.

A Shift of Time

Semyn did enjoy puzzles.

The other two Ansnans, Limoges and Kenton, were senior city administrators as well as guild leaders for, respectively, Mondir's construction and transport trades. They sat back, silent and glum, giving every impression of waiting for an excuse to leave.

At the far end sat their hosts, two Rhothan priests. Unfortunately, the priests let nothing show on their faces but respectful attention during the bedlam following the baron's announcement.

Other than Chancellor Milne and Gore, who expressed their natural shock and dismay, Semyn found it impossible to tell if the rest were complete fools, or ably playing the part. "We know nothing of what happened, m'lord." "Nothing like that could happen here." "You must be mistaken—" their ongoing themes, with mirrored glares implying any fault belonged across the table.

At its head, Semyn beside him, Poppa sat listening, a finger stroking what would normally be a communion table, the glass of its top allowing the display of selected bones for, say, a family's Midwinter Beholding.

Not like the one Semyn had witnessed in Marrowdell, where everyone stood silently in the snow within the tiny village ossuary to admit to their Blessed Ancestors the errors and regrets of the year past, then whisper their most ardent wish for the one to come. He'd been moved to confess a woeful lack of attention to the Eld language of Crucib, with its deliberately complex adverbs.

To, more seriously, confess to teasing his little brother, along with his ardent wish to be better. He and Werfol had shared a further wish for the coming year: to stick together no matter what and never be separated. A childish wish, it now seemed, quickly broken. As quickly mended, Semyn vowed.

There'd been a dance in the mill afterward. He'd played Frann's pipes, Ancestors Dear and Departed. Weed had told him about Wisp's game of hide-and-spy the dragon—which would have been a wondrous memory, if Semyn hadn't lost it outside the edge, but he'd vowed to believe his brother and would.

Any Beholding held here couldn't be further removed from

Marrowdell's, with its warmth and family. This table was for what Momma called *gaming the pious*—a term he and Werfol weren't to repeat—where the weaker members of a family, the vulnerable, were cowed into confessing and taking blame for whatever most benefited the stronger.

Their wishes, being of no consequence and unlikely to come true, were kept to themselves.

This table, therefore, was steeped in lies and power struggles and not a reverent place at all. Semyn kept that in mind as he listened with Poppa to the ten who spouted accusations and protests and called for order.

One or some of them—and he refused to omit the priests in his accounting—had conspired to use dark magic to stop this meeting. Only Momma's precautions had prevented them being delayed—or taken and killed.

With a *click*, the baron set his vial of black dust on the table.

The overlapping babble dwindled then ceased, those gathered staring at the vial like perplexed geese. The priests scowled. "What is this, m'lord baron?" asked the second of them, speaking for the first. A most senior did not to speak to anyone less than the head of their order in Avyo. Semyn imagined it must grow frustrating, to keep silent surrounded by fools. Weed still couldn't do it.

"A sample of the weapon used against my person, that of my son and heir, and our trusted staff." Poppa's calm voice had the slight edge that wasn't temper but meant he was done dancing around the topic. "Do not doubt, had this attack succeeded? We would not be here."

An embarrassingly fervent round of "Ancestors Blessed" and "Beholden to"s followed from the Rhothans, the witness of priests undoubtedly an encouragement to piety. The Ansnans tried to outshout them with exhortations to the Celestials.

His expression bland, Semyn kept his opinion to himself.

As did the seniormost priest at the opposite end of the table, who met his gaze. She was as tall as Momma but round everywhere, as Momma was not. Her brown robes were no finer than those of her subordinate, her rank indicated by a simple braid of gray around the stiff collar that rose behind her bald head, where the other's had black.

Semyn didn't flinch or look away, though the priest's eyes were like chips of granite and her gaze forbidding. He waited for her to blink, then gave a gracious nod.

Her lips twitched.

While this went on, Poppa drummed the table with four fingers until, without warning, he slammed down his hand. "We *are* here, esteemed citizens," he said mildly, "so let us to work. What progress on supplies?" To the Rhothan side. "And on logistics." The Ansnan.

Netej Hase, on behalf of the Rhothans, produced a sheaf of papers, dividing those into two piles, the second of which she pushed as if to shove them down the length of the table.

Not to be outdone, Carde, Gordit's accountant, brought forth wide-bound journals featuring stars inset in the leather, propelling those along.

Omi Derhall, the baron's seniormost guard, stepped smartly to intercept both. Stacking the papers and journals together, he marched around the table to set them properly in front of his lord.

Court protocol was a privilege Poppa rarely insisted upon, preferring to meet with others as one of them.

He must believe those responsible for the attack were here.

Grateful for the looming presence of Dutton Omemee behind his chair, Semyn reassessed the positioning of the other guards. Two stood behind the Rhothans, two behind the Ansnans, while the baron's seniormost had returned to his post tellingly behind the priests, all in easy reach for a deadly strike if so commanded. As well as Dutton, another guard stood behind the baron, while guards in Westietas livery stood at attention by each of the two closed doors into this room. The rest remained with the coach and horses, securing their exit.

Semyn relaxed inwardly. Those here—those who'd ordered the attack—should be the ones nervous. Westietas controlled this space; the baron would see to an accounting.

Which he did, in a way that surprised his son as much as all others. "My heir will check your figures." Poppa slid the papers and journals to Semyn.

Semyn brought out the scribe's kit he carried with him everywhere and set to work, conscious of the reactions around the table. The simmering offense from the Ansnan accountant he dismissed, as he did the dismay of the rest.

The gleam of approval from the seniormost priest? That was worth noting.

He began to scan the columns, a red pencil ready in his hand. Numbers spoke to him, they always had, and as he spotted entries worth questioning, he made a tidy mark beside each, quickly absorbed in the work.

"Where is Engineer Araben Sethe?" Poppa said. "I expressly requested her presence at this meeting."

"The engineer said she would wait in another room until 'you'd sorted this mess,' m'lord baron. Her words," the priest added stiffly, plainly disapproving the informality.

Just like Araben, Semyn thought with glee. The Ansnan had risked her life, coming in secret to the estate to help Poppa finalize his plans, determined to further peace in Vorkoun. Not only was she brave, but she'd treated him and Werfol as equals and, as Momma said with rare admiration, had no patience for fools.

The baron leaned back, steepling his fingers. He regarded those at the table with little favor. "A mess indeed. No one's confessed to the crime against our persons. You—" he aimed his fingertips at the Rhothans "—assert a lack of supplies." At the Ansnans, "You claim a dearth of wagons to move them, should any arrive." The words were measured, but Poppa's tone grew increasingly cold.

He settled back, eyes on the priests, giving an insouciant wave. "Partake of the refreshments, with our thanks to these good priests. We'll pass the time with other news while your claims are checked."

Semyn wouldn't hum or nibble the end of his pencil, faults Master Setac corrected regularly; this was no ordinary assignment. The boy bent to his task with dignity, aware of its importance. The trail of mischief, as Momma would say, was here, right where someone thought to hide it, within the bloated pages in front of him.

He would not fail.

Terst turn-born, Jenn discovered, slept through the dimmings, even when that came unusually early. Nothing would do but all head to bed. In Marrowdell, each harvest, the terst turn-born slept on thick soft pads topped with blankets and pillows, their airy yellow tent floored with layers of rugs. To Jenn, it seemed the most luxurious accommodation imaginable, the more so as all of it arrived in trunks on horse carts. Trunks, moreover, stored in Bannan's—and now her—barn over winter, making the housing of future piglets something of a quandary to approach, especially when those *horses* had turned out to be kruar.

No pads on the ground here. Jenn wiggled her toes, enjoying the smooth sheets. The terst turn-born still slept in a single room, but this was domed with crystal and hung with draperies to grant each magnificent bed privacy and the whole a sense of space.

She'd had to climb a step to reach the top of the bed they'd given her—Tooth's, which was a sad thought and she'd objected, but Mistress Sand insisted—with its feet of round stone, base of inlaid wood, and mattress deeper than her arm. It was like sleeping in a tower.

And the blankets? Lighter than quilts and with just the right amount of warmth, the premature dimming cooler than she remembered experiencing in the Verge, not that she'd ever come at that risky time on purpose to find out.

Yes, this bed would be perfect—

With a resigned inner sigh, Jenn stared up into the dark.

—if she was alone in it.

Wisp, insistent she be guarded and, truth be told, fond of his own comfort, took up more than a person's share of the bed, crowding her to the side and claiming the extra pillow.

Imp clung precariously to a drapery rod passing overhead. Heart's

Blood, any minute she expected the young dragon to fall asleep, loose its hold, and drop on them—not that birds did, but who knew about dragons?

Wisp would not be amused.

It wasn't that she minded sharing with her dragon, but she'd much prefer sharing the bed—any bed—with her beloved. Who she hoped was home and safe or, if not home, then still safe wherever he was, and the only other thing she wanted was—

For Mistress Sand to have listened when Jenn pulled her aside for a quiet word before bed. Wisp had warned her but, Ancestors Prickly and Prejudiced, she'd had to try.

She'd no more than uttered the word "terst" before Sand—who normally was a good listener and patient for her kind—thrust her palm over Jenn's mouth, shaking her head as if that wasn't sufficient deterrent, to then pronounce darkly, "Terst lie, Sweetling. They are powerless and resentful, cowering in their bubbles."

Which Jenn would have said wasn't necessarily the case, had Sand the least interest in another word.

She wasn't ready to sleep. The situation—all of it—made it challenging to so much as relax. Making it worse, the room resonated with a chorus of snores from those who *were* sleeping, namely the remaining terst turn-born—Chalk's empty bed not for dragons, more the pity—a chorus rising in vigor and hilarious snorts until Jenn buried her face in a pillow to stifle the urge to giggle.

Ancestors Blessed, she was resting and safe. Clean as well, with a full stomach, and dressed in a simple nightgown that reminded her of Marrowdell, and if she couldn't fall asleep, she'd much to think about—

Sputtersputter

A snore. An oddly small snore.

Sputtersnortsputter

And it wasn't, Jenn could tell, a dragonish snore nor a turn-born's. And certainly wasn't Kaj's, who slept at the foot of his mistress' bed and gave a wet whistle every other breath.

Snifflesputter

This snore came from under her bed!

Curious, Jenn eased herself to the edge of the mattress and slipped over the side until, bent at the waist, she could peer beneath. Nothing to see but darkness.

The small snores abruptly stopped. There *was* something there.

"I won't hurt you," she whispered, and stretched her hand under as far as she could. A possibly reckless approach, most things in the Verge having teeth and not particularly nice, but Jenn knew herself surrounded by dragons and in the company of the most powerful beings here, other than sei, and wasn't worried.

A damp little nose, feeling much like a baby rabbit's, pressed into the palm of her hand and *sniffed*. A second joined it. Both withdrew.

How charming! She hadn't known the terst turn-born had pets. Or whatever these were, other than cute.

Definitely shy, though. She'd not disturb them further. Jenn pulled herself back onto the mattress.

Or rather tried, for with most of her hanging down from the very tall bed, the effort was in vain and she wasn't to laugh. She wasn't.

A muted giggle popped out.

She swallowed the next. That Wisp hadn't already stirred was a wonder and she'd no idea if the others were light sleepers.

Nothing for it. She'd have to slither off the very tall bed, then climb back up.

Jenn put one hand on the step and the other on the floor, wiggling forward to slide over her knee. Which was as far as she got before realizing she was about to tumble off and, while the fall was unlikely to hurt, the resulting *thump* would wake the entire room.

Oh dear.

All at once, two little lumps appeared near Jenn's nose. Furry lumps with damp noses who sat on their haunches to regard her with beady little eyes that caught gleams from the lamp, eyes that appeared wistful—or hungry—

And she might still have thought *baby rabbit*, but these had very long arms with a trio of claws in place of hands, and she'd seen such creatures before.

Terst cows. Incredible as it seemed, she was nose to nose with a pair of them, each no larger than her doubled fists, and they weren't babies, unless terst cows were like grasshoppers and started out as miniature versions, and she'd have loved to study them longer but her middle was cramping and—

Heart's Blood, if she fell, she'd crush them.

"Shoo," Jenn whispered. She freed a hand, intending to push them gently out of danger, only to slip, and that would have been that—

But the terst cows *GREW*. To the size of a grown rabbit. To the size of Sand's dog. Until they were the size of ponies and their rumps poked through the draperies, their heads well above hers so she faced their round furry bellies.

She held her breath. Not that they were smelly, but she wasn't sure what to expect.

To her astonishment, they took hold of her as gently as could be and lifted her back into bed.

Then shrank and *shimmered* and weren't there at all.

Oh, but they were, she was certain of it, and under her bed. Jenn lay back on her pillow with a smile.

~Trouble sleeping, Dear Heart?~ her dragon asked.

She yawned, her worries lost in wonder. "Not anymore."

While the two terst cows who'd followed their leader into this wondrous strange place, a place filled with those who were not quite *terst*, not enough *terst*—insufficiently *TERST* to require they defend their leader against rivals, were vastly pleased. They savored her smell and the great gift of TOUCH. And, while in truth now very hungry indeed, this made terst cows so content they curled up and went right to sleep.

Gripping the side of the cart, for the path to the main house went first over what felt like roots and stones before smoothing out, Kydd kept silent. Ancestors Blessed, he was grateful: for the handcart brought to convey him, for the cushions someone had thought to put on the bare wood, for the swift and efficient attention of Lila's staff. Guards, by the sounds, in light mail and armed.

He could smell burning oil and wood. They'd lit torches, an illumination he couldn't see. Surely soon. Once his cavalcade left the edge.

Surely.

Bannan and Lila stayed back to discuss the truthseer's plans. Kydd's journals, all nine, went ahead in the arms of the fleetest of her guard, ordered to run straight to the house and lock them safely away.

Kydd listened to the guard's swift sure footfalls, his heart pounding along with them. Waited, straining, until he could no longer distinguish them from those closer, and knew his journals were gone.

Beyond reach. Beyond *his* reach. Ancestors Blessed, he was Beholden for that most of all. Free of their sickly allure, he felt more himself every moment.

Then, gradually, like a finger of chill air, he grew aware of an influence that wasn't the journals—

Kydd quickly shut out his surroundings, from footsteps to the inevitable creak and jostle of the cart, banished any thought but the search, grasping for the shape of it.

"Find more. GO!"

And there it was. Less than a whisper, greater than a shout, an *imposition* on his choices. With a shiver to his bones, Kydd Uhthoff recognized its signature taint.

The Mage Prime. Rose.

First of the Heirs. Leader and ultimate authority. He'd no other name nor a face for her—no student did—only vivid memories of her vicious testing, her slippery, unavoidable meddling magic, painfully fresh to this day.

And how *her* voice came to push at him here and now, to separate him from his duty to Peggs and force him here—

His hand pressed over the pocket with Melusine's pin.

—was a less urgent question than why.

"We're here, sir," said someone. "Home of the Westietas."

Home of a boy with true sight, able to truedream. Of a mother gifted and that, he suddenly and with horror realized, was the answer. In his day, there'd been rumors the most powerful mages gleaned magic from sources other than spells and tokens, rumors he'd dismissed as envy.

Kydd shoved his hand in his pocket, frantic to pull out the pin and toss it away. A sharp prick on his thumb brought him to his senses. It would only be found—a spell as potent as this would make sure of it.

Loathing its proximity, he began to struggle out of his coat. Gentle hands restrained him, the cart come to a halt. "It's all right, sir. We'll take you inside. Do you need help?"

He did, but not from the innocent. Kydd composed himself, reaching out his hand. "I should be steady on my feet, kind sir, but will need your guidance, I fear."

Heart's Blood, he was beyond the edge. Where there'd be lamps lit, light streaming from windows, while he saw nothing but black. Had the Mage Prime blinded him for life? She'd been capable of such cruelty.

Ask Dove, who'd died trapped below ground and unable to scream.

A pair of guards guided him forward, neither carrying his journals. That much, he thought wryly, he could sense without difficulty. As he could the change from gravel to flat stone. "A stair here, sir."

Kydd found it with his foot, stepped up. The men kept beside him, strong hands under his elbows, letting him set the pace. "Into the kitchen now, sir."

Someone had opened the door. Smells wrapped around him like Peggs' warm arms and he felt tears fill his eyes.

"BLINK!"

He did, only afterward realizing it hadn't been reflex but an order, only in that moment fully comprehending how the spell he'd cast on himself had been twisted against him.

To let *her* see!

"Cover my eyes!" Kydd demanded frantically, pulling back to stop his guides. "Quickly, I implore you. The pain—"

"*NO!!!*"

A shouted "Do it!" A soft cloth wrapped across his eyelids, secured behind his head.

"*TAKE IT OFF! WE MUST SEE!*" With a blast of *PAIN* that had him gasping.

He felt a string go around his wrist. Smelled cinnamon and old socks and the pain receded so abruptly Kydd staggered, to be caught by those with him. "Ancestors Blessed," he gasped gratefully. "I'm beholden—"

"Hush, Lad." An older voice, unfamiliar but firm. "Ioana's got ye." Louder. "Donna stand there like oafs. See his lordship t'the guest suite, an'be smart about it. Tixel's drawn a bath." Quieter, just for him. "It'll be all right, Lad. I got ye." Lips pressed Kydd's cheek, dry lips and soft; a benediction as warm as a mother's, and he felt invisible chains drop from his heart.

Leaving certainty. "I shouldn't be here. I must go back," he pleaded. "I must be with my wife. She's having our baby—"

"Ye've help here," the mysterious woman assured him, then he was swept away, up stairs and down a hall, caught in a current. Kydd let it happen, giving into the strangest sensation.

Hope.

A hope coming too soon, had he known. The words writ in mimrol on a pin sent to spy, the pin still in his coat pocket, changed again to read . . .

"*Now to find them. Now to take them all.*"

While behind him, the baroness' capable guards, no longer distracted by a blind guest and magic, discovered to their horror they were first to reach the house.

Kydd's journals, and the runner sent to deliver them, had not.

When Bannan went to walk alongside the handcart to the house, to be there when they crossed the edge and, Ancestors Blessed and Brilliant, the best happened and Kydd could see again, Lila's fingers had found his wrist, anchoring him with her.

She'd have reason, so he stayed—watched nimble-footed Bobbieb dash away into the dark with the journals, watched the cart, friend, and guards take the path behind her, take the light—before turning to his sister, her face a shadow. "You want to know about Gordit," he guessed.

"Oh, I know a great deal about Gordit, little brother. Come back inside."

He followed her through the hidden door. While it had been closed behind them, no one had extinguished the lamp on the table, and he'd have been impressed none of its light showed outside—had he time. "This isn't part of your games," Bannan protested as Lila perched on the table, swinging an idle leg. "There's a threat to Jenn and Delfinn in that place."

"Is there, now," in that tone meaning he hadn't surprised or informed her.

The truthseer narrowed his eyes and took a step to where he could see her face as more than silhouette. "Mistress Sand came to ask for my help. A turn-born's gone missing in Gordit. They won't risk themselves to follow, not if they can help it."

"And you brought her here?" Fingers flicked at their surroundings.

"Your little hideaway isn't the secret you hoped." He took no pleasure in it.

Grimly, "Did Weed see this creature?"

"Sand was gone before he showed up, and no, not that you've asked, I waited until he and Dutton were well out of sight before I—left. Or tried to."

Lila went still. "What's wrong? What happened?"

Bannan dropped bonelessly onto the settee, draping an arm across the back. "My door took me to Marrowdell—but to a Marrowdell some seventy years ago. I tried again and made it home. And it happened when I came back with Kydd. We walked into the past here and found ourselves in the Harrowing. Scourge guided us out." He grimaced. "Bloody Beast refused to come with us a second time."

"Showing more sense."

The truthseer shrugged. "The journals had to get here, to you," he pointed out. "Marrowdell wanted them gone."

A measure how much Lila had learned about Marrowdell's other inhabitants that she didn't question the statement. "And Kydd?"

He turned his hand palm up. "That may depend on what happens to him here."

Her lips quirked. "By now he's in the hands of our redoubtable Cook. I look forward to her report."

Ioana Tagey had ruled their family's kitchen—and been Lila's confidante—as long as Bannan could remember. He thought of the key around his neck. She was one of two holding a charm to respond to a Larmensu in distress. "Did she—?"

Lila shook her head. "We'd no warning of your arrival." She flashed a grin. "I suppose that means you were never in real danger, Dear Heart, despite your malfunctioning door."

And how he'd felt at the time, he thought, not ready to dismiss the vision.

But his sister hadn't held him back to discuss the past. "You promised me passage to Gordit," he replied. "This ally of yours?"

Hands locked around her upraised knee, Lila swung her leg, looking inordinately pleased with herself.

Never a good sign. Tensing, Bannan perched on the edge of the seat. "What have you done?"

"First things first," she replied archly. "As we speak, the good Baron Westietas and his heir should be nearing the end of their meeting in Mondir. Among the, shall we say, *revelations* I expect—our Semyn exceptionally clever with figures—will be the ongoing and critical falsification of reports ordered by Gordit's leader, the slippery Elder Cotalen." Letting go her knee, she planted her hands on the table to lean forward, her light manner gone. "After the war, he closed Gordit's iron mine without explanation or cause given—or argument. Note that, little brother. And the town coffers overflow."

Bannan thought of the abandoned mine beneath the Marerrym estate, its walls dripping with mimrol. "You think they found a new source of mimrol and a market for it."

"What I *think* is irrelevant. What I know is there's unusual power in Gordit, political and otherwise, and it's growing. Something's behind it, and I was due to go there myself when Emon came up with this—" A rude gesture.

"You sent Dutton with Semyn—Werfol told me. You expect danger."

"Always." She pursed her lips, breathing out, then, "And wasn't wrong. I received a bird from those I'd set to watch their route. Emon's wagon was attacked as it entered the Ansnan side of the city. Everyone's fine—" quickly, seeing his face. "We'd countermeasures in place."

Risking Emon he understood, but the boy? Bannan scowled at her. "Heart's Blood, Lila. Semyn isn't a piece in your games."

"This is no game, little brother." As if a knife slid from its sheath. "And my sons are neither pieces nor fools." Calmer. "I expect Emon to receive an urgent invitation to visit Gordit to be—ah—reassured as to the elder's doubtless misunderstood intentions."

Bannan shook his head, but didn't press the point. "If a turn-born went missing there, the mine's within the edge."

Her easy smile returned. "Just so." Hopping from the table, Lila strode over to the small table with the signaling device. Ignoring the device, she picked up the hand-sized black stone and the little hammer next to it, items Bannan had dismissed as ornaments.

A mistake, he chided himself, watching her bring the stone and hammer to the table, setting down the first and lifting the other. Her green eyes slid his way, a challenge in their depths. "Ready to meet your ride to Gordit?"

He sat back, feigning disinterest. "So soon? I'd hoped for a bath—" Though if she'd managed what he suspected—and who but his sister could? His pulse began to race.

Lila tapped the stone with the hammer. The sound was faint at first, a ringing tone that seemed to quickly fade.

But didn't. Contrarily, the high-pitched *ring* grew louder until Bannan gritted his teeth, glowering at his sister.

Who put her hand on the stone to stop it. "That should do," she asserted.

"Do what—" He shut his mouth, the *what* taking place before his eyes.

On the floor between them, an oval appeared, white and shimmering.

And from it rose a serpentine figure, crowned with a helm of stone braids, with a woman's head and upper torso merged atop an opalescent snake-like body. Her face was stern and scarred, a lifetime's experience writ on it, and her bare arms were dotted with glowing pearls.

Edis Donovar.

Who, with a quick glance at Bannan, bowed to Lila. "You rang, Baroness?"

And yes, there was the slightest twinkle in her deep, purple eyes, for this was a friend, unlooked for but most welcome, and rising to his feet, Bannan swept Edis a full court bow, brushing the floor with his fingertips.

She bowed her head in return. "Truthseer. Well met."

"Well met indeed, Edis." Once an Ansnan soldier, she'd been betrayed and almost died, to be saved by a creature of the Verge and turned into this marvel. A marvel able to ferry others with her from the edge to the Verge and back, a feat she'd done to save them from the toad queen.

Resigned to a wearisome night or more in the saddle, Bannan was sorely tempted to hug her. "Edis, I must go to Gordit. Would you take me, please?"

Her expression hardened. "It is no good place." She twisted her body to regard Lila, who, back on her tabletop perch, idly tapped the hammer into the palm of her free hand. "You know this."

Lila shrugged a shoulder. "Man has a mission."

"I see." Edis uncoiled, rising to tower above Bannan, scrutinizing him from head to toe. "Stars know, such dress will draw attention whether you want it or not. And no weapons?" With scorn.

He glanced down at himself. His clothes were dusty but whole, a light summer coat over a fine shirt, and leather pants suited to a visit to the baron's household, if not a day's work in their garden. Rhothan and wealthy.

Without so much as a dinner knife. Bannan gave the fierce and doubting ladies his most charming smile, holding out his empty hands. "Had I but known."

"Here." Lila hopped down, tossing the hammer at him. He caught it midair, bemused as she went to a trunk against a wall and threw open the lid.

"Not a soldier," he reminded his sister, setting her hammer by the stone.

Edis snorted. "We'll always be soldiers," she told him. "Now we choose our battles."

He'd have gladly argued, but Lila produced a sword with scabbard and belt, two throwing knives with arm sheaths, and—Bannan raised his eyebrows—a fat leather purse. "You look a charming rogue," she commented, helping him buckle on the weapons before tucking the purse inside his shirt. "To keep you honest." Her hand flattened on his chest, green eyes intent on his. "I know you're going for a friend, Bannan, but—"

Heart's Blood, no need to ask, not when it concerned family. "I'll watch for Emon and the lad while I'm there," he assured her. "If I'm not back before Jenn comes—" Bannan hesitated, but there wasn't a choice. "Tell her where I've gone. She'll know why. And that Kydd is here. You'll take care of him."

It wasn't a question, but Lila nodded gravely. "Will he be able to return on his own?"

Use his door, she meant. Get home to Peggs and, by Jenn's rules, having passed through it with him, Kydd could find the door again and cross on his own—if still blind and safe from the Verge—

And end up *when*? It was too great a risk, he decided. "Best Kydd waits for one of us."

Edis had tilted her head as if listening, eyes hooded. All at once, she smiled. "The scoundrel's back in the edge."

Roche, mouthed his sister with a wink. Bannan's heart soared. "Can you tell where anyone is?"

"Those who matter to me," Edis replied dryly. "And who contain something of the Verge. Magic," the clarification with reluctance, as if admitting a fault.

A wonder she could do it at all—"Jenn. Jenn Nalynn. Can you find her?"

"I've heard the name," with a bite to her tone suggesting she knew all about Jenn's wishing and Roche's curse. Her face softened. "I'm sorry. That's not enough." Edis offered her hand. "If you're ready, truthseer?" Her smile returned. "I've an appointment."

"Ready as I can be," he said honestly. "What should I expect, where you're taking me?"

"A pleasant view." With that her arm went around him and they dropped through the floor—

If Momma were here—

She'd expect him to handle this, Semyn reminded himself, feeling his shoulders straighten. That his stomach growled, the platters of meat, cheese, and fruits not offered to him while he worked and since whisked away, was irrelevant.

That Kenton and Limoges continued arguing with the guard at the door and others paced, equally irrelevant.

He was done.

"I've finished, m'lord baron." Standing to bow, which stretched his back, Semyn offered the Rhothan sheaf of papers and the Ansnan journals, topped by a page summarizing his findings, to his father.

Who took the lot, looking stern and a little—because the boys knew his face and Momma was right, the baron wasn't perfect when it came to hiding his feelings—sad. Because someone worked against their plans to aid Vorkoun and Mondir, and everyone who lived in them or nearby.

Ancestors Bloody and Brutal, while there were minor scoundrels and weak-minded greedy fools aplenty here, to Semyn only one mattered now. Elder Cotalen of Gordit, who'd initialed the altered pages in his own accountant's report—after clumsily tampering with them. Had he assumed no one here could add?

"I'm prepared to give a verbal report, m'lord baron." To Semyn's relief, the quaking in his bones didn't affect his voice.

Baron Westietas gave a curt nod, his hand flat on the papers, a thumb rubbing Semyn's neat numbering as if in approval. Or taking strength from them.

Which was a new and odd thought, and Semyn had to pause a moment before addressing the room, but that was fine. The pause silenced the few who whispered amongst themselves and gathered every eye to him.

"These accounts purport to show Vorkoun lacks the resources to begin construction of the rail station and servicing areas adjacent to the new railway, and even if that weren't the case, Mondir will be unable to move the goods required to support those endeavors in a timely fashion." Semyn warmed to his topic. "These accounts have been falsified."

Mutters grew, Hase and Moreau exchanging looks, the Ansnans from Mondir doing the same. Mutters that threatened to become shouts, and he stopped, waiting for silence, demanding respect.

When it came, Semyn went on, "There is no shortage of iron or timber in Vorkoun. Ample reserves have been stockpiled in several locations, reserves left out of the final tallies. As for transport?" He didn't look at Cotalen. "It should amaze most present here that the number of Ansnan carts and wagons recorded as destroyed or damaged during the war effort is more than exist in all of Rhoth. That shortage is also a lie."

The Mondir Ansnans looked stunned.

His father swept his gaze over those around the table. "To what end, my son and heir?"

"For profit, my father and lord."

Shouts broke out, and Semyn let the words roll over him, taking note of who said what and the inflection of each voice. "This boy knows nothing!" "He's brighter than you lot!" a warming endorsement from Gore trammeled by, "Only a fool listens to a beardless child!" "Where's the proof!"

Cotalen, he saw, took note as well.

The baron lifted an eyebrow. Silence, brooding and angry, fell. Into it, Semyn said in his clear young voice, "Vorkoun's distributors are hoarding supply in hopes of driving up the price for their goods. Those in Mondir—or rather in Gordit, where the existing and ample number of transports sit—are aware of this and will refuse to bring forth their equipment until they can levee a higher charge. Or so it would seem."

A daring statement, but he was encouraged by his father's tiny nod. "I submit another motive for consideration," Semyn continued. "That those honest folk who came to this meeting felt the need to protect or hide their assets from you, m'lord baron. That they believe—or were convinced—you wouldn't be fair to both sides."

Semyn raised his voice. "I know you will be. I know no one shall lose in this endeavor. In fact, all stand to gain, and I give you my oath as heir that this is the truth."

The quality of the silence changed. Rhothans and Ansnans exchanged darting glances, suddenly uncertain what was happening.

The senior priest smiled behind her hand. Chancellor Milne grinned from ear to ear, Gore nodding.

Poppa chuckled. "Still say I shouldn't listen to a beardless boy?" he gently chided, then grew serious. "My friends, I understand your concerns—none better. What we will construct, from track to service bays to market roads, is to benefit everyone who lives and works here. We will not sit by hapless and impoverished while trains rush past us from Eld to the mines of Ansnor, leaving our boats empty of cargo." He rose to his feet, everyone rising with him. "I join my heir, Semyn Westietas, in vowing to you we will never give up your land or goods to line pockets in Avyo."

Kenton bowed her head. "On behalf of my colleagues and me—" with a telling glare at Cotalen "—Mondir offers our sincere apologies to the heir and will correct our—" a slight cough "—any mistakes in our accounts. Wagons will roll. May the Stars Witness."

A reassuringly fervent echo went around the room, while the Rhothans present circled their hearts. "Ancestors Blessed," Sher Moreau said with a wry smile. "True, we've feared this plan of yours, m'lord baron, and worried over the Eld and their train as well." A sour look across the table. "Thus far, the treaty hasn't been to Rhothan gain, only Rhothan loss. That's why we fiddled our numbers, to stop losing more."

"A fair price. Peace." The baron looked around the room. "Being here together. Building something new and magnificent together. That is what we stand to gain. All of us. What say you to that?"

Nods. Smiles. Someone clapped and Semyn half-expected a cheer—

Gore abruptly stood and leaned forward, tight fists on the table. He swung his gray-haired head to stare around the table, from the priests to Semyn, ending with his father. "I say we've an enemy. An enemy who tried to stop you from coming here, m'lord baron, and is against everything you've said and promised."

"An enemy capable and willing to use the foulest sort of magic," Limoges said next, his eyes flashing. "We'll need protection during the work, all of us and our people."

"You'll have it," the baron promised.

In the midst of this, Semyn felt Cotalen's cold appraising stare. He might, the boy thought, wonder why he hadn't been accused by name.

He might feel safe.

Let him. Semyn smiled Momma's smile, drawing Dutton's attention. The time to out a villain, Momma taught, was when they wouldn't see you coming. They must go to Gordit with all haste. Prove what was still conjecture. He'd make the case with his father once they were alone.

Meanwhile, Poppa said cheerfully, "Find my engineer. It's time to discuss the location for the new bridge. I've brought the latest maps to show you all."

When young enough to be in school with Master Dusom, if done their chores, Tadd and Allin would start a game in the Emms' barn called Siege. Roche, if in a good mood, would jump in; Devins always played; and Jenn be coaxed, not that it took much. Siege was fun.

Wainn would judge. Or watch. Or hide and watch. He'd a gift for hiding in plain sight, even then.

Someone started as siege-breaker while the rest grabbed tokens from a bag and dashed away to hide. The tokens were pieces of paper with words scribbled on them, wadded into little balls. Words like "water," "food," "rope," and "fire." The twins tossed in new ones each time, like "wet wood" or "soap" that might not seem important but could be, if you were clever.

They were all clever.

The tokens came into play when your hiding place was discovered. You stayed in the game if you gave the siege-breaker a combination of supplies that let you continue the siege another turn—food and water, for instance. Or something to thwart the siege-breaker, such as a rope slicked with soap because a good story helped. That had been a game.

The terst turn-born were under a siege that wasn't. When Jenn looked in the cupboards of the enclave kitchen, most of what she saw came from elsewhere, brought across from the edge. Jam from Marrowdell. A barrel of oompah from the Sweet Sea. Jars of pickles and a ham from somewhere in Rhoth.

Food to last on a shelf, which made sense if you had to go and get it.

Oh, they'd some fresh. Loaves of bread. Berries that must have grown in the Verge, changing color every time Jenn snuck a look in the bowl. But not nearly enough. Jenn was accustomed to rationing stores. By the gaps on these shelves, the terst turn-born couldn't hide behind their wall much longer without neglecting their flesh and blood selves.

She had to help them.

That settled, Jenn located the tea Mistress Sand had sent her to find, the group insisting she share their breakfast before leaving. Tin in hand, she went to close the door when she realized she was being watched.

Ancestors Blessed. A house toad. *Here?*

It squatted behind a half-empty sack of potatoes, a single limpid brown eye in view, as if drawn from hiding by her presence to stare at her.

Jenn checked over her shoulder. Alone for the moment. She eased the sack aside to better see the toad. It was gray and smallish compared to those of Marrowdell, with longer claws. "Greetings, esteemed little cousin."

A slow blink. ~Greetings, elder sister. I am a messenger. I have a message for Jenn Nalynn.~

"I'm Jenn." A message from Wen! Impatiently, Jenn waited to hear it.

Another, slower blink.

Toads. "May I please have the message, little cousin?"

Eyes of dark glistening brown faded to become gray and white, centered on black pupils and swept by long pale lashes. Bizarre as those were for a house toad, all at once the rest of the toad vanished as well, becoming a head surrounded by wild, glowing hair and a familiar face indeed.

Wen Treff.

As toad queen, Wen was responsible for a good portion of the Verge as well as the little cousins. Saying "hello" would be, Jenn decided, much too casual. Disrespectful, even.

"Greetings, your majesty," she said instead, giving an awkward little curtsy that almost knocked the berry bowl from its shelf so Jenn had to grab for it, ruining the effect.

"Don't start, my friend." Wen's lips quirked to the side. "I get enough from house toads." Her half-smile faded. "I've had them out looking for you, Jenn. There's something wrong with the Verge. It's gone all—wiggly."

The term she'd used to Wisp, and Jenn nodded eagerly. "The sei tell me I must fix what's broken. I fear it's to do with the door I made

Bannan—but it might be more than that." She checked again. Still alone. Jenn lowered her voice to the faintest of whispers. "Tooth and Chalk have gone missing in the edge, in an Ansnan town called Gordit. Mistress Sand sent Bannan to investigate. Can you?" This with sudden burning hope. "He shouldn't go there by himself but we're having a—a little problem crossing." She'd not mention the snow. "Please, Wen?"

"The *terst* turn-born are a problem," and this not in a friend's voice but a queen's. "They meddle and restrict, their reasons selfish and petty." Hair writhed, filling the space around the disembodied head; Wen's brows creased in a thunderous frown. "They've refused my every invitation to discuss the future."

Being, Jenn thought, besieged and afraid. Words Wen wouldn't want to hear, so instead she repeated gently, "Tooth and Chalk, Wen. Our friends."

"'Friends'? They don't know the word." It wasn't just that Wen was angry; she wanted to stay angry.

Sensing that, Jenn waited, Aunt Sybb fond of saying a temper cooled faster if not stoked by argument, a hint she'd given more often to Jenn, who admittedly tended to be stubborn about being right, than to Peggs, who knew when to leave well enough alone.

And who was, if Imp was to be believed, alone and without Kydd at the worst possible time, though Peggs had Aunt Sybb and their father and the entire village. No number of people could replace the one you loved with all your heart.

With a huff, the toad queen calmed herself. "I like your door," Wen declared, to Jenn's surprise. Seeing it, she came close to smiling. "Whenever it's used, there's a trace left behind of Marrowdell, like the smell of Peggs' pies."

Which was lovely to think, but she had, Jenn reminded herself, to be truthful. "Using it might be breaking time."

"Or be holding it together against other forces." Wen gave the impression of a shrug. "Think of the Verge as a pot of soup forgotten on a stove. It might simmer nicely all day—or scorch on the bottom and boil over—but whatever happens, the pot and stove remain."

Except for needing a thorough scrub in the latter case, as Jenn and Bannan had learned, being easily distracted, and Jenn was unsure of Wen's point.

"As for helping the truthseer?" Wedged between potato sack and pickle jars, the head appeared deep in thought.

Jenn held her breath.

Then Wen spoke. "Alas, I have no ability to affect the edge, Dear Heart, other than to visit myself, which I cannot risk until the Verge calms. As for Gordit—house toads haven't gone there in a long time." Her gaze went vague, then sharpened. "I'm told it's a bad place. I realize that's not much help."

"I'm beholden even so." While an intriguing notion, that house toads might pick where they went and thus might, Jenn deduced, be found anywhere, she didn't like in the least that the wise creatures considered where Sand had sent Bannan to be a place to avoid.

She shook herself. "Again, my thanks. I'll do what I can to stop the Verge from wiggling." A wry grin. "Though I'm at a loss for how, if not my door."

"Everything is connected, Dear Heart. Find our missing friends," Wen Treff said gruffly. "Learn what poisons this Gordit. Fix that, and who knows?"

Heart's Blood, hardly a simple assignment, but Jenn nodded. "Delfinn does well," she said, as she should have sooner.

Wen's face softened. "I know."

There was a pause, time for a mother to consider what she'd given up to be queen, time for Jenn to wonder what else she could do.

Then Wen's eyebrow rose. "You do know you've got cows."

Jenn looked around, but the pair weren't in sight. "They're not mine," she corrected. "They live here."

"Do they, now?" Whatever Wen thought to add, she didn't, though she appeared amused. "It's time I gave this brave toad a rest. Hearts of our Ancestors, hear our heart's plea, however far we are apart—"

"Keep Us Close," they said together.

Jenn found herself looking at a toad.

The toad queen was gone.

Not, Wisp thought peevishly, that'd she'd been here at all—other than as a head that smelled like a little cousin. A trick he'd not witnessed before. And what did it say about other little cousins? Were they *all* her eyes?

This was unacceptable. His clenched claw dug into the ceiling and crystal bled a blue tear. *Unacceptable!*

The crystal tear fell to the floor behind Jenn Nalynn, who failed to notice. From under the counter came a faint, ~Why we spying, Great Lord of Dragons? On *her*? You said I mustn't. I remember.~

Why, it almost sounded like a protest. Perhaps there was hope for Imp's manners yet, unless it had more to do with the toad queen. Who, though once a person, showed herself well on the way to becoming what the Verge had never seen: a terrifyingly powerful being driven by a sense of—the girl had tried to explain it but her dragon hadn't grasped its value until meeting Crumlin Tralee and continued to have doubts—

Justice. That was the word. ~No.~ Wisp deigned to answer. ~We were here first.~

~TO SPY, elder brother?~ accused the little cousin in the cupboard, looking up.

A look that might have betrayed him, but Jenn took out a tin and closed the cupboard door, her expression preoccupied.

Good, Wisp thought.

Finding the kettle, she picked it up then turned in a slow circle. "Ancestors Mystified and Muddled. There's no water. No stove—"

"Wish the kettle full and hot, Sweetling." Sand came into the room, the rest following. They looked the worse for wear, as if the untimely rest had come ill to them.

Unless it was the presence of dragons, unfettered and wild.

Wisp had slept very well indeed, warm and in a fine nest. Except for a moment when the girl's movements disturbed him and another when he'd been wakened by the overwhelming stench of terst, only to remember he was surrounded by them.

They fussed over tea. He came to a decision, swooping down to the doorway. He wrapped himself in light.

"Wisp!" the girl said, the only one glad to see him.

The only one he cared was.

~The dimming is over, Dear Heart, but we cannot trust for how long. We must leave now.~

He ignored the protests of the terst turn-born, meeting the sober gaze of purpled eyes.

"Then that," Jenn Nalynn said quietly, "is what we shall do."

EIGHT

ANCESTORS DIRE AND Dubious, the cave holding the turn-borns' crossing to the Westietas Estate looked less appealing than before and was, purple thorns having sprouted around its black mouth while Jenn was with the terst turn-born. Hardly fair, she complained to herself, to face pointy teeth along with all else, even of a botanical nature.

Not that you knew for sure in the Verge.

She didn't care for dark holes like this cave, was the truth of it, no more than Mistress Sand—who'd reiterated her dislike of the mine at Gordit with unfortunate frequency, given that was where she'd aimed Bannan. A dangerous journey Jenn meant to stop as quickly as possible, at least until they could discuss it and make a safer plan. Starting with going into this hole—

A noisy crunching startled her. "Imp!" she remonstrated.

~My apologies. Elder sister,~ it added somewhat tentatively, as if unsure her reaction.

Ancestors Witness, Jenn didn't mind that—"elder sister" was friendlier and more Marrowdell, while Imp drooled in distress when forced to say "turn-born." A wonder it remained coherent, having been trapped in the enclave with the lot of them.

What she did mind was Imp's random crunching. It must have tucked the hard candies in its cheeks like a squirrel. Not what she'd imagined a dragon doing.

A question for Wisp, as was keeping Imp's taste for sweets under control, those scarce and precious this time of year in Marrowdell.

While the young dragon held everyone's attention, the terst cows dropped from their leader's pouch and hurried to sample the thorns, believing their leader had brought them to food. They chewed and chewed, unimpressed. She would find them better; they'd only to be patient.

As for how they'd managed to follow two turn-born and two dragons in and out of the enclave to this crossing without notice, terst cows had perfected *following* long ago, which was why they shimmered out of sight before returning to the safety of their leader's pouch—Jenn Nalynn's dress having deep pockets—and the cows were content this was so.

Mistress Sand examined the cave opening a third time, appearing more dubious than before. ~Sweetling, are you certain, na?~ she asked at last. ~Stay with us and safe.~

A low snarl from near Jenn's knee.

~Think you care the most, dragon lord, na?" Sand snapped. ~Think you're alone in your concern for our brave Sweetling, na?~

Jenn took the turn-born's hand. Reached the other in the direction of her dragon and was it her imagination, that her fingers brushed scales? "Ancestors Beloved and Blessed," she said gently. "I'm Beholden for the love surrounding me—"

CRUNCH.

"And for all of your care," she finished over it. "However far we are apart—"

Sand's grip tightened on hers. ~Don't say the rest, Dear Heart. Not this time.~

Jenn nodded, finishing to herself, *Keep Us Close.*

Then it was time to let go and stride ahead, which she did and briskly, turning glass and pearl before any of the thorns could touch her, in case, and feeling the whoosh of air as an invisible dragon and probably two swept ahead of her to the crossing.

Along with the two terst cows in her pocket.

"Cook sent me."

A young voice—Werfol! Kydd's head turned, the blindfold safely in place.

"TAKE IT OFF! SHOW US!"

Unlikely but terrifyingly possible, that the distant mage heard through his ears as well as saw through his eyes, and he'd not risk naming the boy. Kydd held out his hand in welcome.

A small callused hand found his, gripped tight. "Marrowdell. Is everyone well? Uncle told us about the flood."

The beekeeper pulled the boy into his arms, burying his face in hair fresh washed, by the scent, and a little damp. "Very well," he replied huskily. "But you, Dear Heart? We heard—your horrific experience—"

"A chance to learn, as Momma says." Werfol patted *him* on the back. "We're worried about you, sir."

Kydd touched his blindfold. "We may be overheard," he warned.

"SILENCE!"

Pain didn't matter, but the volume inside his bones made him wince.

Werfol didn't miss a beat. "I've come to tell you your bath is ready, sir." With the politely distant warmth of a well-placed servant. "Cook suggests you not tarry. You do smell. Sir."

Clever lad. Loath as he was to rise from sumptuous upholstery of a chair like none he'd sat in since Avyo, Kydd put his hands on the arms and pushed. To no avail. Where was his strength?

Someone larger than a boy helped him stand, pulling his arm over wide shoulders to guide him forward. The man didn't speak; Kydd gave a nod of silent thanks. Heart's Blood, the more he could keep from the spy inside him, the better.

In what seemed a smaller room, warm and moist, the man indicated he should feel his way around. Finding the toilet, Kydd was given a moment to relieve himself. When he knocked to indicate he was done, the boy and man returned—if they'd left at all.

He shouldn't be too silent. "Smells good in here." The bath felt huge and luxurious; Kydd felt a twinge of guilt, thinking how there wasn't such in Marrowdell for Peggs.

They'd the trout pond, he told himself, with its sparkling clear water. Delectable sponge baths, in the dark after Radd and Aunt Sybb were abed, and the thought of those lanced his heart with longing.

"Let me help you with your coat, sir," Werfol offered.

He mustn't touch the pin! Kydd flinched backward into the tub. Before he could trip and fall into it, with reassuring quickness the man had him.

Plucking at his coat, he fumbled for the other's forearm, gripped it, mouthed, *Take it!*, then pointed to his pocket, shaking his head violently in warning.

"*LET US SEE LET US SEE LET US—*"

His coat lifted from him. Hand on the wall, Kydd made a shooing gesture, mouthing *AWAY! DANGER!*

In any other house, he'd have been judged rattled or losing his wits, but this was the home of the Westietas and Kydd listened to rapid footsteps, heard the closing of a door, and felt faint with relief they'd believed him.

But it wasn't just relief making his head spin. Ancestors Blessed and Beholden, it was *absence*. The voice—the pain—were gone!

Waving the boy to one side, Kydd tore off his blindfold, blinking at the lamplight, at his reflection in a generous mirror, then spotted Werfol tucked into a shadow and almost invisible.

Clever indeed. "We're safe now," he declared, leaning his back against a wall, relishing the return of his sight and what it meant.

"There's something in your coat," Werfol guessed, taking a step forward. The young truthseer's eyes turned molten gold, ready to catch a lie, and Kydd didn't blame him.

"A pin like flowers. In the lower pocket. It's bespelled—you mustn't touch it," Kydd warned sharply. "Your mother mustn't. I cast a spell to let me pass unharmed through Bannan's door; the pin corrupted it, allowing someone else to use my eyes."

A curt nod. "To find us."

Not a question about spellcasting or magic doors, but straight to the point. "To find those with gifts," Kydd qualified, in case there were others in the building. He glanced at the waiting bath and couldn't help a sigh of longing.

Werfol's lips twitched, the gold in his eyes fading away. "Can you manage on your own?" When Kydd nodded, he raised his arm, sleeve dropping back to reveal a crude string bracelet, identical to the one Kydd found around his wrist. "Don't take it off. I'll warn the guard and Momma about the pin then be right back."

"I'm beholden—"

"Save your thanks, sir, till I earn them."

The beekeeper raised his eyebrows.

Werfol ducked his head, glancing up through unruly hair with a cheeky grin. "It's why I'm here. Cook asked me to check on Peggs for you. I'll need something she's touched."

Truedreamer. Eyes dimmed this time with welcome tears, Kydd pulled off his shirt and passed it to the amazing boy, unable to say a word.

Vowing to protect Werfol—and his family—from the Heirs, no matter the cost.

Her step . . .

Landed on stones. Steadying herself, for the stones formed a slope, Jenn looked around, greatly relieved to find herself where she should be. The Westietas Estate. The forest formed a cup around her, leaves dappled with sunlight—though the sun had gone behind the huge and not yet familiar mountain, making this much later than she'd hoped.

She was losing track of time. Let alone what day it was.

A question to ask—someone. Jenn gazed around eagerly, but there was no sign of her love. Or anyone else, for that matter.

Overlooked, the terst cows hopped from her pocket into the shade of a stone, nostrils flared. Their delighted gaze fell on the lush, if unfamiliar, greenery so close. Their leader had brought them to food!

Without a sound or a tumbled pebble, they lumbered to it. Growing larger and larger, invisible still, they reached up their great arms to harvest what tasted wonderful indeed, if nothing like kaliia. Though as they were nigh to starving they might not have cared. Here was the proof they had chosen wisely and both kept a watchful eye on their leader; they would follow her forever and be content.

A stone *chimed* near Jenn's feet. "My apologies," she said, moving aside at once, though other than during the turn a scree was impossible to distinguish from—for those lacking true sight—an actual rock, of which there were uncountable plenty on the mountainside.

Still, it was someone. She bent down. "Excuse me, where might I find Bannan Larmensu?"

A dozen stones rolled full tilt into one another, producing a melodic series of *chimes* and a distinct *clank*.

Dragonish laughter. A breeze in her ear. "Dear Heart, scree can't talk to the likes of us."

"Wisp!" She waved her hands urgently, to speed her dragon. "Hurry, please! Find Bannan and Kydd!" Heart's Blood, what if her love had gone outside the edge already?

What if Kydd hadn't survived the crossing—

"I will." A more substantial breeze nudged her downhill. "The place he made you is close." Somehow, her dragon managed to add a note of disapproval to what Jenn thought sounded amazing. "You should go there while I search."

"Of course I should," she exclaimed, and began to run in the direction his breeze pushed her.

Behind her the terst cows roused to follow, unhurried and snatching mouthfuls of clover as they shrank.

Jenn had only gone a few strides when something caught her eye. She stopped. There, in the forest.

Between the healthy trees were stumps, mossy and rotting, but big. Stumps she'd seen before, when they'd first tried to cross. "Wisp, I owe you an apology." She pointed. "We crossed here, as you said. But not to now," words sending a shiver down her spine, because it took years and years to regrow a forest, making the snow and burnt stumps from a past before she'd been born. Maybe before Aunt Sybb. "You were right."

"I was." A breeze tossed her hair over her head and into her eyes. "I am. From here on, you must follow me, Dear Heart. The limit of the edge comes close." A note of scorn. "There are stones placed to mark it, but the scree play with them."

Putting the Westietas home close as well, out of sight behind trees. And, there, a path no doubt leading to it—

A path not for her. Jenn had stood high on the Spine and at the edge of the Sweet Sea. Seeing the world beyond the edge, where she couldn't go, no longer felt frustrating. She'd ample places to explore, for one thing.

For another, and more importantly, it meant turn-born magic—her magic—had limits over and above those she imposed on herself. Protection for those outside and blissfully unaware, a constraint against those thinking to come to the edge and use magic for ill.

Jenn nodded to herself, comforted as she went after Wisp. She'd tell Peggs all this, impress her sister with her mature attitude. Of course, Peggs would immediately poke her in the ribs, to make sure she didn't get too mature.

Following her dragon was a matter of catching glimpses; he wouldn't reveal his entirety in a strange place. Jenn glimpsed a spiked tail and hurried after it. A hint of wing. Wisp, her first and oldest friend, kept her safe, and she smiled to herself.

He led her through the first of the trees to a ruined building, about the size of Uncle Horst's home, the smallest in Marrowdell before the addition to house Hettie and her family. Sunbeams painted moss and mushrooms, wood stained with damp and rot, and this couldn't be it. Jenn almost turned away.

But didn't, there being something not right in what she saw. The corners were too crisp. The roof should have fallen in long ago, and why hadn't a tree or several grown up inside?

And now that she thought of trees, why, where were the berry bushes and ferns that should grow against and into the old and neglected logs forming the walls?

A trick. Another time, Jenn might have clapped her hands at the cleverness of it. Instead, she got busy trying to find the way inside, hoping beyond hope at any instant her love would appear and laugh and guide her—

A knot in a piece of wood depressed itself. Pushed by an invisible dragon who'd seen this already, and Jenn almost danced with impatience as the marvelously disguised door swung open.

No one came out. She hurried inside, hardly seeing what was there in her need to find—she stopped in her tracks. Breathed out "Bannan." Inhaled a shaky sob, for despite better sense, how she'd hoped he'd be here.

"There's no one upstairs, Dear Heart," Wisp told her before she noticed the ladder to what had to be a loft and she sat, there being chairs and a table.

They'd missed him. "We're too late." Or too soon. Whatever this was, it felt terrifyingly like failure. "If I'm to fix what's broken," she whispered, "I have to close his door—how can I do that when I don't know where he is?"

A soft breeze ruffled her bangs. "Don't tell my old enemy, but he's one tactic of use now. Wait in ambush," Wisp advised, grim and sure. "Wait here, Dear Heart, and let me flush our quarry to you. If Bannan has come to this place and left, I will find him or, failing that, the young truthseer, who should know where he's gone. If Bannan hasn't arrived before I return, I'll cross to Marrowdell to stop him, then come for you."

"The crossing—" Jenn swallowed, thinking of snow where none should be. Thinking of Bannan's door they dared not use. "What if it—what if it fails again?"

"I'll try twice. That worked, did it not?" Bold, now, her dragon, his blood up for a hunt, and who was she to doubt him?

Fear for him, yes. "Ancestors Blessed, please be care—"

Tinkle.

Jenn jumped to her feet, looking everywhere for what, by the sound, was a rather little bell—

THUD!

That came from overhead. *CRASH!*

Wisp ROARED.

A fraught—all too familiar—silence fell.

Oh dear.

Fearing she knew the answer, Jenn asked, "Where's Imp?"

Crossing with Edis, her muscular arm locked around his waist, was more plunging into a lake than taking a step forward. Familiar with the sensation, Bannan held his breath and closed his eyes, trusting he'd be alive to open them—

—albeit somewhere else.

Edis would cross into the Verge before taking them to Gordit, so the truthseer readied his deeper sight, preparing to see through the Verge's distortion.

But when he opened his eyes, it was to find himself in a lake after all—

Not of water but of boiling mimrol!

He'd no time to draw a breath to scream—magic scalded his skin and boiled his flesh. With a faint *Larmen*—the key around his neck melted and next went his bones—

As all of him *BURNED*—

The soothing bath was wasted on him, Kydd too anxious what Werfol might discover while truedreaming Peggs. After sluicing off most of the dust, he got out and dried himself. Finding a stack of fresh clothing on a shelf, he dressed quickly, finished just in time, by a sudden commotion in the other room.

Doing up shirt buttons, Kydd went through the door to find Lila and her head guard, instead of Werfol, with no sign of Bannan.

He refused to worry. The truthseer had left him in his family's care. Kydd bowed. "I'm beholden—"

"Your journals are gone," the baroness interrupted. "My guard, Ebra Bobbieb, went missing with them." A pause like the lifting of a sword. "But lo, Kydd Uhthoff can see."

The runner. Why hadn't he warned them not to put the foul things in a single pair of hands? The probable answer, that he'd been influenced as well, roiled his stomach and made no difference to the result. "Don't blame your Bobbieb," Kydd said heavily. "It was the journals' influence—or one from outside." He touched beside his eye. "This? The pin I gave your servant. Once it was re—"

"I blame you. You brought curses into my house, to my family." Ice in her voice, fury in her eyes, and, as Lila's hand dropped to her sword hilt, Kydd knew himself in mortal danger.

There was but one way out of it. The truth. "Yes, I did."

Her fingers wrapped around the hilt, tightened.

"I will not use my good intentions as an excuse," he continued. "You've no gauge of my heart. No truthseer could tell you if I lied. If I were you, baroness, Ancestors Witness, I'd kill me."

Those fingers loosened. Tapped irritably as she glared at him. "Heart's Blood, I'm not about to murder Jenn Nalynn's brother-in-law. You know that."

"I hoped that," he replied honestly.

"You've sorely vexed me, Kydd."

"Someone has." Feeling as if he walked on eggs, Kydd took a seat at the small table, with its tray, and gestured to the other chair, tense until Lila huffed and sat to join him.

She poured them each a glass of red wine. Lifted hers, and a challenging eyebrow, at him.

As with Bannan, he'd one chance to convince her. "The pin opened a door, of sorts. I heard a voice. In here." He touched his head. "I recognized it. Mage Prime Rose. Before you ask, I've no other name or a face. When I was a student in Avyo, she led the Heirs—the group

I belonged to then. Not since," this at a glitter in her expressive eyes. "Never again," with feeling. Kydd took a small sip.

"This mage gave you the pin?"

He shook his head. "Peggs did, in all innocence. Magical objects find their way, you see, and the pin was bespelled at least twice. The first was a simple wishing for a child's joy, a gift for Melusine Semanaryas from her mother. Before leaving Avyo, Melusine gave the pin to Lady Mahavar, to keep safe until her daughter was grown."

"To die producing a second."

Did she note his shudder? Probably. Kydd shook it off. "Yesterday morning, the lady gifted the pin to Jenn, who left it with Peggs. None of us knew then a trap lay in wait. The Mage Prime's, to distort to her advantage whatever spell was cast using the pin."

"Whatever spell *you* cast." Lila's brow rose. "Kydd Uhthoff. Here I thought you kept bees and painted."

Heart's Blood, how he wished that were all. "I was—am a spellcaster," he admitted. "I used the pin in a spell to blind myself, to safely pass through Bannan's door and accompany my journals here, to you."

"A trap in a pin, set years ago." She nibbled a piece of cheese. Nodded for him to do the same. A moment passed. "Come now to me," Lila said quietly, fingering a pendant at her breast. "My husband collects artifacts from Channen, items of magic. Small, clever things. I've not noticed any such display of will."

"I can check them, if you wish."

A look. "You aren't joking."

"No." How to distill years of learning—Kydd held up a crisp, balancing a piece of cheese on it. "It's not just the pin. When the journals came out of hiding during the flood, Marrowdell reacted. It—the place, what lives there—wanted them gone and rightly so." He tipped the bread, letting the cheese fall into his open palm. "My journals are more than paper, ink, and binding, baroness. The spells inside are a temptation of the darkest sort—for me in particular, I confess—but they can, quite literally, lure anyone who has taken that path."

"Not Bobbieb," Lila snapped.

"She wouldn't have taken them of her own accord," he agreed. "Ancestors Dear and Departed, I fear she's dead by now, murdered by whomever the journals summoned." Kydd slumped back in his chair. "As for the pin—its malice was guided. Deliberate. It's a spy in your house. If we can destroy it, we must."

"If?"

A knock at the door halted Kydd's response. Just as well, he thought. He'd nothing concrete to offer, only a growing dread they dealt with those more potent than he'd ever been.

"M'lady, a signal from the cottage."

On her feet at once, Lila shot Kydd a questioning look. "Up to greeting whomever it is?"

He knew who he hoped it was. Kydd drained the last of his wine and, as he stood, tucked a hunk of cheese inside his shirt in case of dragons. "If it's Jenn, she can't come here."

A tiny smile. "Ryll, one of Emon's light coats for Master Uhthoff, please, then we'll be off."

Werfol popped out from behind the guard in the door, dressed in a coat and boots and clearly intent not to be left behind. At Kydd's questioning look, the boy shook his head.

No news, then, of Peggs. There hadn't been time, Kydd told himself. He'd nothing to worry about.

And nothing to be done if he did.

BURNING—

He found himself encased in ice.

Not dead. Unable to blink, Bannan fought to make sense of his surroundings.

Ice. Clear as glass and bitterly cold.

Cold but no pain.

Or he was, he thought grimly, unable to feel it, being frozen solid. Ancestors Battered and Bloody, did that make him dead twice over? Tir would be rightly pissed—

—Jenn devastated. He tried to struggle, tried to move—

Was shocked when a face appeared in front of his, a face with purple eyes and a crown of stone braid, and despite the resemblance, this wasn't Edis. Wasn't anything ever of skin and flesh and bone.

Wisps of blue light streamed around it. Lips like his curved in a gentle smile. *Be not afraid, brother.*

Words that filled him, not in the way he heard a house toad in the Verge—or a dragon.

A second face appeared. Edis!

With everything he had, he tried to speak, to beg answers, most of all to know if he was dead and these his mourners.

If he was dead, Bannan reminded himself, close to hysteria, then he was a Blessed Ancestor and by the teachings of priests able to listen to the living he loved. But all he heard was a pulsing beat in his head and he clung desperately to that sensation, to what it might mean.

Stars saw. This is my doing. Edis' lips formed a thin line. *My fault—*

No, sister. A hand of glowing pearl came into view to stroke Edis' arm. *The Verge is broken and took you astray. You pulled him here, that he might survive.* Purple eyes regarded him gravely. *Brother, you are very near death. Do you wish me to heal you?*

Heart's Blood, what kind of question was that?

The kind asked by a creature of magic, the same creature who he'd suddenly no doubt had healed a wounded Edis Donovar in a way that left her alive, yes, but no longer what she'd been. What did it say about him, that he hesitated—

Did he prefer death over such a change?

You won't become part-olm, brother.

Able to read his thoughts, was she?

Stars witness, this isn't fair! Edis rammed her fist into the ice. A crack formed, spreading thin jagged fingers in fits and starts. Bannan watched it, helpless to shift his gaze.

You have now and a promise, sister. Are you not glad of both?

Beyond the cracks, he watched Edis bury her face in her hands, but they weren't a woman's hands, they were something *other* with tiny stubs for fingers and no palm—

—were *hers* again, the hands Bannan remembered, long-fingered, strong, and scarred. She drew them from her face, staring at them as if astonished, then looked at her companion. *I am, sister. For now and a promise, and I thank you.*

The creature turned to Bannan, stroking away the cracks in the ice separating them, colors trailing her fingertip like the sky of the Verge or Wen Treff's hair and he wondered idly at such casual glory.

Wondered if he dared allow it close.

Wondered . . .

You are out of time, brother. Do you want to live?

The rich purple of her eyes was the same as in the depths of Jenn Nalynn's. Wordless, heart-deep longing filled him . . .

So be it.

Wisp flew up through the floor of the loft, surged past the roof, and hovered over the cabin, staring down in disbelief.

The youngling hung, wrapped in the metal thread that had once connected a small tower on the roof to another hidden in the trees beyond, its every struggle tying it tighter while pulling more things down.

The ruckus would draw everyone in earshot.

The girl wanted to find Bannan. On that thought, Wisp perched on a still-intact section of the tower to regard the hapless youngling if not fondly, then with satisfaction. ~Well done.~

Imp froze, staring up. ~It doesn't feel that way, Great Lord of Dragons.~

~The result is what counts,~ Wisp assured it, catching the thud of hooves in the distance. ~Hold still,~ this when the fool began to twist, setting the mass of metal and wood swinging. ~The young truthseer will assist you. Possibly,~ he added, before the notion of being helped went to the youngling's narrow head. ~Be patient.~

A muttered, ~Yes, lord.~

More hooves and, yes, orders. People were coming. *Better and better.* Wisp stretched.

~Lord?~

He canted a reluctant eye back down. ~What?~

~Will the young truthseer have sweets?~

Ridiculous creature. ~The guards,~ Wisp assured the youngling, ~will have swords.~

Maybe the metal thread would wring its neck.

NINE

IT WASN'T HARD to find Imp, though he remained invisible. Moonlight revealed a massive knot of wire and posts and fasteners hanging in midair, an end attached to a post leaning from the cottage roof. The young dragon, Jenn sighed to herself, had got itself into a thorough mess and broken what looked important—much as Wisp had torn holes in the dome protecting the terst village, dragons in general difficult companions—not that she could tell what this had been.

Or could she? She raised the lamp she'd found in the cottage, frowning. The wire must have gone from the roof, in the edge, into the forest, that wasn't. From there, why, it probably continued on to the Westietas home, beyond sight.

Wire was a strong and useful commodity, one the villagers scrounged from any bale or packaging. Davi, their smith, could pull iron into nails but neither bale wrap nor nail looked like this fine, flexible stuff—

—strong enough to snare a dragon.

Ancestors Treasonous and Traitorous, they'd set a trap! "Hold still, Imp," she ordered as the suspended mass shifted unhappily. "We'll get you out."

A breeze stroked her cheek. "Must we, Dear Heart? The youngling will only cause more trouble."

A different breeze, this hot and fetid, found Jenn's other ear. "Leave it to us, turn-born."

Another, slightly higher, "Long since we've tasted dragonflesh."

"As if either of you have," Wisp replied, sounding reassuringly amused.

Two kruar stepped from shadow to moonlight. Dauntless and Spirit—names they'd earned and bestowed by Bannan—now living with Werfol and Lila. When Jenn last saw them, the pair had been near death, having come close to running their hearts out to save Werfol.

In their guise as horses, they looked well-groomed and healthy, Dauntless a chestnut mare with a short black mane, Spirit, a bay with black points. It was in how they stalked closer and closer, heads low and red eyes aimed at poor Imp, forked tongues catching drool from what wasn't remotely the mouth of a horse, that gave away the fact these were fearsome predators.

Inside their leader's pouch, the terst cows shivered, though they knew themselves safe.

Suddenly, both kruar turned to stare at Jenn with—was that *hunger*? While she did owe them for their help in the Verge and Channen, if they wanted bacon or some other snack, she'd nothing to offer, and, Jenn reminded herself testily, they'd a stable of their own—

Spirit took a step. "I smell terst."

Dauntless snorted and stamped a foot. "A turn-born was here."

Apparently satisfied on that count, the two swung their big heads upward. Imp whimpered.

"No one of any sort is being eaten, thank you," Jenn said firmly, fists on her hips. "Can you tell me where Bannan is?" Because while she intended to free Imp, this opportunity wasn't to be missed.

"The truthseer?" Spirit's head lowered, nostrils flaring. "He was here not long ago."

Bother. Jenn couldn't help a glance at where she thought her dragon might be.

"The truthseer's scent is everywhere here, Dear Heart," Wisp volunteered, his tone managing to diminish the kruars' sense while sounding not the least apologetic about his own, though dragons weren't, as a rule, scent hunters.

Dauntless' head jerked around, aimed at the path. A joyful, "She comes!"

"She" could only mean Lila Westietas. "We tripped an alarm," Jenn concluded, immediately self-conscious. She combed her fingers through her hair, pushing back what felt a mess, then brushed the front of her shirtwaist. The skirt—and her bare feet—were soiled, but there wasn't that much light. The baroness might not notice—

And, in the best of outcomes, Bannan came with her?

Her love wouldn't care at all.

Araben Sethe poked Semyn's shin with her booted toe.

Startled, he glanced up from his reading.

The Ansnan engineer tipped her head at his father, sitting beside her in the coach. Despite the lamplight, Poppa was sound asleep—he'd the useful knack of napping anywhere and anytime, according to Momma—and his head had slipped down to rest on Macle's shoulder, which couldn't be a comfort to either man, Macle in light armor and Poppa's head a considerable weight. And responsibility, from the way Macle sat braced in the corner as if afraid to move, and didn't look about to sleep, ever again.

Hiding a grin, Semyn looked back to Araben, who was grinning, a big, bold grin from ear to ear, a grin making his lips twitch in answer, so he kicked her back to remind her of Poppa's dignity and his own.

She stuck out her tongue.

Squeezed between Dutton and Elsa, he felt the latter give a muted chuckle and, with a sigh, Semyn marked his place and closed his book. He'd thought to catch up his study while the coach rolled along the excellent road from Mondir to Gordit, noting to himself that smoothness showed where Ansnan funds were being spent. Their engineer, however, appeared as bored by the journey as his brother would have been.

He and Werfol had taught Araben a few of their hand signs; she'd taught them Ansnan ones, which the guards pretended not to know, that being diplomatic, Momma said. What Semyn signed emphatically to her now was, he hoped, *Stop that.*

Make me. She tipped back her head and slouched in her seat.

If it came to it, Araben might be worse than Werfol.

She didn't act her eighteen years, was the problem. Momma had married Poppa at eighteen to become a baroness and take charge of a household—and her own small army, but no one mentioned that—and would never have stuck out her tongue in public.

Admittedly she did at times kick people under the table, but only when necessary.

He was better behaved at nine, appreciating the weight of responsibility this trip entailed. While he'd planned to ask Poppa to make a surprise visit to Gordit, to confront Elder Cotalen about the transports his town hoarded, this was another sort of venture altogether and far riskier.

Cotalen had swooped in before Semyn could bring up the topic, inviting them all—including those around the table and Poppa's Ansnan engineer—to Gordit's inaugural Peace Day celebration, that new holiday declared by Prince Ordo to mark his treaty. Surely, he'd said, all involved in plans for the Eld train should come.

Sher Moreau and Netej Hase had declined, as had the Ansnan, Kenton. Chancellor Milne, with Jellicoe Dee, Kluet Gore, and Limoges from Mondir, followed in the chancellor's coach. Naturally, Elder Cotalen and his staff had rushed out to arrive first and get ready for them—not an ideal situation.

Because celebrations and parties, Semyn well knew, were about outward civility and pending bloodshed, and you couldn't relax for an instant—or consume anything until a guard discreetly tasted it. Giving those from Gordit time to prepare increased the risks.

Araben pointed to his book. About to refuse, Semyn shrugged

and handed it to her, a little curious what she'd make of it, for the pages inside had nothing to do with the cover, being his watch notes. Words and names Momma wanted him to mark and pay attention to; terms and processes Poppa needed him able to use easily, in a company familiar with one kind of train—but not the sort the Eld would bring.

He watched her turn pages. Odd, feeling exposed by her attention. He shouldn't be. Araben was, by Momma's standards as well as Poppa's, a highly trusted ally. Indispensable, Momma had told Semyn in private before they left, meaning it was up to him to be sure their guards treated Araben with the same care they gave him.

To Semyn's dismay, Araben pulled out the stub of a pencil, licked the tip, then began scribbling in his book!

He kicked her, hard.

Without looking up, or stopping, she signed *Stop that* with her free hand.

Semyn was paralyzed. Heart's Blood, what was he to do? Kick her again? Even their guards might take exception to that, and Poppa—

—was awake. Not only awake, but reading what Araben scribbled in his heir's very private notebook and, to Semyn's dismay, the look on Poppa's face wasn't disapproval.

It was the look Momma described as intrigued.

Araben stuck her pencil stub into the braid over her ear and passed back his book, open to where she'd been writing.

Semyn took it gingerly, ready to be angry. But instead of defacing it, she'd added words. Words in Ansnan.

Words about the operation of trains in their mines, trains that weren't pulled by oxen, but by chains connected to water wheels. Astonishing—

There, she'd crossed out some of the terms he'd had, replacing them with newer, better ones. Heart's Blood, this, THIS, was why she was here, with them.

Looking up, he signed *thank you* before realizing he could speak aloud and felt himself blush. "This is wonderful, Araben. I'm beholden." Then Semyn turned the page and handed his book back to her, rewarded by her big, bold grin.

A guard with a lantern on a pole came first, followed by three figures, those followed by two more guards. Although none were Bannan, someone special indeed had arrived, and Jenn rushed forward with a glad cry to wrap her arms around Kydd. "You're here!"

Then pulled back to scowl at him. "Heart's Blood, what were you thinking, Kydd, to leave Peggs for some books?!" Seeing his face crumple with remorse and grief, she tugged him close again, resting her cheek on his chest. "I am glad you made it through the door safely," which was true and important, much as Bannan shouldn't have let him and they'd talk about *that*. "And that you didn't stay blind," she added, having no faith in spells.

"As am I, Dear Heart," he said shakily, pressing his lips to her hair. "Alas, all was for naught," a whisper. "We lost my journals."

All things considered, a fortunate outcome, in Jenn's opinion. Now, to see that Kydd—

"You broke it."

At that too-familiar accusation, Jenn released her sister's beloved and whirled to meet a glare she most certainly didn't deserve. *This time.* "Greetings to you, Baroness Westietas." She did not curtsy. "Where's Bannan?"

"Jenn Nalynn. I don't know where my brother is, at the moment. What have you done to my husband's equipment?"

"There's a dragon stuck in it," a small voice offered cheerfully. "Hello, Aunt Jenn!"

Heart warmed by the salutation, Jenn bent to take Werfol in a quick fierce hug. "And to you, Dear Heart." Less happy, she released the boy and stood to look at Lila. "You set a trap."

Lila's eyes were green, like Roche Morrill's. Unlike that young man, she didn't have to tell the truth, but Jenn thought she would, to her. Sure enough, "Not its original purpose," lips twisting. "It is—was—Emon's signaling device."

The bell—but to signal what? The air grew chill despite the evening sunshine. "To warn of my arrival."

Werfol took Jenn's hand, his fingers cold, and at that reminder, she thought hurriedly of mucking out stalls and wiping baby noses. The warmth returned.

It left Lila's face. "Why would we need a warning, Jenn Nalynn?"

Jenn didn't need Kydd's flinch to know it wasn't safe or good to have this woman fear her. "Not about me," she replied. "I would never harm you or your family—or anyone," she finished, though that last likely wouldn't impress the martial baroness.

"It's true, Momma," Werfol said vehemently, his grip tightening on Jenn's.

Lila gave him an exasperated if fond look. "I know it is." Her gaze rose to Jenn. "Emon's device sends a signal either from here, or from the estate. A means for you and Bannan to let us know when you were visiting, and when you'd enjoy company."

Werfol looked up at Jenn, gold still brimming in his eyes. "And to warn you if anyone was coming, if you wanted to leave unseen. Did you like it? Inside?" the irrepressible boy continued. "We haven't been allowed in yet, but Semyn and I are to use it when you aren't here as our—" a lightning glance at his ominously quiet mother "—study room. When the house is busy." His gaze came back to Jenn, dipped to stare at her dress.

The stains. "I've been traveling," she mumbled.

But Jenn was wrong about the reason for Werfol's attention. The two terst cows had climbed up to cling to the top of her pocket to peer out with their rheumy little eyes, curious and certain they were invisible.

In that, they were wrong, for the young truthseer saw them very well.

What Jenn saw was Werfol's grin, a mysterious and mischievous grin that made his mother frown. "We need to speak to Jenn about your uncle—in private." Before Jenn could argue she was ready this instant to know about Bannan, Lila added smoothly, "And Kydd should sit."

He did seem unsteady on his feet. Giving in, Jenn took hold of his hand and pointed at the imprisoned dragon. "We must free Imp."

"Without cutting the wire." At Jenn's frown, Lila gave a careless shrug. "It's not easily replaced. Emon would be heartbroken."

An exaggeration, though on the good side, what she could see of the wire looked intact. Because Imp didn't care for the taste?

Before it thought to try, Jenn quickly ordered, "Imp, don't bite the wire."

"Bite?" A brisk breeze tossed her hair. A section of wire developed a sharp bend. "BITE!" Joyous and overloud—

Why hadn't she remembered Wisp's regular complaint that the youngling didn't listen—or didn't hear—what went against its desire? In this case, to be free.

"STOP THAT!" Werfol shouted back.

"There's candy," Jenn offered quickly. "Might there be?" a quick aside to Lila.

Who, after an incredulous look, shook her head and gave the order to her guard. "Candy. Plus a ladder and tools to deal with this." She waved overhead.

"Would this do?" Kydd produced a handful of cheese from his pocket. The kruars' ears perked up.

Imp let out a desperate whimper, which might have been the distance between it and cheese—or any delay in the arrival of sweets—but how could they be sure the wire wasn't harming some more tender dragonish part?

And she wasn't about to wait for ladders and more strangers before hearing about Bannan.

Jenn put her hands on her hips and sent her version of Peggs' most quelling stare at the roof, where she assumed Wisp watched with dragonish glee while not being in any sense helpful. "Wisp, we could—"

A touch on her elbow. Having her attention, Werfol nodded at a moonlit patch of rock toward the crossing and winked.

Lila, now leaning her back on the cottage wall, one foot crossed over the other and apparently ready to wait all night, sighed. "There's two of them?"

"I told you, Momma. Wisp and Imp. Imp is the one stuck. Wisp," Werfol added because it was true and dragons listened, "would never get stuck." A breeze tousled his hair and he grinned.

Jenn turned to face the patch. "Wisp, please free Imp. Without damaging the wire," she added hastily, before her dragon used fire to melt it. "I know you can." More precisely, she hoped he could, Imp having created a tight gnarl with no ends in sight. But if Wisp couldn't do it, she doubted Lila's people could.

A breeze flipped her bangs. "But must I, Dear Heart? It squirms so deliciously. Are you sure?"

"Yes, and quickly, please," to forestall any argument about spoiling a lesson for Imp, who should, at the very least, have learned to avoid strung wire.

But likely hadn't. They'd need to hang ribbons or some such.

A wire twanged. Another twisted. Imp wailed, then promptly stopped.

Doubtless threatened.

Those below watched in fascination as more wires were tugged and bent, but gently. "He's not touching it," the young truthseer whispered in awe. "Wisp's using the air to move them."

Lila's gaze sharpened.

Her dragon, Jenn thought—having untangled her share of wool skeins—was investigating, finding the path taken by any particular wire around Imp, trying to identify the first or the last, those being good starting points.

A pause.

Then every wire danced and jigged, poles and fasteners tumbling free so the people watching jumped back, the guard close to dropping the lantern pole, when all at once—

"FREE! I'M FREE!"

—as everyone winced at Imp's shout, the wire coiled itself midair into a tidy roll to drop lightly at Lila's feet.

"FREE!!! CHEESE NOW???!"

A loud *SMACK* answered that question. Werfol giggled.

Time for hers. Jenn looked at Kydd, then Lila. "Where's Bannan?"

Heights didn't bother him.

Until now. Bannan kept his back pressed to the rock wall of an immense cavern, toes overhanging the ledge where he'd found himself.

Before—was vague and disturbing. Fingers of ice had torn and stitched, and if, as it seemed, he'd been rebuilt from within, he'd no idea from how deep. Had he been mere bones after all? Less?

Impossible. Like this place. Ice filled the space in front of him, a mass reaching beyond the limit of his sight. It shone with its own light, as did the massive icicles looming just overhead. A fool might reach up and touch one.

He hadn't been a fool until agreeing to this.

Black water, white froth, swirled and tossed around the base of the ice, as if an iceberg from the northern sea had been lost and trapped here. *Things* cavorted in those deadly waves. Olms. While familiar with Ansnan myths about the cave-dwelling creatures, these were giants of their kind and kin to the two with him.

Not to him, Ancestors Blessed; the one who'd healed him hadn't lied about that. Easy to tell, for his clothing—his key, Lila's purse—hadn't survived the burning any more than his old scars and farmer's tan.

How much more had he lost? How much had the creature replaced—and with what?

Heart's Blood. How would he know? How could he—

Queasy, Bannan shoved such questions aside, determined to focus on the most pressing one. What next?

Go to Jenn. The speed and overwhelming force of that desire made him dizzy—and terrified. What would she see? The man she loved or something else and while he felt like himself, that hardly constituted proof.

Go to Lila. And what, tell his sister he'd almost died but was fine now, because he owed his continued existence to a magical creature of the Verge without knowing what bargain he'd made—or if he was still entirely flesh?

Naked flesh at that. "I can't go anywhere like this," Bannan complained, it being easier than thinking, startled when motes of blue floated up from his mouth.

The figure dancing within the ice redirected her steps toward him, leaving trails of color. Stepping free, she moved somehow through the air, or he did, or the world did, coming to stand before him on a sheet of endless ice where before had been the ledge.

Unable to trust the footing, Bannan wasn't sure it was an improvement.

Where would you go, brother?

He should have remembered she could read his mind. "As this?" he asked, trying not to sound bitter.

Edis, who spoke aloud now as well, actually chuckled, her voice sending up a distractingly pretty cloud of blue dots. "Don't worry." Curling down, she reached into the ice and produced an armload of clothing, complete with boots.

Our brother fears to show those he loves what he's become, sister. Woeful, this, and Bannan felt a surge of guilt.

He bowed, touching fingers to the ice. Rising, he brought his circled fingers over his heart—hoping it was his. "Hearts of my Ancestors," he managed to say, looking through blue motes, "I'm beholden to you for your gift and truly grateful to be alive. I just—" Only the truth would serve, with a being of such power and grace. "I don't know what I am."

Brother. A hand of ice, or was it warm stone?, rested briefly on his cheek. *Brother I call you and you have always been.* A wave of *caring* swept around and through him, a love without judgment or request, and he didn't deserve it.

Captain Ash didn't.

"Why?" he asked roughly. "Why do you care about me? Why heal me?"

Amusement, gentle and warm.

Edis clapped him on the back, her palm stinging his bare new skin. "Our sister's healed your body. Here, you can heal yourself. Shed the darkness within you, as I did. Lose your hate."

Lose *more* of himself? Repulsed, Bannan shook his head.

She shrugged. "Your choice. Stars know, you might need it, where you're going."

"And where am I going?" he asked wryly, for he certainly didn't know.

"You've a mission." Edis held up a miner's hat.

Mission. The word settled a world tending to spin. "Gordit," Bannan confirmed.

To help the turn-born. To protect Jenn and Delfinn. To learn what he was.

Then he thought of the crossing to get there.

Actually, what he thought was of plunging into boiling mimrol and horrible death, not that he imagined staying here forever, but it seemed better than the alternative—

Go, brother and sister. The creature floated away, the ice beneath Bannan's feet once more the narrow ledge above an abyss of water, ice, and olms. She stepped inside the massive iceberg, spinning on a toe, blue wisps around her, light trailing from her outstretched fingertips. *I will calm the Verge for you.*

Edis curled, lowering her head. "Thank you, sister."

Find your way here again, when that is your wish.

With that, they were alone.

"So we're doing this?" Bannan asked. He looked askance at the clothing Edis held out, there being no room on the ledge to change.

She grinned, tucking the clothes under an arm, boots in that hand, and reached for him.

"We're doing this."

Jenn Nalynn led the way into the cottage. The guards stayed outside and, after a brief exchange of words with his mother, Werfol came in to sit beside Kydd on the settee, hands folded and feet together, the epitome of politeness.

Or judging it safer.

Her stiff back to the room, Jenn stood at the mirror where a window should be. She'd pulled the curtain to find it, stayed there. Studied her reflection or them. Perhaps, Kydd thought, she saw the one she wished were here, instead.

Lila looked at her, then at Werfol. Finally, she shrugged and said bluntly, "You didn't miss him by much. Edis took Bannan to Gordit a couple of hours ago. He said to tell you, if you came."

Jenn gave a tiny nod.

Upset with him, he knew, and in need of answers. "I wasn't—myself," Kydd said carefully. "Not when I had Bannan bring me through his door. When I left Peggs." He braced himself. "She agreed I should go, but neither of us knew then I was being influenced by a spell."

"You'd blame a pin." Jenn's gaze rose to meet his reflection's. "Imp called you a wizard."

"I'm not! Not like Tralee," he qualified, determined to be truthful. "But you're right, Jenn. The guilt is mine. Before Marrowdell I wasn't just a student. I was being trained to cast spells, dark ones. Peggs knows."

"She knows now," Jenn said, and frost rimed the mirror. She traced it with a finger. "Your past. Your secret. It's why you hesitated to court my sister." Her finger stopped. "Would you have told her if the yling hadn't found your journals?"

Breath fogged in the chill air, Kydd bent his head. "I wanted to forget."

Werfol scowled. "The truth. The one he believes," with a calculated look.

"I swear I've done all I can to leave that past behind." Kydd gave a hopeless little shrug. "I thought I had."

The boy's scowl faded. "You made mistakes." A nod. "Everyone does—well, except Momma." This with a sly glance her way.

Ignoring the cold—and her pert son—Lila knocked lightly on the table. "This pin of yours, Jenn, was spelled into a tool to find us. My brother, my son. Me."

The lamplight dimmed. "Where is the pin now?" Jenn asked, very quietly.

Lila brought out a small bag, its velvet worked with mimrol. "Here."

"From Channen," Kydd breathed. In Avyo, mages had used bags like this, impermeable to magic, to carry their most valued tokens.

"Trust nothing from there," Jenn Nalynn said, turning around at last, her hand outstretched. "Give that to me." Her eyes were more purple than blue and the air felt close and heavy, hot where an instant before it had felt like winter. "Now."

And with the word, her hands turned to glass, glass filled with light, and it wasn't the light of this world—

Werfol jumped to his feet. "Stop, Jenn! You're scaring Momma."

Lila raised a brow, her expression serene. A mask, Kydd knew, and not a wise choice, to hide honest feelings in such a moment. Jenn was as close to fury as he'd ever seen her come, and Peggs had warned him her power wasn't always under her control.

Heart's Blood, then there was Wainn, the memory clear and still shocking of when his nephew had spoken for Marrowdell, as Marrowdell. When he'd said, *Time is breaking.*

The crossing. The time shift. A man with half his knowledge would be terrified by that, let alone to think he was in the same room as a being capable of it—and more.

Not a *being*. His dear sister-in-law, Jenn Nalynn. Who'd told Peggs to bake pie until the village filled with the scent and he'd come to the Nalynn kitchen window to beg forgiveness. Who'd soaked his cuffs in dishwater then brought him to every good in his life today, deserved or not.

Kydd got to his feet, walked to Lila and took the bag—relieved she let him and even more not to sense the pin—and handed the foul thing to Jenn, willingly touching her turn-born hand. "Dear Heart," he said gently. "We're family."

Her eyes searched his as if she were lost and his face the map home again, their purple fading to a sorrow-filled deep blue. Her hand became flesh and warm, as the room brightened, as the air returned to the warm caress of a summer's evening, and while part of him shuddered at what seemed a close escape from a force of magic beyond wizards and spells?

The better part leaned forward to tenderly kiss her cheek. "Thank you."

Jenn turned to Lila and Werfol, one hand in Kydd's, the other tucking the bag and pin into her bodice. "Forgive me. It's been a—" she appeared to search for the word.

"A day?" Lila finished for her, lips quirked.

"Yes."

The two were a match, Kydd decided, who wouldn't have thought it before. Determined to protect their loved ones, powerful in themselves, if the pair worked together he doubted there was anything they couldn't overcome.

If only Bannan's sister didn't see Jenn as a threat, a conviction he read in the tiny lines beside her mouth and the way her fingers twitched as if wanting the hilt of a sword. A conviction they had to change.

Kydd plucked a thorn from Jenn's hair. "Before you follow Bannan to Gordit—as I'm sure you intend, Dear Heart—I suggest a wash and change of clothes. Lila?"

A taut spring before, something eased, enough that the baroness' smile seemed sincere. "Easily and quickly done, Jenn. I'll summon Edis for you once you're ready. If that's how you'd like to, ah, get to Gordit?" she asked, having picked up a little hammer and a black stone.

"I don't know." A troubling flicker of unease in Jenn's face. "Crossings aren't safe. You mustn't try it," this to him, flat and sure. "No matter how much we want to know about Peggs."

Werfol jumped to his feet. "I'll truedream—"

"You will not," his mother commanded sharply. The boy sank back down. "I'll check on Peggs. Once," she qualified, "back home and secured."

"Baroness—" Kydd drew a shaky breath and bowed, surprised how much the offer meant to him.

"And I'll find Bannan," Jenn declared.

"Wait." Werfol was on his feet again. "Kydd's a great artist. He can draw the faces of people Jenn should watch out for—those who taught him to do dark magic. Can't you?" And those golden eyes blazed at him.

A challenge that was, worthy of his mother. Prove your worth to us, the boy meant. Protect those we care about.

Most of all, prove he was of Marrowdell.

And Werfol wasn't wrong. He might not have real names—or his journals—but some of those faces were etched in his memory beyond any forgetting.

Kydd sat at the table. "I'll need paper and pencil."

They'd made it, he was alive, and if Bannan needed proof, it was the awkwardness of dressing in front of what should have been disinterested eyes that weren't, by their twinkle.

"You could turn around," he suggested, buttoning his pants.

A chuckle. "Stars blessed, and miss a fine figure of a man like yourself?" Edis curled around herself, elbows on a convenient log—for they'd arrived in a woodland glade—and supported her chin in her hands, the better to leer at him. "Besides, you enjoy it. I can tell."

"When it's Jenn." At the thought of his love—at the thought of her seeing whatever the olm-creature had made of him—Bannan's hands stopped moving. "What am I to do, Edis?" he whispered.

"Shirt next—though I don't insist."

He shot her an angry look.

She made a face and turned serious. "From what I see, Bannan Larmensu, and I've paid close attention, you're just as you were. An ordinary—admittedly, better than ordinary—looking man. Well, other than your hair."

The first was reassuring, but the rest? Alarmed, Bannan's hand shot up. All felt normal and he grumbled, "A poor jest."

"No jest," Edis said blandly. "To eyes able to see, your hair holds the colors of the Verge. It's subtle—" at whatever she read in his face "—but there. I quite like it."

"Says the woman who's half olm." Who did not deserve his ire in any sense. The truthseer dipped his head in apology. "That was uncalled for, Edis. Forgive me."

Her lips twitched. "Been called worse, stars know." She ran the fingers of one hand through the leaf litter and grass, smiling when a cricket hopped away, serious when she again looked up at him. "I'm curious. What do you call Jenn Nalynn?"

Love. Life. "I know what you're doing," he snapped. "It's not the same—Jenn had no choice—"

Edis hooted. "That's what you think?" She shook her heavy head.

Of course it wasn't. Bannan knew full well the many choices Jenn had faced. Continued to face. To let herself die or become sei and turn-born. To risk herself, time and again, for him, for others, for Marrowdell. Heart's Blood, each and every time she chose to govern her incredible power, to decide when to use it—and, harder, when not, to do no harm.

This past Midwinter Beholding, the wonderful moment she'd sat at his side to watch those dancing below, and made the choice to live her life with him.

Softly, no less firmly, Edis went on, "The woman you love isn't just a woman. You don't love her regardless—you love her the more because of it."

Magic-purpled eyes, the way the air turned warm when Jenn smiled at him—then chilly when she'd realized what she'd done, so they'd wrap themselves in a blanket, laughing—"Ancestors Blessed," he said with wonder. "I do."

"Whatever you are now, Bannan Larmensu? Don't take that choice to love you from Jenn Nalynn." Done with sentiment, Edis snorted. "Get dressed. We've work to do."

He finished dressing in silence, more thoughtful than anxious—though Ancestors Witness, the truthseer told himself, he'd worry until Jenn met this version of himself and he knew how she felt.

Edis had brought him miner's clothes like Mistress Sand's, ubiquitous throughout Ansnor. An ideal disguise whether in town or, as he'd promised the terst turn-born, to let him enter Gordit's cursed mine. The pants, with their array of loops and pockets, were held up by shoulder straps, the loops meant to support weighty tools. A simple collarless shirt, but the jacket to go over it was thick and padded; the weather summer warm, he left it open.

The truthseer tried to ignore his new and flawless skin, down a lack of useful calluses on his heels making him glad for the socks and tall boots.

The hat was flat-topped and reinforced to support the small lantern at its front. Seeing the clip on the back, Bannan secured the hat to a pant loop. Done, he took stock of where they were.

The breaking dawn illuminated a peaceful landscape. The glade opened on pasture, verdant and sloping—as every patch of ground did in the foothills of the snow-topped Marbled Range. The Bloody Marbles, they'd called them in the war.

The Ascension Peaks, he corrected himself, shaking off memory and deliberately using their Ansnan name.

Where the pasture leveled out stood a tall festival tent, its sides raised to show tables inside and figures busy among them. Beyond the tent rose the town itself, smoke rising from bake ovens.

Gordit, preparing itself for a party—not what an Ansnan town would do for visiting Rhothan nobility, but tomorrow, if he hadn't lost all track, would be the longest day of the year. Summer's Day Festival, in Rhoth, where celebrants competed in sport, shared meals, and danced the day away.

In Ansnor, the day was considered the last chance to get away with whatever the Celestials would judge foolish or in excess, their attention safely elsewhere until the following night. Depending where in Ansnor you celebrated, it was variously called Fool's Day, Wild Day, or No Regrets.

Bannan took an educated guess. "Fool's Day?"

"More than usual." Edis reared up to look at the tent, her face clouded. "Tomorrow marks a year since I walked out of prison and you left the marches."

She didn't, he noted, say he'd stopped being Captain Ash. "The end of our forgotten little war," he commented.

"Your ridiculous prince has declared it our shared holiday. Peace Day, or some such nonsense." Edis spat, sinking back down to rest her chin on her arms.

Ordo's truce. While he'd no doubt believing the prince would declare a holiday in Avyo—to be ignored by those outside the city—co-opting the Ansnan Fool's Day was reckless even for his monumental ego. Granted, the solstice wouldn't always correspond, but this first year, with most of Ansnor drinking themselves stupid for the entire day and the Baron Westietas and his heir driving right into it?

If anything happened—"It'll start the war again," he predicted glumly.

"Trust me, no Ansnan cares enough. The only ones celebrating will be those who profited from the treaty—or believe they will." With resignation, "Stars witness, who doesn't like a gathering with free food and drink?"

Those who'd lost their lives or their homes, he thought bitterly. Bannan gave himself a shake. "Emon has to be aware." Ancestors Shady and Sly, wouldn't it be just like Lila, to take advantage of Fool's Day liberties—and loose lips—for her husband's first trip deeper to Ansnor?

Shading his eyes, he studied the mountainside rising behind the town, looking for the mine where Tooth had gone missing. There. Above a wide scarp, a rectangle of timbers marked the entrance. An entrance a goodly distance away on horseback, let alone on foot. "Why are we here and not there?" With a nod to the mountain.

Edis shrugged. "Here is where our sister put us, truthseer. She'd have reason."

"Or the Verge went awry. Again."

"Or that." Uncurling, she rose to look toward the mountain and the mine. "The edge goes from here to the town, then dips deep below ground into the mine. See it?"

"I don't—" Bannan closed his lips over the rest. He'd come to know this much about Edis. She'd reason for asking.

He might not detect the boundary, but would see what was hidden. The truthseer gazed out over the pasture and town, this time with his deeper sight.

The landscape peeled away, mountains disappearing, buildings gone. Instead, what he saw was mimrol, silver specks here and there—

—then, deep beneath, a mammoth lake of it, a lake that rushed closer and closer until he saw the surface roiled by angry waves, until he was drowning in it, *BURNING IN IT—*

Being shaken, hard.

His teeth clanged together, pain a welcome reality, and Bannan opened eyelids he didn't remember closing, careful not to invoke his deeper sight.

WAVES WAVES!

He shut his eyes again. Reached out. "Edis!"

A hand clasped his. Did she speak? He couldn't hear over a rising cacophony. The bedlam overlapped, surged up and down; impossible to discern if it consisted of words or songs or a nonsensical buzz. Clapping hands over his ears made no difference.

"Gift—see—too much," he gasped. "Hear—too much. Help—"

Edis pulled his hand from his ear and shouted in it, "I'll get—who can." He felt himself pressed down to sit. "Stay—"

Stay? Bannan choked on a laugh. How could he move when he couldn't trust his senses? "Edis?"

No answer.

The log nearby. Bannan went to shift his position to lean against it. His right arm and leg obeyed him.

His left did not.

Ancestors Battered and Besieged, this wasn't good—

Not, the truthseer assured himself, settling where he was, unexpected. He'd suffered a shock, to put it mildly, and only natural his gift was out of sorts. Injury had repercussions; he'd witnessed cases in the marches where an injured soldier's body became paralyzed or began to twitch uncontrollably, symptoms that passed with time.

Ancestors Witness, the like had happened to Tir, the day after losing the better part of his jaw to an Ansnan sword, and his friend had recovered.

But the thoughts wouldn't stop. What injury had he suffered, to cause this?

No, Edis had said he remained a man—

On the outside. *What about within—*

He'd a mission. People counting on him. He wouldn't fail them.

Bannan forced himself to take slower breaths. To think, Heart's Blood, about what was real and provable. What he'd seen—Ancestors Witness, he'd panicked, that was all, his gift gone wild for a moment.

Embarrassing, for someone of his training and hard-won skill, and he'd prefer his nephew and sister not find out. If his gift had changed, he'd adapt—

He wasn't to have the time.

"Who's this 'ere?"

Jenn had expected Kydd to ask her to return him to Marrowdell, but he didn't. Perhaps being sensible. He couldn't endure the Verge without another spell—*and look where the first had got him—*

Not, Jenn told herself sternly, that she was angry. But Ancestors Abandoned and Alone, her poor Peggs!

Who was surrounded by help and, to be fair to Kydd, he did appreciate how very important it was that she reach Bannan and help *him*.

As well as deliver the page of Kydd's sketches, safely folded and tucked away, a page covered with strangers' faces and false names. Lilac. Lavender. Daisy. Willow. Rose. Kydd had drawn a face for each save Rose, who he said had been foremost of the Heirs' leadership— who might still be, for he'd recognized her voice whispering to him through the pin.

The Mage Prime, he'd called her, saying it was likely she'd been the one who'd bespelled the pin, those years ago. Her hand reaching from Avyo to Marrowdell, and Jenn was ever so glad Peggs no longer had the foul thing—or Aunt Sybb, for that matter.

Lila and Werfol had watched Kydd sketch. The boy had gasped and looked up at his mother, who'd given a tiny shake of her head. They'd recognized someone—or more than one.

Instead of telling Jenn who, which would have seemed helpful and polite, the baroness had ordered her not to tarry for a wash or fresh clothes, but to make all haste to show the page to Emon as well as Bannan, the baron and their other son in Gordit as well.

Ancestors Witness, for a town she'd not so much as seen on a map before, this Gordit was fast becoming the center of trouble for too many of those Jenn cared about, not that she'd the faintest idea why. Lila wasn't about to tell her. The woman thrived on secrets. She'd probably set poor Kydd to make more sketches already. Would order her guard to arms or horse or whatever a baroness did when learning of an enemy, not for an instant relying on Jenn to do as she'd been asked.

Because Lila didn't trust her.

Imp tearing down the wires hadn't helped. Worse, Jenn sighed to herself, had been her misstep, becoming turn-born in the cottage as if the sight would impress the baroness and not make her afraid, which of course it had.

Jenn resolved to do better, once she'd an idea how, and Bannan would surely talk to his sister, not that she was at all certain Lila would listen. Right now, though, she was glad to be on her way. Heart's Blood, she'd happily leave all of it to Lila and forget about Heirs and dark magic, but that wasn't, were she honest, which Jenn tried her best to be, entirely true.

She wouldn't forget this Rose. Not when roses were her mother's flower and gift to her family, the living symbol of Melusine's love and Marrowdell's treasure. Not when this Rose had sent a curse to tear Kydd from her sister and who knew what else. *Rose* would not remain the alias of someone so dreadful. It must not.

Not, Jenn told herself, striving to be sensible, that she herself could or should do anything about it. She couldn't go beyond the edge, a significant handicap in searching for someone who could. And she mustn't, under any circumstances, let ill feelings take hold, as she had when angry at Mistress Sand. The consequences were unthinkable.

And it would change her. She'd only lately begun to learn who and what she was, being a work in progress, as Aunt Sybb would say.

Thinking of that dear lady, Jenn pressed her hand over her bodice, feeling the lump, cold and ominous, between her breasts. The bespelled pin. In a bag bespelled to keep whatever the pin did from any more doing, and it was all to do with—

Magic. Jenn sighed. Tir had been right to suspect it. How was she to tell Aunt Sybb, who'd brought the cursed thing to Marrowdell with such joyful intent, that it hadn't been her idea? Worse, that she'd unwittingly furthered some plot of the Semanaryas'. Of Melusine's mother, their grandmother, who—Ancestors Tormented and Tainted—might be this *Rose*. Or had hired the mage to work dark magic against her family, which was hardly better, and she'd no doubt Kydd and Lila thought the same.

Her head rose. No more. Ancestors Blessed, if the pin was her inheritance, it was hers to deal with, and that was that. At her first opportunity, she'd melt it as she had Crumlin's mirror and be done.

That settled, Jenn paid more attention to her footing as she climbed the slope above the cottage. Streaks of moonlight and shadow made it harder to avoid those she thought might be scree, but she didn't mind going slowly, having yet to decide how to go or where.

A decision to make soon. She'd promised to give Emon the sketches and would, but he'd be in Gordit and easy to find.

Bannan, on the other hand, would strive to complete his investigation quickly, to protect her and Delfinn if there were danger. He might even be done by now and in Marrowdell—

—except that her beloved, though the most accomplished and amazing person in her life, did occasionally underestimate the time a task would require. And had a charming faith in the speed with which those around him would move if they understood its importance. Why, just the other day—

Jenn's breath caught. She'd give anything to be home, on that other day, teasing Bannan while curling his thick black hair through her fingers.

How frustrated he'd been with Anton's slow and methodical squeezing of whey from the cheese curds he'd planned as a surprise for their supper, this after doing his best to speed up Zehr and Davi while they worked together on the Morrill home, the older men in favor of sitting on the porch to discuss the project over raising timbers in the heat of the afternoon, and, why, even Tir had got under his friend's skin, proposing a quick game of nillystones when there was, according to Bannan, no such thing and he'd wanted desperately to be home.

With her. Jenn almost smiled, remembering. So badly had he wanted to create the perfect evening for them before leaving to help with Werfol, he'd overdone himself in the heat and fallen asleep with his head in her lap.

Not, she recalled, that he hadn't recovered very nicely—

—Ancestors Foolish and Frivolous, how dare she imagine going back in time when going back in time was probably what was wrong with the crossings, or the Verge, or both—and maybe the edge as well, though it seemed normal.

For now.

So, was she to go first to Marrowdell? Jenn drew in a slow breath, reassured by the scent of pine and fern, then shook her head.

If to Gordit and the baron, she'd have to follow Bannan's lead. Lila had given her the little hammer and stone to use, as he had, to summon this Edis creature.

Who had, Jenn suspected, something to do with Roche Morrill, who was in Vorkoun at the moment, of all things, studying. He'd barely deigned to listen to Master Dusom—

Who, though free of yling, would be worried about his brother, meaning she should go to Marrowdell and maybe try to take Kydd with her after all—

No, she should go to Gordit. Jenn hefted the hammer. Closed her fist over it. What if Edis was helping Bannan at this very moment? She mustn't risk a summons that pulled her away from him—

A breeze tickled her cheek, sliding up to her ear. "Dear Heart, why are you standing still?"

She was? Jenn sighed. Of course she was. Afraid to make the wrong decision, she'd come to a stop rather than make any at all. Wisp knew her better than anyone, even Bannan. "I'm stuck," she admitted.

Another breeze, really more a small gale, shoved Jenn. "I WAS STUCK! I WAS—"

SNAP.

Silence. "Better," Wisp declared, and Jenn had no intention of asking if her dragon had actually bitten his student, though she supposed if he had there'd be blood and wailing. "You aren't stuck, Dear Heart," Wisp continued calmly. "Sand sent us here. Sand was wrong. We need to go back to the Verge and—"

"Come with me!"

A stranger's voice. Jenn whirled around to face what didn't, at first, seem a person at all.

The stranger curled up from the rocks like an enormous pale snake. She—for the upper torso was definitely a woman's—had a head and face shaped like Jenn's own, other than a helmet of braids. Those appeared to be stone and thus the helmet must be heavy, but there was no sign the weight troubled the stranger. She'd very strong-looking shoulders and arms, the pale skin of the latter dotted with pearls, and eyes of the deepest purple.

Jenn hadn't struck the rock with Lila's hammer, but she knew who this must be. "Edis. Edis Donovar."

Edis bowed more gracefully than anyone with legs or hips could. "And you are the famous Jenn Nalynn, turn-born and sei." She'd a striking face, worn by care and scarred. Though laugh lines creased the edges of her eyes, she didn't look happy.

"It's Bannan." Jenn's heart fell. "What's happened?"

Edis swung back and forth as if restless. Or anxious. "I left him in Gordit. He needs help." She looked up at the moon. "How is it night here?"

Because it was? Ignoring the question and its implications, Jenn pressed forward. "Take me to him!" A gust of wind knocked her back a step. "Wisp!" Jenn protested.

Edis stretched up and up, growing much taller than Jenn while staying anchored in the ground. Her eyes glittered. "Dragon."

For a wonder, Wisp showed himself. He stood nearer than Jenn expected, wings out and quivering. Flame boiled in his jaws and fury filled his wild violet eyes—eyes holding something of the color of Edis'.

Who bowed her head slightly and held out her hand, which Jenn wouldn't have recommended, seeing Wisp's mood.

But her dragon gave a shake and calmed. Extending his neck, Wisp briefly touched Edis' hand with his snout, an unprecedented gesture in Jenn's experience. "Traveler."

And everything seemed to be moving, as Aunt Sybb would say, in a most mannerly and positive direction, but then sunbeams lanced through the forest, making Jenn squint, and confused birds began to sing—

Edis let out a wail and Wisp a roar and the rocks beneath them shook—

—stopping so abruptly, the echoes of wail and roar continued after the world steadied and Jenn had no idea what had just happened, other than a most untimely dawn.

Leaves ripped and rocks rattled, and she didn't blame her dragon, shaking herself. "Heart's Blood. What—what happened?"

"She did," he snarled at Edis. "Go! Your presence disturbs the edge."

"It was dawn where I was—" Edis seemed no happier, writhing from side to side, fists clenched. "This isn't me—not just me," she said in a low, troubled voice. "The Verge is no longer safe. If its unease has spread here, there's no telling what's to come. The dragon lord is right, Jenn. We must leave while we still can." With a wary look at the dragon.

If anything, Wisp's return look was even warier. The two knew one another—or about each other.

What mattered was Bannan. "Can you take us both?" Jenn asked hopefully.

Edis shook her head. "Not with the Verge like this."

"Then take me—"

"Without me?" Wisp's head snapped up. "Anywhere else. Dear Heart, anywhere but there—"

Where turn-born had gone and not returned—a place she wouldn't want to go under any circumstances except this one. Jenn steeled herself. "Bannan needs my help. I will help him," she finished, almost, but not quite, making that a wish.

He lowered his head.

Jenn crouched in front of her dragon, seeing herself reflected in his eye. "Ancestors Blessed, I promise to fix this." This now to include, she supposed numbly, the unexpected sunshine warming her face. "Until I do, please stay here, Wisp. Protect Kydd and Bannan's family. Wait for me."

His jaws opened, flame broiling within, but tellingly, Wisp didn't argue.

"What about ME?"

Jenn looked up, for the young dragon wouldn't land anywhere near a being like Edis. "Stay here and safe as well, Imp." She'd have gone on to implore it to be more careful and to please not break anything else, especially of Lila's, but her thoughts raced ahead.

The terst cows, who grasped feeling and intention, if not meaning, tucked themselves deeper in their leader's pouch. They would not be separated from her, for she needed them; they were content it was so.

"I'm ready." Jenn set the hammer and stone on the ground, leaving them for Lila.

A scree grabbed the hammer and rolled away, tapping its neighbors, the sound mournful and what did that mean?

Edis wrapped her arms around Jenn, whispering in her ear, "Stars grant us luck."

Before Jenn could ask why, faster than a blink, she was pulled into the ground—

While inside a bespelled bag from the Shadow District, a bag nestled between Jenn's breasts and over her heart, the words writ in mimrol changed again, to read . . .

"Such power. Forget the rest. It's you we want."

"Started Fool's Day too soon, stars witness, and sleeping it off," claimed a deep voice, the one who'd spotted Bannan. "I say leave him."

Ansnan. The truthseer tensed, or one side of him did. Where was Edis with help?

"Now, Selwyn, where's the kindness in that?" Lighter, higher pitched. "By his clothes he's a miner like our good mother was, and it's none o' their doing the mine's shut tight, is it? We can't leave him in the damp. Besides, Elder Cotalen will have the ademens out soon for a sweep before the Rhothan lords arrive. They won't treat such as him well at all. We take him back to town, and that's that."

He heard them clearly, Bannan suddenly realized, because all other voices had gone silent. Cautious of strangers?

Implying the other voices were almost certainly those of little cousins. The small ones, like yling, that he hadn't been able to hear before, and, while it felt better to suppose he'd gained an ability that might be useful in Marrowdell?

What else had changed, inside?

"You've too good a heart, Wanda," the one called Selwyn grumbled halfheartedly. "Fine, then, but he's not coming in the house."

"We'll put him in with Honeypie. Come on, then, and be quick. Stars witness, you're slow in the mornings."

Eyes closed and helpless, Bannan let himself be picked up and carried by his shoulders and legs. The pair were careful of him and strong, their clothes redolent of flowers and fresh-cut greens. Farmers, at a guess, young enough to have their own Fool's Day plans, providing a decent entry to an unfamiliar town.

Once he recovered, he'd do what he could to make sure they didn't get in trouble for their kindness.

Positive thinking, that's what got them through the war. The war they didn't win, granted, against those helping him now, but Bannan was willing to move forward if they were.

And, with any luck, bump into one of the "Rhothan lords" about to arrive.

The cavalcade of the Baron Westietas and his heir rolled noisily into the cobbled center square of Gordit midafternoon, cheered by a crowd that looked, to Semyn, to be a bit unsure what they cheered about—though that might have been the bleary, overloud group of those well into their cups and the lackluster effort of those yet to be. Fool's Day wasn't, he'd been taught, a good time to be Rhothan in Ansnor. Until now, he reminded himself.

"Look at it this way, sir," Dutton offered. "A year ago, they'd have shot us."

"Progress," Poppa declared.

Araben didn't look as certain. "You'll likely have to care for the horses yourselves. A town like this won't know much about them." A pleasant smile. "Except as meat."

If she thought to shock him, Semyn thought, she'd have to try harder. Momma made sure he and Werfol were familiar with—and tasted—Ansnan cookery as well as that of other domains.

None a match to Peggs' pies. She'd made special handheld ones for him and Werfol after they'd come in from playing in the snow with Wisp, the dragon, and—

He remembered the dragon.

Along with all else about Marrowdell and magic, making it hard to keep his breathing normal. It wasn't as if he could ask anyone else in the coach. None of those selected for this journey forgot, beyond the edge. Only him.

Making him, Semyn realized with a jolt, the only one who knew, in this moment, that the town of Gordit lay in the edge.

There'd be magic here.

He looked out the window eagerly, then chided himself. Yling and dragons or whatever else was here wouldn't show themselves. He'd have to wait for sunset and the turn to see the creatures of the edge.

What he did spot were the town's obelisks, tall stones marking the alignment of a favored constellation and so that of the square. To his surprise, these were as bejeweled and ornate as those of Mondir, with an archway over the middle to support three more. Unless an endowment, the display wasn't what a town this small should be able to afford, but then, much about the finances of Gordit bore scrutiny.

Semyn looked forward to it. Almost as much as to what he had to tell Poppa.

On approaching the town, they'd acquired a pair of town ademens, keepers of the peace. While Ansnans considered themselves held responsible for their actions by the Celestials, to be judged upon their passing from this world, as Momma said, that didn't mean everyone behaved. The ademens had introduced themselves and been properly courteous. A guide to their lodgings and, unsaid, watchers to ensure they went nowhere else.

Baron Westietas had declined, with proper courtesy, Elder Cotalen's offer to house them in his home, missing the opportunities such proximity offered through, Semyn decided, an abundance of caution concerning his own presence as heir.

Which was a mistake; he and Werfol well versed in the ways people underestimated children and how to take advantage of it. Her best spies, Momma called them, and it was true, at least when he'd Weed to help.

Maybe he'd someone else. Semyn gave Araben a considering

look. She wasn't old like the guards and Poppa, and could pass as younger than she was—possibly even as a servant—if he found her the right clothes.

Noticing his attention, she raised an eyebrow. "I meant it about horsemeat."

Semyn smiled.

Poppa began to wave out the open window, nodding to Semyn to do the same as best he could past Dutton's unyielding bulk. It did liven the crowd to be acknowledged. "Thanks to Limoges, Rober and the others have billets with the dema, who is, I'm told, delighted to house such high-ranking guests. We'll stay at *Sibley's Drift*," Poppa said under the cover of cheers. "The inn has a livery stable with," a wink to Araben, "provision for horses. I'm told Gordit sees a fair number of Rhothan travelers."

Semyn added *why do Rhothans come here?* to his mental list.

"We've no commitments tonight, other than some quiet sniffing about town by some of the guard."

Elsa nodded. "I've picked a couple who'll have no trouble blending in, m'lord."

"Good. The dema is hosting a private supper for his guests and select local businesspeople—an occasion where my presence would only silence those with valuable information to share, so gladly I'll leave it in Rober's capable hands. Tomorrow we will be busy. It's the first anniversary of the treaty ending the war," Poppa went on. "As well as the Ansnan traditional Fool's Day celebration—"

Which, Master Setac had mentioned in passing, included ungoverned behavior.

"—I've been invited to make a brief address. Don't worry," this at Semyn's immediate frown. "Your mother and I agreed we must avoid any action that promotes one Ansnan faction over another, particularly on this, ah, delicate an occasion." Poppa sighed, though still smiling and waving. "The baroness was to speak in my stead. We brought her trunk."

Their parents had been leagues ahead of the scheming Cotalen, knowing from the start about Gordit's culpability and that their journey would see them here on Fool's Day. Semyn didn't know whether to be proud or appalled. "You've sent Momma birds." He hadn't seen any, but her fleet messengers were trained to silence and could travel tucked in sleeves.

"Yes, but we can't receive messages in return. Your mother was to meet us on the road. Something must have come up."

At home, he meant, and Semyn swallowed. "In her place, would an address from your heir suffice?" he asked calmly. Not that he felt calm about it in any way, not in a town of strangers and one where, to quote his guard, he'd have been shot a year ago. Not with Momma failing to be where she'd promised.

That never happened.

But Poppa looked pleased. "More than suffice and thank you, Semyn. We'll work on it tonight."

He'd waited for the offer, trusting Semyn to make it. The boy felt a warm glow. "I'll do my best, m'lord baron," he promised, and would.

Araben held out her hand for his book.

They'd all help him. In better cheer, he leaned over Dutton to wave.

He couldn't wait to see Poppa's face when he told him about Gordit and the edge.

Crossing with Edis, if that's what it was, was unlike anything Jenn had experienced. It took longer, for one thing, and at a certain point she seemed stretched and at another a pinprick—all the while with the sense of a second set of hands holding her as they traveled wherever they went before arriving—

—here. A place dim and warm, with a ceiling of huge timbers and a floor of damp stone, and with no one in sight. At once Jenn shouted, "Bannan!"

Futile echoes skipped away, dying in the distance.

Heart's Blood, he wasn't here. Jenn bit her lower lip. "Where are we?"

Edis swung her head and shoulders this way and that. Her skin glowed, which was, Jenn had to admit, a relief. Otherwise it'd be pitch dark.

"A mine. Gordit's. It's where he and I planned to come, stars witness, but didn't," her companion said chillingly. Her final swing ended to face Jenn. "I left Bannan outside, in a forest. In daylight—"

Jenn grabbed Edis' arm. "Take me there!"

"I don't think I can."

Catching something in the other's voice, Jenn paid proper attention to her, only then seeing how the snake part of Edis was wrinkled and thinner. The glow from dots on her arms was brighter than that of the rest of her body, and her mouth was pinched with pain.

"The crossings cost you dearly," Jenn said remorsefully. She eased her grip. "I'm sorry. Will you be all right? Can I help?"

A snort. "I'm not done yet." Edis flattened her palm on the rock wall beside them. Winced and let her hand fall away, raising her head to gaze into the dark. "Something's wrong here."

Something was wrong everywhere, as far as Jenn could tell. "The rock told you that?"

"I hear what they remember." A shrug. "It's rarely of use. Being tumbled in a stream. Carried in ice. Rock has a long memory." Her tone darkened. "This is different. It remembers the mine being full of people and productive. Laments veins of ore abandoned, and that's normal, but then—"

"'Then'?" Jenn prompted.

"Then evil came."

Heart's Blood, what would rock consider evil, if not miners? More importantly, "And you tried to bring Bannan here?" Jenn protested.

"Be glad I didn't. He's safer where I left him." Edis pointed into the dark. "Scamps have no mercy."

As if her attention roused them from hiding, sickly green streaks whipped along the timbers to disappear into cracks. They made a wet, clicking sound as if vexed or thwarted, reminding Jenn unpleasantly of the hiss of nyphrit when chased away by a toad, and if either foul thing attacked Bannan—

A surely disastrous wish took shape and Jenn tried to smother it. She thought of sunrises and sunsets, of warm sheets and her love's gentle touch—

—not enough

—cleaning the stove and bake oven, those being past due

—nothing worked. Her fear for him was too great, her anguished need to save him out of control—

Disagreement.

Faint. Weak, that denial, but effective. Her half-formed intention melted away and, Ancestors Blessed, that was a relief in more than one sense.

"What just didn't happen, Jenn Nalynn?" Edis asked very carefully, purple eyes fixed on her.

What didn't bear thinking about. At least, Jenn told herself, until they could go to Bannan, there was something they could and should do here.

"We have to search the mine," she announced. "I'm not the only turn-born here."

The girl was beyond his reach, if not the sense of her gifted her dragon by the sei. Attenuated to a thread, but Wisp knew she lived and was sorely upset.

Conjecture served no purpose. She'd grown stronger, this past year, and if the world remained whole, continued to govern her power. An outcome sufficient to let him focus on his own woes.

~But, Great Lord of Dragons, the young truthseer is inside. Shouldn't we be with him? For protection?~

Unclear who the youngling believed would be protected. *Foolish creature.*

~No.~

With luck, a concept Tir Half-face had brought to Wisp's attention if not understanding, Werfol and the rest would stay inside the windowless building, for what they faced was more than a dawn premature even this close to the longest day of summer.

And strange. For night lingered, a velvet darkness bordered by the stones set to mark the limit of the edge—most in the right place, but some dangerously not—and flowed outside it as far as a dragon could see, the forest illuminated solely by the moon and stars.

If he took to the sky, would the misplaced dawn reveal the precise limits of the edge across this land, or this portion alone?

Not that it mattered, the dragon being and staying here.

The ground beneath shook, again. It was becoming a habit. Scree rolled downslope, arms out as if enjoying the ride. Or desperate to find a hold. A dragon wouldn't know.

~Lord——~

~I see it.~ The difference between the sunlit edge and moonlit beyond had lessened. Wisp couldn't be sure if it was the barest start of real dawn elsewhere, or the fading of light here, but the entire business was disturbing and he needed to rend something—

~Lord!~

He whirled on his good legs, mouth agape and more than happy to rend the insolent dragon distracting him—

To find himself snout to nostrils with his old enemy.

Nostrils flaring, Scourge glared down at Wisp as if all this might be a dragon's doing, his flanks frothed with disgusting sweat and sides heaving, as if he'd run all the way from Marrowdell.

Of course he had, the old kruar many things, but never one to take a fool's risk. He'd known better than cross to get here. But to come at all meant he knew Bannan and Kydd had done so.

On that thought, Wisp sat, wings folded and jaws closed, resisting the temptation to taunt his enemy. They'd no time for it. ~Kydd is in the cottage with Lila and Werfol.~

~My truthseer?~

~Went on to a town called Gordit. Jenn Nalynn has followed.~

A great hoof flung stones, scree arms flailing. ~WHILE YOU SIT HERE?~

Imp fled to the roof of the cottage—thankfully free of wire. The other two kruar, the youngsters, watched him go, then returned their rapt attention to their lord and general.

Who ignored them. ~WHY DID YOU NOT GO WITH THEM?~

Understanding Scourge's fury, full of his own frustration, Wisp refused to take offense. ~Why did you run here?~

A growl.

~For the same reason,~ the dragon continued. ~The Verge isn't safe to travel. They left with The Traveler. We do not have that option. The girl asked,~ a heavy pause ~that we protect those here while she finds Bannan and they—fix this.~

The massive head swung around, nostrils working, then back. Scourge looked to the boundary between false day and forgotten night. Shook, clots of vile foam flying. ~Have you ever seen the like?~

~Within the past day, when crossing. The dimmings—time has become unreliable in the Verge.~

And here.

Scourge reared back, then lowered his head again with a suspicious sniff. Apparently satisfied, he nodded. ~The wizard from Marrowdell. Is this his work?~

Unspoken, the threat, but no less real. Kydd Uhthoff's fate was being discussed by the two most terrifying beings to ever eat his wife's biscuits, and Wisp himself had no defense to give—

But one. ~Jenn Nalynn loves him.~

A huff. Acceptance, that was—

For now.

~Lord?~

Wisp lost patience. ~I WILL eat——~

~Theresnooneinside,~ Imp replied hastily.

Dauntless tossed her head. ~They left by the secret door when the turn-born did, lord general. We took them home. The lady rode me!~ With pride.

~Then we followed you here, lord general,~ from Spirit, prancing nervously. ~Was that not correct?~

Scourge and Wisp exchanged looks of mutual exasperation. About to comment on the dimness of the kruar youngsters, the dragon fell silent, a small white moth having landed daintily on his snout.

It might have been an ordinary, if remarkably foolish, moth.

None here believed it.

The moth stroked an antenna over one dark eye. ~You must go to her.~

A command from the sei that answered his heartfelt desire? Wisp refused to believe it. ~Why?~

A tiny leg pointed at Scourge. ~You must go to him.~

The kruar's red-rimmed eyes narrowed. ~How?~

~Terst would undo what is. Terst would return to what was.~ Little wings fluttered. ~They must not!~

A sei, anxious? ~Terst are powerless,~ Wisp told it, chilled inside, but the words were hollow. What did he truly know of them, except deception?

A voice like the shout of a mountain, ~A TRAP AWAITS!~

The moth fluttered, as if startled itself, rising into the air. ~If it claims him and takes her, all is lost. GO!~ With that final thunderous word, the moth was gone.

Imp whimpered.

Wise youngling.

As for why it suited the sei to give *them* the warning instead of the girl and truthseer—he'd put it down to their never doing anything useful, except this time?

This time, it wasn't the warning alone the sei wanted to reach the girl, but their help, and that, Wisp thought with grim satisfaction, he did understand.

He shook himself from snout to tail. ~The younglings will remain here, to watch for the return of Jenn Nalynn and Bannan. Outside the structure.~ Imp able to forget the most monumental upset in a heartbeat.

~Where will you be, Great Lord of Dragons?~

~With me.~ The old kruar curled a lip. ~We go beyond the edge.~

Where he'd forget himself and Wisp be sorely diminished, but there was, the dragon knew, no choice if they were to heed the sei and save the girl and truthseer from the terst.

No choice if they were to help save the Verge and all else.

Flexing his wings, he eyed the kruar. ~Unless you need rest?~

Scourge snorted. ~I'll beat you to Gordit, old fool!~

Wisp soared into the air, dipping down to skim the slope. ~Catch me if you can!~

With that, they left the edge, and daylight, behind.

TEN

SHE COULDN'T HAVE asked for a better guide through this underground world, Jenn realized. Nor could she have taken five steps in any direction without, as Edis casually informed her, running into trouble, of a sort she'd never in her lifetime expected to face.

Like this. Holding onto a timber, Jenn leaned cautiously over the rim of a pit that disappeared into darkness, a pit she would have walked into had Edis not stopped her. "Heart's Blood. The poor miners!"

"They'd be dead without it." Edis pointed up. "It's an air shaft." A shrug. "If the mine was active, there'd be light here and a warning gate across."

Such a gate, broken and covered in cobwebs, leaned against rock to one side. The whole place—come to think of it and Jenn did—felt abandoned, and why would the terst turn-born come here for gems, if that were so?

Thinking of gems, she pulled out the bag with the pin and went to drop it into the shaft.

"Don't!"

Startled, she stepped back, bag still in hand. "Why not?"

"You don't know what's below—or who." Edis frowned at her. "Never drop anything down a shaft, hear me? Never!"

Chastened, Jenn nodded and returned the bag to her bodice. "I meant no harm."

Her companion hesitated, then explained, her voice flat and hard. "Rhothans did, during the war. They'd piss in air shafts. Toss rubble down—or worse. Not a good memory." Another shrug dismissed past horrors. "Stay behind me."

The mine was an organized maze, reminding Jenn of the tunnels ants made in rotten wood. These tunnels were pierced by vertical shafts so often Jenn grew used to walking around them. They passed other tunnels Edis would consider, then dismiss. While it might have been something she heard from nearby rock, Jenn thought it more likely Edis simply knew how mines were constructed and where to go. The tunnels Edis choose slanted underfoot, sides and ceilings reinforced with timber, turning back on themselves. They could have gone up.

She led them down.

And down. The air warmed. Water was everywhere, dripping down walls and flowing into channels carved into the floor along one side. Smaller shafts drained the water away, and seeing them, Jenn had a new and dreadful thought. Bad enough thinking of the weight of rock overhead, but to worry about drowning if those shafts were blocked?

"Miners are very brave," she said abruptly.

"Stars know, most of us are born into the work and don't think much of it." Edis chuckled. "Farming, now. Tried it. That's danger." She feigned a shudder. "As for fishing? Won't find me on top of an ocean."

But Edis *was* brave, Jenn knew. She'd been a soldier and, from what she'd told Jenn as they walked—conversation helping push away her dread—had had the courage after the war to go out and build a new life for herself.

Until that life ended—Edis had shrugged, leaving it at that. As if whatever had happened to change her mattered not a whit compared to who she'd become, a lesson, Jenn decided, having undergone her own changes, worth remembering.

She followed Edis' glow around another sharp turn, hearing scamps rush out of their path, which would be reassuring if Jenn were able to dismiss the constant wet clicks of the creatures from behind. How many trailed them? "Do scamps attack miners?" she asked at last, staring around.

"They get into lunch boxes. Ruin food stores. Their bites leave itchy welts."

Jenn relaxed. "So they aren't dangerous."

"Not those beyond the edge." Edis curled to look back at her, her expression grim. "These are bigger. Their venom would paralyze us and then they'd eat us alive." A half grin. "If we were normal flesh and bone." Her grin disappeared and she moved closer to Jenn. "About—"

CLATTERCLATTER

The sound echoed down the tunnel. Edis broke off whatever she'd planned to say, shouting over the din, "Train!" She dived past Jenn the way they'd just come, sliding forward through the rock floor so quickly Jenn was forced to run to keep up.

The terst cows dug their claws into the sides of her pouch and held on with all their strength.

Ancestors Harried and Hurried, the noise and their pace toward it made it impossible to think of questions, let alone take breath to shout them out. Jenn focused on not falling behind, that and watching for air shafts and scamps and whatever other perils Edis was no longer bothering to show her, though it was a help they retraced steps already taken.

Until Jenn found herself running past that point into the unknown.

While the pin in the bag she'd thought to discard glowed white hot, and the words in mimrol changed briefly to read . . .

"This way. Yes. This way to us."

His second ride on a kruar. Kydd sat gingerly on the kitchen's bench, vowing not to have a third, and took the cup Cook offered with a grateful nod. Sipping what turned out to be spiced wine, he raised his eyebrows. "Thank you."

Her grin showed very few teeth.

Lila held her cup in a hand curled to her breast, pacing back and forth the length of the room. Prowling, Kydd corrected, her every movement restrained and deliberate. "What do we know?"

"That we should have stayed in the cottage." Werfol hid his face behind his cup, feet swinging back and forth.

When older, Kydd suspected he'd pace as well. "We passed through a shift of time leaving the edge," he said at last. That eerie dawn they'd left, night here, through the kitchen windows; to anyone who could remember the edge and magic, troubling was the least of it. Hence the wine.

Lila's free hand waved at a device on the wall. A protest. "Emon's clock hasn't changed."

He didn't like the notion either, but—"Here wasn't part of whatever happened." Kydd picked up a napkin, folding it so the edges touched, and dipped those briefly in his wine. Unfolded, the red-stained edges were far apart. "Bannan saw Marrowdell at a time different from now. We stepped into the great storm that hit the south before any of us were born, and, while the world seemed to return to normal?" He lifted the napkin.

"You think it's Bannan's door."

Werfol's eyes widened, then narrowed. He slammed down his cup. "Uncle has his own crossing to Marrowdell? Why didn't he tell me? You told him not to." A glower from molten gold eyes.

Lila raised an eyebrow. "And why would I do that, son of mine?"

The gold faded. "Because I'd want to use it," the boy replied, not sullen, not daring that, but not happy either.

His mother perched on the table next to him, tucking a finger under his chin to lift his face to hers. "Jenn made a crossing for your uncle as a gift, because he missed us. Not to let us go there. For him to come *here* when needed."

"To deal with me."

"To instruct you. And yes—" she planted a kiss on his forehead before standing "—to help your father and me survive the process. And Semyn." A pause. A hint of a smile. "Not to mention the staff—"

Werfol looked stricken. "I haven't been that bad. Have I?"

"A single gift is a burden. You've been dealing—usually well—with two. Bannan helps us when you can't."

Kydd watched the boy mull this over, then give a sad little nod. "Yes, Momma."

"Now, drink your wine—slowly—and keep our guest company while I look into the matter of his wife." A glance at the windows. A knowing grimace. "At this stage, our dear Peggs won't be asleep much. I should be able to 'dream her."

"Ancestors Blessed—"

Putting down her cup, Lila shrugged off his thanks. "Wait till we see if this first attempt succeeds, Kydd. Excuse me."

The baroness left a room smaller, she couldn't help it. At the notion, Kydd tipped his cup against Werfol's. "I caused my brother no end of trouble and he still loves me."

The boy wasn't ready to be charmed. "Because you did dark magic."

"Dusom doesn't love that," Kydd admitted. After a moment's consideration, he leaned back. "Your uncle isn't too happy with me either. A spell was cast on me as a student, to deflect a truthseer's gift. I can lie to you and you won't be able to tell."

"Can not!" Werfol shot erect, eyes burning gold.

Cook lifted her spoon from the pot.

Kydd held up his hands. "Peace, both of you. I'm telling you this, Werfol, because there's a counter to the spell. I haven't had a chance to teach it to your uncle." Or the pin had deterred him. "I'd like to teach you."

"Why?" with a suspicion far beyond his years.

Ancestors Troubled and Torn. It'd make too heartfelt—and long—a confession. "To protect you from those like me. Like I was."

He'd caught Werfol's interest. "The people you drew for Jenn. This counter you'd teach me—would it reveal them as users of dark magic?"

"You'll only know if they speak the truth."

A nod. "That's a start."

"As for the sketches—there'll be others I never met," he cautioned.

"More by now. They've had twenty years." Kydd patted the bench beside him. "Sit here. I'm going to lie. You try to tell."

Plopping himself down, Werfol stared at him with those disconcerting eyes.

"I don't remember anything strange about Marrowdell. I just pretend."

Creases appeared on the boy's forehead. "You don't remember?"

"I do."

Werfol rubbed his eyes. Stared harder at Kydd. "I can see you, I see your father, and his, I see—" He covered his face. Dropped his hands to show eyes of sober brown. "What was the lie?"

Instead of answering, Kydd held out his hand. Waited for Werfol to lay his on top. "I don't remember anything strange about Marrowdell. I just pretend—"

Eyes flared gold. "You're lying!!" the young truthseer crowed. "I can tell." He tilted his head. "Because I was touching you. That's the counter? That's all it takes?" As if disappointed.

Kydd nodded. "Keep in mind someone relying on that spell will know it as well. You can't be obvious."

"The lad's a clever un," Cook commented, back to stirring her pot. Porridge, by the aroma.

And there it was, dawn peeking in the windows.

The main streets of Gordit ran from the town square outward along lines set by the Constellation of True Vigilance as its stars appeared overhead at midnight of the autumnal equinox, the start of the period when the Celestials took charge of watching and judging those below. There were four streets in and out: Prepare, Behave, Declare, and Submit, the latter worrisome for those non-Ansnans unaware it simply meant accepting the judgment of the stars.

The pronounced slope to which Gordit clung added an adventurous feel to what was, in sum, a pretty place, replete with colorful tiled roofs and window boxes brimming with flowers. Roads running perpendicular to the main streets weren't held to astronomical order, able to wander up and down the slopes, causing Semyn some consternation as he tried to memorize their names, until he spotted a pattern. Those roads were named for the most significant structure along each, a choice subject to time and the whims of business, but useful for travelers.

Sibley's Drift, the tavern housing the Baron Westietas and his retinue—significant as Gordit's largest tavern—took up the block between roads aptly named Drift and Stable, as well as streets Behave and Declare.

The *Drift* was a large stone and timber building with a wide porch on two sides and patio along on the third for dining in view of the stars, when weather permitted. The fourth side backed on the stables and delivery area, with wash basins for those fresh from work.

The street named Declare climbed the foothill to Gordit's mine, the *Drift* a miners' haven today and always.

"Stars proud of it!" the current Sibley, Jas, exclaimed in Semyn's ear, having missed a chance to bend the baron's.

As had Semyn, burning to talk about Gordit and edge, but on arrival Poppa, skilled at politely avoiding entanglements, had signed to his heir to linger.

Momma did say he'd a knack for drawing information from strangers. Resigned to his duty, Semyn chatted with the innkeeper. "Is the name some sort of mining term, then?"

Beaming, Jas rattled off the answer.

Semyn knew, of course. It was in his notebook. The name *drift* referred to a horizontal tunnel reaching to the ore—thus open only at one end—but there was no harm letting the man teach a newcomer, and Semyn hadn't known drift also referred to a tool used to tap cotter pins from machinery.

Weed would like that one.

The dining room was a rectangle with huge fireplaces at each end and backed by a long, well-used bar. What set it apart hung from hooks in the walls and low ceiling: mining gear, from lantern hats to pickaxes. "Quite the collection," Semyn broached in the innkeeper's next pause.

"What? Oh, that. Most of it's in hock," Jas informed Semyn, waggling his eyebrows. "T'pay for Fool's Day drinks tomorrow, if you get my meaning, young sir. Been the *Drift*'s tradition since my great-greats built the place." His cheer diminished. "Stars know we'll be stuck with most of it this year. W'the mine shut down so long, none of the miners can pay their bills."

Dutton looked set to rescue him. Semyn spread his fingers in the sign *wait*. "Good sir," he said earnestly, eyes wide. "I'm confused. I understood Gordit's famed wealth came from its mine. Was I mistaken?"

The innkeeper might have hesitated to answer another adult. Warmed by Semyn's bright young gaze, he leaned in—after a glance to be sure he wouldn't be overheard. "They tell us t'mine's closed, lad, but there be those who come and go from it. An' those making coin in plenty from it, if you get my meaning, w'none coming to—"

A noisy pair approached and Jas harrumphed, briskly ruffling Semyn's hair. "Stop ye pestering, lad," he said brusquely. "I'll send up trays proper quick."

Ducking his head in the Ansnan courtesy, Semyn joined Dutton on the stairs. "Sir?" the guard asked quietly.

"We were right to come here," Semyn answered, sure now.

Despite Fool's Day, which had to bring folks in from the surrounding area, the innkeeper had kept the entire upper floor empty and ready for them courtesy of Elder Cotalen. Implying his plot to get them here had been hatched at the same time as Momma's, and it was an even bet who'd been first.

Their floor had its own staircase. The door at the top landing didn't lock, but they were secure. Nyc Wise, head of the horse guard, stood on the public side.

"There'll be trays coming up shortly," Semyn advised her when they reached the top.

With a nod, Wise opened the door for Semyn and Dutton to pass through, closing it behind them.

Another of the horse guard, Anet Boyes, came to attention on the inside of the door. "Grub's coming," Dutton announced cheerfully, shedding tension.

Ancestors Witness, this wasn't a private space, Semyn knew. They'd been taught to check rooms for peepholes and listening grids; to never assume they'd found them all.

Semyn pointed to the wall, with its fresco of painted stags, then to his ear.

Dutton's lips tightened in understanding. "Save some for me," he said, his voice unchanged.

Boyes, who'd watched this exchange, gave a curt nod. "Will do."

Semyn hurried into Poppa's room, near to bursting with his news. The baron looked up from the papers he'd strewn over the desk. "Ready to work on your—" Reading his son's face, he waved his aide, Mabbs Keit—another of the horse guard—and Dutton from the room, then Semyn to the chair opposite him. Once the door closed, he leaned back. "We're secure. What have you found out?"

"I remember Marrowdell's magic." It was rare to see Poppa speechless, and disconcerting. "Gordit is in the edge. At least where I've been so far," Semyn added, that being important.

"You're sure—of course, you are, Dear Heart," Poppa answered himself, beginning to smile. "Well, this puts a new spin on things."

"There's more. I've talked to—"

The door burst open.

It was Araben, Dutton looming behind. She took two steps into the room then stopped, eyes locked on Semyn. "Your uncle's hiding in the stables. Injured or ill."

Poppa surged to his feet.

So did Semyn. "Wait! My lord baron, please." It was as if Momma whispered in his ear. "You can't go down there and you mustn't send guards. We'll go." He gestured to Araben. "I've Ansnan clothes. No one will notice."

A muscle jumped in Poppa's jaw, but he gave the tiniest nod. "Go."

"Sir," Dutton protested as Semyn went to his trunk for the disguise he'd packed.

"We'll need Macle's uniform," Araben said calmly.

Macle being closest in size to Uncle Bannan. An idea like one of Werfol's, quick and clever, Semyn judged.

Not that he'd tell his little brother.

Bannan Larmensu knew several things in this moment.

He knew he was in a stable, lying on straw under a feed bag. Enormous cloven hooves came closer to his face than he'd prefer, but Honeypie, the massive ox who owned the feet, had sniffed and nudged him gently, and then been careful where it stepped. Thus far.

He knew the farmers who'd put him with the ox had been surprised to find horses in the stable. Selwyn had made a comment about roast horse someone else objected to in a Rhothan accent. The sister, Wanda, had hustled him out with her.

Horses. Rhothans. Help, perhaps.

Enemies, as likely.

Wasn't, Heart's Blood, as if he could ask.

He knew he remained within the edge, for any time he cracked open his eyes it was to drown in light, and he could barely hear over whatever chattered without stopping from all sides, even if the chatter resembled giggles and not growls.

Last and not least, he knew he was running out of time. The paralysis had spread to his right side and his jaw was numb. To forestall drowning in his own drool, Bannan had turned his head while he still could, mouth aimed down, and congratulated himself on more fine and forward thinking.

Someone entered the stall.

"Hey, Honeypie." The wooden floor shook as the ox turned, a ponderous maneuver kicking straw into Bannan's face. He fought to stifle a cough, not that he'd be heard over the animal's happy crunching of whatever treat it had been brought. Choked down a bitter laugh because the business end of the ox was most likely now aimed his way and it was only a matter of time and digestion—

Someone crouched in front of him and brushed the straw from his face. "Don't move," he thought he heard. The straw went back on his face, which wasn't a kindness.

He felt the ox turn around, which, Ancestors Befouled and Beleaguered, was.

Had he dreamed the someone?

A relevant concern, Bannan decided a while later. A dream was a more appealing explanation of events beyond belief, and honestly, he'd be overjoyed to wake up and discover everything that had happened since Marrowdell had been a dream—

A nightmare of BURNING ALIVE—

A dream, he insisted to himself, shuddering inside. For the sake of prudence, in case it wasn't, he'd avoid the Verge in future, assuming he had one—

A touch. "Uncle."

Semyn?!

He should have known rescue would be his undoing.

—darkness swallowed him.

While Araben kept the overly friendly ox from stepping on them, Semyn changed his unconscious uncle into Macle's uniform. One of Momma's games, for him and Werfol, to change clothes on the brother whose turn it was to play dead.

But Heart's Blood, Uncle Bannan was heavy. He didn't want to hurt him but—

Araben dropped to her knees in the straw, methodically pulling off Uncle's boots and pants—with the war over a mere year ago, he wasn't about to ask where she'd practiced *that*—letting Semyn deal with the coat.

A coat the like of which he'd last seen in the *Drift*, along with the pants and hat with a lantern near Uncle's head, and there was but one reason to be dressed like an Ansnan miner. Uncle Bannan was here in disguise, as he was.

Good enough, Semyn signed, when it was.

Leaving Araben with Uncle Bannan, the miner's clothing and hat under an arm, Semyn slipped past the ox into the stableway. Three stalls down he found the Westietas' horses and, as he'd expected, their driver, Cecebe Loring, tending to them with the fourth horse guard, Omas Egind.

He came up and gave a little cough. "Your pardon?"

They turned, regarding him none too kindly. "Go along, lad," Egind said brusquely, in Ansnan. "We're on duty. And have had our fill of brats this day."

Loring seemed to see through Semyn's disguise, bending to squint at him with a puzzled frown. But then she rose with a shrug, tossing him a coin and pointing to the sunlit doorway. "Go along."

Momma was right, as Momma always was. Dirty clothes and a slouch rarely failed as a disguise. Pocketing the coin with a satisfaction he'd let himself savor once uncle was safe, Semyn straightened. As recognition—and chagrin—filled their faces, he said, in Rhothan, "I'm beholden for your generosity, Loring, but what I need are your strong arms. Follow me, please."

When they came out with Uncle, Dutton rolled from his lean beside the stable entry, taking Loring's place so she could return to their horses, which mustn't be left unguarded.

Entering the inn, head lolling and slung between Dutton and Egind—in a matching, if disheveled uniform—Uncle Bannan was the image of a guard in a drunken stupor. Araben and Semyn, ignored by those calling out rude advice and cruder comments about Rhothan capacity or lack thereof, nipped up the stairs to alert the guard and prepare the baron.

Not, Semyn knew, that anything could. Whatever was wrong with Uncle Bannan, it wasn't an injury, nor had he felt a fever. No, this was scarily like what happened to Werfol when consumed by his gifts.

And Momma wasn't here to help.

But in that, he'd underestimated who was.

"Lay him on the bed," Poppa ordered briskly. "Mabbs, Lila's trunk, on the desk. You—" a glance at Semyn and Araben, who'd moved back, out of the way "—well done. Egind, thank you. We'll send supper to the stable." The guard bowed and left. "A hand towel, Dutton."

Poppa opened the trunk, then used four fingers of each hand to unlock a compartment hidden in the lid. Retrieving a leather-bound bundle, he untied it and stretched out an array of little bottles, each secured in their loop.

Momma's *remedies*. Most, Semyn knew, were poisons.

Choosing one, Poppa went to the small camp stove they'd brought with them, part of a collapsible kitchen. His design, Momma's thinking, to travel ready for a siege—or poor service.

The water must have been already heated for tea. After testing it with a finger, his father poured the contents of the bottle into the water and called for the towel.

Not a motion wasted, nothing but focus to read from his face, and Semyn suddenly realized this was far from the first time Poppa had helped someone in the throes of their gift.

Momma—

"Semyn."

He jumped to his feet and hurried to stand by the camp stove.

Poppa handed him the towel. "Might as well show you now," a mutter. Louder. "Hold it out, flat and level." When Semyn did, his father lifted the pot by the handle and prepared to pour.

"Won't it go through?" Semyn asked.

Poppa shook his head. "Watch." He poured.

The water had thickened and turned blue. Wherever it struck the towel, it spread through the fabric without a drip falling past. Passing the pot to Mabbs, Poppa took the towel, still flat and level, and went to the bed.

He wrapped the soaked towel around Uncle Bannan's head, covering his ears and eyes, leaving his mouth and nose uncovered. Done, Poppa sat on the side of the bed. Without looking up, he took hold of Uncle Bannan's hand and said quietly, "Now we wait."

With a nod to Mabbs, Dutton led the way to the door. Araben went with them, stopping once to glance back.

Semyn didn't notice. He sat gently on the bed, on Uncle Bannan's other side, slipping his hand under Uncle's distressingly limp one. He looked up and met Poppa's somber gaze, a question in his own.

"Up to Bannan, now, Dear Heart."

The CLATTERCLATTER of the train came and went, as if it didn't go very far—which was, Edis told Jenn absently, likely the case. Tracks were laid in active drifts, to reach the outer face of the mine, carrying ore back to where it could be crushed and sorted before the best pieces were hoisted above.

When Edis brushed her fingers along the rock, listening to its memories, she'd shake her head and mutter there shouldn't be a train moving at all. The miners were gone, the rocks kept lamenting. The mine was closed.

CLATTERCLATTER

Jenn walked in a tunnel like all the others they'd walked, struggling with what Edis had said about Rhothan soldiers and the air shafts of Ansnan mines. She didn't want to believe it, if she were honest, for the most selfish of reasons.

Ancestors Witness, she'd no difficulty imagining Tir, with his axes and simmering anger, dropping corpses on those hiding in a mine. Or helping tear down homes for refuse to choke a shaft and smother those below.

But . . . her dearest love?

Bannan didn't speak about the war, but his scars did, every time Jenn's fingers found them. One arched around a rib, three crossed deep into his back, and his wrists and hands, like Uncle Horst's, bore nicks from swords.

A soldier's worst scars were on the inside. Jenn had seen it for herself when Bannan transformed himself into Captain Ash, the fearsome interrogator from the marches, at Lila's request. His grief afterward, his terrible pain—she'd been so angry with his sister, until discovering Lila's pain ran just as deep.

All at once, Jenn realized she no longer heard scamps behind her and she could see the tunnel floor and walls beyond Edis' waning glow. "Are we almost out?" she asked, trying to keep a wistful note from her voice. Hard to avoid, when her skin crawled and she wanted to crouch despite the timbers overhead being higher than her outstretched hand; it felt like the sun had been snuffed out forever.

The terst cows, uneasy as their leader, gratefully tucked themselves into the folded leaves she'd put into their pouch for bedding, content it was so.

"Will you look at that," Edis murmured. "Stars blessed, I thought Deter made it up."

Jenn reached where Edis had halted to stare into yet another a drift tunnel. But this one wasn't the same. The entrance was choked with—things. A glossy eye caught the light. Heart's Blood, a horse's head!

She jumped back.

Edis flowed past her to rap her knuckles on the long nose, producing a hollow sound. "Came from a carousel."

The wooden horse was the size of Wainn's old pony, from what Jenn could see of the rest, but it looked nothing like the wonderful painted illustration of a carousel horse in Peggs' favorite book, *Wonders of Avyo*. What paint there'd been was peeling and chipped, the head contorted and mouth agape as if to bite. On top of the horse was the broken half of a bear, also once a ride for children, part of what sealed the tunnel along with shattered poles and planks, rough timber and stone.

The mass looked violent—looked angry. "Did Rhothans do this?" Jenn asked, her voice low and shaken.

"You don't want to know." Purple eyes glanced at her, then Edis—more wrinkled than before—continued her slide onward through the floor.

Ancestors Despicable and Dreadful, yes, she was afraid of the answer. That didn't, Jenn reminded herself, excuse ignorance. "Ansnans died here, didn't they."

"No." Edis stopped. "Rhothans did." Seeing Jenn's face, she sighed.

"Very well. It's known as the Siege of Gordit. Story goes, Rhothans thought to hide here with their prisoners, believing the mine deserted. But voices carry up the shafts." She pointed, and only then did Jenn realize there was—or had been—an air shaft above the blockage. "Hearing the intruders, the townsfolk threw everything they could break apart into the shaft, to trap them." Flowing forward, Edis touched the wooden bear. "Including the town's carousel. At the time, I'm sure they felt justified."

"Did it—"

"Work?" Edis shrugged. "Story goes—and it's just a story, remember—the Rhothans suddenly went quiet. The villagers feared they'd escaped; old, forgotten shafts riddle the spent parts of any mine, so they lowered a miner down the next air shaft, to spy on the soldiers.

"Story goes the miner found the prisoners asleep and safe, but the soldiers were dead, with nary a mark on a body or sign of poison, with full flasks of water and supplies in their bags. The villagers declared it the vengeance of the Celestials. That's why I didn't believe Deter. Once a liar—" she added grimly, and spat to the side.

Heart's Blood, to die, trapped in the dark—Jenn shivered.

CLATTERCLATTER

Edis looked up. "We're close. The edge goes to the top and to the town," as if Jenn had asked.

Trusting her guide, it hadn't occurred to her. "Can you? Go past it?"

"Not and survive." Edis rubbed her jaw. Brought down her hand when it touched her helm of stone braids, and gave her shrug. "Besides, where would I go if I could? The Verge is my home now, the edge a place to visit. I—"

CLATTERCLATTER

Taking the interruption as an excuse to stop there, Edis flowed up the tunnel toward the train—Jenn forced to hurry behind.

While on a pin given to her mother by her own, safe in its bag, letters of mimrol briefly changed to read . . .

"We're waiting. We're ready. Come."

"Peggs is well. She was up at dawn, baking pies with Gallie's help."

To hear the words from Lila's lips, the solid conviction behind them—better still, to hear Peggs was doing what she loved—was a tonic like no other. Kydd smiled so widely, his cheeks protested.

"And, from what I could see, still very pregnant," Lila finished, looking pleased.

His smile froze. Heart's Blood, he'd known how her gift worked, that a truedreamer caught a glimpse through their subject's eyes without being sensed in return, but it wasn't the same, now.

Not since he'd had his own sight stolen and used against those he loved—

Reading his reaction, Lila lost her smile. "Kydd," she began gently.

Werfol, who'd been staring meaningfully at the untouched bowl in front of their guest, blurted out, "Will you want your oatmeal?"

Kydd waved permission, taking a gulp of strong tea before braving the sympathy in Lila's eyes. The night had vanished without time for sleep; this breakfast in the upstairs room felt too soon. "Forgive me, baroness. I know full well in here—" he tapped his head "—that your gift is nothing like the spell that bound me. But—" A hand over his heart.

"A feeling of violation," she said for him. Her lips quirked and she lifted her cup. "Ancestors Witness, my brother has a similar opinion, believe me. Which is why I didn't tell him till this winter."

Her son looked up from dismantling Kydd's breakfast.

"No," Lila said without shifting her attention from Kydd. "You may not 'dream your brother without his permission and mine."

Werfol sat straight, a full spoon poised in midair. "What if it's an urgent and terrible emergency?" His eyes became molten gold. "What then, Momma?"

From where Kydd sat, he caught the little sigh before Lila turned to her son. "If there's an emergency of any significance, I will tell you."

"But—" At her look, Werfol stifled the word with porridge, eyes still aglow.

"See what I have to put up with, Kydd?" Lila leaned back, rolling her shoulders as if easing a burden. "I envy you the years before your child develops such atrocious ambition."

He stole a glance at the boy, trying—and failing—to imagine being a father to someone as courageous and, yes, ambitious, but above all a remarkable person. "I hope we're as blessed, baroness," he said impulsively.

Werfol's face lit up.

"You'll find out soon," the baroness said, her tone businesslike. "When you're done breakfast, I'm sending you home, Kydd." She put a small tile on the table by his hand. "This will see you and my driver through to Marrowdell by the fastest non-magical means at my disposal. You should be home by tomorrow night."

He froze, unable to pick it up. "But—you said Peggs was well."

"Yes, and the size of a house. I remember the feeling." A grimace. "Go home. You belong with her."

Feeling in a dream, Kydd took the tile and clenched it in his fist. "My journals—" choking on the words because Ancestors Calamitous and Crazed, he'd been about to beg to stay until they were found or found him—

What had they made him? "Without my journals—" He'd been a fool to think it was over, that he was safe. Heard the depth of despair in his voice and knew its source was that terrible lust.

Would these good people? Could they? "Without them, it's been for nothing, my coming here." *He* was nothing. "I haven't helped you find the Heirs. Helped you stop them."

"Don't worry," Werfol piped up cheerfully. "You drew faces for Jenn Nalynn. She'll show Poppa and Uncle Bannan. We'll have them then. Won't we, Momma?"

And oh, the satisfaction in the look Lila gave her son. "That we will. Take the tile, good sir. You've done more than your share and we're grateful."

As Kydd flattened his palm over it, there came a knock at the door. His driver?

A message. Receiving it at the suite door, the guard—Lila having kept her seniormost, a sober-faced woman named Ryll Aronom, at hand—stepped briskly to the table. "The boys' tutor has returned, m'lady."

The atmosphere became charged with what Kydd couldn't name until Werfol whispered, "He can't be home yet. Master Setac went to Avyo—" He fell silent at a signal from his mother.

Who looked no happier at this unforeseen arrival. "And?"

"He's at the door, m'lady, with news that can't wait." For some reason the guard glanced at Kydd.

Who got to his feet and bowed. "I'll go—"

"Stay, please. Word will come up when the light carriage is ready. And you, Werfol," Lila commanded, though the boy hadn't budged and looked ready to argue. "Master Setac will sit with us. Please send to Cook, Ryll, for a tray."

"Yes, m'lady."

In any other household, Kydd thought, the boy would be allowed to remain to greet his teacher. But by the frisson of alarm, and the hint of gold shimmering in Werfol's eyes?

Lila didn't keep her son by her side, she kept her truthseer.

Fisting the tile, bringing his fist to his lap, Kydd composed his face as the door opened again, admitting two guards and a compact man in a long dusty coat, with bright blue eyes.

When those eyes met Kydd's, the beekeeper stumbled to his feet. "You!"

Light flooded the tunnel ahead past the switchback, a strange cold light of a sort Jenn hadn't seen before. Edis pressed herself against a shadowed wall, motioning Jenn to do the same.

CLATTERCLATTERCLATTER

The sound rocketed through the tunnels, the echoes deafening. Whatever made it had to be around the corner.

As they stood there, waiting for whatever sign her companion anticipated, Jenn noticed how the glow from Edis' pearlescent skin barely lit the rock behind them. Worse, that skin was wrinkled and folded as if the flesh within her body—if flesh, which hardly mattered, she herself filled with a sei's tears and who better to understand—shrank. Or was Edis being consumed from within? Ancestors Blessed, how much longer could she stay in the edge, if so?

Jenn took hold of Edis' callused hand. "You should leave. To take care of yourself," she whispered, the words firm despite not having the least idea what *take care* meant for whatever Edis now was.

Edis pulled her hand away. "Don't pity me." Harsh and final.

"Why would I?" Jenn blinked, not sure what more to say. Then she thought of Uncle Hane, who lost part of his leg before meeting Aunt Sybb.

Aunt Sybb said he'd hesitated at first to court her, afraid she'd see what he'd lost and pity him, instead of who he was and love him back. A situation, Jenn knew, that had ended very well, Aunt Sybb crystal clear what she wanted in her life even when young and not to be denied.

Well, then.

Jenn Nalynn made herself glass and pearl and light, lifting her palm to Edis' cheek, her own light, the Verge's light, wild colors spilling across Edis' face and over her helm of stone, reflecting in wide purple eyes.

A flicker of astonishment, then Edis snorted. "Neat trick."

Not a reaction to Jenn's turn-born self she'd experienced before, but it was, in this instance, a relief. Once more flesh and blood, she smiled from her heart.

Edis looked away. Slowly, almost grudgingly, she looked back at Jenn. She didn't smile. Perhaps her face softened. "Stars know," a grumble, "might be I pity myself at times. Bad habit. I'm not the only one star-touched." She touched Jenn's cheek. "Bannan will be in good hands."

Jenn stiffened. "Why would—"

"Come on." Edis pulled her forward. "We'll take them by surprise!"

They charged around the corner, only to surprise no one, for no one was there.

Jenn moved forward, captivated by the light emitted from silken bags hung from hooks along the walls. Bags of liquid, without flame, glowing bright. Puzzled, she turned to Edis. "How do they work?"

"Magic. They're filled with Star Blood." Her companion came beside her, reaching out but not quite touching a bag, her voice filled with awe. "What Rhothans call Silver Tears. From the Verge, where it's called—"

"Mimrol," Jenn finished. Bannan had told her of discovering mimrol beneath his family's home—

Heart's Blood, he'd said its worth could start a war. Artisans made devices powered by the tiniest hint of mimrol. The terst's mechanicals had been moved by it, but in the Verge, mimrol was everywhere.

It wasn't here. Or was it? Appalled, Jenn heard herself ask, "How much can they have, to squander it like this?"

"A good question. And who are 'they'?" Edis asked grimly. "The mine's closed. Because they found it and wished to keep the secret?"

Jenn looked around, as if she'd find answers in the rock walls, the timbers above. On the floor were paired metal tracks running in both directions, between them a double chain that went—

She turned to follow, to be confronted by what was very familiar indeed.

A huge water wheel. Of metal, not wood and leather as in Marrowdell's mill, but its dangling cups dripped with recent moisture, and the chain wrapped around a well-greased gear on one side.

The terst cows climbed up, peeking out of her pouch, nostrils working. Surprised to smell the Verge this strongly. Wary.

"Moves the ore," Edis said, seeing her focus. "The wheel turns, pulling the train cars along by the chain."

"I was taught you use oxen."

"In my grandparents' day." Edis swung from side to side, as if she were uneasy. "But this isn't—"

A hatch opened above the wheel, releasing a waterfall.

The terst cows ducked back inside.

CLATTERCLATTERCLATTER

The sound was the filling cups, the wheel turning, the chain moving—

Edis gasped. "Jenn—that isn't water!"

She must have Bannan's ability, to see mimrol in the edge with his deeper sight. To Jenn it looked like water, a mesmerizing torrent of it, flowing within hands' reach to vanish into a shaft below the wheel—

Edis yanked Jenn away from the tracks and the moving chain, mouthing *train!* Jenn looked down the tunnel, eager to finally see one up close—

CLATTERCLATTERCLAT—

The hatch closed. Flow cut off, the wheel slowed to a halt, without a train of any sort in view.

Deflated, Jenn turned to Edis. "Where's the train?"

Her companion sank through the floor to touch the rock. Frowned as she rose. "There is one. Has been for years, stars witness. It stopped running when the miners left."

"Then why still turn the wheel?" Jenn asked, feeling that a sensible question amid what clearly wasn't normal at all.

Together, they looked where the chain and tracks led, a destination hidden by the downward slope of the tunnel.

Edis flowed forward. "Let's find out."

While in the bag laced with mimrol thread and spells, the lettering of mimrol on the pin brought from Avyo changed briefly to read . . .

"At last!"

Ancestors Putrid and Pickled, Bannan couldn't remember the last time he'd been this drunk, unless it was when Lila talked them into trying—

"He's awake!"

Semyn? His nephew shouldn't be in a bar, especially this one. Bad parenting, that was. A complaint he tried to utter, but it came out an incoherent croak.

"Ancestors Best and Beholden, you gave us a scare."

Emon? Who had, Ancestors Witness, come along with them in the past, but not since his investiture as a baron of the House of Keys and becoming no fun. Why bring him along? Another croaked complaint.

"I'm still fun," that familiar voice informed him, by the tone mildly insulted. "Hold still."

People kept saying that, Bannan thought mussily. It wasn't fair—

—Wasn't fair—

—fair, to not know what he was and "Heart's Blood!" he heard himself shout, loud and clear at last.

"You're safe," Emon went on, saying in his calm easy voice what steadied the world and Bannan's badly frayed nerves. "You're in our rooms, in Gordit, and well guarded. Semyn and Araben brought you from the stable. It's late afternoon, the day before Fool's Day. When you're ready, we'll—"

"Is something wrong at home?" Semyn jumped in, grabbing Bannan's hand. "Are Momma and Werfol in danger?"

Bannan opened his eyes to find himself staring into a blue cloth. He fumbled to push it away. Someone else eased away his hand, then began unwrapping what turned out to be a damp towel, gently lifting Bannan's head to remove the rest.

And reveal Emon's face, with those intelligent eyes and gentle smile. "I can see you," Bannan announced, for it felt a momentous accomplishment. He thought at once of Kydd. By the Bones of his Ancestors, he'd be beyond beholden if Lila had lifted Kydd's blindness, too.

He rolled his head to look at Semyn, dressed in rags with his face smeared with dirt. "Street urchin, I take it?"

The boy grinned. "Says the miner."

Emon gave a little cough. "Bannan. Did Lila send you?"

Bannan sat up, Semyn pushing a pillow behind his back, to check they were alone before he answered. "When I left her, everything was well at your home." Lengthy explanations had to wait. "A turn-born went missing in Gordit. I was asked to look into the matter and Lila got me here." Thanks to Edis—an arrangement to be questioned another time—and most of his flesh.

Another question to wait. "Is Jenn here?"

Semyn's eyes widened. Emon cocked his head like one of his curious crows. "Not that I'm aware," he said.

"I remember Jenn," the boy announced proudly. "She can come here. Gordit is in the edge."

The truth. And good come of Semyn's inability to remember elsewhere, something Bannan knew the boy felt acutely. "Thank you. Jenn may join us soon, then." *The sooner the better—*

"Here I envisioned a dry investigation into misplaced funds and support," Emon commented. "I take it there's more going on."

"It has to be the mine, Poppa." Werfol would have bounced on the bed with excitement. Semyn sat perfectly still, only the intensity of his gaze a sign he was ready to burst with news. "It's shut down and boarded up, but the innkeeper told me there are those who go into it, and that it's where Gordit's wealth comes from, to the benefit of few."

"Excellent." Emon studied Bannan, assessing his condition. "I treated you with Lila's potion. A last resort, should she be trapped by her gift. We're glad it worked." He stopped there, though clearly wanting to know what had happened to him to make it necessary.

The truthseer drew a breath, about to tell them, but what could he say? The Verge destroyed me. A creature of magic rebuilt me. But treat me as you did before. Trust me.

There was the rub. How could they, when he wasn't sure he did anymore?

Ancestors Tortured and Tormented, Edis had been wrong—or optimistic—to judge him back to normal. His altered gift, the creeping paralysis? Bannan had seen enough of magic to take them as portents of a change more profound than new skin, change impossible to predict, and, he feared, far from done.

And beyond his control. What wasn't? Accomplishing what he'd come to Gordit to do. Saving those counting on him, and at that better thought, the truthseer released the breath he'd held. He stretched and, feeling no dizziness, rolled to sit on the side of the bed, Semyn hopping out of his way. "Ancestors Blessed, I'm beholden you found me," giving the boy a warm smile, "and to your skill, Emon. And ridiculously hungry," he added, surprised.

"A side effect," Emon assured him with a relieved smile. "Semyn, fetch some supper before the guards finish it all, please. Let them know your mother's brother is back to his normal self."

If only that were true, Bannan thought, managing to keep his smile.

Jenn didn't need Edis' air of increased vigilance to be aware of a threat growing with every step she took down the tunnel, a sensation unmitigated by the mimrol lights. They weren't at all like the lantern Bannan had told her about, that burned mimrol like oil in a lamp. These shed a cold brilliance that made the place eerier, she thought, glinting along the empty track and greasy chains, carving thick shadows between timbers. And while she'd have thought it impossible to be ambushed?

Heart's Blood, anything seemed possible here.

She felt the intentions woven by a sequence of terst turn-born, unusually tidy and small in scope. Like Mistress Sand, perhaps none of her kind willingly lingered in the mine. Some intentions were reassuring and agreeable, this far underground. *Don't collapse. Show the way. Freshen the air.*

Others less so. *Don't steal from us. Don't notice us. Let us pass.*

Large shapes appeared ahead, box-like. They'd found the train cars! Edis' hand came back, pressed down in a sharp *halt*.

Jenn stopped in the glow between shadows, her mouth dry despite the damp, watching her companion sink into the rock floor by the tracks up to her head, then slide forward to the cars.

A head without a body in view, like Wen's trick with the house toad, was bad enough. Watching Edis' glide over rock was, Jenn decided, the most disturbing thing she'd ever witnessed, but she couldn't not look, as if looking might help.

Edis emerged, rising to her normal height, waving Jenn to approach. "There's no one here."

The cars were dark, dented metal, wide and open at the top and narrow below, their large metal wheels sitting on the rails, which she knew train cars did but it was remarkable to actually see it for herself.

There were three cars linked together by a system of large hooks and rings; the first car in line had an empty hook ready, Jenn assumed, to connect to a link on the chain beneath.

Standing on her toes, fingers gripping the rusty rim of the car, Jenn looked inside. Empty save for a few small rocks wedged in the bottom. The next was the same, and she was about to follow Edis past the third and last without wasting more time, when a feeling made her stop. A feeling she must look—

The same feeling alerted the terst cows in her pouch, who knew the scent of illusion and the danger it posed, and, afraid for their leader, they bounced and jiggled, making no difference at all at this size, then used their claws to *POKE!*

"Ow!" Jenn slapped a hand at her pocket.

Edis flowed back to her. "What is it?"

"I don't know. Something pricked me." She shook her dress, on the chance one of the scamps or other pest had climbed inside. Nothing fell out, which was good, except now she'd no idea what might have poked her. "I was about to check this car—"

"Stay here." Edis rose up and up, extending herself till her wrinkled body was no wider than Jenn's arm. She curled over the rim of the train car, hesitated an instant, then dived down like a striking snake, rising again with hands cupped into fists.

Once more Jenn's height, Edis opened her right hand. On the

palm were round stones unlike any Jenn had seen or heard described, with color swimming in their milky depths. No two were the same. "Wicles. They're found in pockets of ore. Worthless." Edis went to toss them away.

Jenn stopped her. "The turn-born came for gems to trade in Eldad. What's worthless here might be rare and valuable there."

A considering look. "I wouldn't know. It's possible. The rest of what's in the car are these. A big pile of them."

She opened her left hand to show the palm covered in little triangles, each with two serrated sides.

Shark's teeth. Jenn stared at them, trying not to believe it. But she'd seen what Tooth was inside, as she was a sei's tears—"It's my friend. What's left of him." She looked up at Edis, tears blurring her vision. "How could this happen?"

Had the terst cows been able to speak, they would have told their leader about such traps. But she'd avoided this one, thanks to them, and they were content it was so.

While the words on the pin didn't change at all.

With no rider to hinder his choices, Scourge ran a straight course from the Westietas Estate to Gordit, crashing through forest and field, surging up and down ridges and hills; his speed and endurance were impressive, even to a dragon.

Not that Wisp would admit it.

Nor did he follow the kruar's peril-filled path, finding it soothing and more efficient to fly the ways of the earth, though the land here turned out to be full of holes dug by people. Passing through those was startling in the extreme.

Good. Outside the edge, his thoughts slowed, as did his reflexes. Having done it once before, Wisp forced himself to pay attention to every wingbeat, every breath. Unsettling, the sense of moving out of sync with his surroundings. Exhausting, the effort to hold steady.

His old enemy had the advantage there, having forgotten what he was with his first hoof strike on the path, a mindless beast driven to Gordit by a single instinct.

Find the truthseer. Find his rider.

A dragon flew its own course and would never be driven—

Other than by his concern for the girl and this nonsense of the sei. Wisp snarled as he flew. A trap? He'd rip apart whoever dared—

What if it were an Old One?

There was a thought to hurry up his blood, not that the Old Ones were to fear. If the tales were true, they'd been first to emerge from pools of primordial magic and remained unchanged since. Ancient, aloof, Old Ones took no interest in the business of younger beings, including the sei, paying no attention even when the sei sundered the world, creating the Verge and edge.

Most, Wisp knew, had forgotten the Old Ones or never heard the tales. Others, like the terst, denied the truth, refusing to acknowledge any had come before.

Fools. He'd met an Old One. A being of unimaginable power and terrifying purity. It smelled like dust and memory—and hadn't noticed his existence.

A dragon could be grateful.

Why would an Old One deign to heal the soldier, Edis Donovar? Why make her into The Traveler, that force of legend able to move anywhere at whim?

Why *now*?

Wisp counted wingbeats and breaths. Wingbeats and breaths.

Fearing the answers.

ELEVEN

JENN BADE EDIS return her handful of teeth to those in the Ansnan train car, being akin to an Ancestor's Bones, which were kept together and deserving of respect. She doubted Mistress Sand and her fellows would want them, sentiment not a characteristic of the terst turn-born, but she would tell them where to find them, should she be wrong.

CLATTERCLATTER

The chains bounced and rattled along the floor at intervals, whatever they moved still ahead. Edis thought it likely an elevator to the surface, but she couldn't be sure.

Jenn was no longer sure she cared to find out but, with no better option, she followed Edis down the tunnel.

Her companion abruptly stopped with her hand on the wall—not as she'd done to listen to the rock, but for support. Jenn caught up to her in a heartbeat, putting her shoulder under Edis' other arm.

Edis' eyes were closed and there was, to Jenn's dismay, no weight to her, nor strength nor glow. Her mouth gaped, taking in light desperate pants. There was no question.

She was done.

"It's past time you left, Edis," Jenn told her gently, but firm. "Regain your strength. Hearts of my Ancestors, I ask you to go. Please."

A sorry sign, that Edis' nod of assent left her head hanging. "If—if it's an elevator, there's—there's a lever—"

"I'll figure it out," Jenn assured her. Heart's Blood, she'd have to, wouldn't she? "What matters most is you." She stepped back.

Without another word, Edis Donovar sank into the rock floor and was gone.

Leaving Jenn alone in the tunnel.

CLATTERCLATTER

A sound she'd come to heartily dislike, but a goal, after all. Aunt Sybb said, Jenn reminded herself, that goals were admirable incentives.

Though she also said they could be daunting. Especially that time when, much younger, Jenn and Peggs had made a long list of ambitious goals to accomplish before their beloved aunt left for Avyo, to show their love, only to exhaust themselves and miss precious time with her, so they hadn't.

The trick, Jenn knew, was to pick a single goal and do your best to achieve it.

Brushing back a stray lock of hair, she began to walk alongside the rail, deeper into the tunnel. An elevator would be excellent, if it provided the way out. She didn't overlook the fact that an elevator also provided the way *in*, meaning there might be others ahead of her.

CLATTERCLATTER

Others who might have water and food, Jenn judged, growing more cheerful, for she was thirsty and hungry, and stretched her legs a bit more.

Or news of Bannan Larmensu, which would be the best outcome of all, and with that thought, she was tempted to run but knew better, the rock floor uneven.

But the wish of her heart would not be denied and the tunnel grew shorter than it had been or was, and Jenn's next footstep took her right out of the tunnel to its end.

And into a vast cavern. A cavern with a floor ending steps away, with a railing to stop anyone from falling into—

Grabbing the metal bar, Jenn stared out over the limitless lake, its dark wavy surface stroked by light from bags hanging from a ceiling far above. She'd heard of underground rivers, of course, but hadn't imagined anything this big.

A great disk of stone, like a miller's wheel, sat atop the water nearby, lapped by waves. The chains ran to a gear shaft running through its heart. Pulleys and timbers supported a crane waiting to one side, its claws sized to pick up a train car, for there were two on the disk, set opposite to each other, and at first Jenn thought both were empty.

CLATTERCLATTER

The chains moved, the gearshift turned, and the stone disk came to life. Slowly, then faster it spun, bringing the car furthest from her around until she could see it was occupied.

"Chalk!" Stripped of his clothing, prone, unconscious. Or dead.

No, she wouldn't think that. She was in time to save him. Jenn ducked under the railing to reach the car, but it spun past. Water soaked her, the lake churned by the disk, and much as she wanted to, she couldn't jump that far.

The crane.

Rushing to it, Jenn was relieved to see it was similar—other than in size—to the one she and her father used in the mill to set the stones each year. She released the brake, turning the control wheel to ease the claws into position. She'd wait for the chains to stop and the stone disk to come to a halt, then take hold of the car. A matter then of swinging it and Chalk to safety on the waiting tracks beside her, the counterweight doing the work.

CLATTERCLATTER

SPIT! HISS! Sparks began to fly! More and more shooting into the air from the edge of the spinning disk!

Jenn flinched back. Sparks could fly from a millstone as well, posing such danger to the wooden structure they'd have water nearby—

With ROAR the lake caught fire!

The terst cows cowered in her pocket, trusting their leader to save them, and hoping she'd do it very soon.

She staggered further away, hands raised and dumbfounded. Everyone knew water couldn't catch fire, so this wasn't a proper lake at all, and she might have thought it oil, but there wasn't a smell—

Edis had claimed the "water" at the wheel was mimrol. Here, then, must be a mammoth lake of the stuff, here, in the edge. *But how?*

Flames licked the train cars, turning them white hot, and this was how they'd murdered Tooth, Jenn realized with helpless horror. They'd melted his glass.

It wasn't to happen again. She wouldn't let it.

Jenn Nalynn made a wish.

While the pin from her mother glowed white hot, singeing the bag but not scorching her skin, and every part of it read . . .

"We must have this power!"

Baron Emon Westietas convened a war council in his bedroom, not, Bannan knew, that any here anticipated a battle—Ancestors Witness, he'd again arrived weaponless should there be one and would have to remedy that—but to adjust a strategy upended by his arrival.

And Semyn's excellent spycraft. The boy—the heir, the truthseer corrected proudly to himself—had slipped away while he'd gobbled not two but three meals' worth of food, reentering the room immaculately attired in a formal summer coat, with a roll of paper in his hand. He brought the Ansnan engineer with him, and Bannan rose to his feet to bow. "Araben Sethe. I'm told without you I'd still be with the ox. My deepest thanks."

She grinned. "I'm sure Honeypie was sorry to lose you. The big fellows like company."

"Come, take a seat." Emon consulted his timepiece. "We've less than two hours till sunset."

With no sign of Jenn Nalynn and, much as he'd give to see her walk in the door, Bannan prayed she'd find somewhere safe to wait out the turn before moving through town.

While they'd take advantage of the evening crowds to make a move of their own. Bannan wore his miner's clothing, grateful for Semyn's quick thinking to retrieve it and the hat.

As he was grateful to Emon who—regardless of Bannan's being comatose on his bed earlier—refrained from questions or doubt of his readiness now.

The baron's confidence in Lila's potion implied a truly distressing familiarity; Bannan fully intended to press his sister on the topic of the near-death experiences she hadn't shared, how many and how dire for a start.

As for being ready? He was, the truthseer vowed to himself. He had to be.

Taking Semyn's roll, Emon spread it on the table they'd pulled away from the wall, Dutton and Derhall watching from the side. It was a map of Gordit, neatly drawn and mostly complete. The baron nodded thanks to his son, who nodded back, a hint of color in his cheeks. "Elder Cotalen?"

Semyn pointed to a large square three blocks from where he'd marked the inn. "Here, on Declare. The road leading to the mine, Poppa."

"Wise reported the elder's entertaining guests tonight," Derhall said. "Rhothan guests and unfamiliar."

"On Fool's Day Eve?" Araben shook her head with disgust. "A town's leader is to host the less fortunate, not serve a feast to rich friends. Not the only duty he's shirked. Why, he left it to the dema to declare clemency! Fah, the man doesn't deserve to be an official, stars witness, let alone an elder."

The "clemency" she spoke of was the Ansnan practice of releasing nonviolent offenders, such as those serving time for debt, to participate in the festival. Word was, all peacefully returned to their incarceration at the end, hungover but presumably happier.

Not a prospect making the baron's guards happier, Bannan thought, amused.

"Who in Gordit might share your opinion?" Emon asked, a little too casually.

"The dema," suggested Semyn, eyes alight.

"I'd planned to visit the Celestial Temple this evening, m'lord," Araben offered, quick as could be. "I might lodge a complaint, without mentioning Rhothan information. A word in the right ear." She looked downright gleeful at the prospect.

"Thank you." The baron gazed at the map, then flattened his hand over Cotalen's home. "We need to know who's in there."

Semyn straightened. "A courtesy call from your heir would be in order, m'lord baron. To arrange final details for tomorrow's speech."

Emon looked to Dutton, who gave a terse nod. He trusted the boy, that said, and be sure Semyn noticed.

"I'll take some air myself," Bannan put in, grinning at the guard. "Might stroll toward the mine."

Semyn waited, eyes locked on his father, face calm and absolutely still. More disciplined than most adults, this lad, and not only due to his mother's teaching. Much as the truthseer wanted to deny it, his young nephew was no longer a child.

"We'll work on your speech tomorrow morning." Emon flashed a thoroughly mischievous smile. "I've a feeling the appropriate wording will have changed by then." His smile faded as he looked at his son. "Visit this thorn in our side. Learn what you can, but get back before I worry, if you please."

"I will." Semyn swept a full court bow, rising with a smile of his own. "My lord baron."

"Rascal," Emon said fondly. "Go on, the lot of you. Stir up the town." A keen look to Bannan. "And find your lady."

"That," Bannan answered, his pulse racing, "I promise."

Ice coated the chains and gear shaft, halting both. Ice spread from where Jenn waited by the railing across the lake, the mimrol drawing itself into long feathered crystals, unable to evade her wish.

No sparks, no flame, but with the mine this warm, she'd bought herself moments, no more, before all thawed and it started again, moments to save Chalk—

Jenn Nalynn ran to the railing and jumped.

Her hands hit stone. Her feet slipped over ice and she heaved herself up, shocked to have made it. Which wasn't, according to Aunt Sybb, how one should proceed in any action, particularly one involving lives and safety—but also applied to carrying too large a pot of boiling water through the parlor—

Jenn pushed herself to her feet and rushed to the frost-rimmed train car holding Chalk. A jump and she got her elbows over the top, then a knee.

And before the terst cows, gravely concerned over her actions, could protest—

With a sensation like slipping through a curtain, she tumbled inside to land on top of the terst turn-born.

Who hadn't melted, as far as she could tell, although he was flesh and bone, which made it a question. His poor feet were burnt and his hands, the hair singed from his head. Jenn touched his cheek as gently as possible. "Chalk. Wake up. We don't have much—"

He seized her wrist, eyes wide. Before she could move, he rolled over, pinning her beneath him, then leapt to his feet and threw himself over the side of the car.

Ancestors Ungrateful and Rude. She could almost hear Wisp, ranting about the untrustworthiness of terst turn-born, though to be fair, she hadn't been the one being melted—

Speaking of ice, hers would be, making it time she got out of here, too.

Jenn went to get up, only to find herself pinned to the floor. No need to panic, she told herself. She'd simply wish for cold again.

She made the wish, forming it as clearly and powerfully as she had before.

Nothing happened.

It wasn't a *nothing* as if Chalk *disagreed* with her intention.

Drips began trickling down the inside of the train car.

This was a *nothing* as if she'd no power at all.
Oh dear.

Horse sweat stained the lower half of his long coat; the man had ridden hard to get here and with no good news, by his expression. He reacted to Kydd's blurted "You!" with a quizzical look, saying "Are we acquainted, good sir?" and Kydd might have imagined that flicker of appalled recognition in his eyes—

—but he hadn't. Heart's Blood, they knew one another, all too well.

Twenty-four years ago they'd studied in Avyo together, done magic together, and, among the up-and-coming Heirs, this man's talent had set him fourth behind Kydd. Whatever name he used now, then he'd been Weasel, as Kydd had been Raven; only the seniormost mages knew their real ones.

They'd been competitors, never friends, and when Weasel vanished without a trace, Kydd, with the rest, assumed he'd died attempting a spell beyond his ability.

Ancestors Sneaky and Sly, what was he doing here?

HERE! WE'RE HERE!

His journals! Once more clawing at his heart, pulling at his mind—Weasel had brought them—must have intercepted the guard—but why return them? *He must mean to use them—to force Kydd to give them up—or kill him, to the same result—*

Unaware, the baroness made a brisk introduction. "Kydd, my sons' tutor, Master Namron Setac. Namron, Kydd Uhthoff is here as our guest."

Weasel collected himself. "Good sir." He bowed his head in polite greeting, raised it to give Kydd a searching look.

Nothing else. No overt accusation. Weasel felt confident, secure in his place here.

Two could play that game. Schooling his expression to one of chagrined apology, Kydd inclined his head. "Master Setac. My mistake."

He sat down, taking hold of Werfol's small hand beneath the table, drawing courage from the touch.

Lila lowered the brow she'd lifted, the only reaction she'd shown. Werfol's eyes, brown with those specks of gold, flicked between him and Weasel.

Who turned his attention to his employer, his expression become grave. "Baroness Westietas, I encountered a member of your guard in great distress on the road. I deeply regret to inform you she died in my arms."

At her post by the door, Ryll took a sharp breath; she subsided at a glance from the baroness, but her stare never left Namron as he went on, "I've given Revis the location of her body, judging it vital to return these to you with all speed." Weasel pulled a satchel from under his coat.

And there they were. "Daring," Kydd accused, unable—unwilling—to restrain himself, "to touch books of dark magic that aren't your own."

Weasel, about to offer the bundle to Lila, hesitated no more than a heartbeat, but it was enough. The baroness folded her hands in refusal. "Grim news, Master Setac," she acknowledged, her voice like a knife. "Leave what you've brought over there." A tilt of her head indicated the desk, then she smiled, a smile that sent a chill down Kydd's spine and brought the guards to alert, guards she kept in the room with a signal. "Sit with us. Cook is sending up a tray."

"Of course, m'lady." Putting the cursed satchel on the desk, Weasel started for the table only to be intercepted by a guard waiting to take his filthy coat. "I'll keep it on," he said. "I'm chilled."

Lila snorted. "Nonsense." She nodded at her guard, who peeled off the coat despite Weasel's belated effort to forestall him—the reason for which became immediately and dreadfully plain.

A bloody handprint smeared the front of his shirt.

Ryll lunged forward, grabbing him by the collar to lift him half off his feet by that choking grip. "What did you do to Bobbieb?!"

"Put him down," Lila admonished.

Gritting her teeth, the seniormost obeyed. She didn't let go. "He knows what happened to her, m'lady."

"Master Setac?"

Weasel shot Kydd a pleading look.

Wanted help, did he? Ancestors Brutal and Blooded, he'd not get it, Kydd railed to himself. Never, for a liar wearing an innocent's blood, this worm who'd somehow become the boys' tutor, trusted with their care and lives—allowed to teach them—

Kydd kept hold of Werfol's hand. "I wasn't mistaken," he stated, flat and sure. "Whoever you pretend to be now, I knew you as Weasel, member of the Heirs and student of the foulest magic."

"Momma, it's true. It's true!" Werfol half shouted, his bottom lip trembling. Kydd's heart went out to the lad, so sorely betrayed.

At the same instant, Ryll freed a hand to whip out her knife, pressing it to her captive's throat. "Watch his hands," Kydd warned quickly.

But Weasel's hands stayed limp at his sides, his demeanor improbably calm, and that couldn't be good, the beekeeper thought, bracing himself. Sure enough, instead of protesting, the spellcaster spat out, "And I know you, Raven! Do these fine people?"

"Stand down, Ryll, please." The guard lowered her knife and took a reluctant half step back.

Weasel shook himself like some harmless, ruffled bird.

Lila Westietas rested her chin on the back of her hand to gaze at him. "You bring us no secrets, Master Setac. Kydd is a family friend who revealed himself and risked his life to bring us the information in those books." She turned her head to look at her son. "As for your tutor, I know what he studied, what he did before taking a different path." Her face softened. "Dearest Heart, do you really think I'd let anyone close to you and Semyn whose life I hadn't scraped bare? Who hadn't earned my trust?"

His small hand tightened around Kydd's, but nothing but intense focus showed on Werfol's face. "He can lie to me, Momma. To Uncle Bannan. Did you know that about him?"

A focus reflected in Lila's. Lifting her head, she regarded Weasel a long moment. "I did not." At her frigid tone, every guard dropped hand to weapon.

"I haven't lied—but you've no need to take me at my word." As if without fear—or seeing his only recourse—Weasel stepped to the table to offer the boy his hand. "If you trust what Raven's told you, Werfol, that includes the counter."

Kydd's warning "Careful!" came too late. Werfol lunged forward, knocking dishes to the floor in his haste to seize his tutor's hand. "Have you lied to Momma?" the boy demanded.

"I have never lied to your mother, the baroness." Was that the glint of a tear? "I have never lied to you, Werfol, or your family or staff. I care, deeply, about the Westietas. You are the hope for us all."

Still linked to the truthseer, Weasel looked at Kydd. "I escaped the Heirs and went into hiding. To my shame, I feared to tell anyone else of my doubts—my loathing for their ways. I should have told you, Raven. Given you the same chance. I'm sorry I misjudged you."

"Ancestors Blessed, don't be. You didn't." Kydd let out a shaky breath as Werfol let go and sat back, bones aching as he dared let go of tension and fear for the first time since seeing Weasel's face. "I'd have turned you in—torn your mind to shreds and been glad of the chance to advance myself. I wasn't—I wasn't what I am now. What I want to stay—" He couldn't help the glance at the desk, at the satchel of his journals, the journals *calling* him.

Weasel's—Namron's face lit with comprehension. "They're yours."

"They were Bobbieb's charge," Ryll snapped, out of patience. "M'lady, he wears her blood!"

A plea for justice, and Lila inclined her head, accepting it. Cold green eyes found Namron. "Explain yourself, Master Setac."

The other man dropped his gaze, lips working.

With a rush of compassion, Kydd answered for him. "Your guard was compelled. Taking my journals was meant to make me follow—to go to whoever was responsible. It might have worked—" If he hadn't Peggs and Marrowdell to pull him a better way. "As for the guard, Bobbieb—" Heart's Blood, a child was beside him.

Werfol tucked his arm through Kydd's. Looked up earnestly. "Momma says we must know the bad things people do to one another, if we're to stop them."

Even Lila had the grace to look discomfited by this. "There are limits," she muttered.

"Not about this," her son said with a most unchildlike conviction. "Not about magic."

After a long, painful pause, she nodded. Ryll stepped closer, folding her arms. Waiting.

"They would have used a spell that turns a person into a stone walker—a shell without will," Kydd said heavily. "With Bobbieb's strong sense of duty—her loyalty to you, Baroness—nothing less would have controlled her for more than an instant." Heart's Blood, if only he could leave it at that—but if he did, there'd be questions. Lingering doubt. "She would have known. She couldn't have resisted. Only death freed her."

One hand pressed to the bloody print on his shirt, Namron covered his eyes and wept, answering the last, unasked question. Ryll Aronson gently guided him to sit at the table, pressing his shoulder in mute gratitude, and the beekeeper felt numb, faced with such grief.

His fault.

OURS! TAKE US UP! OURS!

With searing intensity, and Kydd flinched, holding onto the table edge. "I can't stay here," he pleaded abruptly, though how could he leave? "They're too strong," he gasped, unable to take his eyes from the satchel.

Helpless against the desire to claim that strength again. He started to rise.

Namron lifted his face. "Be free, then. Spell them to me."

"You can do that?" Lila demanded sharply. "Make it safe for someone else to use them?"

In that instant, the wrong path, the deadliest one, yawned in front of them all. The fierce, protective Lila Westietas, untrained and with access to dark magic? As if hearing Kydd's thought, Namron said firmly, "They can only be spelled to a person fully versed in those arts, baroness."

Kydd saw a flicker of relief in her eyes; he wanted to sag in his chair with his own, but there was much to be done. "I'm willing," he said firmly. Heart's Blood, to return to Marrowdell, return to Peggs and their child, with the final link to his terrible past severed?

NO! YOU WANT US! WE ARE YOU!

Kydd pushed himself from the table with such violence he barely stayed in his chair. Wrapping his arms around his middle, he rocked in place, bobbing his head, anything to keep from running to the desk. "They don't like the idea," he said, surprised how calm he sounded. "They're fighting back."

"It's part of how the Heirs controlled us—our journals came from the mages," Namron reminded him—and informed the others. "They put spells to make us keep the journals close in the bindings and pages, spells fed by each stroke of our pens and every word. Or drawing—you drew in yours, Raven. I remember."

"I did more. I put in every name I heard. Every meeting place and time. I wanted to know everything—" Kydd stopped.

Lila's eyes glowed.

"There's a way to preserve such information while removing any threat posed by these books." Namron took a sip of wine. "My masters—oh, yes," at Kydd's raised eyebrow, "I continue to be taught. How to detect and counter dark magic. How to locate those with gifts and—" A look at Lila made him gulp his next mouthful instead of finishing the sentence.

"Pertinent to this situation," Namron continued, "I can erase every spell you wrote in these books, Kydd. Cleanse them of every scrap of dark magic, while leaving the rest behind."

NO!NO!NO!!

For the first time, the beekeeper relished the journals' babble in his head, feeling their fear.

"There is a price," Namron finished soberly.

There always was. Kydd had cast such cleansing spells in his time. He knew what Namron hesitated to say. "To erase spells I wrote, you must erase my memory of writing them. I'll no longer remember any specifics. It's safer that way," this to Lila.

NO!NO!NO!!WE WON'T ALLOW IT!

Namron gave a tiny flinch. Averted his gaze to stare into his glass. "I'm not you, Raven." He looked up with—was that pity?

He deserved none. Kydd nodded, clarity slowing the beat of his heart, putting all into final, perfect perspective. Ancestors Penitent and Punished, how fitting, after all this time, after all he'd done. "I understand. It's fine."

"I don't. What do you mean?" Lila demanded.

That Namron possessed the tokens and words the spell required but not the skill to limit what it erased. That the price to silence the journals for good would be the whole of Kydd's memory—to the point when he'd first set pen to paper, maybe more.

That the price was Peggs.

He'd forget her. Return to Marrowdell a confused stranger, no longer the man she loved, with no right to her love. Though he would always, Kydd swore by the Bones of his Ancestors, be a good father to their child. He'd leave himself instructions—

Making sure he didn't touch Werfol, Kydd straightened in his chair, fussed with his shirt, and found his voice. "My old acquaintance means he'll need my help. I've always been the stronger spellcaster. Time you admitted it," with a glance at Namron.

Who looked sad but proud, as if Kydd had passed a test. *Maybe he had at last*, the beekeeper thought. "I don't want their stain in my head a moment longer," he said. "Let's be done. I'll spell my journals to Namron and accept the cleanse."

NOOOOOOO!

A howl echoing the one in his heart.

Trapped and alone, truly helpless, Jenn Nalynn closed her eyes, the better to picture Bannan's. They were like warm apple butter, often more gold than brown. His gaze sparkled with interest in everything, warmed with a deep, understanding compassion.

Heated with love, that as well. Why, she could almost forget—

CLATTERCLATTER

—her eyes shot open. "Hearts of my Ancestors, hear my heart's plea," she prayed, as loudly as she could. "I'd be Beholden to know Bannan is safe, and Peggs, and Kydd, and Poppa and Aunt Sybb and everyone. I'd be Beholden if Wisp doesn't take my—my melting as his fault—" but her dragon would, not being here "—and if Edis doesn't either—" because she would, having left her "—and if time gets fixed or whatever I broke—"

Losing track, Jenn paused, because the gear shaft she could plainly see towering beyond the train car had begun to turn and her imminent fate was, quite reasonably, a distraction.

She resumed, "—I'd be Beholden if this doesn't hurt—" it would, Chalk having burnt feet and lost his hair, and she'd had her share of scalds working in the kitchen so had some notion "—doesn't hurt for long," Jenn amended.

Were her Ancestors listening?

Whoever had bespelled the pin might—what a horrible thought! Unless—"I'd be Beholden if whoever hurt Kydd and tricked my mother and Aunt Sybb into giving me this pin gets their comeuppance!" she prayed next and fervently, though the Ancestors didn't like it if you prayed for harm to others.

Still, a comeuppance was like *just desserts*, an expression Aunt Sybb liked—

The car moved sideways and she moved with it, meaning the stone was starting to spin.

Oh dear.

"—hear my heart's plea—however far we are apart," she whispered hurriedly, holding tight to thoughts of Bannan, "Keep Us Close."

Jenn closed her eyes.

Their leader falling silent, the terst cows climbed from her pouch.

Growing a bit larger, they severed her bonds, for those were illusion, then grew larger still.

Larger.

LARGER.

Until Jenn realized the warmth she felt down both sides wasn't from flames but something moving. She opened her eyes.

A terst cow. The two of them, stuffed into the car with her, rheumy little eyes attentive as if awaiting instruction.

While she didn't understand how they were here, she knew they shouldn't be. "Shoo!" Jenn said firmly, making the motion with her hands before remembering they were pinned—

But they weren't! The motion turned into a push at each terst cow, who nodded as if understanding completely, and when Jenn squirmed to get out of the car?

One scooped her up in the bend of its very large arm and followed the other over the side, leaving substantial amounts of manure behind as if stressed, and Jenn didn't blame them one bit.

The stone was spinning faster now, sparks beginning to fly. The terst cows held her and each other, gripping the stone with the great claws of their unencumbered arms, but they couldn't hold for long.

"We have to get off!" Jenn shouted, the churning lake adding to the racket. She pulled an arm free and tried to point—the spin making that difficult—to safety.

The terst cows, relieved their leader had such an excellent plan, grew larger.

And larger.

Until they were so LARGE, the stone tipped, tearing apart the gear shaft. Then, it was a simple matter of walking up the slope, hopping to solid ground, then growing smaller again.

And smaller.

Till Jenn Nalynn found herself standing on her own, two tiny cows at her feet. She stooped and picked them up, raising them to her eyes. "Thank you." She kissed each on its round tiny head.

Before hurrying down the tunnel before the stone and gear shaft crashed together with a tremendous *BOOM* and *SPLASH!*

Overcome by joy, the terst cows trembled and made themselves smaller still. Their leader kindly slipped them back into her pouch, and they were more than content it was so.

While in the bag, the words on the pin changed again to read . . . *"We are coming. We will have you."*

Once Araben Sethe left to pray—and lay her timely complaint—in her temple, Semyn Westietas and Dutton Omemee set off for their encounter with Elder Cotalen, the heir a splendid spectacle and the guard not far behind in his dress uniform with polished high boots and unusually large sword. The pair walked slowly, taking in the sights as befitted a young man let out on the town, being seen in return.

Bannan, in his guise as a local, gave the pair a sniff and scornful look, easing after them to follow at a distance. The tang of ox and stable left on his clothing was a bonus, the odors more common than not.

The streets were busy but not yet raucous. Most people were strolling with baskets and sacks, obtaining Fool's Day treats, and paid little attention to the young Rhothan noble and his guard other than ordinary courtesy. Behavior he'd expect in Vorkoun or Mondir, but not here, where battles had been fought and blood spilled.

Lila's peace? Much as he wanted to believe in it, the truthseer suspected it had more to do with Cotalen's guests. A wealthy Rhothan was no novelty here.

Lanterns were being lit on the shaded side of the street, while on the other, the final rays of sunshine imbued stone and timbers with a rosy glow. Musicians struck up light and lively tunes and children began to dance.

Jenn would love it.

At that pleasant thought, when not watching Semyn—more particularly watching for anyone else paying undue attention to the lad—Bannan looked for a head of golden hair. In Ansnor, hair like his love's would be striking—would she hide it? Meaning he had to keep an eye out for any young women of her size and grace wearing headscarves—

Ancestors Foolish and Frivolous, too many were, making him feel the fool indeed.

Semyn paused to exchange words with merchants every few steps, making small purchases he handed his guard to carry, or fervently taking notes as if planning to return. This went on for a block and a half, the boy ably playing the part of someone with a destination, but in no rush to reach it, merchants gazing after him fondly.

His latest stop was in front of a table of small dolls—the sort superstitious, or pious, Ansnans used to even their numbers, and he'd know they weren't toys—

"You there."

Impressive, how two words in that bone-shakingly deep voice oozed menace. *Bad as Tir.* As was Dutton's ability, in full dress, to slink up beside him.

"After sommat, soldier?" Bannan asked in a surly tone, also in Ansnan.

"M'lord wishes to tour the mine." Dutton held up his hand, a coin between two thick fingers.

"Happy to oblige." Snatching the coin, Bannan backed away with a mocking, "Fool on Fool's Day! Mine's closed, ye daft ox."

Dutton made a good show of swatting at him, though if his great fist had connected, Bannan would be flat on the cobblestones. Having escaped, he waved like the rogue Lila'd thought him, slipping into the crowd.

Without delay, Bannan sought a quiet, out-of-the-way place to look at the coin, or rather the folded scrap of paper Dutton had hidden against it. On the scrap, in Semyn's tidy script, were three lines in Lila's code, information doubtless gleaned from those so-casual conversations.

Lad did the family proud.

While Semyn and his guard lingered by the table, Bannan rearranged the letters in his head. Three names. Quot. Urkett. Eldee. Strangers' names, Rhothan but likely aliases. Even so, of use.

He chewed and swallowed the scrap of paper, then made a show of dodging out and past the doll-maker's table, making a rude Ansnan gesture at Dutton, onlookers aware he'd earned the big guard's ire. A few cheered him on, others less amused, but it was all part of the game they played.

Bannan reached Cotalen's house first.

No cobbles here; instead, heavy slabs of stone made a durable pavement, continuing as the street sloped up to become the roadway to the mine. Tracks glinted in the long last rays of sunlight, marking the start of factories and warehouses. Rows of miners' housing stood beyond them. Behind those houses? The wagons the duplicitous elder had "lost" in the record.

Here, though, were the homes of those in power. Unlike other elders' homes he'd seen, with their open doors and provision boxes for the poor, Cotalen's hid behind a tall metal fence with a closed gate. As if that weren't enough to keep out worthy townsfolk, two alert ademens stood watch.

No subtlety here. Was the man bold—or a fool?

Bannan tucked himself in an entranceway, shielded by one of the myriad potted plants adorning the street. There were plants behind the fence as well, larger shrubs, a cluster of imported roses and starflowers, plus a sorry-looking palm tree from Eld, proof wealth couldn't stop winter. There was, he blinked to be sure, an Avyo-style courtyard squeezed into the mix, complete with a tiny fountain before the doors into the house.

The building had to be well over a hundred years old, a structure not only historic but resistant to change. No number of false columns—four framed the doors—or ostentatious scrollwork over the new-looking windows hid what had been an iron foundry in its day. It'd be full of nasty drafts, come the cold weather, like being in a block of ice.

Gooseflesh rose on his arms. Bannan shook himself to be rid of the memory, though it was better than *BURNING—*

Heart's Blood, enough! He'd pushed himself hard, out here so soon; that was all. Lila's drug, Emon's care—ridiculous to be hungry after eating what he had, but it was part of the process and a good sign. Proof he was—

Semyn came in view, walking briskly now, Dutton his shadow. The lad approached the ademens at the gate, and, while Bannan couldn't hear what he said over the music from the street, it worked, for the ademens bowed and let them in—exchanging looks behind Dutton's broad back.

Too easy. True, the ademens might have been dazzled by Semyn's Rhothan perfection or briefed to expect a delegation from the baron, but this didn't feel right.

Why he was here, after all. Bannan pushed out of his hiding place, rejoining the smattering of people on the street.

Dodging around the corner to slip along the fence and hunt a way inside.

Stepping inside the elder's house, Semyn nodded graciously to the servant at the door, somehow not staring at the décor inside. Where exposed, the walls and ceilings were of discolored stone inset with remnants of iron hardware—evidence this had been the site of industry not too long ago. The floors, however, were new and agleam with expensive wood—where not covered in carpet. Someone had tried—and failed, in Semyn's estimation—to impose balance by choosing very large furnishings, most of dark wood, but those were covered with a market's worth of bright cushions and draperies, adding to the visual chaos.

Chaos could be a tactic, Momma taught, flooding the senses to hide significant details; moreover, this was the edge, where magic could be anywhere. Semyn took furtive glances at spots likely to hold a house toad or other such creature, not forgetting to look up into the high rafters, all the while looking for more mundane clues.

"This way, sirs."

Dutton a looming comfort a step behind, Semyn followed the servant through doubled carved doors into a much more welcoming room.

To the immediate consternation of the four already there. Seeing that, the servant fled without making any introduction.

Elder Cotalen. Three Rhothans—strangers, two women and a man. One woman bore a disarming resemblance to Cook, being wrinkled and round, but the lines on her face had never been from smiles. The second, taller woman had sharp features and unusually full lips. She looked so like the man, they might be twins.

He'd caught them about to leave. Semyn kept his expression pleasant, mind racing. The four were dressed for rough walking—no evening's revels here—and burdened with packs and sticks.

The elder turned an interesting shade of gray. The others simply looked hostile.

Semyn swept a deep bow. "Greetings. I am Semyn Marerrym Westietas, son and heir of Baron Westietas of Vorkoun. I've come to convey my father's respects and mine to you, Elder Cotalen. My apologies for the interruption," with such polished and false sincerity, poor Weed would have winced. "We'll leave at once."

Worth a try, Semyn thought, keeping his hand from his hidden dagger. If theirs was an innocent excursion, they'd accept his apology and let him and Dutton leave.

It wasn't, of course. Semyn read it in their faces, in the looks they exchanged. There were no weapons in sight, but menace oozed from the Rhothans.

Dutton took the sidestep that made room for his sword. "You'll be letting us go," the big guard growled, pulling free the blade.

The small woman smiled. Made a languid gesture.

The sword clattered to the floor, Dutton Omemee's arms and hands pinned tight to his body by invisible bonds. He fought to free himself, muscle bulging with effort, his face turning red, only to topple like a falling tree. His head struck the floor with a sickening CRACK!

He stopped moving.

Semyn didn't look at him. Didn't let his face lose control. "Was that necessary?" he asked as if mildly curious and not utterly horrified, because Momma's first lesson to her sons? Weakness armed their enemies.

"We must be in place before the turn," hissed the second woman. "Take the sword. End him."

"No!" Cotalen gasped. "We can't harm the heir." He grabbed Semyn's arm and pulled him close. "We bring him with us. Show him why he must work with us. Yes," as if talking to himself, "that's the best idea."

Semyn didn't struggle, though the elder's grip hurt and there was something not right in the look in his eyes. "Show me what?" he made himself demand, using the imperious tone Werfol adopted when refusing to budge. "More imaginary wagons on your ledger?"

"See? He's bright. He's been acclaimed. We can make him baron tomorrow. Have a seat in Avyo—"

They were going to kill Poppa. His fear vanished as Semyn's blood turned cold, and if any who knew Lila Westietas had been there, they'd have fled from the glint in his eyes.

"We have a seat in Avyo," the man said, unimpressed.

The boy caught it, suddenly, what unsettled him about the three in Rhothan clothing. The deliberate posture, the stilted voice. They were acting. And whether they were imposters or hiding their true identities, he'd seen their faces. No matter what Cotalen said, they wouldn't let him live.

Uncle Bannan was outside. Poppa and his guard would come. He had to buy them time.

Pointedly ignoring the elder, still holding his arm, Semyn spoke to the three.

"We know about the mine."

The turn was coming, a tickle in what would have been bones if Jenn had more than the memory of them; she supposed the sei's tears reacted in their place, but where were the sei in all this? It wasn't at all reassuring to think of the shrunken green dragon and its demand for her to FIX WHAT SHE'D BROKEN.

As if the mighty sei were powerless and afraid.

Ancestors Alarmed and Adamant, she'd her own priorities and Bannan came first, which meant reaching the glade where Edis had left her beloved. If he'd stayed there, of course. If he hadn't, she'd risk Melusine's magic—summoning what was lost to her wasn't entirely reliable or safe, but it had worked in Channen—

—and the turn would complicate matters. She'd need somewhere to hide as it passed. Maybe Ansnans had barns? A thick hedge would do—

Getting ahead of herself would not.

No telling what more could go wrong if she were careless. Though, Ancestors Witness, she was not staying in this dreadful place a moment longer than it took to find the way out. There had to be another exit and, Jenn reasoned, it had to be here.

In the cavern. She'd returned, driven back by the racket as the water—mimrol—wheel continued to *CLATTERCLATTER* futilely, scraping and bouncing the chains along. And, to be honest, she hadn't been able to walk past the train car with its sad pile of teeth, knowing what had happened to Tooth in it.

Jenn stayed to the wall, where the elevator Edis predicted surely should be—if there was an elevator. Thus far, she'd not found so much as an empty air shaft, but, she reminded herself determinedly, there remained a great expanse of dark damp wall to search. She kept going, glad to stay as far from the horrid underground lake as possible.

For one thing, its surface *rippled* as if unhappy they'd destroyed the stone—going calm if she stared at it, which wasn't normal. Not that anything down here was normal, in her opinion, but the ripples were sneaky and she didn't like them.

Feeling sorry for herself, was she? Jenn snorted. The sound echoed through the cavern, making her wince.

Ancestors Adrift and Alone, she'd give anything to have one or both of her magical friends with her right now. Her doing, that Wisp was with the Westietas, but how long did Edis need to rebuild herself?

Too long was very likely. Thinking of Edis, Jenn put her hand on the rock. It remained rock, mute and unhelpful.

Desperate, she put her palm gently against her pocket. "Tiny cows—" *very*, the terst cows preferring a size close to lint "—can you show me the way out?"

The terst cows, thrilled by their leader's *TOUCH* and her *VOICE* addressing them, had no idea what she said, but shared her intent to be somewhere other than here where there was nothing to eat, for they were hungrier than ever. They trusted their leader would take them to a better place with wonderful food, for they were forever in her care and content it was so.

"I didn't think so," Jenn answered for them. Regretting what sounded a churlish response, she added a fervent, "Ancestors Blessed, I'm beholden for your rescue." A gratitude she'd expressed several times this past while, particularly when reminded by a fresh whiff of what they'd deposited in the train car on the precariously tilted stone.

Bending her head, she sniffed warily, grateful the tiny cows seemed to make their noxious deposits where it was appropriate and not in her pocket.

Being bent, Jenn glimpsed something move on the floor, something small that wasn't a scamp, and froze in place lest she scare it away.

A section of rock the size of her thumb stood open like a little door. A head slowly appeared, a head that was mostly a pair of gleaming black eyes and partially beak, with wee sparkling blue gems for skin, making the head resemble an overripe summerberry.

The eyes, lidless, stared up at her.

More doors opened. More. Until she was surrounded by heads like summerberries. Stoneberries, she decided to call them, to herself at least.

After checking there were none directly beneath her, Jenn sank to her knees. A couple of heads whipped out of sight, doors closing behind them to instantly appear part of the rock floor. Shy.

"Greetings, little cousins. I'm Jenn Nalynn." She spoke in her softest voice, not wanting the rest to disappear. Other than the terst cows—and Edis—the stoneberries were the first creatures she'd encountered in the mine who appeared harmless and quite possibly friendly.

The first head to show itself elevated in little bursts, as if the stoneberry hopped up little stairs within its hole. A charming image dispelled once Jenn saw the rest of it.

Its back and sides were plated in flecks of stone matching the rock of the mine—an admirable camouflage except for the liberal sprinkling of blue gems everywhere, forming a glittering inlay of swirls and dots.

Its underside was a twitchy mass of gray segmented legs, a middle pair much larger and bent out like springs past the stoneberry's back. It was this pair that moved it in little hops—which weren't little relative to its size, Jenn discovered when the creature hopped to her knee.

Charming, she decided then and there, smiling at it.

As if smiling back, the stoneberry opened its beak, revealing the tip of a thick sturdy tongue. ~Elder sister, you have cows.~

A soundless echo followed, others chiming in, ~have cows—cows—cows—cows—~

As Wen had said, not that Jenn had grasped the full implication then. "I do, it seems." For now, she assured herself.

The terst cows, having climbed to the opening of her pouch to examine the new creatures, blinked and tucked themselves away again, relieved their leader was in charge.

"I would very much like to know how to get to the surface—"

A faint wind-through-leaves *flutter* as several doors slammed shut at once.

Oh dear. A different approach, then. "I need to find someone who is—" She pointed up, hoping if she didn't mention the surface it might help.

It didn't. More doors closed, and Jenn was at a loss what to try next.

Fortunately, the stoneberry on her knee was of sterner stuff—perhaps a leader, Jenn thought suddenly—for though it trembled, gems glittering, it remained. ~Elder sister, you must not stay here.~

Doors opened. ~stay here—here—here—here—~

The stoneberry sounding very like a house toad, Jenn summoned her patience. ~I don't want to stay here,~ she agreed.

~The cows you lead are hungry, elder sister.~

~elder sister—sister—sister—sister—~

Was that *reproach*? About to argue she'd hardly asked to have tiny cows in her pocket, let alone to be responsible for leading them to pasture, Jenn thought of Wainn's old pony, who'd safely carried every one of Marrowdell's children but to this day couldn't be trusted alone near apples or it would eat itself sick.

~I want to take good care of them,~ she conceded. ~I can't do that here.~ This hopefully.

A little leg tapped her knee. ~The cows see your path, elder sister, but cannot lead you there. Cows follow. That is their nature.~

~their nature—nature—nature—nature—~

Exactly like a house toad, other than the echoes, helpful and not at the same time. Maybe she could put the cows on her hand and walk around, waiting for them to point—

The stoneberry, however, wasn't done. ~First, you must speak with the Great One, who needs your help. He too doesn't want to be here.~

~be here—here—here—here—~

Great One?

Stomach sinking, Jenn lifted her gaze from the earnest stoneberry to look out over the lake.

Vast, inscrutable yellow-black eyes looked back, eyes set in a beaked head no more like the stoneberry's than a grain of sand was like a mountain. Mimrol poured from it as it continued to surface, until a body the size of an enormous island floated in front of her, the top gently bumping bags of light to send sparkles across the rock ceiling.

This needed her help?

~Elder sister. The Great One fell from there.~

~from there—there—there—there—~ echoed the rest, and every stoneberry aimed a small gray leg at the ceiling. Jenn tore her gaze from the monster to look up at what was, as far as she could tell, quite solid, being the underside of a mountain. It seemed highly improbable anything fell from it but the occasional rock.

Rock that sparkled. Which some kinds of rock did, Jenn knew, but, trusting the little cousins, she dutifully squinted, trying to make out more detail. The dazzle from the bags of light made it impossible to be sure, but the sparkles did seem to cover the ceiling.

And were some—twitching?

~Are there more of you up there?~ she asked the stoneberry on her knee.

~Not more of us, elder sister.~

~elder sister—sister—sister—sister—~

Implying something "not-us."

Well, whatever it was could stay there, far overhead, she decided, being more concerned with the enormous "not-us" floating right in front of her.

Jenn went back to staring at what appeared even bigger than an instant before.

Forgetting, in her astonishment, about the bag in her bodice, the bag containing the pin with words writ in mimrol, words changing briefly to read . . .

"Hurry! Hurry, granddaughter!"

"Flower crowns! Fool's Day flower crowns!" chanted a young woman in the street beyond, and he knew her voice. Had Bannan not been about to crawl under Elder Cotalen's high metal fence—some rodent or other conveniently wearing a sizable hollow near the kitchen midden—he'd have gone straightaway to thank the young farmer who'd brought him to the stable with her brother, thus to Semyn and rescue.

Semyn his pressing concern. Something wasn't right here, from the attitude of the ademens at the gate to this building with its blatant display of wealth. He should have stopped the boy—Dutton should have—

They hadn't, making it imperative he get inside. Thanks to Emon's guards, he'd an assortment of easily concealed weapons. Two knives, a garrote—he'd shot Wise a surprised look and she'd grinned at him—and a weighted club.

His jacket snagged on a metal curlicue and he worked it free, careful not to make any noise.

Through. He crouched behind the midden, the back door in view, ready to use his deeper sight to check for magical traps.

Then squeezed his eyes shut, terrified he'd lose control of his gift again. Opened them, furious at himself. *Heart's Blood, gift or no, he wasn't useless!*

The truthseer studied the door. The handle was worn, the wood unpainted. The servants' entrance, probably to the kitchen. No smoke rising from the chimneys implied an empty kitchen at that. The perfect entry—he rose, about to dash to it.

Crouched again as the door opened. Four adults came out, hustling Semyn along in their midst. His heart sank further when there was no sign of Dutton, guessing what that meant.

The group went to the back gate, ordering the ademens there to open it. There was a pause, a brief conversation.

He didn't wait to hear it. Bannan dived back through his hole under the fence, leaving skin and a pocket behind. Jumping to his feet, he made his way as quickly and quietly as he could to the street, the direction they'd have to come.

"Flower crowns for Fool's Day!"

Making a quick decision, he hurried to the voice, catching up to the woman with a tray of wildflower crowns. By the number on display in the crowd around her, business was brisk.

"Wanda."

Her eyes widened with recognition. "Stars blessed! I'm glad to see you're up and about so soon." A wink. "Told my—"

The group emerged onto the street. Bannan turned his back to them, speaking low and fast. "I need you to go the *Drift*, Wanda, fast as you can. Ask to speak to the baron's guard—"

She frowned, edging away. "I'm not—Oh." He'd held up Dutton's coin, enough to buy all her flower crowns plus a good supper for a family. "And what am I to say?"

"Say, 'Dutton's down. Semyn's been taken'—" he glanced over his shoulder to confirm "—'to the mine.'"

Semyn saw him. Looked away without a single indication he'd spotted help, and there was Lila's training, not to give away an advantage.

"The mine's closed—" Wanda followed his glance and paled, seeing who moved purposefully through the crowds, the ademens in the lead using a pole to hurry the non-attentive aside.

Dumping her tray to the pavement and ignoring the coin, Wanda put a hand on Bannan's arm. "Don't let them take the boy inside," she whispered urgently, then turned and ran for the inn, long legs flashing, before he could ask her why.

Ancestors Blessed, Uncle Bannan was coming for him. Had, by the way he stood with the flower seller, arranged for a message to Poppa, and Semyn knew his part was to give no sign he expected aid, to remain calm and focused, and he did it.

Even if his heart hammered in his chest and he felt sick, unable to stop seeing Dutton fall, his blood.

Momma would say to assess the odds.

They weren't good, not yet, the ademens leading them a big brute and well armed, and those with him capable of magic. Those coming for him would need an opening, some opportunity. His job, Semyn told himself, trying not to be afraid.

The road climbed, becoming loose stone with rusty dust-filled tracks to one side, tidy shed-like homes lining the other. Empty homes, those inside gone to town to enjoy Fool's Day Eve, not that Semyn dared shout for rescue. Their destination had never been in doubt. They took him to the mine and he went willingly, having little choice and a growing curiosity.

He did, however, diligently press and twist his left heel slightly with every step to leave a distinctive trail, the motion small and natural-seeming. A wise decision, he discovered shortly after they passed the miners' homes, where, without pausing, the three strangers gestured—

And everything outside their group *blurred* and became indistinct. By the Ansnans' lack of reaction, this wasn't new to them. Whatever they'd done muted the sound of their boots on rock as well, and such magic, to make them unseen and unheard, might foil ordinary pursuit.

Lowin was their best tracker. She'd know to watch for a deeper left heel print. Uncle would, and he'd true sight—which he shouldn't use so soon after being overwhelmed. Semyn might have no gift of his own, but he knew the danger, being tasked with stopping his brother from overusing his. Weed listened to him. Usually. More than to Momma, who wasn't much better at restraint.

The entrance of the mine loomed ahead, sealed behind massive barred doors that let only the rails through. Semyn wasn't surprised when they left the road, taking a narrow path up the rocky slope, but was disappointed they didn't leave someone behind to guard their backs. It would have been useful to know if anyone leaving the group lost the cover of its blurring shield.

The rocks of the path too large to hold his heelprint, he pretended to slip once in a while, leaving a scuff. If they noticed, those with him didn't appear to care. Heart's Blood, why should they? He was to be interrogated somewhere safe from interruption. After that—

Their plans for him were irrelevant. Poppa and Uncle Bannan would come; in the meantime, Semyn would find out everything he could about his captors.

Dragons. Dragons and Marrowdell and house toads. His memories proved they continued in the edge. By the sun's position between the mountains, it would set soon, bringing the turn. What had the woman said? *They had to be in the mine by then.*

Did they fear exposure? Or hurry to some timing of their own?

He needed, Semyn told himself, information. Easing closer to Cotalen, he whispered, "The baron will pay handsomely for my safe return."

"Hush, boy," this with a frantic look at the others. Louder, "I would never betray my friends."

Friends who ignored him. Noting that, Semyn confirmed his own conclusion: the elder was a pawn, the three with him in charge. "Quot. Urkett. Eldee."

Cotalen gaped like a fish. Seized his arm and whispered, spitting the words. "How do you know those names? Are you working for them? Stars witness, are they here?"

Another faction or a former alliance? How many had this fool betrayed?

They'd more enemies here than any had guessed.

One of the strange Rhothans gestured impatiently and Cotalen stumbled forward, ending Semyn's brief interrogation.

Brief but useful, the boy thought. He'd get more, given the chance.

Jenn considered the Great One of the stoneberries. Having not-always-tiny cows in her pocket, and familiar with the sei, who could be, at any moment, moth or mountain, size wasn't a surety in creatures of the Verge. But she'd the impression this was the Great One's proper size, the growth of a lifetime rivaling Wisp's centuries. Or longer.

Unlike the toad queen, who'd been huge and old, the Great One gave forth no sense of menace or malice. If anything, the feeling she had was of a patience so slow and profound it might not notice her fleeting self at all.

Yet did. Jenn couldn't decide if she was flattered or terrified. She'd the urge to curtsy to it—which she couldn't without standing first and couldn't very well do that with a stoneberry on her knee.

The rest of the stoneberries peeked from their doors at the show.

She gave a dignified nod, the best she could do. "I'm Jenn Nalynn."

HUFF!

Blowing her a considerable distance, and onto her back. After a startled pause, Jenn collected herself—pushing her hair from her face—and got to her feet, cautiously staying where she was.

Stoneberry doors popped open again. The one who'd been on her knee gripped the front of her dress like a burr—or confident spider. ~Fear not. I'm with you, elder sister.~

~elder sister—sister—sister—sister—~

"I'm glad," Jenn said weakly, then firmed her voice to address the vast face towering in front of her. "Please don't do that again."

The Great One's nostrils snapped closed.

Manners? A promising development, if so, Jenn told herself. She might as well get right to it. "How can I help you?"

The Great One *ROLLED!*

The motion drove a whoosh of lake over the surrounding floor, up to Jenn's knees and soaking her dress. It whooshed out again, making her stagger to keep her feet.

Stoneberry doors opened, heads nice and dry, once more peeking out. The little cousins had amazing reflexes—or knew what to expect.

What mattered loomed high above Jenn's head. A flipper, mossy and green, and she'd seen a flipper like this before—the Great One was a nyim.

The Nyim, perhaps, ancestor to the much smaller and abundant nyim swimming in Channen's canals. Creatures who snapped up mimrol raindrops—and stole her earrings, for they were greedy things and inclined to mischief, if not watched—though they'd helped her, in the end.

Had The Nyim been drawn to the huge lake of mimrol or the lake come with it?

Whichever came first, it was trapped here. Around the flipper, biting cruelly deep in its flesh, was a massive claw of silver metal from which led a chain with loops bigger than Jenn was tall—a chain going under the stone and gear shaft used to melt turn-born, which, because of Jenn and her terst cows, presently tipped far to one side and looked most unstable and possibly about to sink.

While The Nyim seemed about as vulnerable as the rock wall behind her, it had shown her it breathed air, as she did, making the consequence of that stone sinking deadly indeed.

It would take a wish, Jenn knew. A careful, focused sort of wish, like the one she'd made to melt Crumlin's mirror, but she immediately decided she mustn't envision heat. The mimrol would catch fire—with The Nyim on the surface—

Not fire. It wouldn't work anyway; the stone was impervious to heat—that's why, Jenn told herself, whoever had built this death machine for turn-born chose it.

She thought of her father, more specifically of his stories of his mills in Avyo. Millstones shattered when least expected, and, while that could cause tremendous damage, more often than not it simply meant cleaning out the bits of damaged stone. And hadn't Edis told her rocks remembered being eroded and tumbling and bouncing? Surely in the memory of this stone would be the moment it had been chiseled free of its parent rock, pieces flying—

"I'm going to shatter the stone," Jenn told The Nyim, trusting it understood. "With luck, the chain will come loose and you'll be free."

The flipper, claw, and chain lowered and disappeared, The Nyim righting itself with more care this time, so the lake merely sloshed, splashing the railing.

~Elder sister, is this wise?~

~this wise—wise—wise—wise?~

Ancestors Beleaguered and Beset, the better question was would it work at all and she'd no idea—

Jenn made herself smile at the concerned stoneberry. "You should get off me now. And all of you, take shelter."

It hopped to the floor, head tilted to watch her walk to the base of the crane, as close as she could to the stone in the lake, then all the stoneberries fled behind their doors.

Jenn became glass and pearl and light—in case the shattering proved a bit more than she planned—and made her wish.

DENIED!

Memories slammed into his head as Bannan took the road to Gordit's mine. Memories of bloodshed and shouts. Of smothering darkness and a rain of debris. One of his soldiers had died beneath the mass thrown down to trap them. Another suffered a crushed foot.

A vain effort by the Ansnans. He'd never have led his patrol into the mine without having a way out. They'd entered through a collapsed shaft, open to the hillside. His choice, to linger in what seemed safety to catch their breath and rest—for Captain Ash to interrogate new and important prisoners—but what no one saw coming was the sickness. A malady without explanation or source, robbing them of strength and will.

To this day Bannan couldn't remember how he'd managed to get the still-living outside, into the life-giving open and fresh air, and Tir refused to tell him. He did know he'd gone against orders and set the prisoners free, perhaps even then wondering if they'd been the cause. He'd left behind four Rhothan bodies, to the lasting shame of their Ancestors—but the rest of his people survived. Not a detail in the Ansnan version of events.

The truthseer shook off the past, focused on keeping to what cover he could find on the slope. He'd lost sight of Semyn and his captors, but the boy had marked his trail well and Bannan followed at a steady jog.

Finding himself at the sealed adit, he scouted for another entrance—

There, a scuff on a rock. Bannan vowed to hug his resourceful nephew the first chance he had.

"I'll not argue—"

He ducked behind a boulder.

"Just say'n' I'd expect the elder to lop off a finger before giving the like o'us time off with coin to spend, and on Fool's Day eve."

A jingle, coins in a purse, then four men came into view, the first pair the town ademens who'd come up here with the group, the second, rough-looking miners. "I'm putting mine aside," boasted the last comer.

The others mocked him, the lot in fine humor and unwary.

Bannan let them go. By now, Emon's guards would be on the road behind him. These men faced a rude surprise and serious questions when they met.

He sped up the path they'd taken, no longer troubling with stealth. Dismissing their guard?

Whatever the elder and his companions planned, they wanted no witnesses.

Semyn!

"Chalk!"

Jenn's outraged shout rang through the cavern, bouncing from walls, ceiling, and lake, achieving nothing but to make The Nyim stir restlessly, churning the mimrol.

She felt much the same. "I don't understand," she muttered unhappily, though of course she did, to some extent.

The stone hadn't shattered because a terst turn-born had *disagreed* and that was that.

Not that she'd the slightest clue why, though knowing the terst turn-born, Chalk's reason might simply have been the reflex to deny any intention that hadn't been argued over first. Arguments that could take days and days, the terst turn-born adverse to impulse or haste—especially hers—and determined to search out any and every consequence.

Freeing The Nyim from its painful shackles while saving it from drowning was a good consequence, Jenn was sure of it. Not that Chalk had offered to talk about it. They owed the creature an apology.

As for why Chalk didn't show himself? He'd let her take his place in the deadly train car, a betrayal she'd like to believe hadn't been on purpose.

Leaving instead of staying to help her had been.

Ancestors Tricky and Troublesome, why was Chalk still here? She'd been certain he'd crossed back to the Verge and safety—

"Because crossing isn't safe," Jenn whispered to herself, flesh again and worried. She was missing a piece of the puzzle, she could feel it.

HUFF!

The Nyim's exhalation—or sigh, for it seemed one—rocked the crane. Jenn held on to the upright until the wind stopped, the arm of the crane and its claws continuing to swing.

Heart's Blood. "There's more here. Something I'm not seeing," she grumbled, feeling cross and out of sorts. To feel better, she put her hand in her pocket in invitation, waiting until she felt little pin prickles before pulling hand, and cows, into the open.

Jenn brought the tiny terst cows to her eye level, delighted when they grew large enough to fill her palm but no larger, blinking peacefully. They didn't resemble any cow she'd ever seen or heard about, but did act like cows.

For the most part.

"I'm sorry," she told them. "I'm not doing a good job of leading you to pasture or anywhere safe. I think you should follow someone else."

The terst cows looked at one another as if she'd confused them, then stroked Jenn's palm tenderly with their clawed hands.

Which tickled and she mustn't drop them—

Because—

"I mustn't drop you," she said slowly, wondering why the words, *those words*, felt significant. She looked up at The Nyim, floating patiently—the only way it probably did anything, but she was pleased to think it waited for her. "I mustn't drop you," she told it.

Or the immense lake of mimrol. Something else that should be in the Verge, not here, but *was*. Brought to the edge—

The tiny cows had brought themselves, yes, but the rest?

The terst turn-born had come of their own volition—no, what had Master said? They'd come for gems to trade in Eldad. Gems, she and Edis had discovered, that were used as bait in a trap. Killing Tooth—trying to kill Chalk and almost killing her—

None of it seemed connected—

Bannan wouldn't accept that. It was her love's nature to distrust coincidence and be wary of the obvious, quite like her dragon when it came down to it, and she missed them both dearly.

And had to manage on her own. Well then, Jenn thought, what had gone wrong first?

"First was the crossings," she told the tiny cows and The Nyim and the stoneberries, who'd opened their doors to listen. "They began to connect to the past instead of now."

Eyes blinked encouragingly.

"The terst turn-born would have noticed and objected at once." Stung by Chalk's unhelpful *disagreement*, she'd no doubt of that. "But they didn't, you see, because when Tooth went missing they locked themselves away, pretending nothing was wrong."

The terst turn-born had been absolutely right to hide themselves, being in real danger. "Except for Mistress Sand," she shared aloud, proud of her friend. "She's the bravest of them." Who'd sent Bannan in her place, showing she'd been afraid as well. "With the terst turn-born in hiding, there's no one to stop what's happening to the crossings."

Worrying, that Mistress Sand and the rest hadn't thought they could. More so, that the sei hadn't, and Jenn's stomach wasn't happy at all.

"Those responsible—" She should probably call them villains, except that made them sound scarier and she needed all her courage. "—can do whatever they want."

And what they wanted must be terrible, to involve murder—not to mention crossings and time. All of which scared the sei, not to mention dragons and kruar, and Jenn shivered. *Villains, then.*

"Until we came, that is," she stated, firmly, because she and her cows had interfered with some of the villains' "whatever" when they freed Chalk. Admittedly, it was far too soon for self-congratulation, but she felt better for saying it.

Did the tiny cows nod? No, but they were rubbing their heads on her palm as if in agreement.

The pieces were fitting together at last. Some of them. "Whatever the villains are doing makes the crossings go to the wrong time. And—or because—that disturbs other things. Like the dawn in the edge. The too-early dimmings." Which she and Wisp had seen for themselves, and Wen had confirmed her feeling that the Verge was wiggly.

"Everything's off balance," Jenn concluded, then stopped, stuck. She frowned at the terst cows, who looked a bit concerned.

She brightened and they looked happier. "You know what else is off balance? This!" Just in time she refrained from waving her hands, presently holding terst cows, at the lake and The Nyim. "All of this should be in the Verge." She sagged. "I've no idea how that happened." She didn't expect an answer.

The stoneberries pointed up, giving her one.

"Yes, I remember, thank you." The little cousins claimed The Nyim had fallen from the ceiling. No, through the ceiling, which remained, when she glanced at it, rock and bags of light and those twitchy sparkles, the whole reassuringly solid to someone underneath.

She needed her beloved's true sight—"No offense, but I wish you were Bannan," she told the tiny cows, who weren't offended in the least.

~Elder sister, it's a door.~

~a door—door—door—door—~

Jenn looked over her cows at the stoneberry near her toes. "Which part?"

~All of it, elder sister.~

~elder sister—sister—sister—sister—~ The stoneberries stopped pointing, limbs curled in obvious distress.

The entire ceiling? Of a cavern this immense? Fighting the instinct to crouch, Jenn's mouth dried. "What kind of door, little cousin?" she asked hoarsely.

~Elder sister, there is but one kind that opens to the Verge.~

~the Verge—Verge—Verge—Verge—~

A crossing?

Her door, Bannan's door, was barely big enough for three people—or combination of people, dragons, or kruar—to cross at once. If the villains had accomplished this? "Who was it? Who put it there?"

~We don't know. We didn't come out, elder sister. The mine closed and people stopped coming and everything went quiet. Then The Great One fell and mimrol poured down and many of us drowned in our homes.~

The echoes, when they came, were faint and sorrowful. ~our homes—homes—homes—homes—~

Where they should have been safe. Villains in truth, and Jenn blinked away hot tears, as much of anger as grief. The terst cows on her hand covered their heads with their arms, mourning as well.

"Ancestors Dear and Departed," she said quietly, after a somber moment. "I'm so sorry."

The stoneberries, every one, gazed at her, then stroked two limbs over their eyes as if wiping tears of their own.

Their leader spoke again. ~The Great One called to us and we came out to see, elder sister. The door was sealed shut and we thought we were safe, but we were not and are not. The door doesn't stay shut. Mimrol pours down on us all. More of us drown, and we had no hope. Until you came.~

~you came—came—came—came—~

A joyful chorus it was and, in Jenn's opinion, most premature. "I want to help," she said earnestly. "I truly do and I promise I will, but I need to know more."

So she didn't make a mistake. So she knew the consequences. And what did it say about the state of her self-control, upset as she'd been and was, that it took Chalk's *disagreement* to remind her?

"To start with, I must know why," Jenn said, doing her best to sound like Peggs, who was, above all, methodical and composed. And could tell everything about a person at a glance—which would be handy, had Jenn any person to show her sister, not, she thought hastily, that she'd ever show her a villain. "Why make such a door? Why do any of this?" As for being a crossing—"Does it go to the past now, too?"

The stoneberries and terst cows, who didn't know and couldn't help, were silent.

Above her, the empty claws of the crane caught Jenn's restless gaze. They kept swinging gently back and forth on their chain, like the pendulum weight in Master Jupp's grand clock—or how it would if not broken—

The idea was like a root, Jenn discovered, a root that grew a plant before you noticed or saw, for all at once, with nothing like triumph and every kind of fear, she realized the "why" had been in front of her from the start.

To *change* time.

Heart's Blood, it had to be impossible, but—she recalled snow and burnt tree trunks—maybe it wasn't.

"Each crossing opens first to the past, then to now. It's like a pendulum, swinging from time to time," she informed her rapt audience, who likely didn't have the least notion of what a pendulum was but did, she knew in her heart, believe in her.

Not like a clock, Jenn corrected to herself, her thoughts racing. More like Master Dusom's experimental apparatus, a beautifully made device she recalled with no little awe, resolved on the spot to tell her former teacher how vital his lessons had been.

If they survived—which they would, she thought sternly, pushing aside any doubt but not making it a wish.

She raised her hands, palms level so the terst cows wouldn't tip, and moved them up to her left. "When you pull a pendulum up one way and let go, it swings back and forth for a while then stops." She did the motion, slowly.

The terst cows, enjoying their little ride, sighed to themselves when her hands stilled.

And that was the difference. Things here—and there—kept getting worse. Here, where a vast lake of mimrol hid The Nyim, also vast, and that must be it, Jenn supposed, aware of nothing else in the wrong place.

"I think what comes through the door from the Verge pulls the crossings into the past. And every time the door opens to let more mimrol through, it pulls again, over and over—"

Drowning stoneberries.

Causing agony for the sei holding the Verge and edge together with its own flesh.

"But if you pull too much one way," Jenn warned, her voice dropping to an anxious whisper so the stoneberries leaned toward her and the terst cows raised their heads. "If you do that, then let go, the pendulum swings so far it goes beyond where it should and sometimes right over." As Roche had done, shattering Master Dusom's pendulum.

She stared at the terst cows, who stared back, content in her attention. Looked out over the multitude of stoneberries and last, but not least, at The Nyim, floating patiently.

Heart's Blood, were they already there? With The Nyim and the lake full to the brim—was this the highest point of the swing? When it let go, would everything be sent back in time?

Or would time restart from that point in the past—

Maybe it wasn't too late. Maybe the villains trapped the terst turn-born for more than to prevent their interference. Maybe they needed the turn-born inner light, the Verge's magic—

Ancestors Blessed, they were safe! She'd broken the wheel. No more turn-born would melt. Jenn started to smile with relief.

Only to stop and sigh. The terst turn-born were too smart to keep walking into a trap, meaning the villains didn't need their light, meaning she'd missed something.

The door. Waterwheels. Crane and gears. Railings and trains. What else was here for villains to use?

Her eyes aimed up at the ceiling, the stoneberries' "door," sealed and covered in sparkles that twitched. "That's not just a door," she heard herself say unsteadily. "It's a dam."

There weren't dams in Marrowdell's valley, other than the rockfall Jenn had created with a too-impulsive wish or those children made to hold the water in a puddle to float their pretend boats. Master Dusom had shown his students drawings, dams important structures elsewhere. In those dams, water accumulated behind a wall, held back for various reasons, its outward flow carefully controlled.

But here, mimrol was accumulating on this side, bit by bit. Held back from the Verge by the rocks sealing the door—the villains' dam—but it didn't belong here. In a sense, the mimrol wanted to return, and certainly The Nyim longed to go home.

If the rocks fell from the door—if the villains' dam burst—The Nyim and every drop in the lake would flow into the Verge at once. And if a little mimrol shifting from place to place could turn back years?

The sum of this would turn back centuries.

She had to stop them. It was as simple as that.

And not simple at all. She didn't know how she'd do it, for one thing. And it would certainly help, Jenn thought wearily, to know who, exactly, the villains were. She couldn't think of anyone who wasn't turn-born who'd be capable of—of changing time. "Who would do this?" she said aloud.

While in the bag forgotten between Jenn Nalynn's breasts, words in mimrol written on the pin she'd also forgotten changed to read . . .

"We'd like to meet them."

The team of four raced along the road, unimpeded by the small black carriage with its two huge free-moving wheels and light box. Their pace didn't vary; the carriage bore messenger flags declaring it on vital business of the prince—which this wasn't—but those who bolted aside to let them pass were hardly in a position to ask questions.

Speed blurred the forest on either side of the road—had there been windows instead of holes for air. Inside, two seats faced one another, close enough to make knees bash together despite the carriage's modern springs.

The driver kept such a casual hold on the reins going out a slit in front that Kydd Uhthoff probably should have been terrified.

Had he not been more concerned with their destination. His hands crushed the sheaf of papers given him by the current Baroness Westietas—

—when, to the best of Kydd's knowledge, the baron was old, happily married to his equally old wife, with an heir acclaimed—Emon, that was the young man's name.

The existence of a young, vibrant baroness was a mystery that paled in comparison to the papers in his hands. On one, in a woman's handwriting, a list of names he didn't recognize. On another, drawn by a boy, a map of a tiny village called Marrowdell.

The third, a note of instruction, from himself, fit to upend his world.

[LETTER FORMAT FROM TURN]

I, Kydd Uhthoff, having willingly sacrificed my past, charge myself by the Bones of my Blessed Ancestors to perform these worthy tasks until my death.

I will return home to Marrowdell.

There, I will serve and support Peggs Uhthoff, once my beloved wife, and her child, to the best of my abilities.

To be better.

[LETTER ENDS]

A home he didn't remember—
A wife and child that couldn't be—
Though the writing was, beyond doubt, his own.

Kydd brought his hands to his face and crushed the papers against his mouth, screaming without making a sound until he had to stop for breath. The driver studiously ignored him.

Sacrificed my past . . . Kydd knew his past and his present. He was a student, in Avyo. When not in residence he lived with his brother's family, most certainly not in a northern village—

He lowered his hands. Hands with callused palms and age spots. Hands that had lived a life he didn't remember and couldn't be his—

But were, beyond doubt.

It was his last moments at the Westietas Estate that grew hazy. There'd been blood, murmured words—Naalish, which was strange. A cook with oddments she'd dumped into a wooden bowl—or had it been a pouch? Flame—

He'd been hurried outside to where horses chomped and stamped, eager to run, and Kydd hoped he'd said civil farewells, but his clearest memory was of being bundled into the carriage and the impossible baroness giving a tile and packet to the driver before coming to him.

She'd looked so sad. There'd been a small boy with her who'd cried, and Kydd was sorry for their grief, if he was the cause, but how could he be?

Oh, and the cook had tucked something in his pocket at the last, patting his cheek, seeming not at all upset. He'd have looked to see what, but the door had closed, the whip cracked, and the carriage shot forward. Moving around inside after that was impossible.

The driver's tile produced fresh horses at Weken and Endshere, big and strong and fast. They rushed north to this Marrowdell.

Charge myself . . . Kydd hoped for a wheel to fall off, for someone to stop this mad flight into the void and take him home again. To Dusom and Larell. Little Wainn. His studies. The interesting new group he meant to join.

The latest painting on his easel, unfinished but with promise.

This couldn't be his future.
He let the papers fall.
Not this.

For a criminal, Elder Cotalen's lack of control over his expression was disgraceful. Semyn supposed it came from robbing others with paper and lies, with no personal or physical risk. Until today and too late.

He'd shown his shock when the tall woman dismissed theademens and those waiting at the gaping hole into the mine. His reluctance to hand over his purse until the smaller woman smiled. Then, why, then he'd shown outright fear and stumbled back, keeping his distance.

Had he finally grasped his true role? As a pawn of those with no interest in petty power struggles, wagons, or Gordit—a no-longer-necessary pawn at that.

Too late, Semyn judged coolly, keeping his distance. Someone this close to breaking drew others into disaster, Momma taught, and he could see the truth of it.

"Time to be done," said the Rhothan man, gauging the sky with a look. He gestured at the hole before them with both hands.

Suddenly, it wasn't a hole but a smooth opening, closed by an intricate gate of dark silver.

The man produced a key.

"What about them?" asked the smaller woman as he opened the lock.

"I've done what you asked—" Cotalen wailed. A flick of fingers and his lips sealed shut. Dropping to his knees, he scratched frantically at his face, leaving bloody gouges in his cheeks. Semyn felt no pity.

The smaller woman, who no longer resembled dear Cook, lowered her head to glance sideways at Semyn. Was that *hunger*?

The boy braced, lifting slightly on his toes. He'd marked the nearest shelter, planned a quick dodging run—up slope where they'd least expect—

"Forget them." The taller woman beckoned impatiently. "Come the turn, this place will never have existed."

The three went through the gate, leaving those cold terrible words behind them.

Semyn dashed after them, but the gate shut and locked in his face. Turned to run back the way they'd come, calling for the only hope left.

"Uncle! Uncle!"

Her back against the helpful crane, Jenn Nalynn sat by the lake, thinking dark and terrible thoughts—that unfortunately weren't wrong simply because they were dark and terrible, which would have been wonderful to believe. But she'd never forgotten what Aunt Sybb had said to her brother, late one night when the girls were supposed to be asleep but weren't, for Aunt Sybb would leave the next day and everyone was sad.

Except, of course, Uncle Hane, awaiting her in Avyo.

That night, after several glasses of summerberry wine and her voice uncharacteristically grim and sad, Aunt Sybb had declared the greatest weapon evil possessed was how difficult it was for good people to see it for what it was. The sisters had known she spoke of the prince and his schemes, the worst then being the legislation that exiled most of her family. What they hadn't known, then, was of Aunt Sybb's—Lady Mahavar's—ceaseless battle to overturn it.

Evil, Jenn decided, grim and sad herself, was anyone willing to drown little cousins, melt turn-born alive, chain a marvel like The Nyim, and—she feared—plot to destroy the Verge and the edge, with everyone and everything living there.

In a way not even the sei who held the worlds together could stop—

"It's up to me," Jenn told the tiny terst cows curled on her palm, the stoneberries glittering along her hem, and The Nyim, floating beyond her bare toes. "Up to *us*, dear friends," this with a small smile, for she'd not want them to feel unappreciated. Ancestors Witness, she'd only to recall what house toads had done. They'd stopped the toad queen from stealing the magic of edge and Verge alike.

With Wisp's help. And Bannan's. Imp's too, to be fair, and of course Edis Donovar's.

"Us," Jenn repeated, there being nothing to gain wishing for those who weren't here and wouldn't be, not in time.

Time. She never thought to fear the word.

The turn was nigh. It woke the lake, conflicted waves bouncing against one another. The Nyim sank below the surface.

She'd a very bad feeling—

The terst cows, who also had a sudden bad feeling but, unlike their leader, knowing exactly why and what they felt, grew larger.

Jenn set them on the rock floor before they crushed her legs.

They grew still larger. She stood. The stoneberries hopped away, diving into their homes and closing their doors.

Larger.

LARGER until Jenn found herself in the shade of terst cows bigger than any Wisp had shown her in the Verge. "What's wrong?"

In answer, they crouched over her, arms tight around one another. Half-smothered in hair and quite unable to budge—though this close the terst cows smelled rather like sun-warm straw, which did help—Jenn waited to understand.

Reassured by the trust of their leader, the terst cows did what they knew to do when danger approached.

With a shimmer, they disappeared.

And so did Jenn Nalynn.

The turn was coming.

They were back in the edge where they belonged, and the dragon burst from the ground into the air even as the kruar shook himself from head to tail, ridding his hide of dust and debris.

Remembering who he was and why he'd come. ~My truthseer!~ Scourge let out a roar of triumph, catching Bannan's scent, and ran.

~The girl!~ Wisp replied, not to be outdone, and banked sharply, diving for the mountain, and if the pair raced it was for the joy of having done the impossible.

And a chance to save the world.

TWELVE

IF A STRAY hair—doubtless belonging to a terst cow—wasn't making Jenn madly wriggle her nose to keep from sneezing, and if she could only budge her arms now folded awkwardly and immovably across her front—her last move being an instinctive push against the inexorable press of not one but two terst cows—

Ancestors Amazed and Astonished, she'd have thought herself alone in the cavern—a peculiar sensation, indeed.

Until she wasn't.

Or rather *they* weren't—the terst cows definitely present, if transparent, and she'd the sense she was as well—

The reason being three people had just walked through the rock wall in a spot she knew she'd searched at least twice and found no door whatsoever.

Stretching her neck, Jenn watched them approach.

Rhothans, by their dress, and equipped for walking in a mine. Two were women, of differing ages. The third was a man, who resembled one of them but not the other, thus possibly a brother, and Jenn would have been ever so glad to see them.

If it weren't for the terst cows, who were not. Their great bodies rumbled against hers, a deep, low rumbling, and she'd felt the like while touching Wisp's side when he'd been angry. A growl, though without a betraying sound, meaning the newcomers were villains.

Ancestors Witness, she'd not much experience with villains, other than the horrid Crumlin Tralee. She hadn't thought they'd look like, well, ordinary non-magical people. People who, she tried to think charitably past the growling, could be down here for a host of excellent reasons other than to inspect a turn-born-melting apparatus or time-shifting reservoir of mimrol. With The Nyim, who hadn't resurfaced.

Yes, they'd come through a hidden door, which did, Jenn told herself dejectedly, lean matters toward these people being involved in both—though she herself had arrived here by unusual means, making it hardly definitive.

Safely cuddled, and hidden, by her invisible cows, Jenn knew she should wait and see what they were up to—but the turn was coming. She could taste it. And if the turn was why the three had come *now*, that moment when the light of this world matched that of the Verge? And if they were the villains? Whatever they sought to do might be planned to happen then, meaning soon.

She must be ready to stop them. Jenn used her knee and an elbow, gently at first then with as much force as the tight quarters allowed, trying to persuade the terst cows to release her, but as well use a feather. They rumbled and settled closer together, if anything, making it difficult to take a lungful to shout at them—which might not be a good idea but if she must—

Oblivious, the three walked right past them to stand looking down at the ruined gear shaft and stone, hands on the railings.

"Your monster tried to free itself!" The taller woman glared at the man. "I told you!"

Well, that settled that, Jenn nodded to herself. Or would have, had she been able to move her head.

At a gesture from the man, the chain rose from the lake, taut where it connected to the underside of the stone, quivering where it led to The Nyim. Mimrol dripped from every link.

Jenn ceased her struggles, grateful for the protection of huge invisible terst cows however flimsy it felt against power like this. A strange, unfamiliar power—she sensed no intention, not that she thought them turn-born. Sensed nothing about the three at all—except—

Ancestors Witness, it might be looking through the cows, but, all at once, the three didn't appear as substantial as before, their bodies *shimmering*.

It wasn't the cows. It was the turn.

Jenn Nalynn became glass and pearl and light.

And the three Rhothans became terst.

"Uncle!"

Before Bannan could take another step, Semyn landed in his arms. After the briefest embrace, the boy pulled away. "They've gone into the mine," he said, quick and crisp—a soldier's reporting despite the anguish on his young face. "The three have a terrible power, Uncle. They let me go because they plan to destroy the edge and everyone in it."

The truth. "Show me."

He followed Semyn to the rock face, both ignoring the man huddled in misery against it. Bannan touched the gate. "Mimrol." If they'd enough to use for this—

"We have to get through it. Stop them." Semyn looked toward the town. "They killed Dutton." No tears, not a quiver in his voice.

Those would come later—if they had a later. He squeezed the boy's shoulder gently, receiving a small nod of acknowledgment.

They'd no time for more. Bannan resumed his examination of the gate. Without the key, there was no way past it save bringing up tools from the town. "How much time do we have?"

Semyn shook his head. "They said they had to be inside by the turn."

He didn't need his deeper sight. Night's edge was rolling up the mountainside from town, sunset tinting stone blue-gray, evening birds and insects starting their chorus. Bannan grabbed for the bars, to test their strength.

But his palms flattened over a hard, slick surface. "What—?"

A breeze scalded his ear. "Allow me."

The turn found them.

And Wisp appeared in all his dragonish might, stooping from the sky like a silver falcon. Bannan pulled a wide-eyed Semyn aside just in time.

No delicacy in this landing. Kicking up a spray of rock and grit, as he touched down the dragon raked his claws along the "gate," tearing it asunder like some curtain. His head swung around, a wild violet eye finding Bannan.

Then both eyes came to bear, Wisp staring at Bannan as if startled and Heart's Blood, what did the dragon see? What *could* he see?

Wisp became invisible again, his breeze in Bannan's ear. "She's inside."

Jenn! But as Bannan began to move, a great shadow blocked his way.

"Scourge!" he greeted, relieved. Allies at last and most timely. "Take care of—"

The kruar lowered his head, sniffed, then snarled at him, lips pulled back from his fangs, venom dripping.

If everything native to the Verge was this disturbed by him, the truthseer thought, beyond frustrated, he wanted to know why—

And could wait. Semyn stood with him. He wouldn't take the boy into the mine and mustn't abandon him on the mountainside. "Idiot Beast," Bannan said, making it fond, which wasn't easy, the kruar poised to rip out his throat. "Glad you're here. Semyn needs protection and we've a prisoner."

A snarl rippled his lips—

SNAP!

The dragon. Scourge looked up. Whatever passed between the two in that instant, with a shake that showered Bannan with dust, the kruar went from death incarnate to highly annoyed. His breeze was hot and fetid. "I will protect." A great hoof rattled the stone beside Cotalen. "This one I'll eat."

"No!" Semyn protested. Then, grimly, "Not till we've questioned him," being Lila's son.

Scourge tossed his head, satisfied.

"Take Semyn—and that—to his father," Bannan ordered. "Wisp? Wisp!"

The dragon was gone.

Jenn—

Bannan bolted into the tunnel after him.

Terst—not the individuals she'd met in their village, but there was no mistaking what they were as the turn passed. Their Rhothan-seeming clothes became tunics and pants of straw, the nails of their forefingers long and painted and claw-like. Two had lines of fine scars on their wrists. The hair of all three was black and curly, worn short; the cheeks Jenn could see were bright red, and if they turned to face her, she expected to see the same color on their lips.

And bright blue eyes.

The terst had told her they crossed into the edge. Shown her they used illusion to pass as ordinary people. She shouldn't, Jenn thought, be shocked to learn they'd told her the truth, but she was, more than a little.

Villains or not, she needed to speak with them.

Jenn stroked the terst cows. Perhaps sensing her determination, they eased apart, enough for her to step out.

Suddenly visible.

Busy making complicated gestures with their fingernails, as if drawing words in the air, the tersts' attention was for the lake. So much so, Jenn thought she might—if she were the sort of person who would, like Roche—push at least one over the railing and see if they could swim before they noticed she was there at all.

Of course she wasn't and wouldn't. "Pardon me."

They spun around to stare at her, hands dropping.

"I'm Jenn Nalynn—"

A gesture and her arms snapped to her sides, which was hardly polite.

"A Cursed," snapped the short female terst. She ducked her head and licked her lips. "Why aren't you dead?" As if disappointed.

"She broke the Death Wheel," concluded the other female. "You shouldn't have done that," to Jenn.

They'd made a device to kill their own, their children. "Yes, I should," Jenn replied, in no mood for terst games and riddles. But their being terst was the final piece. "I know what you're doing here."

"I doubt that." The male terst had paler eyes than the others. Colder, if that were possible. He raised his hands over his head, the others doing the same, fingers spread.

"You want time to go back to the Perfect Before." While Jenn could understand the terst longing for the home they'd lost, there was no understanding this. "You can't," she told them. "You mustn't. The cost is too high—"

"The cost? There'll be no cost." The terst laughed at her. "In the Perfect Before, none of you will ever have existed."

Terst lied. Unfortunately, these appeared anxious to tell her the truth—

Their hands clenched and the ceiling *tinkled*.

Jenn looked up, she couldn't help it.

The sparkles weren't twitching—they were moving!

And weren't rocks at all, but clockworks. Everywhere she looked, they were tiptapping along the ceiling—moving quickly and to purpose—their dark metal bits sparkling as they passed the bags of light.

They were gathering together. Linking to form bigger and bigger devices.

Devices with drills. Drills boring into the rock along lines and existing cracks, and rubble began to fall, splashing into the lake.

Where the rocks had been was sky!

Not the sky of the edge, but the brilliant colors of the Verge, and Jenn might not have learned to find a sei crossing on her own, but anyone could see *this*.

Droplets from the splashes began to rain up. More and more, heading for the Verge, and the mimrol lake began to seethe, waves reaching upward. The Nyim appeared at the surface, flippers flailing as if to keep from rising—

The terst were sending it all through to the Verge. Once their devices finished clearing the door, everything would go at once. "Stop!" Jenn shouted, struggling in vain to move. "Please! You'll die, too!"

A fingernail tapped the glass of her chin. "We won't have existed. Not like this. And neither will you. Only the Perfect Before will remain."

"The Perfect Before," the others intoned gleefully. "When All Are Where They Should Be."

She'd no name for what was worse than a villain. No words to reason with people willing to destroy everything, including themselves, in an attempt to return to a time they'd never known, that might never have been, and hadn't been perfect for all. She'd no hope—

She was roses and tears and wishes. Kindness and laughter and love.

It wasn't enough—*she* wasn't enough—everything and everyone would be gone. So much loss, so much never done.

Jenn's great heart began to break. "Please stop!" she sobbed. "Please don't make me do this. Please don't make me end you!"

The terst laughed at her, fingers wiggling.

The terst cows, agreeing with their leader, raised their clawed hands in threat—only to drop them again and shimmer from sight as a fearsome dragon flew into the cavern, a man close behind.

Blind with fear and pain, Jenn Nalynn didn't see help coming. Didn't see any choice—

—but to make her wish. A dreadful wish unlike any she'd made before or ever thought to make, a wish to obliterate the evil standing in front of her—to bring the mountain down on *them* alone! A wish—

DENIED!

Bannan burst into the open behind Wisp and, finding himself in a cavern, for a heart-stopping moment thought he was back with The Dancer in her cavern of rock and ice and believed himself dead—

—then heaved a great breath of warm, moist air. *Not dead*, he told himself. No ice, only rock carved by pick and ax, and shaking off the feeling, he looked for Jenn.

There! A glow greater than any lamp—

Rocks began to fall! They hit the floor and shattered. Some splashed into an impossible lake, a lake of silver, with splashes that sent drops up instead of falling, and his appalled stare followed the mimrol up only to see vast numbers of little machines at work, tearing apart the ceiling.

Covering his head with his arms, Bannan ran to his love.

The dragon found her first.

Chalk! He rose out of a train car, a being of glass and white dust and the light of the Verge, his mask in place to give him a face, set and resolved, and Jenn felt the start of his intention, his wish—

HOLD.

He commanded the mountain to obey him—was it to save the terst? With a denial of her own, she could stop him and end them—

Jenn teetered on that awful brink.

A wind slipped over her glass and pearl and light like a caress. The voice of her oldest, first friend filled her every sense, warm and bright and sure. ~I'm here, Dearest Heart! Bannan's here!~

Changing everything.

HOLD! HOLD! Jenn wished, her intention weaving with Chalk's until rock no longer fell and the sound of drills faltered and stopped.

Droplets paused, glittering midair, then rained back down to dimple the lake.

They'd sealed the crossing. Stopped the terst. Ancestors Blessed and Beloved, Chalk had known what to do.

While Jenn had let her emotions, her fear, create a dreadful wish without thought of the consequences. She owed him a great debt, they all did, not that he'd care or understand. As well expect the mountain to be grateful.

Would its rocks remember any of this? she wondered numbly, becoming flesh and blood, not realizing she'd spoken aloud until—

"I'll let you know," Edis Donovar said, rising up through the floor, full and round and laughing.

She dived into the lake with a flash of pearlescent tail Jenn hadn't known she possessed, and wasn't alone in it. The Nyim had submerged, but the mimrol seethed with creatures like Edis yet not, with wide mouths and gills of red and no eyes at all. Olm!

The terst stood, their mouths hanging open, their plan over, and Jenn almost felt sorry for them.

Almost. She was sick at heart, knowing how close she'd come to evil herself. It didn't matter the reason, she mustn't ever again use her magic to harm. Mustn't become—*again*—what could or would. Jenn vowed that instant never to wish destruction again, on anything.

Which would be easier if she were more vigilant and knew to help sooner than later. And if her arms weren't still pinned, which was a nuisance. "Wisp!"

"Let her go!" roared her dragon, skimming low to flutter tunics and hair.

The terst raised fists, shouted, and began to make their gestures as if to pin Wisp as well.

It cost them. Two lost their heads, their bodies toppling into the lake to the obvious relish of those in it.

The third stared up, past Jenn. "But you follow—"

His head disappeared as well, leaving a bloody tear in his neck, and his body joined the others to feed the olm.

Jenn blinked, her hands free. Metal bits fell from the ceiling, the terst devices breaking apart. Doors opened in the floor and stoneberries dashed out to retrieve gears and rods and other bits, making happy little sounds.

Then she felt something as small but most definitely not harmless climb back in her pocket and wasn't sure how she felt about that. Still, they had saved her dragon.

She smiled, to herself.

The terst cows, who didn't mind the occasional meat in their diet but very much minded any terst who would take away their leader, curled up in her pouch. They would stay with her forever, content it was so.

"Jenn!" And when Bannan's arms went around her, she felt the same.

He hadn't, Bannan decided, the slightest clue what was about to happen—or what had or to whom—

And didn't care. His arms full of his beloved, his face buried in her hair—smelling unexpectedly but pleasantly of sun-warm straw—meant everything was right in the world and he'd happily stay like this forever.

Until he remembered Semyn and Dutton and what he'd become.

"What's wrong?" Jenn asked when he eased back, laying a hand on his cheek to keep him close. His heart sank as her beautiful eyes, their blue still purpled with magic, widened. "Your skin. Dearest Heart, what's happened? Are you all right?"

He captured her hand, pressed his lips to her palm. "I'll explain—"

A breeze, chill and accusing, found his ear. "Can you, truthseer? Dare you?" Wisp sounded—impossible—he sounded afraid.

Not a reaction Bannan would have expected, had he considered the dragon at all. Did Wisp know the Dancer in the ice? "I'll explain later," he promised, trusting the dragon accepted the delay, and kissed Jenn on the tip of her adorable nose. "Emon has a room set aside for us at the inn. It's in the edge," in case she'd doubts.

Her face lit up. "An inn? I've never—I've always—" Going on

tiptoe, Jenn planted such a warm loving kiss on his lips, Bannan came close to grabbing her and running from this place.

But Ancestors Mysterious and Marvelous, things weren't over and he'd urgent questions of his own. "The three who came before me, where are they?"

"Look to the lake, truthseer," Wisp said, this time in better cheer.

Where a pair of olm wrestled over a leg amid blood-stained froth, and Bannan went very still, turning to look to Jenn—who'd never willingly harm anyone, but under the circumstances—

To his vast relief, she looked tired and a little sad. "What happened?" he asked gently.

"They fell in," she said, which wasn't the whole of it, he could tell, but what Jenn said next shook him to the core. "Those you followed here weren't people. Not people like us," she qualified. "It was illusion. They came from the Verge."

Heart's Blood, he should have tried his deeper sight the instant he sensed something wrong about them, but he'd ascribed it to dark magic, nothing like this. "What were they?" he asked grimly.

"Terst. All this is their fault." Her face clouded. "They killed Tooth and—" She looked past him.

Turning, he saw Chalk leaning on the side of a train car, a car affixed to a stone wheel of remarkable girth and presently tilted on its side along with its broken shaft. The terst turn-born, flesh again and naked, lifted a hand in greeting.

A burnt hand. Scorched hair and burnt feet, and something clenched in Bannan's stomach. "He needs help—"

"He needs to cross and go home," Jenn said tersely.

Bannan hid a shudder. *Cross.* He'd not try that again—

"Not," she said, unconsciously echoing his thought, "that he should until all the crossings are fixed." Jenn stepped to the railing and lifted her hand at what was more inland sea than lake. "The terst brought the mimrol here and used it to push and pull time through the Verge. During this turn they'd planned to send all of it through their crossing." She indicated the cavern ceiling. "Can you see it?"

Instead of risking his deeper sight, the truthseer asked, "Why?"

"The terst—these terst—wanted to return to a time before the sei reached out to our world. Before the Verge and edge came to be." Jenn's shoulders straightened, as if preparing to take on a weight. Sure enough, "That threat isn't over as long as there's this imbalance. We have to put the mimrol back in the Verge. And him." She waved.

An island slowly rose from the lake, dozens of olm wriggling in the mimrol rolling down its sides. A smaller island—no, a *head*—lifted.

HUFF!

Jenn caught Bannan, staggered by the force of that breath. "The Nyim," she introduced calmly. "The terst trapped it." She pointed.

A flipper the size of a barge rose up to show the claw and chain affixed to it.

Ancestors Dazzled and Dazed. "I see you've made a new friend," Bannan said mildly.

"You've no idea," Jenn muttered, then smiled from her heart, chasing every worry from his. "I'll explain. Later. First, to fix this."

Loot collected, the stoneberries closed their doors, having survived the turn—which they all had, other than the terst, and Jenn refused to regret the actions of her tiny cows, who'd acted to protect her. Hopefully. If they planned to keep following her around, she'd have to be sure the nipping of heads wasn't something they did on a whim.

They'd survived the turn but weren't safe yet, the lake of mimrol roiled by more than glowing swimmers, though it might be the olm swam in it to keep it from getting worse. Jenn hadn't told Bannan about the train cars or Tooth or how close she'd come to melting, topics better left to the nebulous *later* her beloved suggested for such things.

Including how his summer-tanned skin came to be as pale as late winter and his hair—Jenn squinted at him while his attention was on The Nyim, certain she'd seen something different about it. Delicately, she touched a dark curl.

Bannan whirled around, his face stricken.

Oh dear. "Later," she told him, pretending not to see his distress. Later, when they could hold one another for comfort and in safety, to say what was too difficult apart.

A warm breeze on her cheek. "Dear Heart."

"Wisp! I'm so very glad you're here," she said and was—the how another subject to be postponed. "Do you know how to send the mimrol back? And The Nyim," before another sigh gusted over them. "We must send him home as well. Quickly."

"The terst turn-born who sent you here have a crossing." The breeze chilled, her dragon displeased—though not with her. Chalk gave a cry of outrage as air scooped him from the stone, dropping him at Jenn's feet where he stayed, glowering. "Ask him."

The terst cows, who'd watched from her pouch, being curious about the one who made their leader feel warm and happy, knew better than bite what no longer was terst but power and ducked back down to hide inside their paper nest. Their leader would deal with what came next; they were content it was so.

Bannan took off his jacket—an interesting garment, Jenn thought, as was everything he wore. The lantern hanging from a loop on his pants would, she thought pragmatically, come in handy should they lose the glow of the olm and from the bags of mimrol remaining on the ceiling. And she did like his suspenders—

He gave the jacket to Chalk, who glowered slightly less. But still glowered, this after being saved and partially clothed, so Jenn stamped her foot, out of patience with terst of any ilk. Except her tiny cows.

"You heard," she told the terst turn-born. "We need your crossing to put everything back. Where is it?"

Chalk got to his feet, the jacket covering most if not all of genitals quite unlike Bannan's fine and manly parts. More like Good'n'Nuf's, the Ropps' little bull, but with a pronounced twist—

Heart's Blood, this was no time to be distracted by what she'd seen already in full at too close quarters, even if his bits were oddly more distracting peeking from under the jacket.

"Still can't tell, na?" Chalk sneered and pointed to the airshaft where the tunnel began and trains went. The chains between the rails had disappeared, presumably pulled all the way out to jam the mimrol wheel. She hadn't noticed their silence till now.

"It's too small," Jenn said, disappointed.

Bannan looked from the lake to the airshaft, shaking his head, then went to the railing. "Edis!"

Of course. If they couldn't use the turn-borns' crossing—Jenn brightened. Going to stand beside her love, she called as well. "Edis!"

The olm stopped, blind heads aimed their way, bobbing up and down. "She might be fully olm, now," Bannan murmured. "By her choice," as if Jenn had protested, which she hadn't, but might.

All at once, he turned to take her face in his hands, studying it as if to memorize it beyond any loss.

Kissed her as if saying goodbye. And before she could grab him, alarmed and determined he not leave, her beloved stepped away.

And shouted, "DANCER!"

Every olm, every wave, everything . . . stopped.

Semyn rode behind Cotalen, the tip of his dagger pricked into the skin over the man's right kidney while Scourge took the rocky path as if carrying eggs. Not, Semyn knew, that the kruar, bloodthirsty by nature, would be anything but delighted if he accidentally wounded their prisoner, but the beast understood the need to ask the Ansnan questions.

And hoped to eat him afterward.

Semyn, bloodthirsty himself at the moment, would far rather watch Scourge rip apart the traitor than have Cotalen ride, unarmed, ahead of him as if he'd rescued the baron's heir and returned a hero.

A needful deception. He'd given his prisoner a handkerchief to press over those marred cheeks and frozen mouth. The first time Cotalen went to remove it, Semyn pushed his knife tip through his skin. He hadn't tried since.

Rescue yourself, Momma taught her sons, and rightly so, her eldest thought grimly. There was no guarantee Poppa's guard would greet them first, and they had to pass through a town full of people ignorant of this man's betrayal, people who might not like Cotalen but knew him as their leader, while Semyn?

Naught but a boy, and a Rhothan one at that.

Scourge helped. When they reached Gordit's cobbled street, the crowd fell silent, prudently moving aside to give the massive warhorse ample room to pass. A murmur of voices grew behind, but Semyn didn't turn around.

The gate to Cotalen's house stood open but not unguarded. Better still, Derhall, Poppa's seniormost, stood just inside!

With a rush of relief, Semyn used his heels and legs to send his mount at that welcome. The mightiest of the kruar obeyed without a word, stopping at the courtyard's pitiful fountain, out of sight of the curious crowd.

And in view of Poppa, running from the house.

Semyn half slid, half fell off Scourge, Poppa there to catch him. "Those with Cotalen—they didn't come for wealth," he said urgently, gripping his father's arms. "They're here to destroy the edge and everyone in it. Uncle Bannan's gone into the mine to stop them."

"Alone?"

"He has Wisp—"

As if that stung, Scourge reared, dumping the hapless Cotalen on his own paving stones, then charged the closed gate, lifting into the air to clear guard and fence. Alarmed cries and shouts marked his progress beyond.

"And Scourge," Semyn added.

"You've no—" Cotalen looked shocked by his own voice, reaching up to touch his lips. Before he could say another word, he found the baron's sword at his throat.

Poppa looked scarily warlike in that instant, as Poppa hadn't ever in Semyn's recollection—but in Momma's, most surely, the boy realized—and while it was plain he intended to take the Ansnan's head?

There was no need. "Their magic kept him silent," Semyn said with a stir of wonder. "If it's gone—"

"M'lord! Sirs!!!"

Baron and heir turned together—the former's sword tip still at their prisoner's throat—to see the best sight of all.

Dutton stood in the doorway. His head was bloody and he needed the help of two guards who appeared barely able to take his weight, but his eyes were bright. "What's all this?"

Then everything stopped . . .

The Dancer came, gliding on toetip over the lake of mimrol, freezing wide curves and delicate twirls, color in her wake and blue swirling like a cloud around her.

He'd known in his heart she'd come; feared she would, that as well. What Bannan didn't know—and yes, feared—was what she'd ask from him in return. There had to be a price for summoning such a being into their world.

A being able to stop time.

Jenn was frozen, her lips—those lips he could still taste on his— parted in surprise; her hair, her dress, caught midmotion.

Before her crouched her dragon, wings out and flames *stopped* in his mouth. The Nyim's *HUFF* paused, mist in the air, while the terst turn-born was stuck mid-cower, an arm over his face.

Brother! A glad greeting. *Sister!*

Edis Donovar rose up through the stone, arms wide and no more olm than before, to bow to The Dancer. She shot a look at Bannan, a look saying as plain as words, what have you done?

Whatever he could. Bannan bowed, brushing the rock floor with his fingertips. Rose to find The Dancer close enough to touch and didn't flinch. Wouldn't, for there was no harm in her, only curiosity. *Why am I here, brother?*

"To fix this." No blue motes in the air. He'd half expected there would be. "She can't do it alone."

'*She.*' The Dancer flowed to Jenn Nalynn. Around her. Stopped to touch Jenn's nose with a fingertip, appearing startled when it left a glow. *Sei.*

A question. No, a request, and Bannan answered, "Yes. Sei and turn-born. A woman of this world, not the Verge. She's here to try and save us all."

The Dancer's eyes twinkled. *Your love.*

"My life." He held his breath then, or didn't need to breathe, another aspect paused by The Dancer. If she couldn't put things to rights, nothing could and they were doomed.

The Dancer swirled away and despair filled him, but she wasn't done.

Like a storm she rushed back, taking Jenn Nalynn in her arms, and pulling her into the lake.

Bannan jumped in after them.

Finding himself standing on a sheet of ice.

Edis stood nearby. She gestured.

He turned and there was Jenn—holding hands with The Dancer. The two spun slowly together, with unworldly grace, laughing as if they'd no cares or worries, and his lips twitched, so warm was the sound.

Jenn glanced at him, her eyes purple, and smiled.

Then exploded into a cloud of white moths.

The Dancer showed her the steps. Only a sei could take them and so she became that aspect of herself.

The Dancer sang of love and life. No sei knew life and love like those who were flesh and blood, and so she remembered being those as well. Remembered being woman and sister and friend, daughter and niece and yes, a lover and loved, possessed of a heart able to hold, for less than an instant—

—for all of time—

—everything.

Because she was, because she did and would, Jenn Nalynn danced—as a moth, as many moths, as a shape larger than mountains—each step healing a break in time, the joyous melody in her heart leading the way.

Until she was done.

Everything started . . .

Everything started . . .

The dragon lowered his wings, bowing his head to the Old One who'd appeared in front of him, glumly certain this was the end.

You raised her well, Wisp.

The girl. He risked aiming an eye at the Old One who, disturbingly, *smiled* as if well pleased.

In his experience, nothing good came of the attention of the mighty. He was, however, far too old for caution. ~Leave her alone,~ Wisp growled.

Dear Wisp. The Old One twirled, clapping hands the dragon dourly suspected were this moment's whim—like its unwelcome use of his name—then tapped his snout with a finger.

Leaving a glow.

Thirteen

*E*VERYTHING STARTED...
 And Jenn blinked. She blinked again, what she saw before her surely wrong or possibly illusion, unless she'd cracked her head. Not only was there no mimrol in the lake, there was no lake, and where there'd definitely been a lake a blink ago? Naught but a rapidly shrinking crack in the floor.

"You did it!" Bannan lifted her off her feet.

While that felt grand and was wonderful, she craned her head trying to see past his shoulder, so he set her down and settled his arm around her waist. "You did it, Dearest Heart," he whispered in her ear, warm and sure.

Done what? The cavern itself—she distinctly remembered it being very large—was rapidly shrinking, as were the bags of glowing mimrol littering the floor. Bags being snatched by stoneberries, who stuffed them down their holes, taking the light.

"We should get out of here," she decided numbly. "Before it's dark."

Bannan held up his lantern, its flame burning with a warm yellow light.

A hot breeze. "I'll take you."

"Scourge!" Then nothing would do but Jenn and Bannan make a fuss of the kruar, who pretended not to enjoy it but did, Jenn knew.

"Wait, where's Chalk?"

This breeze was soft and gentle. Her dragon! "Crossed to the Verge, Dear Heart, and no loss. I advised him to tell the others you saved them. You saved everything," with dragonish pride.

Had she? Jenn recalled wanting to help. There'd been—"Dancing?" she hazarded, that her clearest memory, which couldn't be right.

Bannan's arm squeezed. "Fool's Day is tomorrow. We'll dance then, Dearest Heart, all you wish. Assuming Emon's settled the town."

Which might have sounded ominous if her love's voice hadn't been so happy, so perhaps "settling" wasn't a difficulty.

There was, however, a difficulty after all. When Bannan went to lift Jenn up on Scourge, the kruar sidled away, rolling his eyes at her. "YOU HAVE COWS!"

Why, so she did.

Everything started . . .

The carriage pulled by a team of four raced through Marrowdell's always-open gate, scattering the piglets in the orchard. The horses thundered down the village road, waking Master Jupp but not Uncle Horst, who watched them come and had his sword. They plowed to a stop before the home of Radd and Melusine Nalynn and their daughter Peggs, then of daughter Jenn—with regular stays by Radd's sister the Lady Mahavar, Aunt Sybb to the girls—and lately and now, home to Radd Nalynn, his daughter Peggs, and her husband Kydd Uhthoff.

Who stared out the door in back of the carriage, utterly lost.

Marrowdell, the map said. It was, at first glance, an ordinary place. Poor. A dirt road. A few small buildings of squared logs and mossy roofs. Gardens and an orchard with hives. The road—if he could call it that—continued on through a gate into a pasture. Out a second gate—there were animals grazing to be kept in—the road passed a large tree and crossed a river, disappearing into a dark wild forest.

Nearer, neat fields drew his eyes, sweeping along the valley until they reached a row of barren hills the color of weathered bone, that plunged down like enormous claws. An unusual formation—he'd not read of the like—

The driver tapped his shoulder. "Sir, I've orders to turn around promptly. Please take these. Mail for the village."

Mail for people he didn't know but who knew him, and well, if he believed any of this.

Kydd pushed his sweaty papers into a pocket, accepted the packet and tucked it under an arm. The driver helped him step down from the carriage—otherwise he'd have fallen flat on his face, stiff from a day and night of bouncing in it—then slammed the door shut before Kydd could thank him.

Or beg to go back.

He watched the carriage leave, unwilling to take his eyes off the familiar. Alone. Afraid. Winced as doors opened and strangers came out on porches and he couldn't do this, he couldn't face anyone—

Falling to his knees, Kydd pressed his hands to the dirt of the road, head hanging, not caring what strangers thought nor that the packet fell, not caring, not caring—he'd make a wall of it, not caring, and hide—

"Hello."

Startled, he peered through his hair to see a pair of shapely bare feet, topped by very shapely ankles. Lifting his head, he saw a hem embroidered with flowers. The round swell of a skirt stretched to its limit obscured the rest, and he remembered his charge to himself.

Ancestors Cruel and Capricious, why her, first? Why the wife he didn't remember?

"Dearest Heart?"

A voice full of warmth he didn't deserve. He rose to his knees and stared in some dismay at the bulge in front of him. "That's your baby," he got out with an effort. "You haven't had your baby."

A graceful hand stroked the bulge with mesmerizing tenderness. "I'll get to it, now you're home." Her hand paused, then reached to him. "You are home, aren't you?" with good humor.

Kydd shied back. He couldn't bear her touch. He looked up, ready to tell her this wasn't his, none of it—

—struck speechless by a face more beautiful than a dream, framed in silken black hair, set against the clearest blue sky he'd ever seen in his life. Eyes like a starry midnight, warm and intelligent—

Eyes that narrowed. "What's wrong?" She began to lower herself to his level, the motion awkward.

He clambered to his feet, taking her hands to steady her before he thought. Dropped them, aghast at his affrontery. "I'm sorry, dear lady—"

Her full lower lip disappeared between her teeth. Reappeared, moist and impossibly lush—

He mustn't have such thoughts about a stranger, mustn't— "Something happened. I don't remember you," Kydd choked out. "I don't remember any of this." He waved at the village.

Heart's Blood, people on porches waved back, and what was he to do? "Help me," he whispered, the woman before him the only thing real. "Please."

The world stilled. Except for his heart, that treacherous organ, beating hard in his chest.

Her head tilted. To his astonishment, she didn't appear sad or shocked, nor did she question his wild statements. Instead, she gave him a thoughtful, considering look, as if he presented a puzzle, not a tragedy. Muttered, "Ancestors Witness, it would be nice if Jenn were home at times like this."

A name from the list. "Your sister—what could she do?"

Her lips curved, deepening a set of extraordinary dimples. "It doesn't matter. I want you to trust me, Kydd Uhthoff, even if you don't—know me." The little break in her voice gave her away. She wasn't as calm as she pretended, wasn't prepared to give him up, and to be so loved by someone like this—

"I do," he heard himself say.

She stepped as close as her bulge permitted them to be and cupped his face in her hands. Smiled a wise and gentle smile. "I'm a daughter of Melusine. I bake very good pies."

"The best!" came a shout, quickly shhhed. Those watching gave them space. Waited.

"I like pie," Kydd said, mystified but willing.

"I know you do." She drew his face forward until their foreheads touched. "I'm a daughter of Melusine," she repeated. Her voice dropped to a soft, potent whisper. "And of Marrowdell. Trust me, Dearest Heart. I do know you."

With that, images—memories—spun themselves through his mind as if being painted there. No, as if being *lived*, and he gasped and cried. Laughed and grumbled. Smelled old wine and new apples. Heard bees and the music of pipes. Saw black hair tumbled on a pillow and his brother weep as bodies were lowered into the ground.

Felt snowflakes. Felt a hand slip into his, a perfect fit, the only fit.

Tasted pie—*her* pie—for this was—

"PEGGS!" He kissed her like a man drowning fights for air. Dug his hands into her hair as if falling and she alone held him up. And this might have gone on a considerable while, Kydd in no mood to stop and Marrowdell cheering, except he felt his wife's little push and lifted his head.

"We need to breathe, too," she reminded him, smiling, tears on her cheeks.

He left his arm around her. Stroked her hair with trembling fingers. Studied her face, eyes lingering on those well-kissed lips, then buried his face into the crook of her neck. His Peggs. Her magic.

Smelled roses, warmed by sunshine and love.

And Kydd knew himself home.

Everything started . . .

"Dutton!" Semyn Westietas ran up the step to their wounded, brave guard, constrained at the last moment not so much by the blood dripping down that big gruff face as the remembrance of what he was and who.

As heir, he gave a deep and respectful bow, brushing fingertips over stone.

Then as boy, wrapped his arms around his friend, armor and all. And while Semyn succeeded in fighting back tears?

Dutton didn't bother to try.

Jenn listened for the wet clicks of scamps in the tunnel leading from the tersts' once-hidden door to the outside, but it was impossible to hear anything over Scourge's dramatic snorts of disgust, the kruar repulsed by the "stench" of cow. Tolerated this once and only time, he'd informed her and Bannan, in appreciation of their act in battle.

The biting off of heads, Wisp told her, being a kruar specialty.

With Bannan's arms around her waist, his chest warm against her back, and his every breath stirring the hair on her neck, Jenn was too happy to care. Finally—

They weren't done. They were far from done. She'd Kydd's sketches in her pocket, for one thing—not that any of those faces had belonged to the terst, but they were bad persons and likely villains too—and thinking of villains—"Bannan, there could be more terst—"

Breezes collided, snatching her breath away. "I will smell them out!" That was Scourge. "They wouldn't dare," from, of course, her proud dragon.

Bannan moved as if uneasy, then whispered in her ear, "I fear, Dearest Heart, we must rely on our friends. My gift has failed me of late and I can't—We're out," he finished, louder and glad and clearly changing the topic.

She was overjoyed to leave the mine, too, but this was serious. Jenn put her hands over Bannan's. Her love's true sight was part of him and who he was. They must, she decided worriedly, have a complete and thorough discussion of the matter.

And she must show him the sketches, but both had to wait. They rode out into night. A spectacular out-in-the-open-again dark night with stars twinkling above—but not like the terst devices—and lights twinkling below—

More lights than she'd seen since Channen, Jenn realized, lining streets that went this way and that like a picture. There were lights as well in buildings, buildings for the most part taller than any in Marrowdell. All of which hemmed in by mountains and narrow flat expanses she guessed were fields by day.

Part of her loved the sight.

The rest wasn't the least prepared to go where it was busy and full of strangers who might have faces Kydd warned her about—Jenn's stomach did an odd little flip. "Is that Gordit?" she asked, not proud of the little quiver in her voice. "It looks—bigger than I thought."

Bannan's arms tightened, hearing what she didn't say. "We'll go straight to the inn."

Where, Scourge had told them, Emon would doubtless take Semyn and Dutton. Hopefully with their prisoner, he'd purred, licking his lips at this.

Jenn hadn't wanted to know more, but an inn? That was promising. "Tell me all about it," she prompted, eager to think of good things. "What's the food like? Is there music? Where will we sleep?"

Lips found her neck, sending heat through her very core. "Who says we will?"

Most promising, Jenn decided, and snuggled closer.

Scourge gave another dramatic snort.

Heart's Blood, Bannan couldn't believe Jenn was back and whole, despite holding her. Despite feeling her warmth against him and the silk of her hair against his cheek—

He kept reliving when Jenn Nalynn went with The Dancer—when she'd burst into a whirling cloud of sei moths—

When she'd been *gone*, Ancestors Dear and Departed—

He'd felt his heart rip apart—as if the one he'd been born with, the one he'd found and loved her with, and not The Dancer's re-creation of the burnt cinder in his chest.

Take it as reassurance, the truthseer told himself bleakly, pulling out of the memory. But the town, when they entered it, seemed a haze of evening lights and strangers, full of danger—

"Are we safe?"

Bannan shook off the miasma gripping him. Jenn was understandably anxious and likely exhausted. "On this great beast?" he answered lightly. "I'm surprised the townsfolk don't flee the streets." Scourge tossed his head and pranced.

Jenn's hand closed over his. "Dearest Heart, I wouldn't want them to," she replied, being staunch and brave. "It's the perfect night to be outside, and—oh." Her head turned, tilted, her attention caught by the naked figures in a doorway, who certainly weren't about to notice a kruar or his riders. "Does—does that happen often in Ansnor?" she asked, once past the amorous couple.

Or trio. Hard to tell. "It's tomorrow's solstice. They believe—the stars—" He coughed, deciding to avoid details. "A time free of judgment—or much sense." However much he felt inspired to find a doorway of their own. "Do you feel it? The day length," he hastened to add, for until Jenn knew what had happened to him—made her choice—he wasn't about to—

"I feel something, Dearest Heart," with a low rich chuckle suggesting their proximity on Scourge's back made her well aware of his inspiration. "About the solstice, of course," she went on, and yes, that was a smile in her voice.

"'Of course,'" Bannan echoed faintly. Ancestors Teased and Tempted, much more of this and he'd—

"I feel less solid," she admitted more seriously.

Ice water couldn't have done more. "Are you all right?"

"Yes. Yes, it's the light, you see. Since I became turn-born, the light from the edge has been more, the light of the Verge, which is what I am, less. I can tell. I suppose, after the solstice, it'll be the other way—I'm not making much sense, am I?"

Ancestors Witness, how could any of it make sense? Time. Now light. A giggle tried to push up his throat and Bannan swallowed, hard. His love was made of light. The Dancer seemed outside of time or space, yet together, if he grasped events as far beyond his ken as the stars above, they'd saved the world—worlds. He started to say so—

"None of it changes what I can do," her voice suddenly full of grief. "Bannan—I was so angry at the terst—I wished—I wished something terrible. I wished them *dead*. If Chalk hadn't been there to deny me—"

A chill breeze. "They are dead, we live, and time is as it should be. The terst," Wisp continued grimly, "will have no chance to meddle again."

Ignoring the dragon, who'd deliberately missed her point and sounded, if anything, proud, Bannan hugged his love. "Dearest Heart—"

He felt her broken little sigh. "I don't know who I am, anymore. I thought—I thought I was better than that."

The depth of her pain shook him. Bannan could have told her finding a darkness within, then learning to control it, was part of life, but it was too soon.

And she wasn't Captain Ash. "I know who you are," he said instead, kissing her cheek, tasting tears. "Dearest Heart, trust that I know. It's—"

Scourge growled a warning.

They neared the gate to Cotalen's house. Bannan collected himself. "The tersts' ally in Gordit lives here," he told Jenn and felt her tense. "Don't worry, he's no longer a threat."

A happy rumble.

The building blazed with light from top to bottom—a thorough search underway, at a guess. About to move the kruar along, Bannan stopped when a voice called out, "M'lord Larmensu?" A figure stepped from the shadow by the gate.

"Araben," he greeted, at first surprised, then not. Emon would have turned matters—including Cotalen—over to a local authority with dispatch. "All's well, then?"

Grinning up at them, the engineer rubbed the back of her neck.

"Not for some, let's say. Stars witness, the dema and honest town officials aren't at all pleased with the good Elder Cotalen." After a curious look at Jenn, Araben gave a neat little bow to them both. "The baron left word for you to go straight to the inn. Semyn and Dutton are there, and safe. There'll be baths," she added with a wink, then waved her hands. "Off with you, stars blessed. And thank you."

Feeling Jenn tremble, Bannan nodded and set Scourge in motion.

Araben had no idea how much she owed the woman in his arms. Maybe no one else should, he thought abruptly.

Something else to discuss with his love—once at the inn and alone.

After that bath.

The town passed in a blur, Jenn unable, in this moment, to care about what otherwise she'd be eager to explore. Instead, she leaned gratefully against Bannan, high above the crowds on the mighty kruar—who didn't snarl or step on anyone, which was a relief.

At the inn, Scourge, sweat-streaked and tired himself, went directly to the stable, where he condescended to being groomed by someone other than Bannan.

Whose hand Jenn wouldn't let go.

The someone, introduced as Emon's driver, Loring, made a sour face at the extra duty, which might have worried her except Loring then gave Scourge's dusty haunch a comradely slap and promised him bacon, winking at Bannan, so that was well.

The doors to *Sibley's Drift*, as proclaimed by a sign above with crossed pickaxes, stood open and welcoming. Jenn perked up as Bannan led her inside. She'd heard the stories about Palma's in Endshere, and the food did smell wonderful, if unfamiliar, this being Ansnor.

But the dining room was jammed shoulder to shoulder with revelers, which she really should have expected and been prepared for, this being Fool's Day Eve. The crowd and noise bothered Bannan as well, and he fought to make progress without knocking drinks or stepping on feet, though everyone else was less careful and Jenn's toes had near misses.

Bannan suddenly stopped, taking her hand. "Here we go."

Two Westietas guards arrived, the crowd parting good-naturedly, and escorted them to a staircase. Another guard greeted them at the top and Jenn wondered how many there were.

"I'll take you to your room—"

If only, Jenn sighed wistfully, but to herself. "Please take us to the baron," she said firmly. "At once." Bannan gave her a startled look.

The guard merely nodded. "Of course." She opened the nearest door for them.

Looking most relieved, Emon came from behind his desk. "Ancestors Blessed. I'm so glad you're all right—and found each other," he said warmly, taking Bannan's hand and hers. He kept his voice down, Semyn sound asleep on the bed, still in his clothes.

While she longed to do the same, Jenn pulled the page of sketches from her pocket, careful of her tiny cows. "Lila asked me to show this to you both. It's from Kydd Uhthoff." She handed it to Emon.

"Kydd—how is he?" Bannan asked with concern. "Can he see?"

"Yes. And Lila's sending him home. His journals disappeared before he could read them," which summed up a great deal she'd explain later. She gave the paper to Emon. "Kydd drew the faces of people I was to avoid. Dangerous people," with a tiny tremor in her voice. "Not those in the cavern," that for Bannan. Heart's Blood, the terst had been bad enough. The people Kydd had described sought power over others, caused harm to gain it—

Bannan took her hand in reassurance. They were safe here, he meant, surrounded by skilled and dangerous people of their own. Derhall, Emon's senior guard. His aide, Mabbs Keit, armed as well. And while someone meeting Emon in this moment, a man gentle of demeanor and weary, a rumpled sleeping gown over his shoulders, might discount him?

She'd seen the baron in Channen and knew he was dangerous, too.

As was her beloved, who went to lean with Emon over the page and study the faces. Kydd had drawn four, skillful even in his haste: two young men with serious expressions, Lilac and Lavender; Daisy, a woman similar in age caught laughing; and Willow, an older woman who looked preoccupied—or indifferent. Before she could say anything about Lila and Werfol recognizing one or more faces, Jenn realized there was no need.

Bannan and Emon had as well. Neither spoke, but their gazes locked, faces equally grim.

"Who is it?" she asked quietly.

Wordlessly, Bannan pointed to the man Kydd had labeled Lilac.

Emon's lips thinned. "An old friend, or so we believed." Picking up the page, he folded it too neatly in half, then again. "Thank you, Jenn."

He shouldn't thank her, Jenn thought sadly. Not for news like this.

"I have to show these faces to Edis," the truthseer said in a low, strained voice. "She was there when spellcasters brought down our house. She might—"

Emon crushed the paper in his fist and Bannan fell silent. The baron stood a long moment, looking down at nothing but seeing, Jenn suspected sorrowfully, a face he'd trusted until this moment.

As if feeling her sympathy, Emon lifted his head to give her a kind smile, with no outward sign of distress on his face. "Ancestors Blessed, I've kept you too long. Please feel free to go to your room. There's food—a bath. I'll arrange a copy," of the paper he seemed to have forgotten in his fist. "I trust you'll join us at the festival tomorrow. I'll need you there," this with a glance at Bannan.

At his truthseer, Jenn realized. Whose failing gift was currently a problem, one he would wish to discuss first with her, not Lila's husband. On that thought, she gave the baron a wistful smile that wasn't entirely feigned, and indicated her sorely stained dress. "I've nothing to wear."

"I'll take care of that," the baron surprised her by saying, then went on to say what surprised her more. "I suggest you leave your clothes—you too, Bannan—outside the door. Mabbs will do what he can to clean them for you. Assuming you still want them?"

"Of course I do," Jenn protested, cheeks warming to have spoken thus to the baron, but her dress was in fine shape, other than needing a wash, and had been remade from one of Gallie Emms this very spring. Once too worn to wear as it was, why, she'd take the stitching apart and use the fabric for—

Bannan held up a hand. "The stains are Silver Tears. Mabbs should collect what he can."

Mimrol? Jenn frowned, trying to remember. There'd been a torrent, in Wisp's sanctuary—no, a lake—

"Heart's—" Emon closed his mouth then shook his head with a wry look. "I hope to hear this tale of yours some day."

Bannan knew more than he'd said to her thus far. Jenn raised an eyebrow, only to have him close his lips and give a tiny shake of his head.

And what was that, that he'd keep secrets from her? Secrets weren't good to have or safe to keep.

Ancestors Witness, she'd prove it.

Jenn put Lila's bag on the table. "This contains a perilous object, full of dark magic. Magic used to take my sister's husband from her and to let a villain in Avyo locate Werfol and Lila—and Bannan." And to hunt her, but that wasn't the baron's concern. "If you wish to examine it, do so now before I destroy it."

A breeze flipped her bangs, her dragon close by and ready.

Melusine's pin. Bannan didn't need his deeper sight to know the bag's contents. He'd have seized it—thrown it out a window—but instinct warned him not to come any closer. "Careful," he warned.

Glancing at him, Emon paused, about to open the bag. "There's risk?"

"It's a spy," Jenn warned. "We mustn't touch it. I think you'll be safe, baron, but listen to Bannan and be cautious. It's a foul thing."

"I will." Turning the bag over, Emon didn't undo the laces, instead pulling a thread at the bottom to split the fabric open. "Lila," he commented. The pin tumbled out. Rather than touch it with his bare hands, he employed a pair of small wooden sticks to move it back and forth. The little gems winked and sparkled, a pretty piece of adornment, innocent and bright.

A lie.

"The wishing words are on the back," Jenn said stiffly.

Nodding, Emon brought a lamp closer. Producing a hand lens from his pocket, he turned over the pin and bent close. *"A wish for joy to our Melly,"* he read. "The source would appear to—wait."

Bannan tensed. "What is it?"

"How remarkable. The words are changing—now it reads, *'We've come for you, granddaughter.'*" He shot a look at Jenn, then went back to the pin.

"Emon, stop—" Bannan protested.

But Lila's ever-curious husband was already reading for a third time, as if the bespelled pin was a book and harmless. *"And the truthseer we lost. Good."*

Snatching the pin, Jenn threw it into the air. "Wisp!"

Her dragon became visible, hovering over the table and the bed with the sleeping boy, filling much of the room, a wingtip and his tail vanishing into the walls. He snapped up the pin midair, dragonsfire flaming in his jaws. Swallowed gleefully.

But before the pin like flowers, gifted to a child with a wish for joy and an enemy's spite, melted and was gone, the words written in mimrol changed a final, unseen, time to read . . .

"Dragons are rea—?"

"You're all right, Wisp?" Jenn asked, hands clenched together. She hadn't thought of anything but her need to be rid of the pin and whoever controlled it. If her dragon came to harm because of it—

"Tasty," sang the little breeze in her ear, a breeze Emon and Bannan heard as well, from the baron's startled look and the truthseer's tight-lipped nod of approval.

Well, that was good, then. Not that everything was, she reminded herself, with faces to watch out for and a still-unsettled town—and she owed Mistress Sand a visit, if just to confirm whatever Chalk reported and confess what she'd almost done—

Ancestors Blessed, her part, surely, was over. Thinking that, Jenn looked meaningfully at her love, desperate for peace—and quiet together to realize it.

And for answers, of course, but first, a bath. Food and sleep. Or, she warmed inwardly, maybe sleep could wait a while, a thought she saw curve Bannan's lips and bring him near, a strong arm around her waist.

Smiling, Emon dismissed them with a little wave.

A guard opened the door. Another led them down a short hallway, past more guards. Jenn lost count.

A curiosity for tomorrow. Reaching their open door, Jenn flew through it, pulling Bannan after, hearing him be courteous, but she'd no time nor mind for it.

As the door closed, her mouth found his, the distance between them gone at long last—

"Wait."

Then was back. Jenn blinked at Bannan, who frustratingly held her at arm's length. "We've *been* waiting," she pointed out, attempting to be reasonable while feeling very far from it. "Since you left Marrowdell to help Werfol."

Then to help Mistress Sand, then Emon and Semyn and the Ansnan, Araben, and probably others she'd never met and, much as she admired his generous and helpful nature—Ancestors Pent and Passionate, with all that had happened and come all too close to happening—it had to be her turn now.

Words Jenn didn't say, of course.

She didn't need to. With a groan, Bannan bowed his head as if ashamed. "I'm sorry—Heart's Blood—Jenn, I'm not the man who left Marrowdell."

In all their time together, she'd never heard his voice hold such despair.

He needed her help. Taking Bannan's head in her hands, Jenn

gently raised it until lamplight glittered in his wonderful apple butter eyes. "Whatever it is, Dearest Heart, can wait till we're clean and had supper," she told him, deliberately making the words as prim and proper as ever Aunt Sybb said them, which she did regularly and so did Peggs, those ladies understanding the fragile nature of hearts.

Bannan thinking to argue—an intention she read in the flex of muscle along his jaw—Jenn moved smartly into the middle of a room she hadn't, till this moment, bothered to examine. It had a bed wider and longer than theirs, and she immediately wondered—

—what she wasn't, she chided herself, to wonder right now.

There was a round table with two chairs, a stand with a tray with covered dishes and cups, a vase of pretty summer flowers, and a most welcome pot of tea. Though it might be something else, this being Ansnor and Jenn newly aware other domains had their own hot beverages.

Their supper, however, would wait. Not so the endearingly curved and generous tub on clawed feet in the other corner of the room, filled with still-steaming water. While it was summer, the curtains over the window pulled back to let in the air, the thought of that bath—

Without looking at Bannan, acutely conscious of his presence, Jenn undid her laces, gladly pulling her arms from the short sleeves of her dress, then let it drop around her feet. She stepped out of it, mindful of the pockets in case the tiny cows hadn't already gone under the wide bed, and she probably should warn Bannan they'd cows but he'd a great deal on his mind—

And was *so* close—

Jenn couldn't help herself. She turned to feast her eyes on her beloved, disappointed he'd yet to remove any of his clothes.

Because he didn't want her to see him. Because the loss of his tan was only the start of a change he'd undergone, a magical transformation of some kind, and she'd have worried—

—but Bannan gazed at her as if seeing her for the first time, the way he always did and hopefully always would, his eyes filled with such longing and love, her smile came from her heart.

Jenn let her simples fall to stand before him as she was and he knew, very well indeed.

Then, answering to impulse, became glass and pearl and light, holding out her hands to her love.

The woman you love isn't just a woman. You don't love her regardless—you love her the more because of it.

Bannan Larmensu took hands of glass and pearl and light in his, the hands of his love and life in any form, and how had Edis known?

"How did you know?" he asked Jenn, that vitally important. As was, "How could you know?"

Jenn's wondrous smile grew tender even as her hands in his became warm, strong flesh. "You said you aren't the man who left Marrowdell, Dearest Heart." Her eyes, purpled with magic, studied his face as if rediscovering joy. "Ancestors Witness, I'm not the Jenn Nalynn you met that day in Marrowdell's trout pond. If my becoming turn-born didn't separate us, why would what happened to you?"

A challenge, then and there, to show her what he'd become—if, for now, only on the outside. Stepping back, Bannan undressed, every nerve aware of her rapt attention, his blood pounding. He removed his shirt last.

Jenn traced where his scars had been with her fingertip, goosebumps rising in his skin at her featherlight *potent* touch. Skin wasn't all that responded, and she glanced down, a mischievous dimple appearing in one cheek, then nodded to the tub. "Tell me in there."

And with Jenn cradled against him, her toes crowned with bubbles and warmed by her love, Bannan found the words after all.

Burned alive—Bannan had tightened his arms around her when she couldn't help but shudder at the words, and the terst were lucky to have simply lost their heads and been eaten, for the failure of Bannan's crossing had been their fault and she'd have—

—no, Jenn thought, with a deep, settling relief, she wouldn't. Not after experiencing what rage could make her wish, make her become—

"What are you thinking?" her love asked quietly.

He would understand, she realized suddenly, as no one else could. Knew the struggle between the good inside a person and the rage able to turn them into, yes, villains. Her beloved had never been one, Jenn believed that to her core, but Bannan had spent years within that darker aspect of himself. As a soldier, every day he'd seen and done what gave him nightmares still; as Captain Ash, he'd used his gift for what, he'd told her, stained him with guilt and regret.

While she'd spent her life free of care or anger. Well, other than being annoyed with Roche and longing for the wider world—and becoming turn-born had certainly not been easy—but nothing in her life had prepared her to face the truth. That she'd the potential to be a villain every bit as dreadful as those terst.

Unless she refused to be. "I'm thinking, Dearest Heart, that while I've much to learn about being turn-born—and about being sei—being Jenn Nalynn? It's my choice, when to use my magic and how." She drew a line in bubbles down his thigh, matching the line she drew in herself, clear and strong. The line she would never again cross and the breeze wafting through the curtains smelled, all at once, of roses. "From now on," she said confidently, "I choose not to cause harm."

Bannan took a deep breath, then sighed. "Ancestors Blessed, Jenn, I wish it were that easy. I hope it is, for you. For me, it's never been. To protect your loved ones. If you fail, that pain making you lash out, desperate to *do* something, anything. Even—to seek vengeance." He fell silent.

Then, flat and sure. "You'll be tested. Over and over. All your life."

The warning wasn't for her alone. Knowing that, Jenn ran her hand along the bubbles, caressing his smooth new skin, wishing she could as easily soothe his heart. "Then we mustn't fail. I can make that a wish, if you like," she added lightly. "Though I suspect it would turn us into trees. Or bugs. Quite possibly mushrooms."

She was glad to feel him laugh. He went on more seriously, "I'd a chance—to shed Captain Ash. After The Dancer healed me, as she did Edis, I might have said yes to it. I should have. I don't know why I didn't."

Jenn could guess. To have his body rebuilt must have been almost too much to bear, even for Bannan. How could he have accepted more? She was unutterably grateful—hoped, some day, to say so to The Dancer. "While Edis is a wonder," she teased, "I'm delighted The Dancer remade you just as you are, Dearest Heart."

Nice and snug between Bannan's thighs, she felt his breath catch.

Ancestors Blessed, this was the crux of it. Jenn squirmed, water sloshing out of the tub, until they faced one another over their knees. "Tell me."

Making a face, Bannan tugged at his hair. "Edis said I've the light of the Verge in my hair."

"Like Wen?" At his nod, Jenn squinted, tilting her head. "It looks the same to me," she complained. "Not that it isn't very nice hair."

Her disappointment lightened his expression and he pulled her closer. "Werfol will see it," he murmured, lips against her neck and his other parts adding to the distraction.

Jenn pushed away, just a little, breathing harder herself, but if her love sought to change the topic, he'd underestimated her determination.

Also, the water was growing cold, as was supper.

"What else?" Jenn insisted. "Your gift?"

"That, too." He leaned back. "The first time I tried it after—" a wave at himself "—I was overwhelmed, my true sight out of control as it hadn't been since I was a boy. I was paralyzed—Emon saved me from it." Casually, as if in all else, this was a small matter.

It wasn't, in any sense. "And?" Jenn pressed gently, sure there was more.

A finger brushed his ear. "When I returned to the edge, I *heard* the little cousins." A grimace. "All of them, all at once. It was deafening. It's better here."

As if it might not be better elsewhere, but still, "It would have helped with Master Dusom's yling," she said pragmatically.

His lips quirked. "If I can ever control it—or my true sight."

"You will," she declared. "You tell Werfol to keep trying, don't you?" Jenn climbed out of the tub and wrapped herself in a towel. When Bannan did the same, she put a hand on his wet chest. "The rest."

He covered her hand with his, gazing down at her. "That, Dearest Heart, is what I don't know."

"Well, I don't know everything I am either." She gave a brisk nod. "We'll find out together." Her stomach chose that moment to rumble. "After we—"

Bannan, eyes aglow, chose that moment to toss aside their towels and sweep her from her feet, after which they found out their bed was indeed wide and entirely wonderful.

From under it, the two terst cows eyed the greenery just out of reach. They'd wait and not trouble their leader while she was very happy. Knowing they'd eat soon, they were content it was so.

Bannan woke to find himself wrapped in Jenn's arms and under her leg, her beautiful face close to his, lashes sweeping her rosy cheeks, for she was sound asleep and snoring just a little. Everything else felt a dream—this, Ancestors Blessed and Beloved, the reality—

Clunk.

He rose on an elbow. The sound had come from the tray, where a flower was waving back and forth in the vase. It disappeared.

A second one came under attack and the truthseer, ever so curious, thought of young Werfol and dared his deeper sight.

Two shaggy little creatures stood on the tray, one balanced on the pot, the other having climbed up on a dish cover. They'd long arms with claws for hands, and were using those to snag flower stalks, pulling the heads down to be nibbled with every appearance of enjoyment.

He felt Jenn stir. "You do have cows," he whispered wonderingly. Not that the things looked anything like such an animal—Scourge came closer, a comparison he'd never admit to making.

"And you can see them," Jenn said, gladness in her voice.

Bannan nodded, overcome with relief. He'd be cautious, yes, but to have regained this much of himself was heartening—and, he suspected, at least in part due to the woman beside him.

Who leaned on his shoulder. "They've stayed with me since the terst village. They saved me when the terst were—when they—" Jenn sat up, pulling the sheet to her, distressed. "I remember making that—that terrible wish. Chalk's denial. But—I don't remember what happened next. Why? What else did I do?" with heartfelt worry and reason for it, being what she was.

He found her hand. "You fixed what was broken. The Dancer showed you how and I believe she helped, but you did it."

She gave him a dubious look. "I fixed time?"

"If you don't remember," he added, believing this as well, "it's because The Dancer knew you shouldn't, not if you were to be whole again."

"'Again'?" with an adorable squeak.

And while he could have told her about exploding into a cloud of moths and how he'd thought her gone—then discussed the serious nature of life and love—her squeak made it far more urgent and important to press her body beneath his into the very accommodating mattress and discover what other adorable sounds he could inspire.

While the terst cows enjoyed the flowers their leader had provided, content it was so.

Uncle Bannan had returned. With Jenn Nalynn and—"Wisp?" Semyn questioned his father, determined to have the whole of it.

"Yes. He was right here," Poppa told him, waving a hand overhead. He looked understandably bemused, this being his first dragon.

Hopefully Wisp would show himself again, Semyn thought wistfully, recalling his own too-brief glimpse. But it was all good news, the best being Dutton's recovery. "I'm ready to work on my speech, Poppa," he said, putting his scribe kit on the table between them; a task he'd started last night, only to fall asleep and miss the dragon.

"Thank you, but it's no longer necessary."

"Momma's come?"

A keen look. "Your mother is handling matters from the estate." Poppa's lips twitched. "Where another dragon took down our signaling device. An accident, Jenn assured me, but the system will need a redesign before we put it back up. To be dragon-proof," this with a gleam in his eye, Poppa relishing the challenge.

And using talk of dragons and redesign to distract him, Semyn decided, from why the Baron Westietas was now to give the public address when yesterday there'd been good and ample reason for him to decline.

He'd had news. Not of the good sort. The boy sank into his seat to regard his father. "What is it, Poppa?"

To his dismay, his father hesitated. Did he judge him incapable of hearing the news? Worse, was he about to lie? Their parents did, at least when Werfol wasn't around. All manner of lies, from how they were to what was about to happen to whether they'd ever have their home again—

Unacceptable. "Tell me," Semyn ordered, using Momma's sharp tone.

His expression abruptly bleak, his father pushed a piece of paper to him, a paper folded and, by the look, crumpled up as if to be tossed into a fire.

Semyn smoothed it out. Saw the faces of strangers—the one that wasn't.

His gaze shot up to meet his father's distressed look. With an effort, the boy swallowed what he might have said in favor of thinking, hard and fast the way Momma taught, why they'd a sketch of a younger Kluet Gore on a table in Gordit and what it could mean.

Coming up with only one answer. "This came from Momma, making these—" he tapped the other faces "—our enemies. Supervisor Gore—" who'd been their *friend* "—is our enemy." Semyn was unaware how his voice chilled in threat and his face grew harsh lines, aging him years in that instant. Nor did he notice how his father grieved to see it, too busy calculating a response.

"You'll expose him at the festival. Good," the boy said with a nod, as if his father had asked his approval. "He won't be able to hide. How can I help?"

Poppa pointed to the damning page. "Make your uncle a copy—on paper without our watermark.

"Then, Semyn . . ." He stopped, looking sad—which wasn't right, because they'd a traitor to catch. A traitor to bring to Momma for questioning, a gift she'd appreciate and a doom their *friend* deserved.

"You'll want me and Araben in the crowd," Semyn said when Poppa failed to say another word. "To spot any affiliations."

And if their *friend* had *friends*?

They'd all pay for their treachery.

Bannan summoned to the baron and, at least slightly, more confident in his gift, Jenn finished her breakfast in rare and welcome leisure, wrapped in a sheet and late morning sunbeams glistening in her unbound hair.

A spectacle her love had, laughing, accused her of creating so it'd be impossible to leave, and, while that hadn't been Jenn's intention, she'd laughed and told him it was so he'd hurry back.

Being done waiting.

Jenn nibbled a sweet pastry not unlike a pie but more like bread, watching her tiny cows finish the last piece of sticky fruit, then lick one another clean. Cute at this size, but they weren't always either. "What am I to do with you?" she asked them.

They looked up at her much like Wainn's old pony would angle his ears when hearing his name—though the pony, being lazy, wouldn't move a jot more unless he smelled an apple.

A breeze tugged the sheet and blew hair in her eyes. "Wisp!" she protested with a laugh.

The breeze found her ear. "Dear Heart. You're happy."

Her dragon knew she was, but Jenn treated it like a question. "I'd be happier if I knew what to do with them." She nodded to the tray.

A sly, "I'll eat them for you."

The terst cows shimmered and disappeared, understanding dragons and their ways.

"You mustn't," Jenn said at once, adding, "You wouldn't," understanding this dragon in particular. "But I can't leave them here."

"They cannot leave you, Dear Heart," Wisp informed her, sounding vastly amused at her predicament.

Jenn broke a piece from her pastry and tossed it in the air.

SNAP!

Heart's Blood, what of the pin he'd swallowed for her? Did dragons get stomach aches? "Thank you for getting rid of the pin."

"You were wise, Dearest Heart, to give me the taste of its maker," this with such anticipation, Jenn immediately envisioned an invisible Wisp taking nips out of anyone suspicious.

Which wouldn't do at all, especially at today's party, though there'd be at least one person—the baron's false friend—who deserved it. "Wisp, promise you won't taste anyone without asking me first."

"As you wish." Hair flew into her face, her dragon less than pleased.

But not, Jenn knew, about to break his word.

"M'lady?"

She parted her hair with two hands, peeking through to find the baron's aide, Mabbs, standing in the doorway with a bundle, a guard behind him carrying a trunk. "Good morning," she said brightly, as if not wearing a sheet and the once-beautifully appointed tray didn't look as if it had been trampled by tiny cows—which it had. "Is that for Bannan?"

The two came in, apparently reassured. "These are for the good sir," Mabbs told her, setting his bundle on the bed and appearing oblivious to the mattress off to one side and bedding strewn across the room. "The trunk is the baroness'. You are encouraged to select what you wish from it. Will you wish assistance dressing?"

Jenn supposed her appearance made him ask. Fortunately, before she had to reply, Bannan came in the room, took in the situation with a sweeping glance, and gave her a wink. "We're beholden to the baron and baroness. And to you for your aid," he said firmly. "We'll manage."

The guard's gaze strayed to the bed, then snapped back. "Yes, sir."

While Mabbs pursed his lips. "With respect, sir, there is the matter of the lady's hair. Let me know when you are ready to have it done," with a bow to her and a quick exit.

When they were gone and the door safely closed, Jenn pretended to glower at her love, who was trying not to laugh.

"What's the matter with my hair?" she demanded, then lifted her hands to what felt a clean, shiny—

—thoroughly tangled mess, Wisp's breezes not helping.

Oh dear.

After pulling their bed back together, not without an exchange of wistful looks that made Bannan want more than ever to be done with Emon's business and back home, they opened the trunk.

Cautiously. He knew his sister. But it proved to be what it appeared, a small trunk, nicely made and, when opened, containing three waxed paper wrapped packages tied with string, a note in Lila's elegant handwriting affixed to each.

Jenn fingered the top one. "It says, 'In case I make the festival.'" Lifting out that package and setting it carefully aside, she brought out the second, handing it to Bannan as if they exchanged gifts on Midwinter Beholding.

Despite the news about Gore, this day, Bannan vowed, should have that feel to it. "This says, 'In case I have to ride home.'" The package did have the heft of riding leathers—or light armor.

"Bannan, look!" The last package in her arms, Jenn stared at him, then back down at the label. "It says, 'A gift for Jenn Nalynn.' It's for me. But how—?"

"How could my sister know you'd be here—and need a dress? I've no idea," he said. Other than Lila being Lila.

"No more secrets," his beloved chided, stern despite her happily flushed cheeks. "You know your sister. What's this about?"

"Nothing new." He tucked Lila's clothing back in the trunk and closed the lid, tracing her crest—their crest—on the top. "Lila's on the hunt."

"For those who killed your parents," Jenn said very quietly, sitting on the bed. "That's why you brought her Kydd and his journals. To find out if people he—he knew in Avyo were involved. The people he drew for me. And someone was." She rested her hands on the package. "It's why we haven't gone home. Why the festival and Emon and all these guards. Those people are here."

Did he imagine a chill to the air?

If so, she'd every right. "I told Lila I won't be part of this," he said roughly. "That you won't be part of this."

Jenn's eyes flashed. "You don't speak for me, Dearest Heart. Not when there's magic involved. Not when it's family. The pin came from my grandmother, in Avyo. The words it said to the baron—they're coming for *me*. And you! How can I not—?" She stopped, breathing deeply, her expression set and resolved. "I won't wish harm to anyone, Bannan. But I won't allow harm, either."

The truth shone in her face.

How long ago had Lila seen this strength in Jenn Nalynn? Recognized in her a moral compass so true, a goodness of heart so deep, it was hard to conceive they could exist in the same world as their gray and ever-shadowed one.

What a fool he'd been. He'd tried to shield his love from his sister. From the Larmensu heritage of death and hate. Heart's Blood, he'd been not much older than Semyn when they'd lost their parents and Lila'd carved the path for them toward vengeance—but that wasn't enough to call a life.

There was so very much more. He'd the proof, here and now, watching him with blue eyes smudged purple with magic and love.

And Lila had to know. Had to fear her brother changing—unless she'd seen that, too.

He'd been staring at Jenn in silence. All at once, she blushed. "What?"

"There you are," he concluded, the universe settling around him.

Earning a quizzical frown. "Yes, I am. Here, waiting for you to tell me what I don't know, Dearest Heart."

Bannan sat beside her. "The man in the sketch is named Kluet Gore."

Her hands moved, untying the package strings, as he told her everything he knew.

The crowds began swelling after breakfast on Fool's Day, Gordit's townsfolk soon outnumbered by the cheerful and colorful hordes flooding down every access road, not to mention those coming across fields and over the mountain. Drawn by Elder Cotalen's promise of free drink and food for all—as well as the novelty of a Rhothan baron—and Dutton expressed the sentiment held by every guard detailed to protect them when he growled, "Ancestors Disorderly and Doomed, a bloody nightmare, that's what this is."

Much as Semyn agreed, there was no turning back. He tightened his rope belt, again dressed as a poor Ansnan lad, one as likely to be a pickpocket as virtuous on this Fool's Day with no rules and the stars oblivious. "You ready?"

"Waiting on you," Araben Sethe blithely informed him. She wore an embroidered tunic indicating she served the household of the dema, with the addition of a floppy brimmed hat to shadow her face and a curved tray suspended from her shoulders loaded with the spiced dried crisps and curds without which no Ansnan gathering would be complete. A noteworthy burden, easy to discard at need.

Impressive. Semyn focused on their orders. "Come along. We're to watch the chancellor and Jellicoe Dee. Others have the rest." A command direct from his father and, much as he ached to expose Gore and whomever the traitor met at the festival, Semyn was ashamed to be relieved. He wasn't ready. Not to confront a man he'd known his whole life, who'd taught him how to fish and as recently as yesterday made him smile.

He wasn't sure he'd ever be.

They'd reached the festival tent, working their way through servants and others preparing the feast, when Araben pulled him to a halt.

"What?" Semyn demanded.

"Exactly," she retorted. "What's going on? You're supposed to be on stage shortly, by that list." She pointed at a nearby tent post, festooned with flyers about today's events.

He should have guessed she'd notice. "That plan's changed."

Uncle Bannan and Jenn Nalynn knew Kydd's "Lilac" was Kluet Gore, but they were family, and "family only" Poppa'd decreed, taking Semyn's carefully drawn copy to his uncle.

Though Dutton had a look about him this morning, passersby giving him a wider berth than usual.

Her eyebrows went up. "Stage fright, is it?"

Semyn scowled. "No. A surprise." He tugged his rope belt. "I'll be here and useful. At the last minute, the word will go out the heir is ill and confined to bed."

She scowled right back. "Why the ruse?"

The most successful lie is the almost truth, Momma would say. Looking Araben in the eye, Semyn told her, "Everyone has to help, today. Someone in the Rhothan delegation is with Cotalen. We're to note any and all conversations Milne and Dee have with others, no matter how trivial they may seem. If they're innocent," he went on, "hopefully we'll be able to prove it." If guilty, they'd have them.

Araben, like Werfol, was too smart not to know he kept something back, but she shrugged and got moving again, meaning she'd let it go. For now.

Outside the tent was a small stage, presently home to a decent juggler, faced by a line of benches where sat several children transfixed by the flying globes and plates and in no mood to move. Town notables—distinguished from the swell of people moving around by broad sashes across their chests—milled in groups nearby, drinks in hand. They'd take their seats on the benches when time for the various speakers, protected from the masses beyond by some hasty fencing that wouldn't, in Semyn's opinion, stop a child, let alone a determined assassin.

Past that, ribbons marked out squares for various competitions, Ansnans fond of sport, several games underway. One square held a muddy puddle and a herd of squealing piglets being chased through it by eager young people wearing very little.

Or nothing. Semyn didn't realize he was staring until Araben laughed. Cheeks hot, he averted his gaze.

The nearest and largest square had a wooden floor laid over the grass and pretty arches suspended overhead, festooned with flowers and lamps for evening. Music filled the air and dancers filled the floor, as they would until tomorrow.

Spotting the chancellor, Semyn touched Araben's hand to alert her to follow.

She seized his shoulder instead, turning him to see the latest arrivals.

It was Uncle Bannan, cutting a fine figure in the latest Avyo fashion, in an elegant tailed summer coat, snug breeches, and knee-high polished boots.

And with him, Jenn Nalynn, looking like a princess.

"People are staring," Jenn whispered to Bannan in an agony of self-consciousness. "Is it the dress—my hair?"

Did she have stains already? Because she might, Ancestors Tippy and Tripped. She'd had tea while Mabbs dealt with the so-called *matter of her hair*, and been so fascinated to watch him in the mirror—hoping to replicate the intricate twists and pins and all else going into the creation of what became a magnificent crown atop her head, with dainty curls brushing her neck, on Peggs' glorious locks—she might have spilled her cup.

Her love, magnificent in his new clothes, brought her hand to his lips. "Let them stare. They've never seen anyone as beautiful, Dearest Heart."

While she doubted that, it did sound better than stains. Reassured, Jenn lifted her head and smiled back, for people were smiling at her, and waving, so she gave a shy little wave in return.

Despite there being what she now thought of as *unfortunate aspects* to the day, the festival was wondrous. She'd not miss a thing, Jenn was determined, from the tall tent, bigger than the terst turn-borns'—not that she'd tell Master Riverstone—to music in the distance.

Music reminding her. "You promised we'd dance, Dearest Heart." She twirled, for Lila's gift was the perfect dress for dancing, light and airy as a summer's day, yellow like the sun, with the most charming little sleeves and plunging neckline. Which her breasts filled more than usual, being pushed up by, yes, a corset, but one of such quality Jenn hadn't been able to argue.

Bannan, she'd already noted, quite enjoyed the result. She'd keep the corset. And dress.

She wasn't as sure about the slippers. Lovely, yes, of the same fabric as the dress, with laces around her ankles—which showed at every step, sure to scandalize Aunt Sybb—but they felt as if she were barefoot. Which she did enjoy, but it warned they'd most likely have holes in the bottom by tonight.

When, if there was any fairness in the world, they'd finally be home.

Providing Emon settled Gordit, including the detention of Supervisor Kluet Gore of Vorkoun, Lilac the mage in Kydd's sketch—ideally, as Bannan said, without a fuss.

Jenn hoped so. If Gore truly was a spellcaster and the sort of person who'd use dark magic against others? There were dozens, possibly hundreds, of innocent happy people surrounding them. A *fuss* risked them all.

She'd not permit it. Whatever it was. She simply wouldn't. So long as they were gone before the turn, Jenn seeing no place to hide, but Bannan had assured her they would.

"A dance it is, Dearest Heart," her love said with a gallant bow, taking her hand.

In the meanwhile, she firmly intended to enjoy her first Fool's Day.

His old enemy prowled the foothills, avoiding the people massed around the town. Hoping, no doubt, for worthy prey.

Wisp could have told him such prey waited below, lurking within the masses, waiting to strike; the first scream would bring the kruar at a run regardless.

And why share?

He found an updraft and circled lazily above, watching the girl and the truthseer. He'd spotted the nephew and his companion earlier, entertained by their able stealth, as well as the Westietas' force arrayed throughout.

They'd not need help against their own kind.

Against this prey, the dragon suspected, they would. He'd tasted the pin, with its old and lingering malice, and judged those he sought to be kin to it. Flesh and blood and crunchy bone.

But also tricks and traps and the foulest magic.

They'd a face and name—he'd seen and heard. Hunted those he guarded. Regrettably, those Wisp cared about wouldn't want him to strike first and eliminate the threat—*a hindrance*.

One to ignore, the dragon thought more cheerfully, the instant the foul wizard opened his mouth to cast a spell.

While Scourge hunted rabbits.

Wisp tipped a wing, soaring closer to the music, following the girl.

FOURTEEN

"I KNOW THIS ONE!" Jenn took the lead, tugging Bannan after her, heading for the dance floor. "We do it at home." Which might have surprised her, Marrowdell being Rhothan, but her love had told her Ansnor had been a friend once before, and music spread everywhere.

She liked to think, with the peace, it would again.

He lifted the ribbon to let her through, then followed, smiling and taking up her hands as they joined the dancers. They were, Jenn decided happily, being ever so responsible. After all, they weren't to *look* as if they were on the lookout for someone.

And if they really had fun—as they were, Bannan a wonderful dancer and lifting her in the air whenever the dance called for it so she felt as if she flew—surely there'd be no harm to it.

A small white moth landed on the arch above, a creature unnoticed by those below. Four of its little legs gripped a flower petal, the other two busy taking notes, and once in a while it looked up, watching a dragon.

While the terst cows tucked themselves between the tight laces of Jenn Nalynn's corset, holding on as their leader moved with unusual speed and unpredictable direction. But she was happy and they were content it was so.

Jenn, blissfully focused on her love and the music, not moths or tiny cows or even her dragon, danced and danced and danced. And would have danced again, Bannan most willing, but the music abruptly stopped, new musicians coming forward to play while those they replaced were greeted with cheers and given drinks.

As were the dancers, milling about during this pause. Seeing others brought drinks, why, nothing would do but Bannan find some for them.

Jenn stayed to watch the new musicians set up—as well as the pig chase going on in the next square, an event in which she'd great experience and might, had she not been in a gorgeous dress, have tried next.

When a hand appeared in front of her, holding a tall delicate glass, she looked around with a glad smile. "Do you—?"

It wasn't Bannan.

Heart's Blood, it was Lilac, the man from the sketch—older, with friendly little wrinkles beside his eyes and a kindly pleasant smile—but Kydd had captured his eyes, and they were sharp and cold as ice. "For a lovely lady," Gore said with a little bow.

She took the glass, her fingers perforce touching his, but didn't raise it to her lips. "Do I know you, good sir?"

"A fellow Rhothan." He bowed again. And had a bald spot, Jenn noted. "A pleasure indeed." He lifted his glass. "To Peace Day."

Jenn put hers on the tray of a passing servant. "It's Fool's Day here."

"So it is." Ridding himself of his glass, Gore deftly captured her hand as the musicians started to play. "Then a dance. There's no harm in a dance, surely."

He'd need his hands free to cast a spell, Jenn reasoned, having cast one herself last fall. And tokens. Possibly fire—or possibly not—the point being, she couldn't see him casting a spell from the dance floor, not without being stopped.

She made herself smile. "A pleasure."

It soon became painfully obvious whatever Gore was, he couldn't dance, while Jenn—usually light on her feet and, according to

Bannan, a quick study—found herself too stiff and anxious to do more than shuffle to the beat.

She also found, and quickly, that she didn't like this stranger touching her, didn't like his hand on her waist, and most of all, detested her fingers crushed in his clammy grip. *Why if she'd a wish—*

Jenn thought hurriedly of manure. Piles of it. Shoveling it. Better yet, terst cow manure—

"Did you come with the baron?"

He'd know she hadn't. "I was already here," Jenn said, then had an inspiration. "Elder Cotalen invited all his friends." Which wasn't a lie, the terst hardly friends, but neither, Jenn decided, was this man. "Did you? Come with the baron?"

"Our delegation traveled separately. Also at the elder's invitation. Have you seen him?" This as Gore spun her vigorously about, giving Jenn an opportunity to search for Bannan.

No sign of him. "Seen who?" she gasped.

"Elder Cotalen. Our host."

"I'm sure he'll be here for—" Ancestors Blessed and Beloved, the song was over. Jenn stepped free. "—for the speeches." She pointed in the general direction of the stage, hoping Gore would take the hint.

Instead, he seized her elbow, pulling her against him, smiling all the while as if they were a couple. Before Jenn could struggle or object, he whispered in her ear what made her go perfectly still.

"We're here for you, *granddaughter.*"

He'd been gone too long. Drinks in hand, Bannan tried to see past the crowds around the dance floor, moving through them almost impossible. Even going to the tent had been a sequence of bumps and slowdowns, an interference he'd think deliberate if not for this being a Fool's Day gathering and most Ansnans well into their cups.

Unless—it was! Dropping the drinks, the truthseer put muscle into his effort to get through the crowd, earning curses and glancing blows, but not stopping, not when—

He burst into the open. Frantically scanned the dance floor.

Heart's Blood, where was Jenn?

Dutton's big hand fell on his shoulder. "Whatcha doing, cutpurse!" he roared, shaking Semyn.

And holding him up, this being a ruse. Semyn cowered, acting his part for onlookers. Whined, "I dinna touch ye purse, ye fat Rhothan frog."

"Come with me," the guard growled, pulling him along. Once behind a stack of beer barrels, Dutton stopped and let go, giving Semyn's clothes a quick brush. "Apologies, m'lord, but we've a problem. Gore has Jenn Nalynn. Took her from the dance floor."

How was that even possible? "She has powers—she—"

"Risky, here, with all these people. We need to get her away from him."

Semyn nodded numbly. "Araben?"

"Here," from behind him.

Her tray was half empty and she'd taken off her floppy hat, sweat gleaming on her forehead. "What's this about Jenn?"

Bothered by something, Semyn didn't answer. He thought about the dance floor. Where it was.

Dutton, who knew him, held up a hand when Araben went to ask again. "He's thinking," the guard murmured.

Charitable, Semyn told himself absently, though he wasn't so much *thinking* as plotting. How would *he* separate someone from a couple as madly in love as Uncle Bannan and Jenn?

He'd wait for his chance, a time when they were happy, perhaps distracted. Delay the one, take the other.

Gore wasn't acting alone.

But only a fool would risk himself, in public, where he'd be recognized. *He* wasn't a fool—he wouldn't assume their enemy was.

Someone else gave the orders.

Without knowing how much help Gore had, without knowing if any of those others were spellcasters—but Ancestors Poison and Perilous, he'd assume they all were—

Semyn looked at Dutton and Araben. "We protect the baron."

And let Uncle Bannan go after Jenn.

For a third time, Gore paused as if searching for someone—or something—and for the third time Jenn used the moment to berate him, loudly. "I don't know who you think I am, or who you are," she snapped, imitating Lorra Treff, who could be the most disagreeable person in Marrowdell. Aunt Sybb claimed Lorra's tongue could slice ham, but all Jenn wanted was attention. "Let go of me, you—you cretin!"

Spotting what he wanted, the man moved again, his hand a vise on her elbow, dragging her along.

Within the laces of her corset, fastenings strained as their leader took deeper and quicker breaths, the terst cows were sorely conflicted. Their leader had been happy and now she wasn't, but she did appear willing to go with the one who made her unhappy, while the one who made her happy had left. Did it signal a change in their herd? They must wait to find out, they decided, discontent but resigned.

Jenn's efforts thus far were in vain. Gore seemed to know where to go to avoid Emon's guards, and in every direction other people were urging one another along by grips on arms, hands, and even hair—for reasons she preferred not to ponder—and while most were laughing and she wasn't, at all, she doubted anyone here would care to intercede.

Or be safe if they tried. Gore was armed. Or at least wore armor, by the hardness of his shoulder against hers, not that it made any sense when he'd dark magic.

Unless his magic had constraints. More than tokens. Maybe he needed privacy—or maybe, Jenn thought suddenly, he needed partners. Bannan's family home had been destroyed by not one, but three magic users working together, Edis Donovar a witness to it.

Well, if that were the case, she mustn't let him reach anyone else. Jenn lunged for a tent pole, wrapping her free arm around it, then did what she would have done earlier, had she taken Gore seriously. She shouted, "WISP!"

Gore's hold on her broke as he rose into the air with a scream, legs kicking and arms flailing.

Everyone, Jenn noted with satisfaction, *paid attention to that.*

Knowing her dragon, she stepped into the open. "Alive, please."

A breeze tugged at her dress, found her ear and blasted, hot and furious, "HE TOUCHED YOU!"

And she'd have bruises, but that wasn't important. Knowing he'd listen, however outraged, Jenn whispered, "Please, Wisp. I want no more blood on my hands." She looked around, hoping for inspiration.

There! "Leave him on top of the tent, Wisp." Shading her eyes, she watched the struggling form of her assailant fly higher. And higher—

—then drop. He screamed louder as he fell—which she hadn't thought possible and wasn't ashamed to enjoy—landing on the tent, where he slid until coming up hard against a pole. Grabbing that, Gore hung on for dear life.

The crowd, who'd done some screaming of their own as the man mysteriously flew into the air, began to cheer and clap, convinced they'd witnessed a most excellent Fool's Day spectacle.

"I'd hoped he'd land on a rock," Bannan said, coming up to Jenn. He put his arm around her shoulders, tipping her chin with a gentle finger to search her face.

"I can still arrange it," Wisp assured them, his breeze calmer but no less angry, and did she glimpse silver scales in the sky above them?

Jenn went on her toes to kiss her love's cheek. "He's fine where he is," she told them both. "I'm fine," this as Bannan's eyes glowed, so he'd know it was true. "Gore isn't alone," she warned, abruptly aware of the press of people around them.

And what better place to hide than among them?

Taking advantage of the excellent distraction provided by the fool atop the tent—the effort to bring him down underway with a gratifying number of Emon's guards volunteering to help—Bannan drew Jenn with him to stand where they could see the stage and, more importantly, spot anyone approaching.

To his dismay, the stage was full of dignitaries and—Heart's Blood, what was Emon doing up there? They'd now a threat, a credible proven threat, and if Derhall and Ennan hadn't been able to stop their lord, Dutton could have sat on him—

"He's made himself bait," the truthseer whispered. Everyone thought Lila the schemer of the pair—and she was—but Emon? Played the long game, and rare for anyone, even his wife, to predict his next move.

Jenn's fingers plucked his sleeve. "Where's Semyn?"

He scanned those near the stage. "There." He nodded to where the boy stood within a group of similar youths, eating crisps from— "Araben is the one with the tray."

"I'd never have guessed," with admiration.

"She's many skills," he replied absently, his attention drawn by the group being shown to their bench. "Gordit's leaders have arrived." Elder Cotalen among them, well dressed and impeccably groomed, and he might have thought the man's fortunes changed if not for those who sat to either side of him, the dema and the *Drift's* innkeeper, Jas Sibley.

Emon's subtle hand. Avoid a public denouncement and any taint of Rhothan interference, while demonstrating to the entire town their elder was in disgrace and would pay for his actions.

If his other enemies didn't get to him first. "Cotalen worked for the Heirs," he whispered to Jenn. "That's why he's been stalling the rail project—why he won't reopen the iron mine. He's been selling the Heirs mimrol since the end of the war—and maybe during it," with a dark scowl.

"Until the terst came," Jenn said quickly. "They had magic—he must have thought they were Heirs as well."

"He'd no reason to question it," Bannan agreed. "My guess is the terst refused to let anyone else into the mine, and that cut off the Heirs' supply. It's why Gore's here, to restore it."

She looked up, eyes somber. "That's not the only reason. The pin told them we were here. Bannan, he called me *granddaughter*."

Heart's Blood, he felt her pain. To grow up knowing your mother had been betrayed by hers own—to live with the fear of coming to the notice of the Semanaryas, who'd the power and wealth to send soldiers to Marrowdell—now this? "Trust nothing he said, Dear Heart," he told her gently. "A poisoned source—"

A blare of horns drowned the rest he might have said, pulling all eyes to the stage. In the ensuing silence, the Baron Westietas of Vorkoun strode into the center, sunlight catching the gilt and insignia of his full regalia as a member of the House of Keys. Those who thought the baron to be out of favor and in exile had to be rethinking, and fast.

Emon bowed to the crowd, a perfect Ansnan bow. But instead of rising, he crumbled to the stage—

—and no one shouted or cried out, because everywhere, everyone was crumbling, falling as if so many discarded dolls—

Bannan grabbed Jenn or she grabbed him. They were, he realized in horror, the only ones standing.

Except for the three watching from the pasture.

"Wait," she heard Bannan say, his voice faint and distant and pleading.

So she did.

As she did, she realized the people weren't dead after all. Chests rose and fell with peaceful breaths, as if everyone around them had fallen asleep at once, slumped against one another or on the ground.

And once she did, something hotter and darker than a dragon's rage left her heart, the heart she had to remember, being glass and pearl and light and trembling on the cusp of—

"They're coming," Bannan said next, sounding closer.

—of—

"Let them," he whispered, warm and sure in her ear.

—of what she wasn't ever to be. With a sigh, Jenn found herself flesh and blood and glad of both. "Their spell didn't affect us."

"Or they want us awake," her love countered, which wasn't at all reassuring. They held hands as the three approached, which was.

The absence of her dragon was not. Ancestors Witness, wherever he was, Wisp should have swooped to their rescue by now, and she greatly feared he was lying nearby, spelled asleep like the rest. Jenn reached out her slippered toes but found only grass.

They'd have to help him, too.

She gazed sternly at the cause of their plight. The three were dressed for the festival, in the same bright colors as everyone else, the better to hide among the innocent. Their heads were veiled but the fabric revealed their faces—no, a series of faces, disconcertingly changing with each step. Another spell and what more could they do?

The leftmost spoke, their voice distorted—answering part of that question. "Truthseer. Granddaughter. Come with us and no one will be harmed."

"We won't," Jenn told them, not believing a word.

The rightmost spoke next, veil aimed at Bannan. "The truthseer knows mountains are treacherous." The one in the center raised her hand to point, as if they might miss the giant mountain Gordit nestled against.

A mountain reinforced by turn-born expectation, *HOLD,* hers and Chalk's, and Jenn knew what they didn't. These spellcasters couldn't budge a stone, no matter how much magic they tried—they'd have better luck with a pickaxe.

"Quot. Urkett. Eldee. Was it you?" Bannan demanded, rather than *Daisy, Willow,* or *Lavender.*

He knew better than reveal they knew those secret names. If they belonged to these individuals at all, Jenn thought, there being every reason to believe there were more Heirs, which wasn't a good thought at all.

The truthseer took a step forward, his voice low and full of menace. "Did you kill my mother? My father? Our friends?"

The rightmost shrugged. "Does it matter?"

Her love tensed, on the balls of his feet as if ready to charge.

What mattered, Jenn knew in that instant, was saving him. The three goaded him to enjoy his pain, but also this, to make him heedless with anger, for it seemed to her Bannan didn't see how their hands moved, readying another spell. A spell against him.

They were, she decided then and there, as nasty as nyphrit.

And thinking of nyphrit, and the grass under her feet, and the lovely green pasture beyond, and the pretty forest crowning it, Jenn Nalynn knew exactly what to wish.

Rabbits? *RABBITS!*

He half staggered to avoid the furballs, a motion sending the three bounding over the grass toward the forest. Bannan stared after them moodily, unsure whether to laugh or rail at Jenn for stealing his—

—what, revenge? He'd been caught off guard—blinded by it—wanting it more than anything else in that moment, forgetting love, risking the innocents around them, his living family. Jenn had listened to him. *She* hadn't succumbed to fear or anger.

How dare he complain, Bannan told himself, feeling all at once strangely light, to find she'd saved him from himself?

"Are you all right?" his beloved ventured, heartrendingly uncertain.

He spun to take her in his arms, raining kisses on her lips, forehead, chin, anywhere he could until she sputtered and laughed, pushing him back. "That's yes," she gasped, eyes bright with joy, then looked around. "Bannan, they're waking up."

She was right. Everyone was moving, slowly at first, looking around with dazed expressions. The stories to come from this—

A breeze found his ear. "Rabbits, Dear Heart? Again?"

"Wisp!" Jenn turned with a relieved smile, looking for the source.

Bannan simply looked deeper. Her dragon sat a mere arm's length in front of her, head tilted as if daring him to say so. "I'm sure he's close by," the truthseer said, giving a little nod to their friend. "As for rabbits?" he continued, straight-faced. "Excellent choice. Hard to work spells without hands, you know." He fluttered his fingers.

On the stage, Emon got to his feet and, seeing them, gestured a brusque summons.

Wanted an explanation, did he?

The truthseer laughed.

Having righted their instruments, again, the musicians went back to work filling the air with lively music, drawing dancers to the floor and making it feel, almost, as if nothing unusual had happened. Lines formed again for free drinks and food—at Elder Cotalen's expense—and Fool's Day in Gordit resumed.

With no one seeming to mind the planned speeches had been canceled.

Because, Jenn knew, those who'd been about to speak were now to listen, the baron inviting them to the inn for a private discussion concerning dark magic, secrets, and how near calamity those had brought them.

Would he mention the rabbits? Her wish had, as Bannan said,

prevented further spellcasting, but she'd had to tell the baron that no matter how important it was he question them, she couldn't change the three back into people.

Goodness, how could she, when she'd no idea who they'd been?

They'd deserved their comeuppance. Maybe, Jenn thought hopefully, they'd be happier as rabbits.

The terst cows were, as it happened, happy too, having fallen asleep at a moment of peril, only to wake with their leader full of joy and relief. They knew she'd lead them next to more food and were content it was so.

Jenn saw Bannan give Semyn a final hug, then head to where she waited.

And had waited. There'd been three different dances—a fourth starting now, her foot tapping the beat—since he'd gone to take his leave of Emon and the boy, and while she was glad he did?

It was time to go home.

"Yes. Yes, Poppa, I'm fine," Semyn insisted, but there was nothing for it but his father take hold of him and turn him this way and that before they went into the inn, as if worse had happened than falling down and scraping his chin on Araben's tray.

By her mocking grin, she'd not let him forget it either, managing to sit neatly when the spell knocked her out.

A spell cast by—Semyn looked at Dutton, who shrugged haplessly, then at his father. "We didn't catch *any* of them? They got away?"

"Gore slipped from the guards in the confusion. We know him now," this grimly, and Semyn understood. The traitor couldn't show his face in Vorkoun or anywhere the Westietas and their allies would be hunting. Momma would see to it.

"He didn't do this." Semyn waved around at the mass of revelers gradually sorting themselves into those done with Fool's Day and those believing it the best in memory. "They'll attack us again, Poppa. You know it."

To his surprise, Poppa smiled. His easy joy-filled smile usually reserved for when Werfol did something unexpectedly good or Semyn solved a tough puzzle, and the boy felt his own lips twitch in response.

Then tightened them. "Poppa, they're dangerous."

"I've your uncle's report." His father leaned close to whisper in his ear. "Rabbits. I'll explain later. But all's well, lad. All's very well."

Jenn looked out over the pasture, her arms wide. "And this is within the edge, too?" she asked wonderingly.

Smiling, Bannan looked deeper. His true sight came more easily each time and, though he'd need practice to understand everything it revealed, if he pushed a little, the boundary between the edge and the wider world beyond showed itself as a rippling curtain, one that sank into the ground and soared up to the sky until it vanished from view.

"The edge runs up the slope over there." He gestured back at Gordit. "And crosses the road to Mondir outside of town." Where Semyn had remembered Marrowdell and dragons.

Where he'd forget them again, come the morning when the baron took his son home, business done. For now, at least.

Jenn ran ahead a few steps, then spun around, her dress swirling. "And the glade where Edis left you? Can you show me?"

He raised his eyebrows. "Why?"

She stopped, the dress wrapping itself around her slim form. "Unless you are able to see crossings Wisp can't, Dear Heart, that's the only one I know of—other than in the mine." Where, by her grimace, they'd not go again.

A feeling he shared. "It's this way. I think," Bannan qualified, taking her hand. He'd seen the town from the glade and the mountain—the dreadful waves of mimrol—

The truthseer focused on here and now. Walking in the afternoon sunshine with his beloved, warm grass swishing around their ankles. No reason to rush—

—and his next step took him into the forest. He stopped in his tracks, raising his eyebrows at Jenn.

Who blushed. "I guess I'm a little impatient."

He wasn't. If anything, Bannan was willing to linger for days here, to build up the courage to follow her into the Verge—

Maybe if he mentioned the bathtub—

Then Jenn exclaimed, eyes wide, "Peggs might be having her baby! Oh, we must be there, Bannan. We must!"

He let out a long breath. So be it.

The rabbits darted, as rabbits did, or tried to freeze in place. Wisp intercepted them, redirecting their path with the flick of a wing, or moved them along with a puff of hot breath.

And the occasional snarl.

This wasn't their meadow. These weren't *her* rabbits. These were the outcome of the girl's wish to render the wizards harmless. Her dragon might have told her it wasn't as simple as transforming nyphrit, who were, after all, ordinary beasts.

He might have told her that what had power and magic didn't lose it, that what felt malice and spite kept feeling it, emotions seething in the beady eyes glaring up at him. Might even have warned her how darkness drew darkness to it and these would do the same.

Wisp chivvied them closer and closer to the trees.

He chose not.

~Old fool!~

The kruar stepped from behind a tree. Saw the three plump rabbits cowering in front of him and began to purr, drool dripping from his jaws.

A dragon with the *taste* of a greater enemy clinging to his tongue would not stoop to eating rabbit.

But his old enemy?

~Enjoy.~

FIFTEEN

SHE HADN'T MEANT to rush away the pasture. Hadn't, Jenn thought worriedly, reading Bannan's face, meant to rush him either.

"We'll see if it's there," she offered gently. "Decide then."

His lips quirked. "There's no decision to be made." Bannan traced her cheek with his fingers. "We're going home. If it's a bumpy ride?" A shrug. "I've you to guide me." A quick kiss.

Let's get this over with, that meant, and Jenn wholeheartedly agreed.

It turned out they'd a guide after all, the footprints of the two who'd found Bannan and carried him to the ox stall leaving a trail through the greenery. Following it, they arrived at the opening in the trees, full of wildflowers reaching for the sun, and, after crouching to look into the distance at the tent and town, he nodded. "This is the place."

The terst cows, in full agreement that this was *the* place, climbed down from their leader's laces and began to feast. So luscious was the vegetation and so many the flowers, the pair grew larger to reach more.

And larger.

Until they were the size they'd been when they'd met their leader, able to reach the delicious lower branches of the trees.

"Jenn."

Hearing something odd in Bannan's voice, Jenn—who'd been staring at the ground as if a crossing would cooperate this one time and show itself—turned.

To find Bannan looking *up* at her cows.

Oh dear. "They must like you, to show themselves," Jenn said quickly, earning a look of disbelief from her beloved.

At this size they were, she had to admit, a tad daunting. And certainly enjoying their food, so they really should be going before the terst cows left another massive pile of manure, a puzzle to local farmers who'd never have encountered anything quite so—pungent.

She turned back to where Bannan insisted he'd crossed, seeing nothing. "We'll wait for Wisp," she decided. "Unless you can see it?"

"I don't. There may not be a crossing. Edis brought me." He came to her side, a wary eye on her no-longer-tiny cows.

She'd thought of that, but there was a problem. "I lost Lila's hammer and stone." Not that she'd used it, thanks to Edis coming for her at the Westietas part of the edge. "We can shout her name."

Bannan flinched. "I—we shouldn't call someone like that. Not by shouting."

Unsure what was wrong, she'd have taken back the words if she could. Jenn reached for him instead, holding him close. "I'm sorry, Dear Heart. We'll find some other way—"

"The two of you are slightly ridiculous."

They broke apart, staring at the being coiled around a tree, arms crossed. Bannan recovered first. "Edis! How did you—" He closed his mouth.

Seeing Edis' half smile, Jenn smiled back. "You've been here, waiting for us."

A snort. "It's a nice view." Edis glanced at the terst cows, who'd frozen in place like oversized rabbits. "Still have cows, I see."

"It seems so, yes."

Then Edis turned her purple gaze at Bannan. "Well, Captain Ash?"

Under Edis' knowing eyes, pinned by that name, Bannan felt in his pocket for Semyn's copy of the sketches. She'd shown him this choice before, to shed what he'd been and heal his heart along with his body, and he'd refused.

Bringing out the paper, he tore it into pieces, letting those drift to the ground. Let his hate drift away with them, taking his pain and the last of his fear—

Brother—

The Dancer wasn't here, but was. As she would always be, he thought, startled to find that a comfort. Less startled to see the pieces of paper—*those faces*—disappear into the ground.

His next breath felt like his first. In a sense it was, being the first since that dreadful day he'd taken without feeling guilt or anger, and he circled his heart with his fingers, "Ancestors Blessed and Beloved, I'm beholden—"

Edis snorted. Was abruptly in his face and pressed her mouth over his. She tasted a little of dust but mostly of friendship, and he gladly kissed her back. And Jenn was there, getting her own kiss and hugging them both, or trying to, her arms not reaching quite around, but it was fine, for Edis' strong arms did the job quite well.

Then let them go. "Stars witness, you're a mushy pair," Edis half-scolded, but her eyes glistened and he knew she was touched. "Get out of here. That way," she added.

Bannan felt Jenn's hand take his.

Prepared to take that step, seeing before them the Verge, its blazing sky filled with dragons—*Heart's Blood, he'd burn—*

But his love drew him gently forward, and, trusting Jenn Nalynn and Edis and The Dancer—

Bannan stepped...

Jenn found herself in the Verge, dragons overhead, gripping Bannan's hand so tightly he should by rights complain but didn't. She eased her hold very slightly, wondering how to tell him this might not have been the best plan, for she'd no idea where they were—

Nor did the terst cows, who followed their leader and bolted, again tiny, for her laces without being noticed, that being their skill. They would stay with her, hidden and content to be so.

—then a dragon—her dragon—flew by overhead, scattering the flock of those already here, and Scourge appeared beside them, tossing his head at those fleeing.

Ancestors Blessed, she might be lost, but they weren't and couldn't be.

~Where would you go, Dear Heart?~ asked her dragon, sounding ever so smug.

~I'll take them!~ offered the kruar, sounding suspiciously the same. ~Wherever they choose!~

Jenn looked into the glowing eyes of her love and he into hers, and knew the answer. Marrowdell and home.

Soon. First?

"We must pay our respects to Mistress Sand," Jenn said. She had to be sure Chalk had made it home—not that he'd understand or appreciate her concern—and express her condolences over Tooth, Ancestors Dear and Departed, who'd been the start of it.

She turned to Bannan, knowing he'd unfinished business as well, having almost died and returned, and a family anxious for news. Not to forget Kydd Uhthoff, who must be almost mad with worry about Peggs and need to get home.

Her love smiled as if hearing her thoughts. "And make one more stop."

Wisp and Scourge, of course, made it a race—Jenn in her dragon's claws and Bannan plastered to the kruar's back—but neither would let them fall. In what seemed no time at all, they arrived at the terst turn-borns' enclave, and Jenn was relieved to see the crystal barrier replaced by the usual low fence and the gate standing open.

With Sand, Riverstone, Clay, Flint, Fieldstone, yes, Chalk, waiting in welcome.

Wisp set her down and Jenn ran to them, swept up in hugs from Mistress Sand then the rest in turn—even Chalk, though he was stiff and possibly embarrassed. Jenn didn't care, hugging him back.

"Sweetling," Mistress Sand greeted aloud when they were done, her voice husky as she held Jenn's shoulders. "All we asked of you and here you are, having done that and more."

"I'm sorry about Tooth, Ancestors Dear and Departed. And not sure what I did," Jenn replied honestly, though the Verge felt back to normal—however strange that might be—and their crossing blissfully uneventful.

"Sei," Riverstone said, as if in explanation and probably, Jenn agreed, not wrong.

Meanwhile, Mistress Sand stood looking up at Bannan, who hadn't dismounted but reached down his hand. Taking it in both of hers—Scourge rolling his eyes but behaving—she said, "Our thanks, truthseer." Then paused, giving him a keen searching look. "Or are you, na?"

Heart's Blood, what did she see? Before Bannan could ask, Wisp landed nearby, wings beating as he pranced more than walked closer. ~We met The Traveler,~ the dragon stated. ~Are you sure you want to know more?~

Mistress Sand dropped his hand as if burnt. Stepped back. "Myth—"

Seeing Jenn's distress, Bannan slid from Scourge's back. "Man," he said firmly, lacing his fingers with his love's. "And truthseer." His gift showed him the Verge in all its unpredictable beauty, only now without effort.

Showed him the truth of the beings before him: glass shells stuffed with bits taken from the edge, aglow with this realm's light, faces that were masks. Strange and otherworldly, but he chose to see them as Jenn did, as a group of friends stricken by loss and uncertainty. "Tooth will be missed, Ancestors Dear and Departed."

Riverstone nodded, rubbing his eyes. Mistress Sand looked sorrowful. The rest—didn't know, Bannan realized, sad for them, what they felt or missed feeling. That they were again safe, the Verge fixed, mattered most to them.

"Will you be all right?" Jenn asked, her voice full of emotion as if to make up for their lack of it. "Will you need—" She hesitated.

"Your help, Sweetling, na?" Sand replied. "See how great her heart, na?" she demanded of her kin before smiling at Jenn. "You take care of Marrowdell, Sweetling. Our number will be replenished."

The color drained from Jenn's face. "But—you mustn't," she said. "Not like before."

"How and what we do, how and what we've always done. These are none of your concern, Sweetling," the terst turn-born said sharply.

Brother.

Less than a whisper . . .

Listen.

Almost an echo . . .

Bannan knew what he'd heard. Be replenished, Sand had said, to Jenn's objection. She'd told him what that meant, to rip the next terst child born at the turn from its family. To repeat the ugly pattern that had led to this—*to them*—

"*Talk to the parents,*" he heard himself command as if he'd the right to order such powerful beings. Heard his voice as what wasn't just sound, but somehow light and possibly time. "*Show them where their child will live when ready. Promise your love.*"

Jenn looked up at him, admiration shining in her eyes, but he hadn't done that—hadn't, Bannan thought queasily, done that *alone*.

The dragon gazed at him with a wild violet eye, then stared at Mistress Sand. ~You've heard The Listener. I suggest~—and oh, the wicked triumph in his tone—~you pay attention.~

Her dragon was very full of himself, strutting before the terst turn-born he'd once served, and what was this about? *The Traveler.* Well, Jenn told herself, that was easy. He must mean Edis Donovar, who'd brought them all where they'd most needed to be.

But to call Bannan *The Listener*, as if he'd some new calling or task ahead—when her dear love had almost died and been through so much—

The Dancer. This was her doing, whatever she was, and Jenn had half a mind to visit her—and soon—for an explanation and possibly apology.

First to get Wisp away before he disturbed the situation further. "Peggs will have her baby any minute now," Jenn announced brightly, that sure to shift Mistress Sand's attention. "We must get moving!"

"I expect you to come and tell us all about it, Sweetling," Sand said agreeably, her glance at Bannan thoughtful to say the least. The other terst turn-born remained stunned, making it high time to be gone before they weren't and had questions.

Scourge snorted and half reared. ~This way!~ He wheeled and ran.

~ Old fool!~ snapped Wisp, launching himself into the air.

Grabbing Bannan's hand, Jenn took off after them. "It's not far," she promised.

The terst turn-borns' crossing to his family's home wasn't far. It was, Bannan discovered, decidedly unpleasant.

"The cave is in there. With the crossing," Jenn insisted, though equally taken aback.

Purple thorny plants covered the rocks, woven into an impenetrable barrier, and if there was an entrance behind them, Bannan couldn't see it. "Is there another way?"

~No.~ from Wisp. The dragon didn't look eager to approach the mass either. Scourge kept well back.

The kruar tossed his head, then muttered darkly.

~What did you say?~ Wisp asked with suspicious glee.

~I SAID THE COWS!~ Scourge roared, as if out of patience.

Jenn perked up. "Do you think they'd clear it away? Could you?" she asked, looking down at herself.

Four sets of tiny claws appeared at the top of her dress, then two tiny heads, and Bannan found himself jealous of their proximity to the beautiful curve of Jenn's breasts. Which was, he knew, ridiculous.

Still jealous.

"No one will hurt you," Jenn cooed, holding her hand to help them climb out.

The terst cows, terrified to be *seen* by a kruar, let alone a dragon, nonetheless climbed onto her palm, gratified by their leader's TOUCH and hoping for her approval. Aimed at the mass of noxious vegetation, they sighed briefly, but accepted her offering, there being no other food in sight.

They grew larger.

She put them down.

Larger.

At the kruar's snarl they trembled, but still they grew LARGER.

Until the terst cows were of a size to easily rip apart the thorny growth. They shoved it into their mouths and, though they had to spit out chewed wads of it, their leader felt pleased. Finished, they shimmered and shrank, needing no help to climb back where they belonged, holding on to her laces and content it was so.

"That's better," Jenn said, nodding at the cleared entrance. She smiled at Scourge.

Guessing she was about to thank the kruar and quite sure how his old friend would react, Bannan ducked his head and stepped into the cave. "You're sure this isn't another mine?" he half joked, looking over his shoulder.

"I'm sure." Jenn made a face. "Though our first time, there was snow."

He'd have to look up the date—

The dragon whooshed past Bannan. ~Follow me!~

And they did...

...stepping out on the scree-covered slope, the Westietas Ossuary high on its ridge, the forest exactly as it had been and the secret cottage there, beyond the trees.

Beyond that? Bannan stopped, staring at the curtain rippling from sky to ground, where the sun caught it sending fierce glints of light—

The edge. This close. Too close, and he reached for Jenn, to keep her here and safe, for out there she'd cease to exist—

Edis would cease to exist—

Heart's Blood, did that mean—

"We won't be able to signal," Jenn reminded him, blissfully unaware of the new and frantic turn of his thoughts. "I'll make us tea while you let Lila know we're here. Dearest Heart?"

He looked down at her face. Kissed her nose and found a smile. "I'll come with you. For all we know," he added lightly, "Lila's waiting for us inside."

Just when she'd thought everything was right again, or about to be or as close to as made no difference, Jenn knew something was wrong. Bannan's face had gone sickly pale when he'd looked at the path leading to his sister's house. Now he urged her to the cottage for all the world as if—

As if he feared to step beyond the edge. Not for her sake—*not only*—but for his own, and what would that mean, if he no longer could?

Whatever it meant, she told herself, they had to know. Be absolutely certain, for this wasn't like a crossing that spat you out in the past so you went back and tried again. If Bannan was now like a turn-born, like her, beyond the edge he'd—

The breeze went from summer soft to a bitter snap, and Jenn thought quickly of the smell of terst cow manure, that becoming her quickest way to stop reacting.

Bannan, meanwhile, had opened the door and peeked in. "No one here." He stood holding it open for her and looked unexpectedly shy.

Oh. Jenn felt the blush roar up her neck to flame her cheeks, and most likely involve her bosom by the involuntary dip of his gaze, because this was to have been—why, now it could be, the crossings fixed—their new and second home.

Shedding an entirely new light on there being no one else in it, this moment, and them about to be. She moved forward, feeling a few stones through the pretty slippers that hadn't, as she'd suspected, held up to much walking.

Took Bannan's offered hand, his arm slipping warm around her waist so they'd enter together, and Jenn hurriedly made sure of the one thing left to make this perfect.

"Privacy, please, Wisp."

The dragon curled himself in front of the door, pleased to find a sunny spot, but he'd have stayed on guard even if there'd been—shudder—snow.

The girl deserving every happiness.

Scourge paced to the path and back, head low and swaying as if gaining courage to run to the house, where his wordless presence alone would ensure someone came.

~Be still or go,~ Wisp said at last, tired of watching.

Contrarily, the kruar half reared, staring up at the roof. ~The youngling's up there. Asleep. Shall I wake it?~ with a more cheerful snarl.

He'd noticed Imp and been pleasantly surprised to have an order obeyed for once. ~Under no circumstances,~ Wisp replied, resting his jaw on his good leg. ~Where are *your* younglings? Weren't they to stay?~

~Doubtless hunting, as they should be,~ Scourge countered. His nostrils flared. ~Ah. They know I'm here. ~ He flexed his proud neck. ~They approach and quickly.~

Wisp closed his eyes. ~Tell them to slow down.~

SIXTEEN

*F*OOTSTEPS RANG OUT below. Jenn burst into giggles and Bannan covered her mouth, looking past the bed to the loft stairs.

As if there was any hiding where they were or what, she thought with delicious satisfaction, they'd managed to already do. In this lovely bedroom, with its most comfortable bed—and the floor didn't squeak under it, as it did in their Marrowdell home, which she considered a most excellent feature—so Jenn nipped his palm. When he snatched it away, she called out breathlessly, "Down in a minute!"

Then took hold of her love to claim a last kiss.

A short time later—it being necessary for Bannan to help with her corset and she to help with his shirt, and they had to give up the search for his socks and one of her slippers, not that there was much of either left—Jenn followed Bannan down the stairs to the main floor.

Where Lila and Werfol were waiting. "Where's Kydd?" Jenn asked at once. "We're taking him home—"

"He's already there," Bannan's sister announced, adding, "A bird arrived," lest Jenn disbelieve her. "As did one from my dear husband. You two have been—busy." An expressive eyebrow lifted.

Heart's Blood, she wasn't to blush again.

Bannan took pity on her, striding forward to hug his sister. But when he stooped to open his arms to his nephew, Werfol took a step back.

Then another, eyes molten gold and face stricken. "What's wrong with you?"

Bannan had known he'd see the truth—what he'd become—in Werfol's eyes. But Ancestors Desperate and Despairing, he'd never thought to horrify the boy.

"What's wrong?" Lila asked sharply. "Werfol—Brother, what does he mean?" searching his face, hers growing anguished and tight. "What's happened to you?"

How did he—

"I'll make tea," Jenn said. "Then we'll sit down to tell you. Properly," this aimed at Werfol.

Who wore his sullen and angry look, that vow not to cooperate in the slightest with anything—until a breeze where one shouldn't be tousled his hair. Whatever Wisp said to the boy, it wiped some of the stiffness from his expression, if not all.

Werfol flopped down on a chair, arms crossed, eyes glaring and gold.

Lila sat with less than her customary grace. Jenn, who must have wished the water to boil, brought the teapot over on a tray with four cups. She sat and poured, adding a dollop of honey he'd not known was in the cottage to Werfol's cup, putting that in front of the boy, then pouring cups for the adults before sitting back.

Making herself at home. Bannan, sitting across from his unhappy nephew, wished he was sure she should.

But there was no going back—and nothing but the whole truth would do.

"I fell into boiling mimrol."

Werfol looked from the steam rising from his cup to Bannan. "You aren't burnt," he accused.

"I was. I—" He hadn't gone into detail with Jenn; she'd filled in the rest for herself. But a truthseer, a young truthseer, required absolutes. He couldn't leave anything out, not without causing needless pain. "My flesh boiled away and I should have been dead but I wasn't, not quite. Edis took me to The Dancer—a magical creature of the Verge—who saved me. Rebuilt me." He put his hands, palm up, on the table. "I'm who I was, Werfol, other than losing my scars and calluses, that is."

A rare occurrence, his sister speechless.

Werfol, of course, wasn't done. "You aren't. You aren't the same."

"I feared as much." Bannan folded his hands. "But I don't know what's changed. I can't see myself the way you can."

A glimmer of interest. "Your hair's different. It's full of colors—like the sky in the Verge."

"That doesn't sound so bad."

With a strangled sound, Lila hid her face behind her cup.

Werfol leaned on the table, edging closer, his eyes ablaze. "Your bones are silver. I don't usually see bones," he admitted. "That's new, too."

Heart's Blood. Mimrol. He'd mimrol *inside*. "I suppose The Dancer needed to replace those as well," Bannan heard himself say with a calmness he assuredly didn't feel. Was there anything left of him?

"It's like armor," the young truthseer declared. "Inside armor. Poppa would like to know about that," with a wicked little glance at his poor mother.

Lila slammed down her cup, tea spilling. "Your father does not need to know any of—this." She fluttered her hand at her brother. "Or Semyn."

"Or Dutton?" Oh, the cheek in that question. Bannan fought back a smile and saw Jenn bite her lip.

An eyebrow lifted, Lila signaling she'd ignore it, this time. "Is there anything else about your uncle I should know?"

A vital question and Bannan chose to take the answer seriously, using his own true sight, seeing recognition flare in the boy's eyes.

"He's much stronger," Werfol breathed. Focused. Suddenly grinned. "And happier!"

This time, when Bannan opened his arms, his nephew didn't hesitate at all.

Lila, on the other hand, narrowed her eyes. "'Happier'?"

He understood. Felt, for the first time, pity for the one person who'd shared his pain and grief, and would now carry it alone—not that she'd appreciate the sentiment. "I'll always protect our family," Bannan told his sister, her son, and Jenn. "I'll no longer pursue vengeance."

"It's true," Werfol said, looking at his mother. Understanding there, too, Bannan realized. What did that say about this remarkable boy, that he could?

Lila's lips thinned, her green eyes bright. Then she gave a slow, gracious nod, conceding, at least for now, his boundaries. "Before he—left—Kydd and Master Setac disarmed the journals. I've a trail to follow. Both to Glammis—and Kluet Gore and the Heirs. Their time is almost up."

"I've no doubt of that." He'd let Emon tell her about the rabbits and how there were three less evil mages to seek out. It didn't matter if he doubted they'd been responsible for their parents' deaths. Lila would discover the truth.

Her lips gave a sour twitch. "Why, brother, are you always *difficult*?"

"That's what you say to me!" Werfol exclaimed, delighted by this bit of news.

Jenn, timing it perfectly, rose to her feet. "We must take our leave, Baroness. We're forever beholden to you and the baron for this beautiful place." And gave her a glorious, heartfelt smile.

Melting Lila's temper. "Wait," she said, rising to her feet. A glance at Werfol, who looked suddenly not happy at all, then back to Jenn. "Before you go home, to Marrowdell, there's something you need to know. About Kydd. He regained his sight," this with a quick nod to Bannan.

"A relief," the truthseer said. Jenn had said so, but to have confirmation—

"But?" Jenn said faintly, ahead of him.

"To rid his journals and himself of dark magic, he asked Master Setac to cast a spell. As a consequence—Kydd's lost his memory of everything since being a student in Avyo."

"He knew. He didn't tell us that would happen," Werfol added in a very small voice. "We thought he would be fine."

The beekeeper had sought atonement. If this was how, it would be a sad blow to his family. Bannan turned to comfort Jenn.

Surprised to see her gazing thoughtfully at Lila. "Your doing, that Kydd made it home safely to Peggs?"

"Yes. We didn't—I didn't know what else to do."

"Momma wrote down everyone's names for him." Werfol looked close to tears. "And I drew a map of Marrowdell."

"That was very kind of you," Jenn told him. She didn't smile, seeing the boy's dismay.

But Bannan had the sense she wanted to, though he couldn't understand why. "Dearest Heart?"

"You sent him where he had to go." How her eyes sparkled! "Ancestors Tested and True, never underestimate Marrowdell—or my sister. Kydd will be fine."

"The truth!" Werfol crowed, jumping up.

"I trust you, Jenn Nalynn." Lila looked slightly appalled to hear herself say so and covered it with a firm, "We'll want news of the baby."

Werfol ran to Jenn, throwing his arms around her. "Do you have to take Imp?"

Please! Lila mouthed.

"Imp belongs with Wisp. For now," Jenn said, not to disappoint the boy, and kind. "We'll all be back," with a questioning look at Lila.

Who'd apparently learned when not to argue about dragons. "Until then, Keep Us Close."

"Keep Us Close." Bannan took the chance and opened his arms in invitation.

Shaking her head, Lila stepped up and gave him a hug, her head, for a fleeting moment, resting on his shoulder. "I'm glad you're happier," she whispered.

Then clapped him hard on the shoulder. "But work on those calluses."

Walking up the slope to his door, Bannan was quiet and Jenn let him be. As Aunt Sybb would say, when someone had a great deal to think about, there was no better help than giving them time to do it.

And time they'd have, she thought peacefully, once home.

A subject—she stepped over what might be a scree—she'd not given its due before, other than to notice how quickly time flew when she needed more or tried to hold still, or how it crawled when waiting for, well, anything. Jenn resolved to pay greater attention.

As now. There'd been some disturbing irregularities recently and a great relief to see the sun still up, though it wouldn't be much longer. One thing to have to fix the Verge—she wasn't at all comfortable with anything being broken where she lived.

Jenn snuck a peek at Bannan.

Wherever they did.

They'd be happy, no matter where and how they were, she decided, not needing to make it a wish.

"We're here," Bannan said, stopping. "The scree mark it." He pointed to a pile of small rocks. "Unless *someone's* moved things again."

A couple of scree rolled into each other, producing a mischievous chime.

Jenn smiled. "Not this time."

And they took the step through together...

...stepping out into her meadow, thinking of Wen and the smell of pie, and Jenn took a great glad breath—

~Elder sister! She's waiting!~

Her house toad. "Peggs?"

~Elder brother!~ chimed in Bannan's house toad, making Jenn blink, for that guardian rarely left the house. ~She's waiting!~

"'She's waiting'?" Bannan echoed.

His toad's eyes widened in astonishment. ~You can hear us in the edge, elder brother?~

The turn was coming! "No time to waste." Scooping up her toad, Jenn hopped up and down until Bannan had his, then took his hand. Began to walk through the meadow—

Wanting to be with her sister.

—and there they were, in front of the Nalynn house.

The porch and steps were full of people, with benches brought to add more seating, a birth a momentous event and not to be missed. Jenn smiled and touched shoulders but they made way for her and for Bannan, knowing where she should be.

And was.

Peggs was on Aunt Sybb's bed, that worthy sitting at her feet with their father, Radd.

Kydd Uhthoff hovered over Covie Ropp, the village healer, looking as normal and anxious as ever he should. Jenn might have worried—being far from as sure as she'd let on with Lila and Werfol—but Peggs gave her a happy, if tired smile, and a wink.

Being magic in her own special way.

"Glad you're here," she said.

And with that—though how toads might be involved, Jenn was determined to find out—her sister got to work.

The brothers raced each other into the house, grabbing the hunks of fresh bread Cook held in their path, and ran up to their room, closing their door before Petrill made it to the stairs after them. They heard him sigh and lean against the wall.

Werfol started. "Uncle Bannan was here. He's different. But all right," this hastily, and plainly he was ready to burst with news. Instead, he took a bite and chewed. Slowly.

Wistful.

Guessing why, Semyn pulled his watch notebook from his shirt, turned it upside down while his brother stared at him, and opened the book to the page at the back. He passed it thus to his brother, then sat back on his bed to eat his bread.

Weed wasn't the fastest reader.

After a suspicious look, Weed bent to the page, eyes darting back and forth, back and forth. Stopped. Looked up again. "This is fantastical. You," with emphasis, "don't write fantastical things."

"I don't," Semyn agreed. "But I did. That's my handwriting, isn't it? And Momma's code, to prove it was written without duress."

"Yes, but—" Head cocked like one of Poppa's crows, Werfol went back to the book.

Semyn knew what he read. A story about a town where people cast spells. About a secret door into a mountain. Best of all, there was a—

"Dragon!" Weed's eyes blazed. "You saw Wisp! And here—you wrote—" Overcome, he launched himself at Semyn, hugging him tight. "You wrote about Jenn Nalynn!"

Once his brother calmed, Semyn explained. "It was Araben's idea. I told her how I forgot, outside, and that I didn't want to—that I mustn't. I had to remember what happened in Gordit. She suggested I take notes. I like taking notes."

Werfol, who knew this about him, nodded sagely. "She's smart."

"She is. It was her idea to say everyone fell asleep during the festival because the mine had been improperly closed and should be reopened, with proper maintenance. And not—" He struggled to say it, but the proof was there, he'd written it to himself. "Not dark magic."

Weed, who couldn't sit still when excited, jumped to his own bed and picked up the book. "You wrote here that Jenn Nalynn turned the evil spellcasters into—" he started to giggle "—into—" he lost it completely and flopped like a fish, laughing.

"Rabbits," Semyn finished, smiling at his brother.

Then had to laugh, too.

The sun hung safely high above the Bone Hills when Bannan Larmensu stepped out the front door of the Nalynn house, two bottles of summerberry wine in each hand and Tir behind him with glasses, to announce, loudly enough so even Master Jupp would hear, "Please welcome Marleen Nalynn Uhthoff to Marrowdell!"

Everyone stood and clapped. Most dabbed their eyes, grown tearful with joy—and relief, Peggs having *waited* longer than expected, for someone expecting, and everyone concerned.

"Not twins?" Hettie shouted back, as if disappointed.

Everyone laughed.

And then it was time to pull out instruments and celebrate, not too loudly so the new mother and babe might rest, along with a new father who'd worn himself out to be where he should.

To remember who he was. Because of Peggs. Because of Marrowdell.

Bannan looked forward to *that* conversation.

Jenn sat with her sister, entranced by the baby nuzzling Peggs' full breast—though she seemed equally interested in the twine and flower necklace around her sister's neck, the Westietas' cook having sent a wishing with Kydd for abundance, which was practical and kind. Lila had sent along a small packet with sealed letters for Aunt Sybb, Master Jupp, and Lorra Treff, which might or might not be, not that any said.

Nor were any letters more important than this. "She's a good size," Jenn declared at last, seeing not much else yet to compliment.

"That she is," Peggs murmured. "And has the most beautiful eyes. Look at your Aunt Jenn, now. Show her." It took a little help, Marleen more interested in her first supper than looking, but finally the baby's head flopped around.

"Oh," Jenn said, hands to her heart, for Peggs hadn't exaggerated. Marleen had indeed the most beautiful eyes she'd ever seen, blue as the crystal in the Verge—not that she'd say so—and alert. "Is she supposed to be looking at me like that?"

"She's been waiting, too," her sister said comfortably.

And born before the turn, to grow up free to be whomever and whatever she wanted. Feeling it, Jenn sighed and stood. "I have to go."

Peggs gave her a keen look. "Stay."

"But—" Aunt Sybb and their father were in the room, Kydd in a chair though half asleep, and Bannan and Tir chose that moment to walk in the door for more wine. "—the baby," Jenn protested.

"Will know everything about her wonderful aunt." In the voice Peggs used when supper was on the table and people better be on time. Gently, "As do I."

As do I. Words Jenn heard as larger than they should be and deeper than they could, in fact words sounding suspiciously like Wainn—or Wen, when it came to it—when they spoke for Marrowdell.

Peggs? Who, unlike their mother Melusine, with her gift for finding the lost, and Jenn, born at the turn, hadn't shown an inkling of magic her entire life.

But had, every minute. Her baking, Jenn reminded herself, was a power not to be underestimated and, yes, Peggs' insights about people, topped off with this business of restoring Kydd's memories—which Jenn had known in her heart her sister could do.

Being magic.

Peggs smiled, composed and waiting on her answer. Sure of it, that too.

"I'll stay," Jenn agreed, rather faintly. Bannan came to stand by her, his hand light on her shoulder, a comfort.

Aunt Sybb, sensing something unusual was about, stopped chatting with her brother about cradles and an endowment—for she took her expanded duties as a *great*-aunt most seriously—to look at her youngest niece. "What's going—"

The turn came.

Jenn went from flesh and blood to glass and pearl and light. Light reflecting in Marleen's alert blue eyes and did the baby smile?

Surely too soon. Gas, Jenn decided nervously. Better than tears. Better than—

"Jenn?"

She turned to face the others. Because she did—as she did—her light caught the sigil and danced Melusine's name across the wall. Their mother's roses surged into the windows, dropping petals on the bed but not on those in it, as if they'd waited, too.

The Lady Mahavar, regal and poised, reached out her hand. Jenn reached out hers. For an instant, flesh touched glass—

—then glass was flesh again.

And the lady, their aunt again, said very clearly, "I'm going to need more wine."

Then opened her arms, Jenn stepping within them while careful not to squeeze, for Aunt Sybb was precious and felt oddly fragile. "I hope you aren't upset," she whispered.

Or overstimulated, their aunt having a delicate constitution.

"My precious girl," Aunt Sybb said. "Upset? Your mother would be so proud of you. As am I." Then she frowned. "Wait. Are there toads in here?"

And everyone laughed.

Meanwhile . . .

The terst cows were on the move.

They'd stayed with their leader, grateful to have been brought safely away from dragons and kruar to this perfect place. Stayed, that is, until she'd passed through a pasture.

A pasture with cows.

Cows with their own leader, a leader feeding them with his own hand, and what he fed them was the most delicious-smelling food the terst cows had ever smelled, better even than the kaliia nearby.

A leader, moreover, who not only TOUCHED his cows, but crooned to them. A leader who felt calm and felt safe, which was all a terst cow ever wanted.

The two moved closer and closer, enraptured by this, their new leader. They would be cows like his, be part of *his* herd, and content forever it was so.

"Bannan. Bannan!"

The truthseer filled another glass of wine before turning to Devins. "It's a girl," he said, the other man arriving late.

"Wonderful. Glad to hear it. You have to come with me," seizing Bannan's arm. "Hurry."

"They're tiny," said Wainn Uhthoff as he wandered past and overheard, Delfinn asleep in her carry sack.

Making no sense—or—*Jenn's cows*. "Has anything been hurt?" Bannan asked warily. "Do we need Covie?"

Devins gave him a blank look. "Why would we need Covie? They're perfect."

Not what he'd expected to hear. Curiosity roused, Bannan kept up with Devins, who walked from the party, then broke into a jog once past the fountain, pausing only so both could dip their fingers in thanks.

Bannan stopped dead at the commons gate. "You've got cows."

"I know that. Jenn brought them, didn't she? She promised to watch out for new stock for me. Aren't they wonderful?"

Gazing back at the truthseer, with the placid content of truly happy bovines, were indeed a pair of cows. They were brown and shaggy, as the terst cows had been, with stout curved horns and sturdy cloven hooves, unlike the terst cows, and in every other respect resembled the other cows in the field. Who stared at them as if puzzled, but not alarmed.

The terst, Bannan told himself, had been people in the edge. Their livestock could disappear and change size—why not, he supposed, become *actual* cows? "They're rather small."

"Tiny," Devins agreed gleefully, already through the gate. The cows waited for him, big brown eyes agleam with love. He went on his knees, arms over their backs. "Tiny! Don't you see? They're the right size for Marrowdell. And this wool?" He dug his fingers into their hair and Bannan could have sworn the cows leaned into the man. "I'm going to breed them to ours. Good'n'Nuf isn't really, you know, anymore," in a hushed voice. "Not at his age."

The tiny cows—the tiny bulls—*winked* at Bannan.

Right for Marrowdell indeed. "I'll tell Jenn you'll be keeping them. She'll be happy."

Devins looked up, smiling broadly. "I can't wait to show them to Elsinore," he blurted, then blushed redder than an apple. "You won't repeat that, will you? I haven't had a chance to, you know, talk to them. Either one. The sisters."

Bannan drew a finger across his closed lips.

Wishing the earnest farmer luck.

Stars lit their way home, frogs chirruped, and night birds sang from the hedges—where the efflet let them. Yling danced along the branches over Jenn and Bannan's heads, celebrating new life and found love—and quite possibly that the journals were gone and Kydd no longer did spells, being honorable defenders of Marrowdell and resolved.

Conscious of time, filled with wonder and joy, Jenn refused to rush a single step, she couldn't when it came to it, no matter how much home beckoned, being preoccupied with Bannan's attempts to tickle her. "You—aren't—helping—" she gasped, not that she minded.

He relented, his arm around her shoulder. A happy man, her love, as he should be. "Devins has cows," he informed her, stealing a kiss.

"My cows?" She hadn't realized they'd left.

"Tiny cows. And they're smitten with each other. I'm guessing you won't get them back."

It was, all things considered, a relief. But, "Are they safe? They're—they've magic. You've seen."

"You do know where we live." He let her go and began walking backward in front of her, which was safer since the path was raked but still risky. "There aren't any biscuits, I fear."

They'd eaten their fill at the birthing party. And drunk wine. How many glasses, Jenn wondered, did it take to make her love this giddy?

"One," Bannan told her as if hearing the question. He spun about, his arms wide, to prove his sure-footedness. "I'm happy. Happier," he corrected, "as Werfol rightly observed."

Then he picked her up in his arms, spinning them both. "Guess what will make me happiest?"

With that, Jenn Nalynn did shorten the road, knowing what would make her happiest, too.

And they were home.

~I guarded, Great Lord of Dragons. I guarded when those foolish kruar got bored and left. I guarded when——~

~Enough!~ Wisp grumbled. A mistake, to praise the youngling. He'd know better next time.

If there was a next time.

~I did.~

SWAT!

Ah, silence. Wisp settled back, tail curled around the chimney of Jenn and Bannan's home. There being no biscuits or cheese, he hadn't bothered to go inside.

And she was happy.

~Might we see the baby of Peggs?~

This was new. Wisp cracked an eye. Imp was halfway up the tree in the farmyard, clinging to branches, looking toward the village.

~No.~

A pause, then ~Might we see the new cows?~

New cows? He'd been relieved the girl no longer smelled of terst. Had neglected to check for it elsewhere and it was, Wisp decided, annoyingly praiseworthy, that the youngling had spotted them first.

Not that he'd say so.

~All cows belong to Marrowdell and are not prey.~

~Yes, Great Lord of Dragons.~

A disgruntled rumble from the shadows. ~Cows. Bah.~

Scourge would endure the presence of the terst cows for the truthseer's sake. And because the girl cared for them.

Brother.

Wisp cocked his head, a chill running through his body though the summer air was pleasantly warm. A whisper, an echo. Nothing worth his attention.

As, he firmly hoped, nothing here was worth the further attention of an Old One.

But a dragon would be watching, nonetheless.

Concerning the Denizens of Marrowdell

Alyssa Ropp, child, daughter of Mimm and Anten, sister of Hettie and Cheffy, stepdaughter to Cynd, stepsister to Roche and Devins. Born in Marrowdell. Helps in dairy.

Anten Ropp, brother of Cynd, father (with Mimm) of Hettie, Cheffy, and Alyssa. Widowed then married Covie. Stepfather of Roche and Devins. Tends the dairy.

Aunt Sybb (the Lady Sybb Mahavar, nee Nalynn), sister of Radd, aunt to Peggs and Jenn. Lives in Avyo with husband Hane Mahavar where they own several of the better riverside inns. Spends summers in Marrowdell.

Bannan Marerrym Larmensu, son of Maggin and Gyllen, brother of Lila, rider of Scourge. Former Vorkoun border guard who went by the name of "Captain Ash." Truthseer and, in Marrowdell, farmer. Beloved of Jenn Nalynn.

Battle and Brawl, Davi Treff's team of draught horses.

Cheffy Ropp, child, son of Mimm and Anten, brother of Hettie and Alyssa, stepson of Covie, stepbrother of Roche and Devins. Born in Marrowdell. Helps in dairy.

Covie Ropp, mother (with Riedd Morrill) of Roche and Devins, stepmother to Hettie, Cheffy, and Alyssa. Widowed then married Anten. A baroness in Avyo. Tends the dairy. Village healer.

Crumlin Tralee (the Lost One), once resident of Marrowdell. Disappeared under magical circumstances. Currently in a box guarded by house toads.

Cynd Treff (nee Ropp), sister of Anten, wife of Davi, aunt to Hettie, Cheffy, and Alyssa, aunt to Delfinn. Gardener and seamstress.

Davi Treff, son of Lorra, brother of Wen, husband of Cynd, uncle to Hettie, Cheffy, and Alyssa, uncle to Delfinn. Village smith.

Delfinn Uhthoff, baby, daughter of Wen and Wainn, granddaughter of Dusom and Lorra, great-niece of Kydd and Peggs.

Devins Morrill, son of Covie and Riedd, brother of Roche. Stepbrother of Hettie, Cheffy, and Alyssa. Stepson of Anten. Came to Marrowdell as a boy. Tends the dairy.

Dusom Uhthoff (Master Dusom), father of Wainn and Ponicce, husband of Larell (widowed), brother of Kydd, grandfather to Delfinn. Formerly professor at Avyo's Sersise University. Village teacher and helps tend the orchard.

Elainn Emms, baby, daughter of Hettie and Tadd, twin of Torre.

Frann Nall, former business rival and later friend of Lorra Treff. In Avyo, holdings included riverfront warehouses. Village weaver and quilter. Died of natural causes.

Gallie Emms, mother of twins, Tadd and Allin, and baby Loee, wife of Zehr. Author (pen name Elag M. Brock) and sausage maker.

Good'n'Nuf, Ropps' bull.

Hettie Emms (nee Ropp), daughter of Mimm and Anten, sister of Cheffy and Alyssa, stepdaughter of Covie, stepsister of Roche and Devins, wife to Tadd, mother of twins Elainn and Torre. Came to Marrowdell as a child. Village cheese maker.

Himself, boar.

Imp, youngling dragon Wisp has been ordered by the sei to teach.

Jenn Nalynn, daughter of Melusine and Radd, sister of Peggs, sister by marriage to Kydd. Born in Marrowdell under magical circumstances. Turn-born. Beloved of Bannan Larmensu.

Kydd Uhthoff, brother of Dusom, uncle of Wainn and Ponicce, husband of Peggs, father of her baby, great-uncle of Delfinn. Came to Marrowdell as a young man. Formerly a student at

Sersise University. Tends apple orchard. Village beekeeper and artist.

Larell Uhthoff, mother of Wainn and Ponicce, wife of Dusom. Died by misadventure on the Northward Road.

Loee Emms, toddler, daughter of Gallie and Zehr, sister of Tadd and Allin. Born in Marrowdell.

Lorra Treff, mother of Davi and Wen, great-aunt to Hettie, Cheffy, and Alyssa, grandmother to Delfinn. Formerly head of Avyo's influential Potter's Guild. Village potter.

Marleen Nalynn Uhthoff, daughter of Peggs and Kydd, born in Marrowdell.

Melusine (Melly) Nalynn (nee Semanaryas), mother of Peggs and Jenn, wife of Radd. Died by misadventure.

Mimm Ropp, mother of Hettie, Cheffy, and Alyssa, first wife of Anten. Died by misadventure.

Peggs Uhthoff (nee Nalynn), daughter of Melusine and Radd, elder sister of Jenn, wife of Kydd, great-aunt of Delfinn. Came to Marrowdell as a toddler. Village's best baker and cook.

Ponicce Uhthoff, baby, daughter of Dusom and Larell, sister of Wainn, niece of Kydd. Died by misadventure on the Northward Road.

Radd Nalynn, father of Peggs and Jenn, husband of Melusine, brother of Sybb. In Avyo, owned mills and a tannery. Village miller.

Riedd Morrill, father of Roche and Devins, husband of Covie, cousin of Riss, great-nephew of Wagler Jupp. In Avyo, was a baron and served in the House of Keys. Died by misadventure.

Riss Nahamm, cousin of Riedd, great-niece of Old Jupp, wife of Sennic. Came to Marrowdell as a young woman. Creates tapestries and cares for her great-uncle.

Satin and Filigree, sows.

Scourge, the Larmensu war horse. In Marrowdell, his true nature is revealed.

Sennic Nahamm (nee Horst), former soldier, husband of Riss. Took the name of Horst from baby Jenn, who continues to call him Uncle Horst. Hunter and village protector.

Tadd Emms, son of Zehr and Gallie, brother of Loee, twin of Allin, husband of Hettie, father to twins Elainn and Torre. Came to Marrowdell as a babe. Miller's apprentice.

Tir Half-face (Tirsan Dimelecor), former Vorkoun border guard. Bannan's friend and companion. Has taken service with the Lady Mahavar in Avyo.

Torre Emms, baby, son of Hettie and Tadd, twin of Elainn.

Wagler Jupp (Old Jupp, Master Jupp), great-uncle of Riedd and Riss, great-great-uncle to Devins and Roche. Former Secretary of the House of Keys in Avyo. Currently writing his memoirs.

Wainn Uhthoff, son of Dusom and Larell, brother of Ponicce, nephew of Kydd, father (with Wen) of Delfinn. Came to Marrowdell as a young boy. Injured by misadventure on the Northward Road. Communes with edge.

Wainn's Old Pony.

Wisp the dragon, once Wyll the man, Jenn Nalynn's dearest friend and protector.

Zehr Emms, father of the twins, Tadd and Allin, and baby Loee, husband of Gallie. A fine furniture maker in Avyo. Village carpenter.

Concerning the Denizens of Endshere

Allin Anan (nee Emms), son of Gallie and Zehr, brother of Loee, twin brother of Tadd, husband to Palma Anan. Came to Marrowdell as a babe. Now lives in Endshere as barkeep in Palma's inn.

Arrmand Comber, distant cousin of Dusom and Kydd's grandfather, father of Cammi. Deceased.

Bliss, not a nice person.

Cammi Comber, daughter of Arrmand. Postmistress. Corresponded with Larell.

Dinorwic, thief and smuggler.

Elsinore Anan, sister of Emo, cousin of Palma. Born and raised in Endshere. Drover. In Marrowdell to take livestock to summer pasture. Courting Devins.

Emo Anan, sister of Elsinore, cousin of Palma. Born and raised in Endshere. Drover. In Marrowdell to take livestock to summer pasture. Courting Devins.

Great Gran, (Caryn Anan), great-grandmother of the family. Former resident of Marrowdell.

Hager Comber, son of Harty, village smith.

Harty Comber, father of Hager, village smith.

Larah Anan, young boy, Palma's brother. Clears tables in the inn.

Palma Anan, sister of Larah, wife of Allin. Born and raised in Endshere. Owns and operates *The Good Night's Sleep* inn. Author.
Shedden, village healer.
Upsala, unscrupulous trader who sold Bannan his ox.

Concerning the Denizens of the Bay of Shades, Eldad

Dawizards (dire-ones), dedicated sect who come to the Bay of Shades hunting for magic to contain and destroy.
Flesie, child, lives in Shadesport. Communes with edge.
Granny Bunac, lives in Shadesport. Best cook.
Heathe, lives in Shadesport. Waalum hunter.
Lenzi, lives in Shadesport. Waalum hunter.
Marni, lives in Shadesport. Waalum hunter.
Nonny (Noemi), lives alone on her boat, the *Good Igrini*. Originally from the deep south of Eldad. Dives for mimrol. Friend to Urcet.
Symyd, lives in Shadesport. Waalum hunter and finder of magical things.
Urcy (Urcet a Hac Sa Od y Dom, Urcy Shade's Ass), former scholar and author exiled to Shadesport after visiting Marrowdell with Dema Qirmirpik. Friend to Nonny.

Concerning the Denizens of Ansnor

Author's Note: Names marked with an * first appear in my Night's Edge novella, "A Pearl from the Dark." Those with a + first appear in my Night's Edge enovella, "A Dragon for William." Both of these stories take place between *A Play of Shadow* and *A Change of Place*. All other names come from the novels themselves.

+**Araben Sethe**, engineer consulting with Emon.
*__Calym Lapec__, resident of Loudit, lensmaster. Token smuggler exposed by Roche Morrill.
Dema Qirmirpik, visited Marrowdell with Urcet the Eld. Resident of temple near Loudit.
*__Deter Elenyas__, former Ansnan soldier released from prison. Traveled with Edis and Jon. Betrayed Edis. Deceased.
*__Disel__, resident of Loudit, smith's apprentice. Friend of Roche, Flam, and Lenert. Received scholarship to attend Vorkoun's Riversbend University. Currently a student there.
*__Edis Donovar__, former Ansnan soldier released from prison. Traveled with Deter and Jon until being betrayed. Befriended by Roche and saved by the magic of the edge. Now a magical creature known as The Traveler.

*Flam, resident of Loudit, musician, friend of Roche, Disel, and Lenert. Received scholarship to attend Vorkoun's Riversbend University. Currently a student there.

Gerhen, Ansnan family granted the Westietas tower in Mondir by treaty.

Idat Cotalen, Elder, town leader in Gordit.

Jas Sibley, owner and innkeeper of *Sibley's Drift* in Gordit.

*Jon Palyenor, former Ansnan soldier released from prison. Traveled with Edis and Deter. Betrayed Edis. Currently with Dema Qirmirpik at his refuge.

Kanajuq, servant to the dema, resident of temple near Loudit. Came to Marrowdell.

Kenton, senior city administrator representing construction and transportation in Mondir.

*Lenert, resident of Loudit, miller's apprentice. Friend of Roche, Disel, and Flam.

Limoges, senior city administrator representing construction and transportation in Mondir.

*Noabi Lapec, resident of Loudit, runs post office.

Panilaq, servant to the dema, resident of temple near Loudit. Came to Marrowdell.

Selwyn Kada, brother of Wanda, farmer, resident of Gordit.

Seter Kilsyth, Elder Cotalen's scribe, resident of Gordit.

Wanda Kada, sister of Selwyn, farmer and flower seller, resident of Gordit.

*Wibler the Great (Master Wibler), resident of Loudit, senior glassmaker.

Concerning the Denizens of Vorkoun

Author's Note: Names marked with an * were first mentioned in my Night's Edge novella, "A Pearl from the Dark." Those with a + were first mentioned in my Night's Edge enovella, "A Dragon for William." Both of these stories take place between *A Play of Shadow* and *A Change of Place*. All other names occur first in the novels.

Adrianna Morven, former nurse of Lila and Bannan, related to their mother.
Ally Ennan, Emon's personal guard.
Anet Boyes, Westietas horse guard.
+Aunt Kinsel, Emon's father's sister, great-aunt to Semyn and Werfol.
Bish Fingel, one of Emon's trusted companions. Betrayed him in Mellynne and was killed by Dutton.
+Breeta, new Westietas smithy.
Cecebe Loring, Westietas coach driver.
+Chancellor Rober Milne, chief administrator of Vorkoun.
Cheek, one of Emon's trained crows.
Dauntless, kruar who came from the Verge to carry Bannan to Marrowdell. Now lives on Westietas Estate to be close to Werfol.
Dutton Omemee, Emon's senior guard, assigned as companion to Werfol and guard to Semyn.

Ebra Bobbieb, Lila's guard known for her fleetness.
Elsa Lowin, Emon's guard, assigned to guard Semyn on trip to Gordit.
Emon Westietas, father of Semyn and Werfol, husband of Lila. Baron, holding the seat for Vorkoun in the House of Keys. Currently in disfavor and exiled by Prince Ordo.
+Fullarton, head of Vorkoun's Potter's Guild.
+Kluet Gore, administrator of waterworks and bridges in Vorkoun. (See "Heirs.")
Gyllen Marerrym Larmensu, wife of Maggin, mother of Lila and Bannan. Died in landslide.
Jellicoe Dee, Guild Head for Vorkoun warehouse owners.
Jarratt, aide to Gyllen Larmensu. Died in landslide.
Herer, one of Emon's trusted companions.
Ignace, aide to Maggin Larmensu. Died in landslide.
+Ioana Tagey, sister to Nam, former cook at Marerrym estate. Escaped landslide and now head cook for the Westietas.
+Issan, Semyn and Werfol's former tutor.
Kimm Larmensu, uncle of Maggin, great-uncle to Bannan and Lila. First to ride Scourge in battle. Deceased.
+Lady Estaire, member of a Vorkoun noble house.
Lila Westietas (nee Larmensu), daughter of Maggin and Gyllen, sister of Bannan, mother of Semyn and Werfol, wife of Emon. Baroness. Truedreamer.
Mabbs Keit, Westietas horse guard and Emon's aide.
Maggin Larmensu, husband of Gyllen, father of Lila and Bannan. Truthseer and rider of Scourge. Died in landslide.
Nam Tagey (Tagey), brother to Ioana, former groundskeeper at the Marerrym estate, friend to Bannan. Escaped landslide and works for Lila in Vorkoun.
+Namron Setac (Master Setac), tutor Lila hires for Semyn and Werfol. Member of a secret society concerned with preventing another catastrophe in the edge. Former student of the Heirs.
Nimly, scullery boy at Westietas estate. Mute.
Omas Egind, Westietas horse guard.

Omi Derhall, Emon's seniormost guard.
Petrill Lan, Lila's guard assigned to Werfol during Dutton's absence.
+Revis, Westietas housekeeper and only original house staff left.
Roche Morrill, son of Covie and Riedd, elder brother of Devins, yet to be acclaimed rightful baron to represent the Sensian District of Avyo in the House of Keys. Former resident of Marrowdell, lately of Loudit, now of the Westietas Estate. Attending Vorkoun's Riversbend University. Dreadful dreamer. And truthteller, by the wish of Jenn Nalynn. Friend of Edis.
Rowe Jonn, soldier in Lila's personal guard. Killed protecting her sons on the Northward Road.
Ruthh, former seamstress to the Larmensu. Lila had her sew Bannan into his bedroll for a prank.
Ryll Aronom, seniormost of Lila's personal guard.
Seel Aucoin, soldier in Lila's personal guard. Killed protecting her sons on the Northward Road.
Scatterwit, one of Emon's crows.
Semyn Westietas, young boy, elder son of Lila and Emon, brother of Werfol, nephew of Bannan. Heir to the baron and thus to represent Vorkoun in the House of Keys.
+Sendrick, Westietas' new seniormost servant.
Sher Moreau, former soldier and foundry owner, resident of Vorkoun.
Spirit, kruar who came from the Verge to carry Lila to Marrowdell. Now lives on Westietas Estate to be close to Werfol.
+Tess, twin to Tixel. New staff.
+Tixel, twin to Tess. New staff.
Vin Macle, Emon's personal guard.
Werfol (Weed) Westietas, young boy, younger son of Lila and Emon, brother of Semyn, nephew of Bannan. Truthseer and truedreamer.

Concerning the Heirs, Users of Dark Magic

Daisy, spellcaster, Mage Elect.
Dove, student spellcaster in Avyo, killed by Rose.
Eldee, Rhothan spellcaster working with Cotalen in Gordit.
Lavender, spellcaster.
Lilac, spellcaster, alias of traitor to Westietas.
Quot, Rhothan spellcaster working with Cotalen in Gordit.
Raven, student spellcaster in Avyo, alias of Kydd Uhthoff.
Rose, Mage Prime.
Weasel, student spellcaster in Avyo, alias of Namron Setac.
Willow, spellcaster.

Concerning the Denizens of the Verge

Chalk, terst turn-born.
Clay, terst turn-born.
Fieldstone, terst turn-born.
Flint, terst turn-born.
Mengeeo, terst elder encountered by Jenn Nalynn.
Ollaha, terst elder encountered by Jenn Nalynn.
Riverstone, Master, terst turn-born and friend of Jenn Nalynn.
Ro, terst elder encountered by Jenn Nalynn. Crosses to Channen as Rhonnda Taff.
Sand, Mistress, terst turn-born and friend of Jenn Nalynn.
The Dancer, Old One.
The Listener, what The Dancer makes Bannan Larmensu after his transformation.
The Traveler, what The Dancer makes Edis Donovar after her transformation.
Tooth, terst turn-born.
Wen Treff, daughter of Lorra, sister of Davi, mother (with Wainn) of Delfinn. Came to Marrowdell as a young woman. As the toad queen, she lives in the Verge.

Going Deeper Underground

My beloved grandfather was an engineer who, in his spare time and among other interests, had a passion for mines. As far as I know, he wasn't a prospector—though I inherited some well-used prospecting tools, along with a number of books on Canadian mining, so maybe there's a secret to be discovered yet. It wouldn't surprise me. He'd be pleased to know Roger and I have lived these many years close to the Canadian Shield, where mines abound.

Tools and books from Ernest A. Lace. Photo credit: Roger Czerneda

I didn't know when I wrote *A Turn of Light* that I'd end up going underground. I'd referred to the domain of Ansnor as having mines simply because I'd given that part of my map that sort of geography, and mining (especially to a Canadian) is important. Then DAW Books contracted me to write four more novels in what was now a series, and I'd the notion to set each in a different domain from my original map.

Then, as one does, I sketched out my overall arc for five books and decided Book #4, which you hold in your hands, should be the "darkness before all is resolved," and why not be literal and make that Ansnor and mines? I even called it *A Fall of Darkness*. Ooh. Foreboding.

Years passed. Times changed. While writing Book #3, *A Change of Place*, I realized the last thing I wanted to do was go dark in this series. Suspenseful, impactful, sure, but never grim. I quickly sent in a new title, *A Shift of Time* (because there's a pattern to them and that worked), with the plot I'd proposed essentially the same. A threat to the turn-born, deep in the mines of Ansnor. Moving forward the thread of Bannan and Lila's pursuit of those who'd destroyed their family home by dark magic. Cool creatures and fun magic and pie. Oh, yes.

I started seriously researching mines and mining of the late 1700s/early 1800s, material I used in my novella, "A Pearl from the Dark," and which helped me prepare for *Shift*. I read autobiographies and descriptions, but I really wanted to go into a working mine, to get the feel for it.

Well, not *really*. I'm a bit queasy when it comes to caves, tunnels, low ceilings, and such, but I did try, only to find those in reach of me were closed to visitors until after the book's deadline. (Fancy that!) On the plus side, I gave Mistress Sand something of my feelings on the matter.

I did, however, want to feature what my granddad loved most. Those who do the hard jobs. The mines that not only produce needful minerals but also are the heartblood of their towns and industries. (And the railways built to reach them.) The courage, skill, and determination of miners. Thank you.

As for cool creatures? Following along the rock theme and the notion of time shifting, for my latest entry in the Verge I came up with . . . tiny cows. Not, I hasten to add, the bovines we have on farms today, but another herbivore. I based the grazers of the Verge, my terst cows, on *Megatherium americanum*, the extinct giant ground sloth first discovered in 1787 by Manuel Torres in Argentina. While I added a few magical attributes, including becoming tiny, the initial creature you meet is as accurate a description of the source animal I could provide, including that it burrowed. Nature is amazing!

Oh, as for how my tiny cows appear at the end of the book? Roger went to Peavey Mart (a Canadian farm store) and found two adorable Highland cattle statues to inspire me. I love my life.

We Can Help With That

While I didn't go into a mine, I did lean on others for help with details. My thanks to Ginette Cyr, who came up with Tir Half-face's "bog tea" as a beverage sure to assault the sinuses. I owe the name *Sibley's Drift* to the fine people who follow my Marrowdell FB page, who, when asked to name an establishment frequented by miners, came together to select the best name. From Jason Simcoe: "Alexander H. Sibley was the president of Silver Islet Mining Company, which ran an underwater (!!!) silver mine in Lake Superior, near Thunder Bay, Ontario. The mine is no longer in operation, and is fully submerged, but you can see the shaft and stuff under the water if you go there. Creepy!!! But also cool!" I couldn't agree more! Janet Chase provided the term "drift," which, to a miner, refers to a tunnel that ends on a vein of ore. Thank you both—and all who voted.

I also had the very helpful staff of Canada's Museum of Nature hard at work, trying to find me a piece of *Megatherium* artwork I could include for you. That didn't pan out before going to production, but, bonus? I now know exactly who to email the next time.

There's always a next time.

Put Me in the Story!

A veritable host of dear and familiar folk have wound up in Marrowdell, Endshere, Channen, and now beyond! Some generously bid on a character name in support of charity. Others are here as part of a tribute to my now-ended and beloved sff.net newsgroup (which lives on as the Grey Stone Tower on Facebook, if you've missed the company). Several namings are special gifts, from me to you, most recently when, in thanks, I offered to include anyone who submitted a tavern name in the book—which was super helpful to me, because in the story, Emon was heading off with a cavalcade of staff who needed names!

To all, I'm privileged to be trusted with your names, or variations thereof, and thank you for any character details you provided. I hope you enjoy the result. (The usual proviso applies, in that I make stuff up to serve the story first and foremost, so it's most likely you won't recognize yourselves. Hence the following list. However, any resemblance you do spot? Please take it as the compliment I intend.)

Here's the full list to date because I'm so happy to share it. Some are characters who are mentioned, but don't appear in the story. Others walked in and took over the place. A few wound up on a map. Again, thank you to all, and I hope you enjoy!

Marrowdell:

Alyssa Ropp—Alyssa Donovan
Elainn Emms—in remembrance of Elaine Lones, from Lance Lones
Hettie Emms (nee Ropp)—Henri Reed
Jenn Nalynn—Jennifer Lynn Czerneda
Marleen Nalynn Uhthoff—Marleen Beaulieu
Torre Emms—from Henri Reed
Treff (friend) Frann Nall—Fran Quesnel
Treff, Cynd—Cindy Hodge
Treff, Davi—David Trefor James
Treff, Lorra—Lorraine Vivian James
Treff, Wen—Gwen Veronica James

Outside Marrowdell:

Ally Ennan, guard—Sally McLennan
Anet Boyes, guard—Janet Boyes
Bish, Emon's companion—Anne Bishop
Caryn Anan (Great Gran)—Caryn Cameron
Candlas Bridge—Janet McCandlas
Clairr River—Claire Eamer
Dawnn Blysse, artisan—Dawn Bliss
Ebra Bobbieb, guard—Bobbie Barber
Edis Donovar—Edith Starink
Elsa Lowin, guard—Elsa DieLöwin
Flesie—Florence Giles (Flossie-Mae)
Gerthen, Ansnan family—Roger Henry Czerneda
Heathe—Heather Dryer
Herer, Emon's companion—Robert Herrera
Jas Sibley, innkeeper—Jason Simcoe
Jellicoe Dee—Bob Milne's wife Dee
Jym Garnden, astronomer in Avyo—James Alan Gardner
Kimm Larmensu, Bannan's great-uncle—Kimm Antell
Koevoets and Moniq, fair goers—Monique Koevoets
Kotor and Mila Rivers—Janet, Willem, Leo and Mila Chase

Larah Anan, Palma's little brother—Lara Herrera
Lehman, infamous author—Susan Lehman
Lenzi—Julie Lenzi
Leott, artisan—Elliot James Godfrey
Lianna, wife of Stevynn—Liana K
Lippet, Rhothan barony—Philip Peter Czerneda
Loiss, Bannan's former friend—Lois Gresh
Lornn Heatt, Lila's assumed identity—Lorne and Heather Kates
Mabbs Keit—Keith Mabbs
Marni—Marni Cooper
Neb Carde, accountant—Ben Carde
Netej Hase, industrialist—Janet Chase
Nonny (Noemi)—Noemi Hope (thanks to Blaine Fleming)
Nycharl, Rhothan barony—Tony Charles Czerneda
Nyc Wise, guard—Cyn Wise
Omas Egind, guard—Thomas Wiegard
Omi Derhall, guard—Naomi Elder-Hall
Palma Anan, innkeeper—Shannan Palma
Petrill Lan, guard—Alan Petrillo
Renee, Bannan's former friend—Renee E. Babcock
Rhonnda Taff, artisan—Rhonda Donley
Rowe Jonn, Lila's guardsman—Jonathan Crowe
Ruthh, infamous seamstress—Ruth Stuart
Sarra River—Sarah Jane Elliott
Seel Aucoin, Lila's guardsman—Jennifer Seely
Sher Moreau, industrialist—Sheri Moreau
Stevynn, artisan—Steven Kerzner
Thomm, artisan—Thomas Czurgai
Vin Macle, guard—Kevin Maclean
Wanda Kada, flower seller—Kada McDonald and her daughter Wanda

Thank you all!

We'd Like to Invite You...

What a book tour!! My sincere thanks to all the booksellers who hosted me in 2024 as well as the wonderful readers, old and new, who came for their copies and received "toad swag"! Yes, Roger made fantastic limited-edition house toad cards, featuring Jenn Nalynn's house toad and Bannan's, and they were most happily received.

I breezed into the following stores to sign stock and was delighted by the warm response. Thank you Amanda (Chapters St. Catharines), Amy (Indigo Stoney Creek), Maggie (Indigo Burlington Centre), Sherrie and Kathleen (Indigo Brant), and Kristal (Chapters Belleville).

I had a great time signing and chatting with readers at several events. My thanks to Scott, Catherine, and Michelle at the Ancaster Indigo (which is Czerneda-central, believe me). There were toad cookies and celebrations at the official launch, hosted by Becca at Bakka-Phoenix Books in Toronto. Thank you! I did events for Shelley at Indigo South Keyes and Emma at Chapters Barrhaven. Last but not least, thank you Bailey and Tori at Indigo Kingston for letting me bring out my model of Marrowdell for readers (and the large number of Lego enthusiasts, there being an event nearby in the mall), and to Melissa at the Kanata Chapters who also welcomed my rather large model.

Marrowdell out in public for the first time in a decade!
Photo credit: Roger Czerneda

I was honored to be a judge for the annual Muskoka Novel Marathon—a difficult task indeed, to choose between such great entries, and warm congratulations to all! I'd also like to take this opportunity to congratulate Christy Climenhage on the publication of her debut SF novel, *The Midnight Project*, from Wolchak & Wynn. I was privileged to read her wonderful book in its early stage and couldn't be more delighted to see it in the world.

Writers supporting writers became a theme, this year. My thanks to fellow scribe Richard West, who put my name forward to the Niagara-on-the-Lake Public Library. As a result, I did a presentation, arranged by Debbie Krause and ably hosted by Sarah Bowers, who was a little surprised to receive the library's house toad. Yes, we'd love to come back!

My sole swing south of Lake Ontario last year was a great success. My thanks to Doug and Kasia at Pittsford, NY, Barnes and Noble. I was also at World Fantasy in Niagara Falls, NY, and had a splendid time. My congratulations to the concom and all involved. So many people we hadn't seen (in person) in ages, including Anne Bishop and Kristine Smith, among many others. Thank you, Maree Pavletich, for reminding us how much we miss our New Zealand family and for your gifts (and that tasty gin). Martha Wells, you were most kind, letting me fangirl all over you, and I won't ever forget. (You probably won't either and will keep a wary eye out for enthused Canadians in future.) And hearty congratulations to our talented friend, Janet Chase, whose amazing 3D art was featured in the Art Show—most going home with happy purchasers as well.

Can*Con in Ottawa wrapped up the year's celebration of all things book and friend. As usual, Marie Bilodeau, Brandon Crilly, and their host of brilliant concom made it perfect for all. See you this fall!

The More Usual Acknowledgments

With exceptional joy! I'm delighted to have the most able assistance of my new editor at DAW Books, Madeline Goldberg, for this book. Madeline not only "gets" all things Marrowdell, she's a fantastic editor. This book is significantly better thanks to Madeline's insights and suggestions (and "Julie, do you really mean that?" moments). Can't wait to work with you, Madeline, on my next. Allons-y!

I'd also like to thank Laura Fitzgerald, DAW's publicist, for their tremendous efforts to be sure my work is out there in the classiest and most fun ways possible! (So many toads, so little time.) As well as for suggesting the toad cards—thanks, Roger, for doing those photo shoots (again, so many toads) and for creating the final wonderful product. And congratulations, managing editor and friend Joshua Starr, from both of us. (You know why.)

Matthew Stawicki came through—I knew he would—with this fabulous cover that includes my very odd list of crucial items: party tent, summer northern forest, crossing to the Verge with dragons, and, most importantly, Jenn's regency gown! Bannan looks quite spiffy as well. Oh, and thanks Matt for not blinking an eye when I asked you to add a giant ground sloth. Thank you, Katie Anderson, for wonderful art direction. (And to Madeline for the swish.)

While Night's Edge rolled along in book form, thanks to the tireless efforts of DAW and my incredible agent Sara Megibow the novels began to come out from Tantor Audiobooks, read by Jen Jayden. This includes *A Turn of Light* as well as the remaining four, and it's a joy to offer such continuity to my audiobook readers. (Jen, I hope you still enjoy my work after all these months of reading it aloud!) My thanks also to Kim Budnick of Tantor for her enthusiasm as well as the new covers and wonderful promotion. A grand experience!

Friends and family put up with my intense periods of "poof" to make my deadlines this year. Thank you not only for understanding, but for cheering me on the entire way. Not to mention hosting us during the tour, especially Mike and Debi Lamarre, who showed me what has to be on the next book cover (it's a secret). Toad cookies for all!

As for my other half, Roger? Couldn't have done it, wouldn't have done it, really can't fathom a moment without *you*.

However far we are apart,

Keep Us Close.

Photo by Roger Czerneda

An unabashed romantic and optimist, **Julie E. Czerneda** finds something remarkable wherever she looks. Dragons and magic—and house toads—hold a special place in her heart—and in the heart of her Night's Edge series. As a former biologist, her studies of the natural world heavily influence the imaginative landscapes in these books. *A Turn of Light* and *A Play of Shadow*—the first two books set in Julie's magical world of Marrowdell—won international Aurora Prix Awards for Best SF/F novels. Shortly thereafter, she was awarded membership in the prestigious Canadian Science Fiction and Fantasy Hall of Fame.

Julie sends her earnest thanks to you, her dedicated and kind readers, as well as to the tireless and passionate team at DAW Books who have shepherded both her fantasy and science fiction novels into bookstores for over twenty years. She is represented by Sara Megibow of Megibow Literary Agency and can be found wilderness camping, gardening, or online at: www.czerneda.com